THE EMPRESS OF THE LAST DAYS

Jane Stevenson

Jonathan Cape
London

Published by Jonathan Cape 2003

2 4 6 8 10 9 7 5 3 1

First published in Great Britain in 2003 by
Jonathan Cape
Random House, 20 Vauxhall Bridge Road,
London SW1V 2SA

Random House Australia (Pty) Limited
20 Alfred Street, Milsons Point, Sydney,
New South Wales 2061, Australia

Random House New Zealand Limited
18 Poland Road, Glenfield,
Auckland 10, New Zealand

Random House South Africa (Pty) Limited
Endulini, 5A Jubilee Road, Parktown 2193, South Africa

The Random House Group Limited Reg. No. 954009
www.randomhouse.co.uk

A CIP catalogue record for this book
is available from the British Library

ISBN 0–224–06142–9

Typeset by Palimpsest Book Production Limited,
Polmont, Stirlingshire
Printed and bound in Great Britain by
Clays Ltd, St Ives plc

THE EMPRESS OF THE LAST DAYS

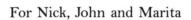

For Nick, John and Marita

Mongrel as I am, something prickles in me when I see the word Ashanti as with the word Warwickshire, both separately intimating my grandfathers' roots, both baptising this neither proud nor ashamed bastard, this hybrid, this West Indian.

Derek Walcott, *What the Twilight Says*

I

For who can tell but the Millennium
May take its rise from my poor Cranium?
And who knows if God may please
It should come by the West Indies?

Thomas Spence (born 1750),
revolutionary Christian

'. . . in the last analysis, it is the wisdom inherent in their sacred blood which provides the basis for the "divine right" of the Great Royal Dynasty. And as I think I have contrived to demonstrate, this is a year in which we may hope to see great things. The last year of equivalent importance in history is 482, in which representatives of three highly significant lineages become visible at one and the same time – King Arthur triumphed at the Battle of Mount Badon, as you will doubtless recall, while Clovis, Emperor of the Franks, took power in France, and the erstwhile lands of the Queen of Sheba were reconquered by her illustrious descendant, Ella-Asbeha, also known as Caleb, the Negus of Ethiopia.'

'I used to like Arthur Negus. He did that lovely antiques programme – Neville, do you remember what it was called? The one with the bird in a cage?'

'*Going for a Song*. Marion used to watch it every week. Of course, she was brought up to take an interest; her parents had some very nice things. Most of the furniture in here's from her side, you know, and it'll go to Michael in the fullness of time. But speaking of blood, Harold, the Foxwists are a very old family. From

1

Carmarthenshire originally, I believe, though my lot are from Cheshire. There's a Manor of Foxwist somewhere north of Macclesfield, though I've never really looked into it. Michael, you found a Civil War Foxwist in Carmarthen, didn't you?'

'Yes. He wasn't anybody very special, just a bog-standard backbench MP. Kept his head down, didn't sign the warrant for the execution of King Charles, and made his peace at the Restoration. A lesson for us all in trying times, really.'

'I always think Wales is so peaceful. Neville, do you remember that lovely holiday we had with Mummy and Daddy at Portmeirion?'

'I do indeed. It must've been the year after the war. It was before I went up to Oxford, and I rather think you were just out of school.'

'That's right. It's funny we haven't been back. Michael dear, your young lady's Welsh, isn't she? Such a pretty name, it's Celtic, I suppose?'

'Eimer's Irish. But I'm not seeing her any more.'

'Oh. Perhaps it's all for the best.'

A rattle of sleet banged against the window, but Michael could stand no more. Only an absolutely uninterrupted flow of conversation, however random, could keep his great-uncle under control, and the old man had seized a politician's advantage of Aunt May's momentary embarrassment to resume his inexorable lecture.

His family were sitting where they always sat on festive occasions, his father in his usual chair, but with Great-Uncle Harold, as senior guest, at the other side of the gas fire, while Aunt May and her silent husband sat on the sofa, presiding over the remains of the Christmas cake and the wreckage of tea. He himself was over by the Christmas tree in the window, where he was in a draught, but away from the television. If May had not mentioned Eimer, he thought to himself, he could have stood it, on the basis of sheer familiarity, even though it was still only ten-thirty. A long hour and a half to the twelve strokes of Big Ben, 'Auld Lang Syne', 'Absent Friends', the ritual drink, the mince pie nobody wanted, and then ho for indigestion tablets all round and so to bed. I am the only person under seventy in this room, he thought, not for the first time. I cannot take another minute of this.

'I'm just going out for a bit,' he said, and could not resist adding, 'I may be some time.'

'I hope I haven't spoken out of turn, pet. She'd've been very welcome here, you know that.'

'Don't worry, May. I want a breath of air, that's all.'

'You'll be back by twelve?' said his father automatically.

'Of course I'll be back by twelve.' His great-uncle was prosing serenely on: '. . . and you will realise that, in order to interpret the evidence correctly, it is necessary always to remember that the epochal cycle of eighty-four years, which goes back to the Babylonians, is of far more intrinsic significance than the century, which is a mere unit of convenience . . .'

'. . . We're all very excited here in Birmingham . . .' yipped a voice from the telly.

Michael fled, and heard no more. After the stuffy warmth of the drawing-room, it was very cold on the stairs. He fumbled himself into his waterproof coat and a scarf, and stuffed a torch into his pocket. The moment he opened the front door, he heard the roaring of the sea, and the sleet smacked him in the face.

It was coming down diagonally, glittering orange in the glare of the street-lights. Head down, he pulled up his hood, crossed the road, and kept going, away from the light and into the vast, windy dark. The turf crunched underfoot, stiff with frost. He was moving briskly despite the darkness, crossing a wide expanse of grass, heading for the promenade. When he reached the shelter of the Scots pines, he paused to look back the way he had come. Criffel Street looked absurdly theatrical viewed from the cavernous dark-ness in which he stood. It was a backdrop to a Dickensian

Christmas panto; a parade of Victorian seaside villas, with the lamplight picking up details of the stucco-work and wrought-iron balconies. Since it was Old Year's Night, nearly every window shone warm and yellow; few houses had drawn curtains. Even at a distance of fifty yards or so, he could see the Christmas trees standing in all the front rooms, and guess at the tinsel and the strings of coloured foil shapes swagged across the ceilings. Some householders had strung lights outside, a neighbourly, cheerful gesture.

Viewed from so far away, his father's house looked just like anyone else's. He turned his back on it, trying to put it out of his mind. At least the worst was over for the year. Christmas was always at May and Harry's, and since he had to drive his father and Harold home from Aspatria in Harry's geriatric Vauxhall, the interminable day had to be endured on one sweet sherry and a glass of wine with the meal. After the ordeal of Christmas, therefore, Old Year's Night, on which he could at least blur the edges a bit, was something he could normally put up with well enough. But what was really getting him down, he realised, threading his way cautiously through the dark trees, was not the tedium, or even May's gaffe, but the forlornness of it all. They would start dying off eventually, probably Harold first since he was by far the oldest, but year by year, the survivors would sit where they always sat, and say what they always said, clinging to their terrible ritual while their world melted around them.

Once he was on the other side of the shelter belt, on the concrete promenade, the sea was much louder, and Criffel Street was out of sight. The invisible Solway growled and grumbled in its bed; he could hear gravel churning in the undertow. He switched his torch on, lest he fall off the edge in the dark and break a leg, wishing that he had remembered to bring his gloves, as the wind chilled, then froze, his exposed hand. The cone of whitish light in the darkness before him showed little but the sharp edge of the sea-wall along which he was walking, and below him, the diagonal lines of the wet groynes disappearing into the night. Black, grey, falling diamonds of almost-snow caught in the meagre light. At that moment, alone and cold in the booming dark, Silloth seemed so peculiar and so much itself that it was almost possible even to love it.

In February, on a morning when the ice was melting at last to glass lace on dark ground, and the branches were turning from black to burgundy before the breaking of the leaves, Michael awoke from a vivid near-nightmare, momentarily confused about where he was. In the syntax of his dreams, the escape of Mary, Queen of Scots across the Solway had merged with the escape of Henrietta Maria across the Channel, and perhaps Garbo's last scene in *Queen Christina*; he remembered seeing, or being, a queen in the prow of a boat, a sense of flight and urgency, and across the sea, potential safety: a star-formed town of the Netherlands, snug behind its walls, and soft light glimmering over the sands. Fighting free of the clinging vision, he became conscious of muted sun, an unaccustomed brightness on the ceiling, and a perception of softened air.

Above Oxford, the gulls were moving amongst the crows, skeins of geese passing and unravelling in the sky. On that quotidian morning, while Michael was making his coffee and dumping books into his briefcase, spring had finally arrived. He was aware of a sense of hope, though, as yet, it was baseless: he knew nothing of how the dead would reach into his life. Astrea, who lay at rest among the poets in St Paul's. The Winter Queen, under marble at Westminster, her name half-read among the half-read names. Prince Omoloju, far from his Africa, beneath a slab smoothed blank on the floor of the Groote Kerk at Middelburg. And the last Emperor, under the wind that blows for ever from the Old World to the New, in the churchyard of St John's, attended by the sistrums of the shak-shak tree and the responses of Atlantic waves.

He was also ignorant, for the time, of the prophets and the madmen who dreamed with open eyes and exchanged visions: the just king who sleeps beneath the green hill, airless dirt and spores of old disease that wait their moment in unopened rooms. He had forgotten what his Great-Uncle Harold had so often and so pertinaceously told him, that the past was not dead, but only sleeping; that no cause, however lost, can die gently, that no dream is wholly gone at morning.

In fact, the real story began on that morning, though it was some time before Michael knew anything about it. Not in Silloth or Oxford, or even in Middelburg, but in Utrecht University, where Corinne Hoyers' life changed direction without warning on a perfectly ordinary day. She had just got back from coffee when the phone rang in the little paper-strewn office she shared with the other Book History graduate student and a linguist who couldn't be fitted in anywhere else.

'History of the Book project. You're speaking to Corinne Hoyers.'

The voice at the other end of the phone was educated, but with a slightly provincial flavour. 'Mevrouw Hoyers. I'm glad to have reached you. I got your name from your excellent exhibition catalogue – *Published in Middelburg*? I realised you were just the person to help us out.'

'Yes?' said Corinne. 'And who's speaking, please?'

'Oh, sorry. I'm Piet van der Velde, from the architectural restoration committee of the Middelburg Civic Trust. We're doing some work on a group of old buildings off Sint Janstraat, and we've made a very exciting discovery.'

'Mmm,' said Corinne encouragingly. Her heart was sinking as she listened; her mind chattering through a familiar litany of self-reproach for her own lack of judgement. At nearly thirty, she was still a doctoral candidate with an unfinished thesis. She had written a couple of articles, back when she thought she had all the time in the world, then she had got into curating an exhibition . . . all well worth doing, but the doctorate had kept on getting shelved, and until it was done, she could not get a proper job. Now it looked as though the exhibition, which had forced her to drop out of her PhD programme for a year, was all set to generate some kind of horrendous secondary complication. Fortunately, van der Velde was in a sufficient state of excitement that he wasn't listening.

'We were working on one of those old houses with a set of outbuildings on two sides of a little courtyard, you know the sort of thing? Anyway, we were taking a look at the stables, and we found a pile of stuff in the hayloft. There's whole cases of lead type, piles of unbound printed sheets tied up in bundles, some ledgers, and other bits and pieces, all absolutely filthy.'

'Hey,' said Corinne, getting interested despite herself. 'Date?'

'Certainly seventeenth century. We haven't opened up the bundles – we really wanted to get an expert before we touched anything. We've taken it all to the town archive, just as it is. They're very good, as you know, but they haven't time and resources to work over something like this. You have IT expertise we don't, and we'd like to end up with something like that online virtual exhibition you did for *Published in Middelburg*. It must've belonged to a printer, because of the lead type, and we thought we'd better get a university in on it. You know what things are like. You academics can access funds we can't.'

Yes, thought Corinne to herself, but only if we happen to be professors. She would have to cross that bridge when she came to it; meanwhile she changed the subject.

'Can you see what language it's in?'

'Some of it's Dutch but quite a lot of it's English.'

'The printer may not be easy to identify, then. There was a lot of English-language printing going on in seventeenth-century

Middelburg, as I'm sure you know, and because it's mostly political comment and pornography, the printers lied about absolutely
everything just to keep the English authorities confused.'

'Yes, we thought we needed some help. Is there any chance you
can come down to Middelburg?'

Corinne sighed, and looked at her calendar. She worked three
days a week for a software company called 'Logistik' to keep herself
afloat financially, but she had made herself a firm promise that the
other two days were sacred to her thesis . . . and what was more,
it was a long and tedious journey, involving at least three trains.
'Are you paying my fare?' she asked experimentally. It was a way
of getting fate to make the decision for her.

'We can do,' he agreed, surprising her. 'If you give me the receipt
for your ticket when you arrive, the secretary will organise your
reimbursement.'

Oh, well, she thought. 'Then I can come on Friday.'

'Excellent. I will meet you at the town archive – you remember
where that is, I'm sure. I'll come before twelve, and we can look
at the stuff together, and have some lunch.'

By dint of a horribly early start, Corinne was walking through
the hi-tech steel and glass doors of the Middelburg town archive
at twenty past ten. She had spent a lot of time there three years
previously, working on her exhibition, but she had not set foot in
the town since. It was looking sprucer and smarter than it had
been, under a huge spring sky mackerel-marked with scudding
clouds. A miniature fortress snug within the fantastic geometry
of rebated, circumflexing walls dear to seventeenth-century mil-
itary engineers, its charm remained intact. She had had the odd
sense of walking with a ghost of her earlier self as she traced the
once-familiar route from the station, and 1999-Corinne had been
desperately annoying company. Her earlier self had been so smug,
so certain that she was in the first stages of a life going according

to plan. But all the same, the depression lifted when she entered the archives and found that Marijke the receptionist seemed to remember her with some affection, so that it was necessary to stop and exchange news before she was able to hang up her coat and go up the stairs into the reading-room.

They hardly needed to direct her: the whole of one of the big grey tables was piled high with dusty paper, with more waiting on another beside it. Corinne got out a pack of surgeon's thin latex gloves and her notebook and pencil, rolled up her sleeves, donned a pair of the gloves, and began to undo the ancient, dust-greyed twine on the nearest bundle, thinking that she had been quite right to dress in her housepainting clothes, overalls and an ancient shirt. The old enthusiasm, the excitement of finding things out, tugged at her. She had learned circumspection very late, perhaps too late. It would never come naturally.

After an hour, the dim beginnings of a picture was beginning to form. The watermarks she found – the paper was mostly Dutch, with a bit bought in from France and Germany – suggested dates in the first half of the seventeenth century. As she turned over the pages, their actual contents pointed in the same direction; she found pages from an English-language satirical almanac, violently anti-Parliament, *The School of Venus, or Madame Aloysia's Sotadical Dialogues*, which she recognised as a version of a pornographic classic of the time, something else called Mercurius Aulicus, *The Stewes of West-Minster discover'd*, a sort of gazetteer of politicians' mistresses, occasionally funny in an awful sort of way. She noticed that the same set of worn-down pornographic woodcuts, crude versions of Aretino's *Postures*, seemed to be doing random duty as illustrations to all the filth, an indication of the generally down-market character of the enterprise. The word 'hermaphrodite' caught her eye as she turned over the pages, and she stopped to read a passage which made her laugh:

Hermaphrodite Freschville with Lowther her friend
With Catzo and Dildo, full often have sinn'd,
But hearing at Court, that maids there are many,
Shows 'em her P——k, & crys will you have any?
It once was my fortune to turn up her clothes
Three inches of P——k hard by her C——t grows.
You Ladies who have not yet heard of her name
At her house may be sped with a Man or a Dame.

Smiling, she scribbled it down for her friend Ankie, who was always pleased to hear about early references to gay women, wondering who Freschville was, and what Catzo meant. Just for a change, the next collection of pages she looked at turned out to be bits of a perfectly genuine, proper Dutch almanac called *The Honest Farmer's Vade-Mecum and Guide*, with nothing satirical in it at all as far as she could see. As she had explained to van der Velde, the alleged authors were almost certainly falsely identified; the places of publication (given as London and Paris; only the *Vade-Mecum* owned up to Middelburg) were obviously wrong, and the dates were probably not reliable either.

Well. At least she now had a sense of what was in the collection; all pretty typical in its way. The next thing was to look at the ledgers. As she had expected, when she opened the first of them, she found a pig's-breakfast. It was in an illegible, scratchy secretary-hand, so closely and carelessly written that the words looked like dead spiders, the columns of figures straggled down the page and there were abbreviations all over the place. She concentrated on trying to find some familiar words: the man would have had to buy paper regularly, so if she could identify paper transactions, then she would have an idea of how the book was organised.

She was bent over the ledger in a state of complete concentration, when a voice behind her made her jump.

'Good morning.' Van der Velde was standing behind her, a neat, smiling man, far too fair, with white eyelashes, wearing a very 1970s tan leather jacket. When she stood up, she realised that she overtopped him by about twenty centimetres. 'I'm glad you could come,' he went on. 'What d'you make of it all?'

'Well. What you've already seen for yourself. This is someone doing business with the English royalists. Most of what I've found's obviously intended for the English market, a mix of pornography and political comment, which is pretty normal for the time. They were illegal in England, so they both got printed abroad and smuggled in, and of course, the pornography acted as a support for the political material by giving it a wider audience. Look. Here's a bit out of a classic example, *Henry Marten's Familiar Letters to his Lady of Delight*. Marten was a republican, so this is actually anti-parliament, but it's being put over as straightforward filth.'

'Interesting. But you don't know who the printer is yet?'

'It's going to take for ever to make sense of the ledger. It must all be in there somewhere, but it's so badly written and disorganised, I can't get the hang of it. If you've come to give me a hand, let's try some of the loose material.'

There were several unbound notebooks, and quite a lot of loose papers. Together, they began to look through: most of the papers appeared to contain financial information.

'I've found a bundle of letters,' said van der Velde after a while. 'They're mostly statements of account. I think we've got our man. He's called Petrus Behn.'

'Means nothing to me, but there's an article by Arnold Wiggers listing Middelburg printers, now we've got a name we can look him up. Let's have a look . . . oh, good. It's the same hand as the main script in the notebooks.'

'Shall we take a look at the satchel? It may be more personal material.'

'Fine.' Carefully, she restored to their original bundles all the papers she had disturbed, and moved them to the other table out of the way. The satchel was grey with dirt, the leather so dried-out it threatened to crack as they cautiously attempted to lift the flap. They prised it up at last without its breaking off, and van der Velde held the bag just open, while Corinne slid the contents out bit by bit. Together they peered with interest at the result, an indescribable muddle of paper which reminded her of her own desk. She looked at her filthy hands.

'I'll just change these.' She dropped the used gloves into the wastepaper basket, put on a fresh pair, and began to look at what they had found.

There was a bound book, small octavo, plain vellum. It seemed a good place to start. She opened it; the binding was in poor condition, cracking open along the top of the front cover, but it was written in a handsome italic script, completely unlike the terrible hand of the ledgers, and it had a neatly set-out title page: *Notatiunculae de vita tribulationibusque magistri Pelagii van Overmeer, necnon scala redemptionis animae felicissimae infaustae.* She looked through: page after page of beautifully regular writing, utterly infuriating.

'What've you got there?' said van der Velde, peering over her shoulder.

'It's so annoying. It's the first thing I've found that's as clear as print, but it's all in Latin. I can't read it. What I think it is is one of those sort of Calvinist spiritual diaries. It's got that feel to it, just look at the way it's set out.'

'Can I look? I took alpha at school.' He took her place, and gave it his earnest consideration. 'Mynheer Pelagius van Overmeer. They both mean the same thing, actually, "someone from the ocean", or "someone from overseas", I don't know if that's significant. "Notes" – little notes, but I think that's just a way of putting it – "about his life and misfortunes". The last bit's peculiar . . . "or a ladder of redemption"?'

'Could be. It's quite a seventeenth-century sort of idea.'

'OK. "Or, a ladder of the redemption of a soul which was most fortunate and most unlucky"? It doesn't make sense.'

'Lucky in one way and unlucky in another? Maybe he went bankrupt and found God? Don't worry. If I can get a microfilm made, I'll find someone who can read it. There's no hurry. It's obviously not part of the main problem, and I doubt if it's interesting in itself.'

The next thing to merge from the bundle were three letters, folio sheets folded into small squares, addressed to 'De heer Pelagius' in Middelburg. They were very dirty, in a way which suggested that they had been carried about for a long time. She undid one carefully: the paper was thick and strong, and she recognised it as fin double croisé de Troyes, far better quality than the stuff used by Mynheer Behn, but it had been folded for so long that it was in danger of wearing through at the creases. The inner surfaces were still creamy white, written in a hasty, highly individual hand, in English. The letter began, 'My dear Pelagius', and was signed 'yours to command in love, Candace'. It was an affectionate document, that much was obvious even at a glance. A sentence caught her eye, 'I see your Face now so often in my dreams, that I wonder if you have contrived a Fetch or Spirit that can cross ten leagues in a breath.' Beyond that, the writer was female, troubled with her lungs, in debt, and annoyed with her son. Doubtless reading them properly would clarify what was going on. She folded it up again, with care.

'This is all personal,' complained van der Velde. 'It's got nothing to do with the printer. Goodness knows why it's here.'

'Keep on looking,' advised Corinne, having paused for a moment in vain hopes of inspiration. 'Once we've seen everything, we'll maybe have an idea of how this all fits together.' She put the book to one side. The other papers from the satchel were written in a practised but non-professional script, mostly writing in English, sometimes in Dutch or French. She'd seen the same hand in some of the other documents, and began to suspect that it belonged to a secretary, or perhaps a partner. 'I think I've got someone else, he seems to be handling the English business. Maybe Behn's English agent?'

Van der Velde was riffling one of the notebooks, as she continued to sort documents. 'There's a bit in this hand signed A.B.'

Corinne sighed. 'Better than nothing, I suppose. Still, we're getting on. I think all this could be very interesting.'

Van der Velde perked up. 'This is good news. You think we might be able to make it into an attraction?'

'Oh, I should think so. It'll be a horrible job reading the ledgers, but I'm sure the pornography will be a draw. Oh, good.'

'What?' said van der Velde, looking hopeful.

'I've found another notebook.' It was a dirty little object with no binding at all, and when she opened it at random, it turned out to be in A.B.'s script, written continuously, in English. She began to read.

<u>Bianca</u>	Prithee no more, my Sister, to thy prayers,
	Oh, that my fate were yours!
<u>Clarina</u>	—— and your fate mine.
	O sister, you are meat for Convent walls,
	Where you might chastely dream among your books,
	But I sigh for a handsome proper man,
	I long to dance, to love and be a Wife.
<u>Bianca</u>	But not a wife to old <u>Antonio</u>,
	Our father's friend, and my unwelcome Spouse.
<u>Clarina</u>	But wherefore not? Once married and no maid,
	No fair Venetian needs to sigh for love,
	Some brisk young squire will surely ~~come to sigh~~ haunt
	your door,
	Hail you your Gundilow at <u>Carnival</u>,

Press you at church, come masquing to your gate,
Sure, an old husband's head's soon decked with horns.

'Piet, I've found a play!' she said, excited, and turned to the beginning. 'It's called *The Female Rosicrucian.*'

'I've found a name. One of the letters in the A.B. hand is signed, I think. Affara? Is that a woman's name?'

'It's got to be Aphra Behn!' exclaimed Corinne, after a moment of standing blankly, fishing about in her memory.

'Who?'

'An English play-writer. Hey, this is a real find. We need an English expert. I'll ring round my friends.'

'We have made a literary discovery,' said van der Velde, as if he was trying the idea on for size. He had smudges of dirt all over his face and his once-immaculate white rollneck jumper, and looked a great deal more human than he had at first – his obvious pleasure was of course to do with potential profit to Middelburg rather than any desire to do her a good turn, but she was not inclined to grudge him it. She smiled at him dazzlingly.

'A good moment to stop. I want my lunch. Is "De Goudene Sterre" still open?'

'Er, yes.' Clearly, little van der Velde had had in mind a frugal cheese roll with a nice glass of cold karnemelk on the side, but she wasn't in the mood. It had been a long day already, and she felt she was owed a treat. She took her gloves off, and threw them away, dusting her fingers together automatically.

'Come on, then. I'm starving.'

By the time Corinne got rather reluctantly onto the last northbound train of the day, much progress had been made. The chief archivist had agreed to pay for the photographic department to microfilm *The Female Rosicrucian,* the other notebooks, and some of the papers, and a certain amount of excitement was already beginning to be generated. Piet van der Velde, after two beers at lunchtime, was basking in visions of extended funding in response to the obvious importance of the material they had found, while Corinne spent the afternoon scribbling down as many details as she could that might help her to make something of it. She was perfectly well aware that she would have to enlist her supervisor, since she couldn't get any funding assistance without his help, but it would take careful handling. Professor Derksen was principally concerned with the religious politics of the Eighty Years War, and had no interest whatsoever in England. Indeed, though he had flawless French and Spanish, she was not sure he actually spoke the language, not everyone of his generation did. However, for the first time in two years, some of her erstwhile buoyancy had returned; if she was clever enough, there was a chance that this material might get her out of her current dead-end and give her a future. By the time the last of the day's trains arrived at Utrecht Central, she had more or less decided what to do.

It was almost nine when she got home to her lonely little flat, all she could afford, even with a little guilt-money from her father to help out her half-time salary. It was lucky in one way, she reflected, hanging up her coat, that he still put his hand in his pocket, considering her age, but she also felt bought off, as if it meant she wasn't allowed to bother him. Her parents' divorce had been reasonably amicable and had not occurred till she was into her twenties, but it occurred to her frequently when her father came into her mind that, much as she loved him, her talent for manipulation was one she had inherited. She very much wanted to tell him about what she had found, but she could no longer be certain he would be interested. He had a new life in Australia, new work, new wife, new babies, new everything; he was practically a new person himself. Anyway, it must be about seven in the morning for him. He would be getting up about now, thinking about going to work, not a good time to bother a man.

She took a look in the fridge. There was the end of a packet of sliced ham, some leek salad from the deli and a packet of rye bread. Keeping-going food, enough for supper, even if unexciting. Later, once she was freshly showered and changed, she looked at her watch. Quarter to ten. Excellent. She curled up in her favourite chair, notebook balanced on the arm, and rang her best friend.

'Pieternelle? Oh, hi. Could I speak to Ankie, please? Is this a good moment?'

'It's fine. We were just watching TV. Ankie! it's Rina.' There was a clunk, then she heard Ankie's voice, dour, reluctant to be charmed.

'Rina. What do you want this time?'

'Ankie, I don't always ring because I want something, do I?' she asked, injured.

'Not always. Usually. What is it now?'

'I have to say, *schatje*, there's just one tiny little thing. But I think you'll be really interested.'

'Spit it out.'

'Do you know about England in the seventeenth century?'

'Sure. I've been teaching a course on Anglo-Dutch relations for the last two years.'

'What d'you know about Aphra Behn?'

'She's quite important. From some of the writing, it looks as if she was one of the first Englishwomen to be a dyke, or at least bi. Anyway, gay history aside, she wrote a lot of plays, and got them performed. She was a spy for the Stuarts.'

'Why was she called Behn? It's not an English name?'

'Some husband or other. Nobody really knows. Her maiden name was Johnson, I think.'

'Ankie. What if I tell you I know she was married to a pornographer in Middelburg?'

'Nelle – darling, my cigarettes, please. Rina, what've you got yourself into?'

17

'I've been looking at an archive of stuff which has just turned up in Middelburg. It's the papers of a printer called Petrus Behn who was selling red-hot royalist propaganda and porn. He seems to be involved with someone called Affara, or A.B. That looks about right, doesn't it?'

'Shit. It does, doesn't it? Congratulations, Rina. This is wonderful.'

'Do you know if there's a play called *The Female Rosicrucian*?'

'Not that I've heard of . . . you've got one, have you?'

'Yes. It's a notebook in Aphra's hand.'

'Oh, Rina. This is serious. We're going to have to think very hard. I'm a historian, and you're a pig-ignorant specialist in printing and bibliography. You need someone in English literature.'

'I was thinking of ringing Michael Foxwist.'

'That pretty-boy of yours, the one from Oxford?'

'I know you don't like him, but he's an English literature person, and he's not in the Netherlands, which is a major plus. I don't want to spread this information around till I've thought about it properly.'

'I don't dislike him, Rina. He's OK, for a man, and he seems reasonably bright. I just didn't know you were still speaking to him.'

'Oh, yes. You never know when you might want a friend in England. I kept in touch.'

'Rina, you really are completely shameless. But I thought he was eighteenth-century? Wasn't he working on Defoe?'

'Well, he's bound to know something, isn't he?'

Ankie sighed. Corinne could visualise her clearly: the severe, freckled face under its light-red cap of straight, flyaway hair, the inevitable cigarette burning down in her left hand as she sat on the floor by the phone. 'Ask him, then.' Corinne could hear the shrug in her voice as clearly as if she saw it. 'He's not an idiot.

18

If he thinks he'd be out of his depth, he'll tell you.'

'Ankie, you really don't approve. What's wrong? – oh, I almost forgot. I found you a lovely seventeenth-century dyke. Mrs Freschville.'

Ankie refused to be distracted. 'You've made a significant discovery for women's history, Rina, and all you're thinking of is being the queen bee in the middle of her web. Sorry about the metaphor, but you know what I mean. It really ought to go to a sister, and here you are, dumping it on an ex-boyfriend just because you'll be able to keep some kind of control.'

Easy for you to say, Ankie, you've got a job, Corinne thought. 'OK, OK. I see what you mean. But . . .'

'Oh, skip it. I know you think I'm too serious about all this. Keep me informed. This sounds fabulous.'

'I'm getting some microfilms made. I'll show you some samples if you've got time.'

'I'd like that.'

'Love you, Ankie.'

'Love you too, Rina.'

The last job of the day done, Corinne put the phone down, and closed her eyes. She could now let herself think about what she had discovered; release herself, for an hour or so before bed at least, from the distraction, the paranoia, and the trainlike chatter of 'Get it done, get it done, get it done', which seemed to have become her permanent companions. It had been lovely talking to Ankie, who at least both cared up to a point and understood her problems, which was more than anyone else did. It was hard not to cling to her, though; she had to keep reminding herself to ring only when she had something specific to talk about, not to make excessive demands, and not to upset Pieternelle.

At that moment, it seemed to her as if everyone who had ever loved her had gone into other relationships, leaving her behind. It had been a long time since she had let a man become really important to her, and even Mam had remarried; she was involved in a new life now, and reluctant to hear bad news. She still believed academics led the life of the mind, that her daughter was all right, what she'd been told till a couple of years ago. For all his elusiveness, her father at least had a better sense of the realities of her position. But for once, this evening, Corinne thought, she had occasion to remind herself that there was a real reason why she didn't just admit defeat, go and work fulltime for 'Logistik' and get a life. In spite of all the downsides, and even if it was as boring as hell some of the time, working in a university still gave her the chance to discover, and to initiate new research. That day, she had found something wonderful, a heap of infinite possibilities, a love-affair of the mind which might spring any kind of unforeseen surprise, and would certainly challenge her skills and knowledge in unpredictable ways.

In the weeks that followed, Corinne returned to her own affairs, and gave Middelburg no further thought. Nothing much could sensibly be done until she had stuff in hand to show people, and meanwhile, her work was as time-consuming as ever. At least Utrecht was still giving her access to a room and facilities for that academic year, which helped, but there weren't enough hours in the day as it was. All the same, when she walked into the secretary's office one day, Yvonne hailed her.

'Corinne. There's a huge package for you. I've got it here. I couldn't get it into your pigeon-hole.'

'Goody!' Corinne, all other concerns temporarily forgotten, seized the bulky padded envelope Yvonne fished from beneath her desk, and scuttled back to her shared office. When she pushed open the door, her heart sank. It was unusual for all three of them to be using the room at the same time, but as sod's law would have it, Ruud was at his computer with a number of books lying open around him, and Cees was sitting in the one comfortable chair making notes. There was not a single surface in the room that didn't already have something on it.

'What've you got there, Corinne?' asked Ruud.

'A lot of stuff from the archive at Middelburg. Sorry, guys, I'm going to have to spread it all out on the floor. Hope I'm not going to be in the way?'

'Don't worry,' said Cees. 'I'm going down to help Derksen with a printing workshop in a little while, so I'll be in the basement. What're you up to, Ruud?'

'Trying to get this article finished. I'm afraid I'll be here or in the library for the rest of the day. Since the baby came, it's been hard to work at home.'

Corinne put her packet down on her chair, and ripped it open. Then she got down on the floor, with due care for her skirt which was straight and on the short side, and started pulling the contents out and sorting them. It was absolutely typical of Cees, she thought angrily, that he had assumed the question was addressed princip-ally to him, though he was actually junior to both herself and Ruud. It was also characteristic that he had taken the opportunity to rub her nose in the fact that if their professor felt the need of help, it was always Cees that he asked.

Fighting down the acid rush of resentment which Cees always produced in her, Corinne tried to think through what she was doing. Most of what was before her were spools of microfilm, each in a numbered tin, plus a typed list from Marijke, telling her what was on which, but there was also some paper. She had managed to persuade Marijke to make discreet xeroxes from some of the most interesting microfilms for her (which she would otherwise have had to pay for herself), so she had, among other things, A3 copies of the English letters to van Overmeer, and A4 copies of the first few pages of van Overmeer's diary. Film three, *The Female Rosicrucian*, could go straight to Michael in England. He could bloody well make his own hard-copies though, she thought in passing, Oxford had money coming out of its ears.

'Ruud, could you pass me down some of those folders? And a marker-pen?'

'Here you are. You winning?'

'Just about.' She began filing the hard-copy into cardboard folders.

'What've you got involved with now?' asked Cees, shutting his notebook. He sounded as if he were asking a child about a game.

Patronising little wanker, she thought. 'I'm not really involved,' she temporised. 'I've just agreed to do some preliminary sorting-out for someone.'

Cees got up to have a look; she was very conscious of him standing over her while she grovelled on the floor at his feet. 'I don't know how you find the time,' he said. 'I'd've thought you had enough on your plate without taking on any more. Looks quite interesting, though.'

Corinne ground her teeth and waited for him to go away. Cees did not believe in wasting his own precious time, so after a few moments more of enjoying his superiority, he went back to work and left her in peace. Goodness only knew where she was going to put it all. By lunchtime, however, everything had at least a temporary home. The microfilms stood in a tottering pile on the overcrowded bookshelf, except for the Aphra film, which was already on its way to England. She had made room for the paper in the filing cabinet. Glancing at her watch, she took one of the folders out again, and tucked it under her arm. Somewhere in the concrete Gulag which was the humanities block was a rather nice Renaissance Latinist she had recently found herself talking to for ages at a faculty drinks-party. With any luck, she would track him down in time to take him to lunch.

'Come in.'

Corinne pushed the door open, and surveyed with interest the man who turned in his chair to look at her. He was much as she had remembered, very tall, moustached, with short black hair, pale, greenish eyes severe behind elegant glasses with narrow black rims, probably in his early forties: he was some sort of almost-professor, so he could hardly be much younger. She was not sure that he remembered her. 'Professor van Waesberghe? I'm Corinne Hoyers, from the Book History project.'

'Oh, yes. Call me Theodoor. Well, what can I do for you?'

'Can I take you to lunch?'

'I haven't really got time for lunch.' Without standing up, he extended one immensely long arm, and reached a packet of *speculaas* down from the bookshelf. 'Here. Have a couple of these if you're hungry, and tell me what you want.'

Corinne took a cookie, and began to tell him about Middelburg, in a carefully edited version. 'So you see,' she wound up, 'I have to catalogue all this stuff, and one of the loose ends I need to tuck in is this Latin journal. I've got the first ten pages printed out from the microfilm, and if you could just give me an idea what's going on . . . ?' She trailed off hopefully, looking up at him.

Theodoor shrugged. 'Early modern spiritual diaries are ten a penny, and they're as often in Latin as not. But you knew that. Practically everyone who could write kept a notebook, so when he caught a cold after he'd groped the scullerymaid, he could ask himself whether it was the judgment of God. Hand it over and I'll take a quick look.' Corinne handed over the folder, and he opened it up. 'Nice clear script, isn't it? Just give me a minute. Have another biscuit.'

Corinne contented herself with watching him. She was pretty sure he was gay, a pity, since she found him mildly attractive. She was so pressed for time that her sex-life was pretty well on hold unless fate actually threw someone into her path. He was a bit old for her, but he had nice eyes, and she liked the way his dark hair clung to his head like fur. Never mind; the thought was almost certainly irrelevant. Theodoor, unconscious of her scrutiny, frowned and bit his lip as he read, then looked up at her.

'I take it all back. This is something special after all.'

'It isn't a spiritual diary?'

'Of course it is. But the writer's a black slave. Or was.'

'What?' Corinne scrambled up, and came up to peer over Theodoor's shoulder. He smelt nice, clean shampoo smells, with a hint of vetivert.

'Look,' he said, indicating with a long knobbly finger like a piece of bamboo. 'We start with a prayer. "Considering the great goodness and justice of God in his dealings with me", blah, blah, blah. "That I was brought from earthly happiness and the vain hope of a crown to the living death of slavery." The word's *servitudo*. "Like the first sons of Israel, I left the fleshpots of Africa with no willing heart, and wandered long in the desert wilderness of waters. But it has pleased the Lord to raise me up from that captivity, and in place of an earthly crown, to make me heritor of a heavenly diadem."'

'Wow.'

'Well, this isn't solving your problems, Corinne. It's just doubled them. Can I have the rest of the text, please?'

'Certainly,' said Corinne, shaken. She leaned against the wall, thinking furiously, while he turned back to the photocopy, skimming the remaining pages.

'There's quite a bit more theology,' said Theodoor once he had got to the end, 'then he starts talking about his origins in Africa. He was the son of the King of the Hoiones, whoever they were. Something about treachery . . . he was made a slave by some people he calls Nubiae, Nubians I suppose, and got shipped overseas to Batavia – the East Indies Batavia, he must mean – and became a Christian. The print-out ends here, you must let me have the rest of it. You're going to have the post-colonial people down like a flock of vultures, you know. I'm not a specialist, but I think that thesis of Capitein's is the first known narrative by a

Dutch ex-slave and it must be a good hundred years later. This is in an early seventeenth-century hand.'

'Who's Capitein?'

'He was a former slave who got himself an education, wrote a Latin treatise on Christian slavery in the 1740s, and became a predikant. This fellow must have a similar type of story. His Latin's very good.'

'Theodoor, I thought I was in enough trouble already,' wailed Corinne. 'What am I going to do?'

'You'll get there. Don't worry.'

'The trouble is, you know, I have to get the thesis done by the end of the year. I can't get a job till I've got it. I haven't *time* for major discoveries.'

Theodoor shrugged. 'I never give advice, Corinne. But this isn't just any old heap of rubbish. Get it sorted out.'

'Oh, God. It's such a gamble.'

'Give me Pelagius, and I'll let you have the gist when I can. If the rest's as good as this, then I wouldn't worry too much.'

'But it doesn't fit.'

'It must fit. It was in with the other texts. It might take a lot of work before anyone can get the hang of it all, though, so you need to make it into a project you can get a grant for. You know the rules, Corinne. If you're bringing in money, your professor won't give you any grief. Who is he, anyway?'

'Hendrik Derksen. He's not very pleased with me. I took a year out of my graduate programme to do this exhibition in Middelburg, and now I'm completely out of time and money. It's Cees that worries me.'

'Who's Cees?'

'The other Book History AIO. He started two years later than me, and he's just about finished, so, of course, he's Derksen's blue-eyed boy. He acts as if getting a job's just a matter of time, and he even goes to faculty meetings. Derksen hasn't really done much to build up the school, and the way things are now, there's not going to be room for both of us.'

'Oh, that Cees. Pushy little git, isn't he? But Corinne, if you get ahead of him, what d'you think he can do about it? Lie on the floor and scream? The trouble with you women is you get invested in this nonsense about being a nice girl. It's a waste of time. I'd start empire-building, if I were you.'

II

Before you can say 'Come' and 'Go',
And breathe twice, and cry, 'So, So',
Each one, tripping on his toe,
Will be here with mop and mow . . .
Do you love me master? No?

William Shakespeare, *The Tempest*, IV.1

Michael awaited Corinne's package with interest. He had been very surprised to hear from her: they were on terms, roughly, of two or three emails a year, and he was under no illusion that she thought of him any more often than that. Two years previously, he had spent a sabbatical term working in the Netherlands on Daniel Defoe's nefarious career as entrepreneur, smuggler, Williamite activist and possibly industrial spy, in the course of which she had surprised and gratified him by picking him up in the canteen of the Koniglijke Bibliotheek. But the relationship, pleasant enough while it lasted, had died a natural death once he went back to Oxford. All the same, he often thought of his months in Holland: especially after he had met Corinne and got more inward with the culture, he had found it a brief but precious experience of an academic world that was structurally fairer, more socially responsible, and capable of adapting to new methods and new ideas. Acculturated as he was to Oxford, the way Corinne's professor had been able to set up a unit to develop an innovative way of looking at texts and recruit bright graduates had been an exciting revelation.

When she rang, he had been delighted by the news of the archive and the project she sketched out to him. 'When d'you think you'll get it online? Professor Edzell and I are trying to get a new course through the Faculty Board on "The Roots of the Novel". We're wanting to put early fiction in context by teaching them about popular literature, chapbooks, romances, travel-writing and so on. You'd be a fabulous resource. I take it quite a lot of it's in English?'

She had been quite amused by his enthusiasm. 'Not for years. We haven't even started yet.'

'Oh, well. Maybe in the future.'

'I hope so. But there was a special reason I wanted to talk to you. We found all these things I have told you about, but we also found a play by Aphra Behn.'

'Aphra Behn?' he had said. 'Janet Todd's the person you want, really. She's at Glasgow now. Or Germaine, at Warwick.'

'But Michael, I think this is something completely new.'

'Oh.' A fluttering sense of excitement had begun to steal over him. Though he was not by nature unscrupulous, the idea of presenting the world with a completely new discovery was one he was no more proof against than the next scholar. 'Well, how about if I find out? I'll check with Todd's edition, and if it's not there, then you've really got something. It's a manuscript, you said?'

'Yes.'

'I'm in the right place, then. There's some kind of Behn common-place book in Bodley. As soon as I get your microfilm, I'll check the handwriting against the book we've got here, and get in touch.'

So for a while, that had been that, till, one morning, he checked his pigeon-hole in Balliol and found in it a small, rotund padded envelope with Dutch stamps. It was a teaching morning, so he shoved it in his briefcase and went on up to his study, where a gaggle of undergraduates were already mooching about on the landing capping one another's stories about recruitment fairs. From what he overheard, you got more points with your peers for an interview with Price Waterhouse than for one with the Foreign Office, and he wondered in passing how long that had been the case; since the 1980s, perhaps?

Later in the day, when the last of them had been successfully pushed out of the door, he went to the college library and made himself a complete photocopy of the microfilm, which he then took over to the Bodleian Library to compare with their manuscript Firth C 19, 'Astraea's Booke for Songs and Satyr's'.

After less than half an hour's work, he was in no doubt whatsoever. The hand of the Middelburg manuscript was very close to the hand that joins Firth C 19 in around 1685, which he knew to be Aphra's. The new play's similarity to such of Aphra's work as he had read was striking, and a brief trip over to the English Literature section of the Upper Reading-Room made it clear that no one had ever heard of it. Pleased and excited, he reflected that it had come into his life at an excellent moment. He had recently finished a book on Defoe, and though he had some ideas about what to do next, they would keep: he had nothing in mind as interesting or as potentially important as Corinne's discovery. By the time he shut *Aphra Behn: An Annotated Bibliography*, he had made a firm decision to commit himself to editing the new play.

Back in his room later that day, he locked the door, unplugged the phone, and settled down for the peculiarly intense experience of meeting a new text to which he had already pretty well decided to give a sizeable chunk of his life. Aphra wrote a nice clear hand, so it was possible for Michael, who was used to late seventeenth-century manuscripts, simply to skim through *The Female Rosicrucian* almost as fast as if it was in print, despite its crossings-out and interlinings, gulping it down in a state of complete concentration, getting the feel of it. Details were for later, but his first impression was highly intriguing. It was in blank verse, like several of her early plays, not her best medium, and it must, he realised, be her first attempt at a play or not far off it.

After the first run-through, he started working out the dates with the college's copy of the recent Behn biography open beside him. Aphra had returned from Suriname, apparently unmarried, in 1663 and then she had vanished for a while. Three years later she popped up in London as a spy, using the name Mrs Behn, and after that, she was reasonably well documented. In 1670, she had erupted into the world of the London theatre as a fully fledged professional writer. The play in front of him must date to the lost years, 1663–6, which had therefore presumably been spent in Middelburg. His enthusiasm for the project rose and rose. Aphra Behn, like his own first love, Daniel Defoe, seemed to have had a complete command of her style from her first appearance in print. How wonderful to be able to get behind that, and look at an early modern writer putting herself together.

The Female Rosicrucian turned out to be set in Venice, and to feature a royal black villain called Ali Puli. This interested him greatly, since Behn had come back to a royal black villain in 1675, in *Abdelazar*, and had also written about a royal black hero in her much later *Oroonoko*, which suggested a lifelong interest. In the play before him, Ali Puli was a magus figure, an ex-king vowing revenge for his enslavement, so he was more like Abdelazar than Oroonoko. But he brought other characters to mind as well, from plays which Aphra might well have read: since he was the seducer of Bianca, the daughter of a Venetian merchant, Michael wondered if Aphra had partly modelled him on Othello, speaker of enchantments to a pale Venetian lady. And *Othello* was partly set in Venice, of course, as was another possibly relevant play, Ben Jonson's *Volpone*, with its manipulative anti-hero. The heavy father in *The Female Rosicrucian* was a Venetian merchant, so it would also be wise to be on the lookout for echoes of *The Merchant of Venice* – especially since in that play, one of Portia's unsuccessful suitors was black, the Prince of Morocco. In fact, he thought, making a note, if you looked at the history of black men wooing white women on the English stage, it was hard to get away from Venice.

The other thing that struck him at once about the play was its interest in women's lives. It had a pair of strong heroines, sisters, one destined for the convent, the other a learned lady being forced into an unsuitable marriage. So she'd been interested from the start in women's lack of choice . . . He glanced at his watch, and shuffled his notes together reluctantly; there would be a knock on the door any minute, more students.

That evening, he rang Corinne.

'Corinne? I got the play. Thanks so much for sending it my way, it's absolutely wonderful.'

'Hallo, Michael! Great to hear from you. Have you read it yet?'

'Only once, at a gallop,' he warned. 'I've not got much time to myself during term.'

'Oh, tell me about it. There's so much I want to do with my end, but I just can't touch it till I'm through with the thesis. Anyway, it is interesting?'

'Gripping. Your printer was called Behn, wasn't he?'

'Yes.'

'I'd guess he must've been Aphra's husband. I wonder if she left him. Did you know she was a spy for the British government in '66? The idea was for her to find out stuff about the Dutch, but she hovered around in Belgium and wouldn't set foot in the Netherlands. Nobody seems to know why, but if she'd a husband in Zeeland she was trying to avoid, that might explain it. I really need to see some of what you've got, though. I think in a way the context's almost as important as the play.'

'Mmm.' He got the impression that she was not best pleased. 'Tell me about the play. Remember, I haven't read it.'

'There's a lot of what you might expect from a Restoration play, sex 'n' cynicism, masses of plotting, but the central character's this tremendous black anti-hero, and I'm wondering why. The Dutch West India Company had a base in Middelburg, didn't they?

I'm wondering if she knew someone black, or if it's based on a story someone told her?'

'Oh, Michael. I think this may be coming together. One of the other things we found was a journal by a black man.'

'Was he a king?'

'Yes – is that in the play?'

'Yes, listen,' said Michael, scrabbling through the pages of print-out:

'My father's blood cries in me for revenge,
The blood I saw as he lay in the dust,
Throne, life, son, ravished by Lorenzo's men.
I was a child, though old enough to grieve,
But not avenge, nor yet defy my fate.
The years that passed have taught me many things,
The magic arts, the gift of coz'ning men –
They have not taught a king's son to forget.'

'That's fascinating,' said Corinne. 'What else does it say about him?'

'He's called Ali Puli, and he's the son of an African king who gets enslaved by the agents of a Venetian merchant called Lorenzo. I don't know that the Venetians were actually involved in the Atlantic trade, but I think she had reasons for wanting to put the play in Venice – one of the heroines ends up becoming a learned courtesan like the real-life Veronica Franco. Anyway, the play opens with Ali Puli vowing revenge on Lorenzo, and saying he's got a way into the house at last, because they've acquired a maidservant who's from his people, and she knows he's her rightful king.'

'The diary isn't like that,' objected Corinne. 'I don't read Latin, but my friend Theodoor says it's all about resignation and Christian stuff.'

'I don't think that's a problem. It's typical of the way dramatists treat sources. They're like journalists, they just take people and situations and put them through the mincer to make a good story. But Corinne, I really must see this thing. It's obviously relevant.'

'Can you clear a few days and come over? You can stay, if you like.'

'Er, no. I don't think I'll do that, Corinne, thanks all the same. I'd rather be on my own. If I do come, I really will have to work all the time.'

'That's fine. If you can give me some dates, I'll see what I can do about getting you a visiting scholar's room.'

Once Michael had rung off, Corinne picked up the phone again, and got in touch with Theodoor.

'Hi, it's Corinne. Listen, does the name Ali Puli mean anything to you? We're in the seventeenth century.'

It was a while before he replied. She could hear a piano somewhere in the background, twentieth-century classical music of some kind, and was momentarily curious about Theodoor's life. Did he live alone? The texture of the sound suggested someone playing, not a recording. She must ask Ankie, who always seemed to know a lot about gay people in the university. 'Alipuli? . . . Yes. He's supposed to be a black Rosicrucian. He wrote a book called *Centrum naturae concentratum*, I've never read it. Are you thinking about him as the author of the memoirs?'

'Well, what d'you think?'

'Off the cuff, the dates aren't going to fit. Anyway, someone called Ali Anything's surely going to be a Muslim, so he was probably from North or East Africa. Your man goes straight from pagan to Christian. Good try, though.'

Michael, negotiating the painless anonymity of Schiphol, began to tune his ear in to Dutch again, its mouth-filling phlegmy vowels and guttural rasps. He bought himself a train-ticket, and found the platform for Duivendrecht, where he would change. Once on board the train, he alternately looked at the free magazine, trying to resurrect his knowledge of the language, or stared out of the window at the flat, waterlogged panorama of willows and motor-ways skirting the southern industrial hinterland of Amsterdam. A sense of familiarity began to settle around him only when he reached the strange two-decker train station at Duivendrecht, which he had forgotten all about. They had started to build a motorway since he was there last, huge concrete Ys marched across the landscape, waiting to cup a future road-bed, interrupting the familiar perspective of rectangular, moated fields, cows and pylons.

It was still only mid-afternoon when he arrived in Utrecht and emerged into the middle of the ugly, bustling shopping-complex called Hoog Catherijne, which was no better and no worse than it had been. Fashions in busking had changed; there was still at least one black drummer, but there was also a pair of sturdy women in what was possibly Ukrainian peasant costume, singing incomprehensible folk-songs in sweet, robust voices, and a little further along, a group of white boys were playing didgeridoos, producing a curious deep booming and buzzing which seemed to disturb the fillings in his teeth. Once escaped from the tentacular embrace of Hoog Catherijne, he was able to walk to the university, get his key, dump his bags and go to the Studiepunt Letteren in reasonable hopes of catching Corinne.

As he climbed the stairs, he found himself swallowing in nervous apprehension, even while he told himself he was being idiotic. Corinne was making casual use of his mind, skills, and connections, as she had once made casual use of his body. With an effort of will, he tried to discipline his mind into starting over with her. Still, there was a jolt – relief or disappointment? – when the office door was opened by a a short, dark-haired man, rather well dressed. He was struck, as they exchanged cautious hallos, by the crowd-edness of the hutch-like office he could see over the man's shoulder – though of course, he reminded himself, Corinne was still only a graduate student, even if she was not much younger than he was, and therefore not entitled to much.

The man, who had introduced himself as Cees, returned to his laptop. Looking around, Michael carefully moved some papers off a chair and sat down. There was a copy of *Dutch Crossing* on a desk nearby, the only visible thing written in English, so he began to leaf through it.

'Michael! Hi!' Corinne had arrived at last, barely visible behind an armful of books. A pair of over-designed glasses with blue-and-green frames were perched on her nose, making her look as if she was playing at being a lecturer, an impression which was strengthened when she dumped her armload on top of a filing cabinet and immediately took them off. She was wearing a 1960s-style stripy dress with batwing sleeves, very short, which suggested that she still had a weakness for showing off her excellent legs. Her hair, which had been quite long, was now worn in a bob coming just under the ears, but otherwise, she had hardly changed at all; she was still a slim, blonde, attractive witness to the irritatingly high quality of the national genotype.

She came over, looking genuinely pleased to see him, and he scrambled to his feet self-consciously. He tried to kiss her on the cheek, but she moved her head, and he found he had met her lips. 'Hallo, *schat*, what've you got there – oh, *Dutch Crossing*. Ruud's got an article in it. He's the other AIO who uses this office. C'mon, let's leave Cees in peace.' She opened the bottom drawer of her desk, and took out her bag, slinging it over her shoulder. Linking her arm with Michael's, she practically towed him out of the room, chattering brightly about the weather.

'Sorry about that,' she said, pausing to look up at him once they had put a flight of stairs between themselves and the office. 'I don't want to talk about any of this stuff in front of that slimeball Cees. If he knew what I was doing, I'd have him in my knickers till he'd worked out how to take all the credit.'

Michael looked at her in surprise. 'You never used to think like that,' he commented.

Corinne met his gaze sombrely. 'I didn't use to share an office with Cees. My professor really likes him, and gradually I realised what was happening. We've had lots of cuts over here, you know, and there's a feeling among us juniors we won't all make permanency. In Book History, really it's him or me, and he's determined to get ahead. Well, I don't want him stealing my thunder – you say that in English, don't you?'

'Yes. Corinne, where are we going?'

'We're going to go and have some coffee, and then we need to do some shopping, I've asked Theodoor to have dinner with us. You'll like him. He's a neo-Latinist, and he's been looking at the diary for me.'

Michael followed in her wake as she set off briskly for the café, surprised and disturbed. Either Corinne had become remarkably paranoid, or there were important things about the system which he had failed to grasp on his previous visit.

He imagined that when they were settled, Corinne would start to tell him what she was thinking. He remembered her as up-front and communicative, but now she was stirring her coffee with unnecessary concentration, apparently unable to spit out whatever was on her mind. 'Tell me about the other things you've found,' he said, hoping to get her started.

Her reaction was not what he expected. 'It's all at a very early stage,' she said. She looked defensive and mulish.

'For Christ's sake, Corinne. That never used to stop you having an opinion.'

'Well, maybe I've changed. Everything's so difficult now. You've got to be so careful.'

'Don't worry. I'm sure you'll be all right. You're very talented, and you've done an awful lot.'

She looked him straight in the eye, and he realised that she was genuinely distressed. 'Michael, it's all changed since I started. You're not supposed to have done a lot, you're supposed to have stayed on track. I think it's different in England – can you teach there if you haven't got a PhD yet?'

'Certainly. I must've been in post for eighteen months by the time it came through. I hadn't realised you couldn't – is that why you're working for these software people?'

'Yes, of course,' she said, rather impatiently. 'It's only you English who are allowed to be amateurs.'

'It's better than being civil servants,' he said and wished he hadn't, it was an argument they had had in the old days. But he sensed with relief that she, like he, realised they had fallen into a pattern; she drank off the rest of her coffee and put the cup down decisively.

'Let's go. I need to go to Albert Hein and get some stuff for tonight. You like Indonesian food, don't you? I was going to make gado-gado.'

'Excellent.'

He was tired; what with one thing and another his day had started early. It was in a state of mild disassociation that he followed Corinne down alleys and along canals to the supermarket. The un-Englishness of it closed over him, mapping comfortably onto his memories from his sabbatical: the lovely fruit and vegetables, the umpteen varieties of yoghurt and custard in this dairy-dependent country, the word '*Reclame!*' at every turn. Corinne filled a basket efficiently with vegetables, rice, eggs, beancurd – tahoe, he remembered the word suddenly – and cruised the condiments shelves with a dissatisfied air.

'I was too late to catch Toko Centraal, so we'll just have to make do,' she said apologetically, collecting satay powder, ketjap manis, sambal oelek and other bits and pieces whose names he had forgotten. 'You remember Ankie? Well, her girlfriend Pieternelle taught me how to make fantastic gado-gado, but it really needs fresh sereh and laos, and proper palm-sugar.'

'I'm sure it'll be delicious. Shall I get some wine?' he volunteered.

'Oh, yes. Thanks.'

They took a bus out to her flat, a characterless, tiny studio with pale wooden floors, enlivened rather haphazardly by a mixture of seventeenth-century printed pages and black-and-white Hollywood glamour pictures, which seemed almost unchanged in the two years since he had last seen it. It was tidy and very clean, but not welcoming; looking at it with a newly analytic eye, it struck him that Eimer, his last girlfriend, must have managed to teach him much more about interior design than he had realised at the time: he could now see how the space might be better used, though it would hardly be tactful to say so. The furniture was also now instantly recognisable.

'I wonder if there's an academic in Europe who doesn't own at least one Ikea bookcase?' he commented, carrying the bags through to the minute kitchen. 'We should teach the kids to assemble a "Billy" as part of skills induction.'

'They're good, aren't they? Even if the name's idiotic. Actually, just about everything in the flat's from Ikea.'

He didn't want to ask her what was wrong with the name, since he was obviously supposed to know. 'That must be one of the headaches of international capitalism. I always wondered who was stupid enough to buy a Toyota Cressida? I mean, anyone in their senses would know it was bound to go wrong. But tell me what I can do to help. Shall I open the wine?'

'If you like. Maybe you could do the beans, and cut up some carrots?'

While he worked, Corinne got out the steamer and a couple of pans, and began putting together the sauce. Despite her disclaimers, it smelt delicious. Half-way through the carrots, he remembered suddenly that *billen* meant 'buttocks' in Dutch, and grinned to himself.

Theodoor arrived punctually at seven. When the doorbell rang, Corinne was in the middle of slicing onions as thinly as possible, so he answered it for her.

He took to Theodoor on sight. They introduced themselves to one another, since Corinne called that she had to finish doing the onions and would come through when she could, so Michael poured the newcomer a drink, while he folded his great height into one of Corinne's little modern armchairs.

'Tell me about *The Female Rosicrucian*,' he said without preamble, once Michael had sat down. He obliged, while Theodoor listened quietly, asking only pertinent questions, and the smell of frying onions drifted through the tiny flat.

'It seems very likely that your playwright knew this journal,' he remarked, once Michael had finished, 'or perhaps, knew of it. Do you think she can have read Latin?'.

'Janet Todd thinks it's very unlikely.'

'Then perhaps there was someone who gave her the gist. It is clear that Ali Puli in the play is not a portrait study of the author of the diary, but the fact that she kept it suggests that it is relevant.'

'As if she used it as a jumping-off point.'

'Precisely. By the way, I have found out a little more about the real Ali Puli. He is supposed to be "a moor out of the East Indies", but nobody knows any more. He wrote a treatise which is usually dated to 1682. But I took a look at the website of the Herzog August Bibliothek in Wolfenbüttel, since there is so much Rosicrucian activity in Braunschweig, and it turns out there is a single surviving copy of a first edition, dated 1661. The '82 edition is a reissue. Would you like to guess where 1661 was published?'

'Middelburg?'

'Correct.'

'So it's not impossible Aphra could have seen a copy?' said Michael.

'No. It would not have been much good to her, since it is in Latin, but if the book was around, someone may have talked about it to her. She was obviously moving in literate circles. Who knows how people get to hear of things? It is as if little pieces of information about black men came together for her, and resulted in this play. Also, did you know there was a second notebook from Pelagius in this collection?'

'No. What is it?'

'A little book, used at both ends. One end has the text of an oracle or divination, called "The African Sibyl", the other has notes on plants.'

Just then, Corinne came through to put a blue-and-white bowl of rice on the table, and as the two men got to their feet, she returned triumphantly with a large platter, heaped with a symmetrical arrangement of steamed vegetables, fried tofu and halved hard-boiled eggs. On her third trip she brought the peanut sauce, and a collection of little bowls containing crisp-fried onions, sliced bananas, cucumber and fiery sambal.

'Wow. This looks wonderful,' said Michael.

'Enjoy your dinner,' she bade them, clearly pleased.

'Corinne, what about this other notebook?' asked Michael, once they had filled their plates.

She frowned. 'It's in the "Pelagius" hand, which we're identifying as belonging to a black man. I can't see where it fits in at all.'

'Except that it suggests that Pelagius was some kind of magician,' said Theodoor. 'The real Alipuli was a Rosicrucian, and Aphra Behn's Ali Puli is an alchemist and magus. It is the divinations and not the diary that make the connecting link, and tell us that her black magus and one-time king is a composite of these two figures.'

'You've got to be right,' said Michael. 'My guess is, she knew this man in Middelburg in the 1660s. He must've been very conspicuous, and he was obviously scholarly. Possibly they were brought together because he was involved with Behn's publishing business in some way.'

'He was quite elderly by then,' observed Theodoor. 'His script is based on models from the first half of the century.'

'She got interested in him, and they got to know each other. Perhaps he was down on his luck, and sold her his books. She seems to have been working for the press, so she presumably had money.'

Later in the evening, once they had finished with dinner, Theodoor went unexpectedly on what Michael had to think of as the offensive.

'Corinne, you will need to think carefully. On one hand, you have what you first saw, a printer's archive. This you can study very efficiently. But you have also a play by Aphra Behn and a Latin narrative by a black man which is more than a century earlier than the thesis of Jacobus Capitein, and these things are connected in some way. How can we deal with this?'

'If I can put my oar in,' added Michael swiftly, 'I'd have to say, together, not apart.'

Corinne reached out for her glass of wine, which had stood until then untouched on the coffee table, and took a long swallow. 'This is my whole chance of a future,' she said.

'Yes,' said Theodoor. 'So how are you thinking of handling it?'

'The key person is my supervisor. Professor Derksen.'

'*Seker*. So consider his weaknesses. He is honest in his way, and what he has written is good, but I have known him for fifteen years, and he is a dull man, fixed in his own little groove. He knows a great deal about Antwerp, the Spanish Netherlands, and the religious politics of the Eighty Years War, but he does not know about England or the Netherlands and the Atlantic world, and he will not want to learn. On the other hand, if you have a plan which clearly benefits him, and you are prepared to do all the work, he will certainly be prepared to put his name on it.'

'Theodoor, do you know if he has any friends in English studies?' asked Corinne.

'Certainly not here. He is on very cool terms with the professor of English and American. I don't think he will want to do any favours there. You are thinking effectively, Corinne. You must calculate what everyone wants. Derksen would be pleased to have more glory, if he did not have to do any extra work. The Middelburg Gemeente want a catalogue and a wonderful website, that is straightforward. For your own part, you must finish your thesis, but you want to come back after six months or so and walk into a job building the website and running this project. Michael, what do you want?'

'I want to edit the Behn play, and I think that's going to involve knowing quite a bit more about the "Pelagius" manuscripts. I'd welcome your help.'

'Yes, but where have you got to in your career? Are you thirsty, like Corinne?'

It was an unexpectedly blunt, un-English question. 'Up to a point,' he said slowly. 'I'll have to think – it's not the kind of question I ask myself. I finished my research fellowship last year, and for now I'm a sort of "locum tenens" lecturer, because the woman who had our junior English post got a Chair somewhere else. That's a great opportunity, because when the job's properly advertised, I'll be the sitting tenant, so I'll have a very good chance of being made permanent, and that in turn means I've a real chance of staying in Oxford. On the other hand, I'm not sure I want to. I've got personal reasons for wanting to be further north, and anyway, you can't go on renting for ever, and you can't buy a house anywhere in the south of England on a lecturer's salary. So just in case something good comes up, I'd like to be looking lots more exciting. I've written a couple of books, but there's only one thing so far that's attracted attention. Is that what you mean? Sorry if that was a bit incoherent.'

'Yes. Your reasons are not so urgent, but they are real.'

'And you, Theodoor?' he asked.

He shrugged. 'Well, I am not very thirsty, so to say. I have my own concerns: I am editing Spanheim, and I am part of a big international project on humanist correspondence. I have no desire to snatch the *Notatiunculae* from Corinne, though I am happy to lend a hand with finding someone who could work on it. I certainly do not pretend to any great knowledge of the Netherlands and the Atlantic – I think, Corinne, your friend Ankie Hoogstra might be some help on this.'

'Yes – and Pieternelle, Ankie's partner. She did a PhD on early modern Curaçao, and she works in black studies.'

'Well, then, Corinne. Can you see that you have made some very lucky choices in trusting the two of us? What Michael is telling you is that he has a clear area of interest, enough to make him do his share of the work, but it seems that his needs are satisfied by editing the play. You will have to learn to make this kind of assessment even of your friends, if you are going to succeed in the present climate. Actually, you are very fortunate indeed, because in general, your friends are better informed than your un-friends, and that means it should be possible to draft a proposal which is attractive to Derksen, and leaves you in control. By the way, the young man Cees, has he any relevant expertise?'

Corinne snorted. 'No. He works on the Spanish Netherlands, of course – staying close to daddy. He has some English, but his Spanish and French are better.'

'So you are the obvious liaison person. You have the knowledge, you have links with English and post-colonial. It will certainly take six months, if not a year, to put the funding package together, so if you are clever and work hard, you should be in a position to take charge just about when there is something to take charge of.' Theodoor reached out and deposited his empty coffee-mug on the table. 'Thank you for a most pleasant evening. I think I will say good-night now, I have some way to go.' Unfolding like a deck-chair, he got to his feet, followed by Michael and Corinne.

Once they had said their farewells, Corinne shut the door behind him. Michael was very conscious that, as they had both gone to wave him off, they were necessarily standing very close to one another.

'Come on,' he said, as she looked as if she was about to say something, 'I'll help you with the washing-up.' He brushed past her, and went to clear the table, pouring himself more wine in passing.

As he handed her the last dish for wiping and putting away, he said, 'Theodoor's right, you know. I don't pretend to understand how university bureaucracy works over here, but everything he says is making the right noises.'

'I suppose so,' she said unhappily. She reached up to put away the dish, then suddenly swung back to face him. 'Michael, I feel completely boxed in. I've got to get it right with Derksen or I may as well give up, and he doesn't really like me. Do you know what it's like to depend on someone like that?'

'Up to a point. English professors don't have that sort of individual power over their grad students, but you certainly can't go around offending them. You see, you need references to get a job, so if you get up people's noses then there's nobody to write for you when you need it. It's a bit less direct but it means we certainly can't afford to speak our minds. Personally, I've got to stay the right side of the entire English Faculty for the time being, because I don't know who'll be on the selection committee when my job's advertised. And I suppose Robert Edzell's potentially got total control over my future, because he's our senior English Fellow. It's never come up in those terms, because we get on terribly well.'

'I see. It's funny, you never really get to understand how other systems work, do you?'

'No. I've been thinking all day that I certainly don't understand the Netherlands. Anyway' – he drained his glass – 'I'd better be going. I've been up since quarter to six. Quarter to five, your time. It's the 23 bus I want, isn't it?'

'Yes. But Michael, you could stay.'

The offer was half-expected, but it jolted him all the same. 'No, love. It'd be a complete fiasco. I can't do that sort of thing.' Turning away, he caught a glimpse of her face out of the corner of his eye, and was horrified to see that her eyes were filling with tears. 'Oh, Corinne. What's wrong?'

'Michael, do you not like me any more?'

'Of course I do. And of course I still think you're very attractive. But the trouble is, to me, the idea of going back to a relationship that went cold feels a bit – I can't think of the right word. Icky. Indecent. Sorry if that's rude.'

'But Michael, it is just a pleasant action, we are not committed,' she protested.

'If it's just an action, then why do you want to do it? I mean, I'm not special to you.'

She stared at him for a moment, then suddenly blurted, 'But how can I trust you?'

Michael sighed, retrieved his glass from the sink, and poured the last of the wine into it. I'm too tired for this sort of scene, he thought. 'Shall I make you some tea, Corinne?'

'Please.' She snuffled into a piece of kitchen-roll, and dropped it in the bin while he put the kettle on.

Once tea was made, they went through to the living-room. He realised he had slipped into the role of impersonal comforter, so familiar from work. 'You've got very frightened, haven't you?'

'Yes,' she said slowly, 'I think I have. I'm all alone, you see. My mother doesn't really know what's going on and my father is in Australia. I don't want to talk to anyone in the university, just in case they have friends who are friends with Cees, and nobody else understands. I think I've maybe ruined my life, and now I must gamble again. So it's not surprising I want you to be friendly and pleased with me. But I think you've not understood me either. I do like you, and I thought we had a good time.'

'Of course we did. But I don't have the temperament for casual sex. Please understand, Corinne. I'm not trying to make you feel guilty. We're just different.' He looked at her with compunction; she was starting to look very fragile. 'If it helps, you know, you really can trust me. I've said I'm on your side, and it's true.' He stood up, half-thought of touching her, and decided against it. 'I'll say good-night now. Sleep well, and I'll see you in the morning.'

'Good-night.' She did not see him to the door.

Michael slept badly, though he was very tired, replaying the scene again and again in his mind's eye. The new facts he had learned about Corinne's life had come as a shock. Over the last couple of years, he realised, his occasional thoughts of her had been coloured by resentment. He had seen her as the child of a successful democracy, healthy in mind and body, supported from cradle to grave by democratic socialism, and unencumbered by the hang-ups and difficulties that came as part of the package of being an English ex-public-school misfit. It was not, he thought, examining his conscience, that he had seen her as smug, so much as that he had believed she had been rendered obtuse by taken-for-granted, lifelong good fortune. He now felt deeply sorry for her.

The following day, he went to Middelburg. He was familiar with the town and the Zeeland archives from his previous experience: he had needed to go down there to work out the back-history of the seventy musk-producing civet cats which Defoe had smuggled into England in 1688, hoping to revolutionise the English perfume industry. He was no stranger, therefore, to the oddities which a Dutch archive might contain, but on this occasion he asked for, and was given, the contents of the Behn satchel, now a box-file full of loose papers, together with the three manuscript books which looked even more interesting than the surreal ups and downs of the great civet-smuggling enterprise. The Behn book was the least of his worries. It was the two 'Pelagius' books that he had really come to see.

He leafed through the first of them, regretting that he had only a smattering of Latin. The fact that his father would have been the one to teach him A level Latin if he'd opted for it had been, to him, reason in itself to drop it at sixteen, a typical teenager's mistake, looking back. He looked carefully at the botanical notes and the meticulous drawings which went with them: he did not recognise the plants, but someone would know. The text at the other end of the book was evidently oracular, possibly, he thought, some of the Sibylline verses, though he knew next to nothing about Sibylline verses except that they had existed. He copied out a couple, noting that they did not, to his amateur eye, seem to be metrical, for later identification. There were still one or two people in Oxford who were walking concordances of classical poetry; surely he could find someone who would identify this material. Moving the book a little more into the light as he copied, he noticed that there were annotations in silverpoint: Dutch words, in a most unattractive script, apparently glosses on the Latin text. Corinne, he remembered, had indicated that translation was part of the overall business of Behn's firm, and he made a note to himself to check with the Netherlands short-title catalogue and see if anything existed which looked like a possible Dutch version. Maybe Pelagius and Aphra had met when he sold the Behns his books.

The third book that he opened was the *Notatiunculae*. He handled it with care, alert to what it might tell him. Dutch paper, Dutch binding; and the script maintained its even beauty for page after page, showing that his man was a highly disciplined and fluent writer. The binding, he noticed, was in oddly poor condition for a book which had lain untouched for most of its three hundred years of existence, almost coming apart. He shut it and turned it round in his hands. No; on second thoughts, the back was tight, the covers were tight. It was the top of the front cover which seemed to be the problem, it was actually coming away from the board. No again – by that time, his nose was very nearly touching the book in the intensity of his concentration – it had been slit, probably deliberately, and there was something between the leather of the cover and its board. The glue must have failed as the leather dried out. He got up, and went to the desk to explain the situation. In the end, the head of the reading-room and another colleague actually came over and sat on either side of him while delicately, with the book flat on the table, he withdrew first one piece of paper, then another, using tweezers. He unfolded the papers, then the archivist produced a sheet of perspex and laid it over them so that he could look at them without touching.

The larger of the two sheets of paper was in Latin, but it was clear enough; the record of a marriage. He looked down to the names at the end, and a wave of scalding heat rolled down his spine; there was the familiar handwriting and name of Pelagius van Overmeer, and the other signatory was Elizabeth Stuart. Not, surely, *the* Elizabeth Stuart . . . ? It would be the simplest of tasks to find out, since there would be dozens of extant documents with the Queen of Bohemia's signature. Intrigued almost beyond bearing, he turned to the second piece of paper, which turned out to be an eloquent sequel to the first, a memorandum of baptism for a child, Balthasar van Overmeer, dated less than a year later, 25 March 1640.

He copied the contents of both sheets and drew, as well as he could, the signature of Elizabeth Stuart. He had an excellent memory for such things, he would know it if he saw it again. The trip to Middelburg had justified itself beyond his expectations. The plot of *The Female Rosicrucian* had turned, he recalled, on a secret liaison between the Machiavellian black magus Ali Puli and the aristocratic Bianca, daughter of the Venetian senator Lorenzo.

Aphra must have known these documents – had it in fact been Behn herself who had concealed them?

For the rest of the afternoon, he made a series of notes about the loose pages from the satchel. Some were deeply gratifying to his original academic purpose, since they were notes for plots or jotted scraps of conversation, but for the time being, he had lost interest in them. The group of letters – there were three altogether – clearly in the hand of 'Elizabeth Stuart', claimed all his attention, since the contents left him virtually certain that he was dealing with the Winter Queen. He knew very little about her beyond the basic facts that she was Charles I's sister and in her widowhood had lived as an exile in Holland, but there was sure to be a biography.

On the train back to Utrecht, he brooded over the day's finds. Poor Corinne was anxious to keep the Latin/black culture material and the Aphra Behn material in parallel tracks; this was partly a basic Dutch desire to organise work into discrete and sensible units, partly a more personal, and pathetically obvious, desire to ensure that she, as co-ordinator, was the only person in possession of the whole picture. Unfortunately, the problems did not seem separable. The papers concealed in the binding of *Notatiunculae* seemed to be leading him, in some bizarre fashion, back to England, and he wondered what Corinne would say – he wondered, in fact, if he was going to tell her just yet. Before he shared it with her, it would be nice to be able to work out a bit more of the story. The archive staff had not observed the significance of the name Elizabeth Stuart; they had merely noted that the author of the diary had concealed his marriage-certificate and their child's baptismal record. Now that they had assigned numbers to both pieces of paper, their professional concern was at an end, they would hardly ring Corinne up to tell her. And Theodoor; should he tell Theodoor? It was more directly his concern, in a way, but he had already signalled that he was far too busy to want to take on editing the diary. Theodoor puzzled him. Everything about his manner and body-language suggested that he was homosexual; he worked in a completely different department, and yet he was going out of his way to help Corinne, when there seemed no good reason why he should. Pure interest in the material, perhaps?

It was a long journey back to Utrecht Central, but he was so absorbed in his notes that he hardly noticed it passing. By the time the last train pulled in, he had decided to keep his new finding to himself till he had done at least some preliminary research on context. Once he had escaped from Hoog Catherijne, the university was not much of a walk. He bought some bami goreng and krupuk at an Indonesian take-away, and headed for his bare little room in the visitors' quarters. As he passed through the university precincts, a pair of double doors swung open, and he found himself surrounded by a small, chattering crowd. An evening lecture or event, just breaking up.

'Hallo, Michael,' said a voice in his ear, in English, making him jump. It was Theodoor. 'Have you had a good day-out in Middelburg?'

'Wonderful. Look, would you have time for a drink, and I'll tell you about it?'

'Yes, a quick one.'

Theodoor called a goodbye to a couple of the people he had come out with, and they strolled off together, Michael mildly embarrassed by his cooling supper in its plastic carrier, wafting the scent of garlic and ketjap as they walked. The stuff was, fortunately, edible cold. 'I will have to go home quite soon,' Theodoor warned, 'we keep a dog, and it is my job to take him out at night.'

'That's a bit of a tie, isn't it? I'd love to have a dog, but I don't know how people manage.'

'We lead a very quiet life, and Diederic is an antiquarian bookseller, so Olivier can go to work with him. He has a basket under the desk, and snoozes there for most of the day. If Diederic is at a bookfair or there are other problems, I take him to the univer-sity. He is not strictly allowed, but the secretary kindly pretends she has not seen him. But mostly, because Diederic has him in the morning and at lunchtime, it is only fair that I should take him last thing. Here we are – this is a quiet little place, and I see they are not crowded.'

Once they were settled with a beer apiece and, at Michael's request, a bowl of peanuts to still his growling stomach, he began to tell Theodoor about his discoveries, with the exception of the marriage and baptism certificates. 'I'm absolutely certain', he wound up, 'that there's a strong connection between Behn and this man.' A thought suddenly occurred to him: Behn was born in 1640, and so, as he had just discovered, was Pelagius's son Balthasar. Was he the link? 'I'm sure there's more we can find out about him. There may be a Dutch translation of the oracle-text.'

'Mmm. And remember the botany. There are not very many botanical works on the New World printed in seventeenth-century Holland, and these are notes on tropical plants, rattan and pandanus. There is a great botanical institute at Leiden, and I have a friend there. I can easily find out if the notes correspond to any published work. Our Pelagius becomes more and more interesting. I will have to think very carefully who could edit this work well. Corinne cannot supervise it effectively, so I will have to find her someone who is good enough to work by himself. Or herself, of course.'

'Theodoor, can I ask a rather personal question? Put it down to being an ignorant foreigner.'

Theodoor raised his eyebrows. 'Ask what you wish. I will not answer, if I think it is intrusive.'

'Well, I'm puzzled by why you're supporting Corinne to this extent. You're being incredibly kind to her. I wish I'd had that sort of mentoring when I was younger. Frankly, I could do with it now.'

'I think you are saying you would expect any protégé of mine to be a young man?'

'I suppose so.'

Theodoor looked at him severely. 'Michael, I do not ask for favours from graduate students.'

'Oh, God. I didn't mean –'

Theodoor waved the apology away. 'No. I do understand you. In England, I think that homosexual men, particularly at your ancient universities, are often homosocial – this is a familiar concept?'

'Oh, yes,' said Michael.

'Such men are hostile to women, but I am not, and I am very concerned about the future. It seems to me that almost all the decisions which have been taken recently are bad, because they favour predictability above everything. Not long ago, even in this bureaucratic nation, a graduate student who wrote and published and curated an exhibition would have been rewarded for talent and initiative. Now, I fear that Corinne has put herself at serious risk by not being conventional, and professional advancement will go to her rival, who has never done anything wrong, but will never do anything right. Intellectual timidity and lack of imagination are becoming virtues. I do not admire the English cult of the amateur, but over here, we are drawing the boundaries too narrowly. If I were fifteen years younger, I do not think I would get a job. Perhaps if Corinne had been a beautiful young man my feelings would be more personal, but as things are, they are strong. She is the type of person that I want to see coming into the academy, because she is capable of being surprised by what she does not know, she has a little bit of courage and she has an instinct for what is interesting. If we lose people like that in our desire for precisely quantifiable ability, we will have lost everything that really matters.'

'I see,' said Michael slowly. 'I hadn't thought of Corinne that way, but she is rather special, isn't she?'

Theodoor shrugged. 'She is a child of her time. Her education is limited and superficial – though in saying that, I maybe just show my age. Even in the time of Horace, it was possible to say *"nos nequiores, mox daturos progeniem vitiosorem"*, so it seems as if learning has always looked more difficult in the present than it was in the past. But truly, I think that we are in danger of destroying ourselves. Corinne tries to look beyond the narrow groove of specialism, and that is now very rare over here. She is owed my support for that reason alone.'

'I think that's tremendous. To be honest, I hadn't realised how vulnerable she was. Or the system as a whole.'

'All systems have their own vulnerabilities, because, sadly, the good is necessarily the enemy of the best. Over here, now that we are trying to do more with less, our concern with the equitable distribution of resources leaves us intensely at risk from mediocrity. Your system has its own forms of arrogance and complacency, and I would say, a higher degree of corruption. But perhaps this means you are pursuing excellence.'

'That's probably the basic justification,' said Michael. He was suddenly very weary, and even though the subject concerned him deeply, he had had all he could stand of earnest Dutch mulling over principles. He drained his glass, and set it down. 'Theodoor, I'm very interested in what you're saying, but I'll have to go, I'm absolutely knackered. I'm very glad we met, though. You've been extremely helpful, and you've given me a great deal to think about. Perhaps we can pick this up another time.'

'Good-night,' said Theodoor. 'Enjoy your noodles.'

III

It is a simple arithmetical fact that, though all the details of the route are unknown, Elizabeth Stuart is almost guaranteed to have an uninterrupted descent from King David. We all share that honour.

Steve Jones, *In the Blood*, p. 82

In the weeks that followed his return to England, Michael worked on the Dutch material whenever he had a spare moment. Since one of the British universities' five-yearly reviews of research activity had only recently rolled over them, no one was requiring him to account in detail for his time; 'research at an early stage, following up some trails suggested by my earlier work in Holland' did nicely. He typed the play into his computer and began to edit it, while simultaneously pursuing other lines of enquiry when time permitted, and he remained in email correspondence with both Corinne and Theodoor. Corinne followed up his suggestion that 'Sibilla Africana' might have been translated, based on the Dutch annotations he had spotted, and some time later, she triumphantly reported that the national library in The Hague had a copy of a book, or rather a pamphlet, issued by Petrus Behn, called *Het dertiende Sibille, of een nieuw en waerachtige waerschouwings-boeck*: 'The Thirteenth Sibyl, or, A New and True Book of Prophecies'. Theodoor's friend in Leiden did even better; the drawing of pandanus and some of the wording of the note on it was successfully identified with an illustration in a book published in The Hague in 1638, the *Oost-Indische Kruyd-boeck*. Theodoor commented that his friend had described the book as something of a bibliographic curiosity, since the plates were of an infinitely higher standard than the text, but the publisher was one of the known villains of the seventeenth-century book trade, so almost anything could have happened.

What he himself was most interested in, apart from the play, was Pelagius, Elizabeth and, increasingly, what had happened to their son Balthasar. Pelagius had clearly been someone remarkable. Both his deep learning and his profound religious commitment were witnessed by the diary, and it seemed he had also been a botanist. He had been sufficiently extraordinary to be loved by an ex-queen, though God only knew how they had met. As an historical individual, he both demanded and resisted interpretation; whatever one found out about context, the central mystery would remain. Elizabeth was more accessible in the sense that there was a great deal known, and knowable, about her. Her lively personality was strongly apparent from her letters; she was a person who loved deeply, and was loved in return. Even apart from Pelagius, she seemed to have inspired romantic gallantry in the most unlikely breasts.

The marriage certificate told him that the ceremony had taken place in 1639. As far as the historical record went, Elizabeth was stuck in The Hague all that year, muddling along from day to day in the Wassenaer Hof, contemplating England's slide into civil war and writing remarkably sensible letters in all directions; her sons were variously in England, imprisoned in Linz, and in Paris, her daughters living elsewhere in The Hague, or at school in Leiden. Moreover, all witnesses were agreed that her household was extravagant, disorderly and chaotic, with a floating population of dependants and hangers-on of all kinds. Putting all these facts together, the combination of place, time and circumstances seemed to be one in which the addition of a scholarly African to the personnel of the Wassenaer Hof could genuinely have passed uncommented-on, and therefore unrecorded. Balthasar had been born in the following year, and before 1647, Pelagius had become resident in Middelburg. It became clear from Michael's researches that during the course of 1640, the various sons had come home to their mother; and it therefore seemed a good guess that at some point in or after that year, since she evidently, and understandably, had not wished to make her second marriage public knowledge, Pelagius and their secret son had made their home in Middelburg, though Elizabeth's continued commitment to him was witnessed by the very affectionate letters.

Pursuing the wider context of this marriage, he became aware of an unexpected variety of stories about queens' secret affairs that had washed about early modern Europe. Elizabeth herself had been rumoured to have become the wife of Lord Craven, her sister-in-law Henrietta Maria was said to have married Lord Jermyn, and the French queen, Anne of Austria, was credited with giving birth to a blackamoor baby in 1664. If any gossip of this kind had circulated about Elizabeth and Pelagius, then presumably she had successfully shrugged it off as yet another tale. Their relationship had occurred at a point where Elizabeth was less effectively supervised than any other royal lady in Europe, and in a context where scandalous gossip was both to be expected, and so prevalent that it need not have carried any conviction.

Elizabeth, then, was the best-attested, the most knowable, so for the time being, she could be treated as a known quantity. Michael therefore concerned himself principally with pursuing Pelagius and his son. He had gone back to the Middelburg archives before leaving Holland, to look them both up in the persons index. Pelagius was revealed as a person of good standing: his name appeared three times in lists of the members of town committees, the first such appearance being in 1647, though no details of his life were given. Balthasar's name appeared only once, but the entry turned out to be pure gold from Michael's point of view: a letter sent from Daniel Everaerts in London to his cousin Joachim

Nicolaeszoon Everaerts, president of the Middelburg Town Council, dated July 1672, enquiring into the background and conduct of Balthasar Pelagiusz van Overmeer, doctor of Leiden. It was in Dutch, and had been very hard to read, but the proper names could not be mistaken, and the archivist, with the smiling condescension which the Dutch tend to deploy on such occasions, had been kind enough to help him with both transcription and interpretation.

The letter told him that Balthasar's trail led to London, but the Leiden link obviously needed to be explored. If Balthasar was known as a doctor of Leiden, he had presumably passed his final examinations, and that meant that he had written and published a thesis. The next step was therefore the Netherlands short-title catalogue. Michael got online, found the catalogue, looked up 'van Overmeer' in it, and got the shock of his life. Not only was there a Leiden thesis by Balthasar on the surgical procedures for recti-fying club-foot and related problems, dated 1663, there was also one by Pelagius dated 1639, *De Theologia naturale: dissertatio theo-logica, qua disquiritur, num gentes cognitionem habent de natura Dei, nec ne.* Michael puzzled over this title for a while, but was finally able to translate it as 'On natural Theology: a theological disser-tation in which it is investigated whether the pagans have know-ledge of the nature of God, or not'. Michael then checked the Leiden matriculation records; Pelagius duly appeared in 1634 – earlier than he was expecting, the man must have dropped out for a while – and was listed merely as a resident of The Hague. Since The Hague was not officially a city he could not be a citizen, but that fact left his status ambiguous, possibly a fully enfranchised person, or possibly a client or protégé, or even a slave. Balthasar, on the other hand, appeared in the records as a citizen of Middelburg.

At that point, Michael had had to get back to England, but he ordered microfilms of both theses from Leiden, and seized eagerly on them as soon as they arrived. Balthasar's was most disappointing;

merely a slender pamphlet ornamented with a page of vaguely horrible engravings illustrating twisted feet and recommended procedures for straightening them out. As far as Michael's very limited Latin extended, the text contained no personal information of any kind. Someone would doubtless be able to tell him in time whether Balthasar's surgical theories were up to the minute, advanced, or archaic, but for the moment, that was a side-issue; the thesis confirmed that he had been a qualified member of his profession which was all that really mattered for the time being.

De Theologia naturale was quite a different matter; and as he looked at the pages in the microfilm reader, Michael began to curse his lack of Latin. It did not seem as if Pelagius had wandered into autobiography at any point, any more than his son had done, but Michael could get no further. It was a substantial book, much bigger than Balthasar's modest work, perhaps seventy or eighty thousand words, and the mere appearance of the pages said a great deal. The text was littered with brackets holding complex references to ancient and contemporary authors, sometimes four or five cited in a single note, it was sprinkled with quotations in Greek as well as Latin, and most of the sentences seemed to be at least half a page long. It would have to go to Theodoor, the only person he knew who was able to deal with it.

He half-thought of asking his father to take a look at it, since Neville certainly possessed the necessary grasp of the language, but on reflection, realised that it was pointless to expect him to tangle with Baroque theology. He clung to the old-fashioned classicist's belief that nothing written after Tacitus was worth reading. Michael had tried to discuss neo-Latin texts with him from time to time, and had always found it a waste of time: his father, after umpteen years of marking Latin proses, was only capable of assessing texts on the basis of whether the author did or did not express himself exactly as Cicero would have done, while issues about the content or significance, or even what it basically meant, were treated as secondary going on irrelevant. So Michael sent the microfilm back to Holland, to Theodoor, with a note of what it was and where it had come from. It reinforced the conclusion he was reluctantly arriving at, that Pelagius was Theodoor's problem, or at least a problem Theodoor would have to solve, on grounds of linguistic competence. So, with Elizabeth more or less accounted for and Pelagius handed over to Theodoor, it seemed to him the obvious thing for him to do, apart from editing the play, was to find out about Balthasar, especially since, as it seemed, he was in the right country to do so.

If Balthasar had settled in London, Michael reasoned, ten to one he had been a member of the Dutch church, and as he knew from his work on Defoe's Dutch contacts, the church records had been edited in the nineteenth century. An afternoon in the Bodleian Library with Hessels's *Ecclesiae Londino-Batavae Archivium* showed him that his reasoning had been quite correct. Balthasar's name turned up seven times. His marriage was mentioned in 1672, then in 1673 and 1677 he appeared as a member of the school board, then three times as a regent of the alms-house, and as one of the signatories of a joint letter to the Archbishop of Canterbury. His death was also recorded, in 1704. Another obscure middle-class life like his father's, rendered interesting only by the fact that both men were black. Hessels also produced a crucial fact, that from September 1675, Balthasar had chosen to be known as Balthasar Stuart. A marginal note at the first mention of him after that date gave '*olim* Balthasar van Overmeer'. Michael, sitting with the bulky book in the Upper Reading-Room, felt a prickle of excitement. Balthasar knew who his mother was, he thought. It was the first personal fact which he had to give him any kind of a picture of the man. What had provoked the change? Had he found out only in 1675, thirteen years after his mother's death, that he was the son of a queen?

The Upper Reading-Room of the Bodleian is lined, above the

bookcases, with a seventeenth-century frieze of portraits of early modern worthies, painted directly onto the plaster. Sitting back in his chair to think, Michael was conscious of the row of white faces looking down, framed by ruffs or linen collars. He thought of seventeenth-century Dutch pictures, pale, doughy faces and strong hands thrown into relief by their wearers' plain Calvinist blacks. There was a black man working a few places down from him, a tubby, round-faced person with very short hair, wearing a suede blouson jacket and jeans. Squinting at him covertly, Michael tried to imagine his dark face and hands emerging from an early modern Dutch costume. The effect was deeply incongruous; how startling had the van Overmeers seemed, in their own time? They must always have been outsiders to some extent, unable to conceal their difference. Balthasar perhaps doubly so, as a black Dutchman in Restoration London. But one who knew he was the king's first cousin.

Leaning back in his chair, Michael wrested his train of thought into less speculative channels. He now had two names, Balthasar van Overmeer, Balthasar Stuart. The Dutch STC had done all it could for him, but had Balthasar ever published anything in England? Stuart was not that uncommon a name, but still, it would not take long to check. Slipping a notebook into his pocket, he went off to find the short-title catalogue. There was nothing there under either name, or even under B.S. It would have been a lot to hope for, he reflected. Still, it was worth doing the job properly. The STC went up to 1700, but in 1700, Balthasar had still had four years to live. While he was at it, it was just worth checking the eighteenth-century short-title catalogue as well.

It was with a glow of peaceful self-congratulation that he got a hit, second time lucky. Balthasar Stuart, *A Caribbean Flora, with a Guide to the Uses of Plants*, printed in Bridgetown, Barbados, in 1743. His man, or perhaps a son of the same name? Either it had been printed long after his death, or there was more than one

Balthasar, but in either case, there was one copy of the book still in existence. The code for the library that contained it was unfamiliar to him, and he looked it up, praying that it wasn't in America. No, thank God, the *Flora* had found a home in the Wellcome Institute for the study of medicine, so it was in London.

Trudging home at the end of the day – the college was unable to provide him with rooms on site, and he lived in a flatlet a long way up the Iffley Road – he reviewed the story so far. *The Female Rosicrucian* was coming along nicely; he had an increasingly clear sense of what Behn had been reading and how it had been written. She had been friendly, when in Middelburg in the early 1660s, with either Pelagius or his son. One or other had given or sold her the books; Pelagius perhaps? He would have to do more work on context, Michael thought parenthetically, was the father perhaps intending to protect his son from the fact of his royal birth? Perhaps he feared for him, after the Restoration? In any case, she had evidently profited from the contact, and acquired an interest in royal black men which had recurred more than once in her later writings. Behn was in London from 1663 or so, Balthasar from at least 1672, so it was possible that they had been lifelong friends.

Strictly speaking, in terms of his bargain with Corinne, his interest might be held to end there. He was preparing an edition of the play, that was all. But he was deeply curious about Balthasar, and also, for all kinds of reasons, he seemed the best placed of the three of them to find out. The trajectory of a life spent in London and apparently ended in Barbados took one a long way from Corinne's essential business of sorting out a Middelburg pornographer's archive. He wanted to know more, and it also struck him that if the excellent Theodoor managed to find a competent Dutch neo-Latinist to do the linguistic work, it might be possible to bargain for collaborating on the edition, or editions, of Pelagius if he had done the groundwork on the family and historical context.

The Behn play would give him a publication in central women's studies territory, if he had another on the early history of black people in Europe, it couldn't hurt his c.v., especially since he was conscious that the peculiarity of Oxford's way of doing things left him short on a lot of teaching and lecturing experience that other universities would normally expect a man of his age to have.

As he trudged up the Iffley Road, almost unaware of his surroundings, he was thinking that it had become extraordinarily easy to find things out. Certainly, the crucial starting-point had been physically going to Middelburg, but there was nothing but money to prevent the likes of Corinne from working through even small provincial archives in time and putting them all on the Internet. Some day, everything would be connected by the Web, though at the moment, the situation was something of a trap for the unwary; certain categories of information were easily available, so that in consequence the very existence of others, not yet part of the new world order, was easily forgotten. Still, it was remarkable what had been achieved since the '80s. If he had found a reference to Balthasar's book in the days before the eighteenth-century short-title catalogue, how long, he wondered, would it have taken him to locate the only copy, given that it was in a library he had no other reason for visiting? Now, in 2002, a relatively small amount of work, mere hours if you put it together, had taken him from a name on a memorandum of baptism to the entire trajectory of a life involving professional training, a change of name, and two changes of country.

But the other thought which preoccupied him as he walked was how little one can ever know of any individual in the past. A memory from school drifted into his mind . . . and some there be, which have no memorial; who are perished, as though they had never been born . . . the sad bit of 'Let Us Now Praise Famous Men', which they used to sing every year on Founder's Day. How few names lived for three hundred years, let alone for 'evermore' and in 'imperishable memory'? Pelagius and Balthasar must have been strangely visible in their time and place, black faces in a white men's land. They had been professional people, members of town committees, published writers, but all that remained were names and meaningless, contextless fragments. Yes, it was possible to get a sense of 'the early modern Dutch world-view', or 'the Calvinist outlook on life', but how did that illumine the lives of men who were, by definition, exceptional? Balthasar was a vacuum in his mind, asking to be filled. He would have to be extremely careful to ensure that he did not fill it with miscellaneous fantasies imported from the twenty-first century.

Home. He let himself in, tossed his briefcase onto a chair and scooped up his mail; apart from the junk, there was a postcard from Paris, this month's *Men's Health*, and a familiar but surprising object: an envelope addressed in looping pink felt-tip, which could only have come from his ex-girlfriend, Eimer Cannon, a designer by profession who habitually wrote with the nearest thing capable of making a mark. They had had an off-and-on relationship for about a year, ending abruptly the previous summer when he had stayed in Oxford to finish a book, leaving her to go on holiday by herself. A fortnight later, she had sent a postcard saying she thought she had met the love of her life and he had never seen her again. For all he knew, she was still on Skiathos.

He ripped open the letter, which was brief and to the point; she apologised for not being in touch, she had moved back to Galway and successfully imported Stephanos to Ireland where they had started a small company; she was pregnant, blissfully happy, and wanted to know how he was. What a leap into the dark, he thought. But Eimer had never been short of bottle. He had long since got over the wound to his self-esteem, and he was glad to have an address for her. She could go on his Christmas card list, and doubtless, in due course, he would send the baby the *Oxford Book of Nursery Rhymes*.

Going through to the kitchen, taking *Men's Health* to depress himself with while he cooked, he pinned the letter to his corkboard to remind himself to answer it and began making a pot of Bolognese sauce, with the magazine propped open on the work-surface. 'Feng Shui for Great Sex' . . . 'Abs Fab?' . . . 'The Silent Killer' – that would be prostate cancer again, no doubt, they couldn't leave it alone – 'Rock'n'Roll Wallpaper' . . . 'Fatbusters' . . . the issue seemed to be veering randomly between the surreal and the predictable. He was mechanically stirring mince and onions, fascinated against his better judgement by their notion of what better shu could do for him, when the phone rang. Moving the pan off the heat, he went through to the living-room to pick up. 'Michael Foxwist.'

'Michael? It's Auntie May.'

'Hallo, May,' he replied, stomach knotting. 'What's happened?'

'Your father's had another episode, Michael. Mrs Denton found him when she went in this morning.'

'Is he in the C.I.?'

'No. They don't keep older people in unless they have to, these days. It's their new policy. He was taken in, but they just did some tests and sent him home in a taxi.'

'But that's ridiculous. Is he on his own?'

'Yes, of course, Michael. There isn't anybody. He's got that buzzer thing, but when he was taken poorly this morning, he'd forgotten to put it on.'

'Oh, God.'

'Michael, I really think you'd better pop up when you can. I keep an eye out as best I can, of course, but it's not the same . . .' It was a familiar litany, he knew it by heart. '. . . it's not as if Marion was there. You can't expect too much. And Harry's not a well man either. I've a lot to do, you know.'

'May, I'll do my best,' he protested. 'I've got another week of term, and there's sheds to do here as well. I'll get away as soon as they'll let me. You know, we really are going to have to start looking around for some kind of home.'

'But Neville wouldn't hear of it!'

'For goodness' sake, May! He can't manage. You can't get over from Aspatria, I do realise that. And I'm at the other end of the country. We're going to have to be realistic.'

'He wouldn't hear of it,' she repeated, as if she had not heard him, reminding him that she had obeyed her big brother all her life. If there was any help to be had with levering Neville into sheltered housing, it would not come from her.

'Well, he should've had a daughter, then! What the hell are we all expected to do?'

'Michael, don't you use that sort of language to me.'

'Sorry, May. I get a bit wound up. Don't think I don't care.'

'I know, pet. You're a good boy. He's very proud of you.'

He made an indeterminate noise, then pulled himself together. 'Thanks for ringing, May. I'll be in touch when I've made arrangements.'

'God bless.' She rang off. May never prolonged long-distance phone calls, the frugality of her generation.

Michael realised his hands were shaking. He went and took the half-finished sauce off the stove and shoved it in the fridge, pan and all. He would have to eat, he thought, pouring another glass of wine, but it would need to wait till he had calmed down.

Bitterly, he thought about all the people he knew who went about as apparently free as if they had hatched out of eggs. Corinne might have plenty to worry about, he reflected, but at least she wasn't trying to protect an old man from the casual cruelties of a disintegrating welfare state.

His feelings for and about his parents were so complex that they hardly bore investigation. They had been on the elderly side when he was born, and throughout his teens, his father's health had dominated family life: as a child, he had learned to play quietly, and later on, he had turned down his music like a good boy and tolerated petty trantrums, all on the grounds that Daddy wasn't well. Yet two years after their retirement, it had not been his father, but his ironic and humorous mother, who had suddenly dropped dead of a stroke, while Neville lived on, cranky, vulnerable, hypochondriac and demanding. His mother had once observed – she must have had just about enough at the time, he realised suddenly – that the old chap had set up a bivouac at death's door, and it seemed to be true.

He would have to go north as soon as term was over. He put his glass down abruptly; getting drunk would make things worse not better. He went to put on his tracksuit instead, since experience suggested that a run out to Iffley village and back would leave him feeling a great deal more human, even if it solved nothing. Running had entered his life as a way to get school to leave him alone; in the long term, he had learned to be grateful for it.

It took him nearly ten days to get clear of Oxford business, and most of a day to get to Silloth. As the first of the day's trains pulled out of the station, he was filled with the most crushing sense of depression and futility. It was ridiculously far. His thoughts slipped into a well-worn path; things might be easier if he lived further north, but if they had done it on purpose, his family could hardly have put themselves anywhere less near a university. Birmingham was one possibility, since at least it would do away with one change of trains, so were Warwick, Manchester, Liverpool and Durham; Lancaster was too appalling even to be considered a last resort, though it was nearest. The new Behn project probably put Glasgow out of the question, he realised, since they already had a Behn specialist.

From Carlisle, where he had arrived forty minutes late, thanks to his Virgin Trains connection, it was a question of getting over to the bus station and catching the 38 bus to Skinburness, each leg of the journey more inconvenient than the last. It made no sense to run a car in Oxford, but it would almost be worth the ludicrous expense of hiring one, he thought, waiting in the bus station, just to break this appalling sense of winding further and further back into the adolescent misery and helplessness of his personal past. The bus chugged slowly through the reticent lands of the Solway floodplain, a flattish, dull countryside of rolling hills and gorse, with well-concealed, ground-hugging houses tucked discreetly into folds of land. As they entered Allonby, he noticed that local kids had modified the sign by the road so that it read 'please d i e carefully'. It made him think of his father.

A little later, he saw the distant radio masts over by Skinburness, always the marker that he had finally reached home territory. After his adventures of earlier in the year, the approach to Silloth, with the church spire and Carr's flour-mill rising strongly from a flat surrounding area, reminded him of the way Dutch towns sit in the landscape, though far in the distance, the blue hills of Dumfriesshire over the water told him he was home.

The bus let him off by the church, and he walked over the cobbles of Criffel Street towards his father's house in the early evening light, wondering if he would have liked the place better if he had been brought up there. But he had been brought up in Cartmel, in the headmaster's house which went with the job; his parents had bought the Criffel Street house and moved to Silloth only when his father retired and he himself was eighteen and bound for university. He had never put down roots in Silloth, though even if he had, he thought, he would still have found it peculiar. He was walking up the esplanade of a smart little Victorian watering-place, all bright-painted stucco and wrought iron. On his left, a good fifty yards' width of grass, hulking masses of shrubbery and wind-sculpted Scots pines separated him from the esplanade and the Solway Firth, which was not even visible. On his right, the impression of smartness was, as he well knew, skin-deep. The Victorian development was one house thick, and behind it was street after street of bleak pebble-dashed terraces.

He let himself into his father's house – he still had his own key – and went up the stairs to the drawing-room. As a long-term resident in Oxford colleges, he was no stranger to ugliness and inconvenience; none the less, the desolate hideousness of his father's house closed round him like the tomb. The previous owner's dreadful vinyl wallpaper had been relatively new and 'still good' in 1987, so it was still there, as were the hardwearing Axminster carpets. If his mother had lived a little longer, she would doubtless have insisted on getting rid of them, but she had not. Since nobody of his own social class ever came to the house, apart from family, Neville had never seen the need to replace them. So they had stayed, clean though now shabby, having never, he suspected, given a moment's actual pleasure in their fourteen or fifteen years of use. His father would spend money on maintenance when he had to, but he had no use for frills.

'Is that you, Michael?' Neville called, hearing his feet on the stairs.

'Yes, Father.' He came into the drawing-room, and put his bags down by the door, stretching his arms. 'Ug. Long day.' His father was, as he had expected, settled in his handsome leather armchair by the gas fire. As usual when he saw the room again after a spell away, its incongruity made itself forcibly apparent; the way that the furniture, his mother's Canton porcelain on the mantelpiece and her rosewood coffee-table, relics of some seafaring ancestor, quarrelled strangely with the inherited wallpaper, silver-and-cream stripes. Only a man possessed of the most brutal indifference to his surroundings could have tolerated it, but Michael suspected that his father was completely unaware of the way it looked.

'I thought you'd be here at five-thirty,' Neville remarked. He was looking thinner, Michael noticed. He stuck to the clothes in which he had lived his life, tweed jacket, cavalry twill trousers, shoes glossy as chestnuts, but he seemed to be reducing within them to a sharp outline of bone.

Michael decoded the remark with the ease of long practice. 'You haven't had your cup of tea, Father.'

'I thought I'd wait.' There was no direct reproach, there never was; gentlemen do not complain, any more than they apologise, carry a pen, or take off their jackets without immediately rolling up their shirt-sleeves.

'The main-line came in late at Carlisle, so I had an hour to wait for the bus. You know what it's like. I'll go and put the kettle on.'

He turned to go, infuriated, as always, by his father's appalling gift for making him feel guilty. Just as he was leaving the room, he heard his voice again:

'I'm very pleased to see you, Michael.'

He pretended he had not heard, and went down to the kitchen. The kettle was, of course, not electric, it had to be put on the stove and watched. So he leaned against the wall and watched it. Would things be easier, he wondered, if his father disliked him, or vice versa? Might a bit of honest hatred have simplified matters? There was something very dreadful about Neville's limited, teacherly gestures of approval or affection, and he felt the terrible ambivalence of a dutiful child. He had always been good – he had had little or no option – and yet his father's status during his childhood, his poor health, and his helplessness in recent years had made the old man the great burden of his life. The kettle-lid bounced a little, and a plume of steam jetted from the spout.

He reached for the brown teapot, the worn silver caddy, the cosy, all the familiar paraphernalia. There would be biscuits in the tin in the larder, abernethy or currant shortbread; Neville would want two. Fetching the biscuits, he was touched to see that his father had made a gesture towards a cooked supper. Two chicken pieces lurked flabbily in a white enamel pie-dish beside a melting packet of frozen peas and a saucepan full of new potatoes. A slightly more appetising prospect than Wonderloaf, corned beef, and beet-root out of a jar, though these would doubtless come round in time. After a lifetime of shovelling down school dinners, his father had no interest in the aesthetics of food, and in his widowerhood had never learned to cook. Michael looked at his watch, turned on the oven, and put a light under the potatoes. It would be supper-time in about forty minutes.

Once restored by tea and the supper which followed shortly upon it, his father made conversation. The subject of cardiac episodes was, it seemed, to be avoided.

'I went down to Cartmel last month, you know. The Old Boys' Association asked me back. I noticed the old house has been done up very nicely, they've put in modern windows.' Hideous replace-ment ones, no doubt, thought Michael, but his father was only ever interested in practicalities. 'Your mother's roses are still there. That "New Dawn" by the door covers most of the front of the house now.' He remembered her planting it. She'd been interested in the garden, and he had been expected to mow the lawn, so they had spent quite a lot of time together out there. 'I met Bob Fowler at the Association do. He was rather a pal of yours, I seem to recall? He was asking after you.'

Michael looked at his father bleakly. The headmaster's son doesn't have friends. He is tarred with the brush of authority, and still worse, he is removed from the private life of his House and goes home every night after supper and second prep. They had merely been lumped together for some school purposes by alphabetic proximity; at this distance in time, nothing about Fowler's face, personality or interests had stayed in his memory. 'What's he doing now?' he asked, for the sake of something to say.

'Solicitor in Cockermouth. Doing very well, I believe. Tell me, Michael. How is your work going? Are you still working on this play you found?'

'Yes, Father. It's going very well. It's turned out to be very interesting, and it's throwing up all kinds of issues.'

'I have been wondering if it's of real importance. I speak merely out of concern, you understand. Defoe is a classic author, though of a low order, and if a mere layman may venture an opinion, your last book seemed to me excellent. A man should stick to his own furrow, no good ever came of chopping and changing.'

He decided to tackle this by trading one schoolmasterly cliché for another. 'On the other hand, one needs breadth as well as depth.'

Neville moved his head irritably. 'Of course, and if you had moved to some more significant figure now that you are fully the master of your craft, Pope, perhaps, or Dryden, I would have seen the point of it. But how does your work on this play illumine the study of English Literature? Is it not merely an instance of *obscurus per obscurioris?*'

'Father, I'm actually moving into the mainstream here,' explained Michael patiently. 'Defoe's not even on the syllabus. I've been trying to get him on for the last year. Remember, I was telling you about the "Campaign for Real Fiction"? There's probably more curriculum time given to Aphra Behn than there is to Dryden or Pope.'

'Good Lord, what on earth for? Ah. It'll be this "political correctness", no doubt. Perhaps in the fullness of time, you'll all be allowed to teach literature again.'

There had been a time in his life when he might have tried to explain that literature as a concept was no longer bounded by the covers of Palgrave's *Golden Treasury*, but he had long since given up. The idea that a canon of literature could change was one his father could never be made to understand: since the list of classic Greek and Latin authors had stayed the same for two thousand years, it was natural for him to assume that English would behave the same way. There was no point going round the old argument again, so he changed the subject.

'You've still got Mrs Denton coming in? How's that working out?'

'Mrs Denton is an excellent person. She keeps me tickety-boo, as you can see for yourself, and of course, there's the Meals-on-Wheels three days a week, so I get something hot half the time. One can't complain.'

His father's tone was final; and Michael reflected that any kind of an argument as to whether the old man's life-style was sustainable had better wait till he was less tired. Accordingly, he changed the subject to his other principal incubus. 'How's Harold getting along? I thought I'd go and see him tomorrow.'

'He's in fine fettle. There's sound stock on your mother's side. He must be a good eighty-seven now, and he still gets out and about. I wish I had his lungs. The mind's still active, and he has his interests.'

That was one way of putting it, thought Michael. 'He's still being properly looked after, though?'

'Of course. There's plenty of money there, and he has someone coming in every day.'

Michael looked at his watch. 'Excellent. I think I'll go up now, Father. It's been a long day.'

'Good-night, Michael. There's whisky on the sideboard, if you want a nightcap.'

Michael went up to his room, which was a sad little place. It was cold and a little damp from being kept shut up, and the furniture of his childhood, the white-painted wardrobe and chest of drawers, the Lloyd Loom chairs, had been redeployed in the new house in, as far as possible, the same places to create a purely ersatz continuity with his actual past. The books on the shelf were a sorry mixture of dog-eared Eagle and Blue Peter annuals, Edgar Rice Burroughs, A level set texts, and things that had seemed important when he was eighteen; Hermann Hesse, Tolkien. None of them, with the exception of *Sense and Sensibility*, would bear rereading. In a sane world, he would throw them out, but if he started throwing things out, it might be hard to stop. The damp smell, he thought, sniffing suspiciously, was merely the result of counter-productive frugality, though he intended to check the attic, just in case. And it would be an idea to find someone to clean out the gutters.

The following morning, he opened the curtains (blue cotton printed with little white boats, his mother's choice) onto a bright, sunny morning. From this second-floor vantage point, he could actually see the Solway shining silver beyond the trees. As he went down the stairs, he could hear his father's morning coughing session well under way, deep, fruity and disgusting.

After washing up the breakfast things he made his escape, leaving Neville settled with *The Times* crossword. The wind off the sea ruffled his hair; there were already dogs scampering on the grass. Only a few yards beyond his father's house, Victorian Silloth came to an abrupt stop, and the street continued on the other side of the through-road as much smaller houses, 1940s postwar development. Michael kept going. A little further on, cutting down the side of the park, he came to a development of 1930s bungalows strung along the seafront north of the original town, facing Scotland across the water and exposed to the scouring gales from which the Victorians had sensibly shielded themselves. The street-plan flowed round a large square eighteenth-century house, which stood like a boulder among the little bungalows in its garden of grass and windblown trees; it must once, even within living memory, have been completely isolated. Michael let himself in through the creaking iron gate, and rang the doorbell.

A woman he didn't know answered the door, looking politely enquiring.

'Hallo. I'm Mr Boumphrey's great-nephew, Michael Foxwist. Have you taken over from Mrs Oulton?'

'That's right, pet. Mrs Oulton moved to Hartlepool to be near her married daughter. I'm Alice Whitrigg. You'll find Mr Boumphrey very well for his time of life.'

'Has he tried to convert you to anything, Mrs Whitrigg?' Michael enquired. 'I hope he's not being too tiresome.' She looked nice, a sturdy, grey-haired woman in slacks and a cardigan, rather an improvement on Mrs Oulton, who had been a moaner, and he hoped she would stay.

'Bless you, lad, I don't mind him. I just say "yes yes", you see, and let him talk. That's all he wants, poor old gentleman.'

'He's in his study, I suppose?'

'That's right. I'll bring you both some tea in a bit.'

'That would be very kind.'

Michael went up to the erstwhile drawing-room, a splendid room which occupied the entire frontage of the first floor, a good fifty feet or more in length, lit from three sides. Long before he had even been born, Great-Uncle Harold had shelved it from floor to ceiling in solid mahogany, and redefined it as the study. It contained perhaps eight or nine thousand books in at least five languages, many of them rare and valuable.

'Who is there?' enquired the high, fluting voice of his great-uncle, as he knocked and came into the room. Harold Boumphrey was sitting at the enormous table which occupied a good twenty feet of the space on the window side of the room, and was perpetually littered with paper. Michael observed with relief that it was not disfigured by a computer terminal. Harold loose in the chat-rooms of the World Wide Web hardly bore thinking about, but fortunately, it was unlikely to occur to him to learn to type. He was an old-fashioned wind-powered loony, a writer of long letters in a shaky but well-formed copperplate script, rather than the new electronic variety, and thus restricted to contact with others of his kind, a dying breed. Physically, he was the convex variety of old man: cheeks and throat pouched like a hamster's, healthily pink, with tufts of white, thistledown hair sprouting at odd angles.

'It's Michael, Uncle. I've nipped up from Oxford to see you all.'

'My de-ar Michael. Of course I remember you. You are very like your poor mother.' Harold Boumphrey struggled to his feet as Michael crossed the room, and held out his hand.

There was a bit of a tremor there; incipient Parkinson's? thought Michael, as he shook it. They were all falling apart. But Harold was certainly extraordinary for his age.

'You have come at a most opportune time, my dear boy. I have some questions for you. I have been in correspondence with His Sacred Majesty, and he has suggested some interesting lines of enquiry.'

'This is Prince Michael of Albany we're talking about?' asked Michael resignedly. To the best of his knowledge, the soi-disant prince was a self-invented Belgian adventurer born with the name of Michel Lafosse, a fact that he had endeavoured to insert into his uncle's world-view on more than one occasion.

'Of course. His Sacred Majesty has been graciously pleased to take an interest. I think that I have now demonstrated beyond any possible doubt that he is the present representative of the house and lineage of David, and therefore the inheritor of the promise which the Almighty made of old to David and his descent. It has been some while since we spoke about this, so allow me to remind you that this Royal Line in Perpetuity passed through Solomon to Zedekiah to his daughter Tea Tephi. You doubtless know that the Irish Annals tell us that Tea Tephi married Eochaid, King of Ireland, who of course is the ancestor of Conn of the Hundred Battles, and therefore of Kenneth mac Alpin. King Kenneth's descendant James VI is the progenitor of the Stuart line, now in exile, of whom His Sacred Majesty is the present head.'

'What sort of time-span are we talking about, Uncle?'

'A little over three thousand years.'

'That short? You're not going back to pre-Adamite masters of the universe?' asked Michael mischievously. 'Do you know, there are people who think that your Royal Line is really a reptilian master-race who can switch their lizard DNA on and off when they feel like it? I've even found someone on the Web saying she's personally seen your mate the Chevalier Labhran morphing into a pointy-headed dinosaur. I thought you might quite fancy the idea of Uther Pendragon as a Dragon King.'

Harold Boumphrey looked a little put out. 'Pernicious nonsense,' he said firmly, 'with no basis in any scientific discipline. These people are merely redacting the speculative fiction of H. P. Lovecraft and Linwood Carter. I trust you can tell the difference, Michael. You are an educated man.'

He opened his mouth to apologise, already a little sorry for winding Harold up, but fortunately, the old man's attention was diverted by the arrival of Mrs Whitrigg with a tray of tea, which she put on the small table near the fire. 'Shall we sit down?' he invited his nephew courteously.

'Thanks.'

Michael poured the tea, while his great-uncle settled himself in an armchair.

'I have become convinced of the importance of tea,' Harold announced. 'There is good reason to think that the active principle of tea, methyl-theobromine, may be a mutatory agent which, as it were, "brought home" the Godhead into Methodism. The early Methodists set their faces against the pagan and deluding influence of wine, but in their advocacy of tea, God was working within them. The congruence of names is highly significant – we have on the one hand, the syllable "meth", on the other, the syllable "theo", shortened to "tho", which as you will know, is Greek for God.'

Michael pinched the bridge of his nose. 'Theobromos means "food of the gods", doesn't it? So God's got to be in there somewhere.'

'God is in everything somewhere,' said Harold serenely, as if he had proved a point.

Michael looked up at the picture over the fireplace; a view of Silloth before Harold Boumphrey's father had taken up speculative building. Both the painting and what it depicted, the carriages and glossy horses spanking along the front, the children with their hoops and the girls in bonnets, had enormous charm. He had often half-hoped that, even if the old dear had left all his money to the White Rose Society or some such organisation, which was more than likely, that picture would come to him eventually. But meanwhile, the possibly sacramental status of tea didn't seem to be getting them anywhere much, so he looped back to the previous subject.

'What was it you wanted me to help with?' he asked.

'His Sacred Majesty informs me that the Chevalier Labhran has argued that King Arthur is a direct link in the Royal Line, but I fear I have doubts about the evidence at the moment. The chevalier is a man of vision, but not quite a scholar. All the same, it is obviously significant that tradition informs us that the king consummated a sacred sister-marriage.'

'But Guinevere wasn't his sister, surely?'

'No, indeed. That union was sterile. I refer to the *hieros gamos* with his sister Queen Morgause, the mother of Mordred, which occurred in the year 477. The Royal Line shows many such unions, by a particular dispensation of Providence, perhaps due to Egyptian influence, to prevent the sacred bloodline from being dissipated. Yet the records do not tell us of any son for Mordred. I fear that the chevalier has been unable to demonstrate that the Arthurian line is any more than a cul-de-sac.'

'Yee-es,' he said cautiously. 'But I think you'll find that if I ask the Celtic History people, they won't be very helpful. All that stuff about Morgause and Mordred comes out of the Arthurian romances, surely? To be honest, I don't think the actual historians are sure Arthur even existed.'

Harold Boumphrey sighed. 'None so blind, as those that won't see. But they will not deny that Gildas existed, and as you perfectly well know, Gildas, who is known as Gildas the Wise for good reason, is quite clear on the subject. I have spent a great deal of time with him of late, and it seems to me that there are meanings hidden beneath the surface of the text. The fact that King Arthur undertook a sacred sister-marriage is in itself evidence that God had marked him as a link in the chain. It became clear to me that there are strange correspondences within the text of Gildas's great work: there are patterns of number.'

'Oh, God,' said Michael to himself, but his uncle failed to hear him, and continued serenely.

'I will not trouble you with my methods, but I have found the word ARTORIUS concealed beneath the surface of the text, quite clearly. As I proceed, using the same methods, which are entirely mathematical and therefore scientific and not to be disputed, I expect to find Mordred, or Mordredus, or Medraut, and most importantly, the name of the son.'

'I see,' he said. As with earlier 'investigations', Harold had already decided what he intended to find, and would simply go on adapting his methodology until he found it. 'Where do I come in?'

'I am informed that, in the Bodleian Library, there is a manuscript called "The Prophecies of Gildas". I wonder if you could look at this for me? No one has ever brought it into consideration in this context, and it may contain vital information.'

'Uncle Harold,' he protested, 'I really don't think that anything called "The Prophecies of Gildas" is going to have anything helpful. It's going to be some sort of medieval Welsh rant about how much they hate the English.'

Harold was not to be diverted. 'I do not take your point, Michael. Gildas the Wise was the master of St Iltutus, and the school of Iltutus taught all the saints of Wales. His name was cherished and revered, and there is continuity. We have no reason to assume that Welsh tradition would fail to preserve the words of the master.'

Michael conceded defeat. It struck him, as it often did at these points, that arguing with his great-uncle was like lobbing cricket-balls into a black hole. The material was simply absorbed and made part of a self-referential system. It seemed deeply unfair that the old man should have such a mastery of Latin, and waste it on twaddling around with Gildas. 'I'll try and find it for you. It may take me a while, because there isn't a unified manuscripts catalogue. And you do realise I'm an eighteenth-century specialist? If this is a medieval manuscript, I'm probably not going to be able to read it, even if it's in English which it probably isn't. But I'm fairly sure I could find you a graduate student who'd make you a transcription, though he or she would need to be paid.'

'That would be most satisfactory. Money is no object, in a work of this kind. You will, I am sure, know what honorarium is appropriate.'

'Ten pounds an hour.' Well, some good would come of it, anyway. He could put some work the way of a graduate student; there was always someone in Oxford who would be glad of it, and also, he felt on the whole that it was safer for his uncle to be puttering with manuscripts than with living Rosicrucians, Jacobites, Dragon Kings, and free-range nutters – from bits of correspondence he had seen at one time or another, some of the people Harold was in touch with were quite clearly mad and possibly even dangerous. It was one thing to be carrying a torch for the Stuart cause, quite another to be corresponding with a German professor convinced that Queen Elizabeth was the Beast of Revelations, who had in the course of a chequered career been declared legally insane, excommunicated, and deported as *persona non grata* from England, France, and the United States. It was another of the things he worried about.

After a morning spent in AD 500 or thereabouts, he could not face lunch at home. He wandered back down Criffel Street, trying to decide what to do with himself. The Balmoral Hotel posed a distinct risk of meeting some crony of his father's, so the Criffel Café Bar, currently offering a roast dinner, sausage and mash, or chicken curry at a mere £2.99, was probably the best bet. Sausage and mash was even vaguely tempting; sea air, no doubt, performing its traditional function of making you hungry. He went in and sat down.

The waitress came over, asking, 'What'll you have, lad?', with the impartial friendliness of the north-west. Michael placed his order, and was surprised to hear her say, 'It's Michael, isn't it?' Startled, he looked at her properly.

'Elaine?'

She smiled at him, pleased to be remembered. 'That's right.' In the late 1980s, she had been queen of Silloth. His father had put an absolute ban on his going to the disco at the Solway Lido, which had in his youth represented the acme of such night life as there was, but even so, no one could miss Elaine. A natural blonde with a perfect figure, she had been no lily maid of Astolat, instead, she had perversely chosen to dye her hair black, shave it up the sides, and clump around town in a black lycra micro-mini, biker boots, and chains. But despite the gothic tat, the unearthly perfection of her willowy back and bottom had lingered in his dreams for years. Now at, he presumed, somewhere between thirty-one and thirty-three, she was an ordinary ponytailed woman in a sweatshirt and jeans, an easy size fourteen, and wearing a wedding ring.

'Good to see you,' he said. 'Have you time to sit down a minute?'

'We're not exactly crowded,' she replied, slipping into the chair opposite. 'You went away to college, didn't you? What happened after that?'

'More college. I'm still at Oxford. How about you, Elaine? What happened to putting on the style?'

'Oh, I got bored with all that. I married Dean in the end, d'you remember him? The one with the tattoos? You should've seen him in white tie and tails at the wedding, it was enough to make a cat laugh. I've got a lass and a lad now, Chelsea and Tyler. We're fine.'

'Glad to hear it,' he said. 'I fancied you for years. Well, we all did, you know that.'

She laughed. 'I suppose so, lad. It's a long time ago now, isn't it? Chelsea's ten now, going on eleven. I still see that dad of yours around. You'll be up visiting, I suppose?'

'That's right. He's not as young as he used to be.'

'Well, I must get on. I'll get you your dinner, Michael. It was the sausage, wasn't it, and a lager?'

She pushed back her chair and went off to serve him, a decent young matron, with not a movement or mannerism left to stir the memory of what she had once been.

IV

The invalid assumption that correlation implies cause is probably among the two or three most serious and common errors of human reasoning . . . The vast majority of correlations in our world are, without doubt, non-causal.

Stephen Jay Gould, *The Mismeasure of Man*, p. 242

Corinne, meanwhile, who had thought herself stretched to the limit between her job and finishing the thesis, now found that with the Middelburg website added to her problems, she had no time to herself at all; she set her alarm an hour earlier every morning, lived on sandwiches and things that came in packets, and tried never to wear anything that needed ironing. It was vitally important to get some rough ideas in place; if she had enough put together to make it look exciting, then the project might be fundable.

The real trick, as she told herself exhaustedly, sitting on the bus one morning, was to produce something transparent enough to be comprehensible, but complicated enough to ensure that the powers that be would immediately conclude that it needed to be left in her expert hands. Fortunately, the problems of the website were something which she could think about in odd moments at 'Logistik', since it was, after all, a design problem; if anybody passed behind her desk and caught her doodling with possibilities (the perpetual hazard of life in an open office), it looked perfectly legitimate.

As the site began to take shape in her mind, she realised that she was thinking, on the one hand, about information and, on the other, about politics. From her point of view, Michael and Ankie, let alone Derksen, were inhabitants of an older and simpler world, and not merely because they had jobs, and she did not. Michael, as his emails told her, was getting on with editing *The Female Rosicrucian*, which he was basically doing by sitting in a beautiful old library, getting up once in a while to look at a book and writing down words on paper, quite as if nothing had changed. Ankie was studying Anglo-Dutch relations or the history of Dutch imperialism, and was doing much the same. They had taken to the Web, in their separate ways, as most academics by now had (though Derksen, she knew, refused even to use email). To be an academic was to be expert at extracting information, and they treated the Web like a glorified encyclopaedia. Though they were competent at judging individual sites, as far as she could see, they were all completely naïve about the ways the Web filtered information, unsure about how to judge the integrity of the information it gave them, and quite possibly unaware that any kind of structures existed within it. They made occasional use of databases, but they certainly did not see the computer as an alternative way of structuring, distributing and thinking about knowledge. As far as she could see, Ankie believed people just 'put things' on the Web, and Michael probably did too; by implication, therefore, they thought the work she was doing was basically mechanical, a matter of shovelling facts from A to B.

Things looked very different from where she was sitting, red-eyed in front of a screen, mouse in hand. Her job was not at all like writing a book, but she was far from sure that it was actually easier: what she was attempting was to produce a system capable of giving precise answers to unknown questions. The starting-point was a physical archive, several thousand bits of dirty, fragile, irreplaceable paper, which, for the time being, was mere archaeology, a heap of artefacts from a known point in the past, and as long as it remained in that form, effectively meaningless. If some scholar chose to write a book about it, he or she would choose their material and tell their story on the basis of unconscious assumptions about what an academic book actually was. Corinne, on the other hand, could do no such thing, because she was not working within established parameters. She had to transform the raw material into findable information, profoundly aware that to do so, she had to impose a narrative, and that it was decisions taken in the very earliest stages which would define the usefulness or uselessness of the site. She had to ask herself what people might want to know, both short-term and long-term, and how the material could be calendared and presented so as to allow users actually to question it. All levels of interest had to be catered for simultaneously, from specialist academic use down to semi-literate curiosity, and she also had to bear in mind the possibility of access by quite young children. Users might come in from any direction, with questions that hadn't occurred to her at all, and whereas people who wrote books could at least assume that readers started at page one, turned pages, and read from top to bottom, the site she built would have to be able to offer transparent and coherent information to people who landed in the middle of it, who might or might not realise that this was the case, and who, in the two or three seconds they would be prepared to spend on problem-solving before they gave up in disgust and flitted off somewhere else, might not even notice or understand conventions such as pull-down menus. There would have to be a set of internal protocols, easily perceived and understood, which would draw on users' experience with the Web more generally. The only thing she could be certain of was that users would insist on navigating the site in ways that she had not anticipated, to answer questions that she had not anticipated either.

She would certainly need to give it a search engine, a site map and an index, since different users would approach the contents of the site in different ways. The whole question of links was another major issue. Links to other Middelburg websites, of course, including the Tourist Board, and to the Golden Age of Amsterdam project and so forth. Plantijn-Moretus, the big Dutch museum sites, the bookshops, timelines, images . . . the list of possibilities was endless. The protocols of website design, what she chose to include or exclude, were also, as she was well aware, political decisions.

The politics of personal survival were also much on her mind. It was vital to put together a support group of people important enough to have some influence over budgets, not easy for a lowly graduate student. Theodoor, fortunately, was already convinced of the value of the work, and although he was not strictly speaking a professor, she was aware that precisely because of his detachment from day-to-day politicking, his was a voice that was heeded. Derksen had a long-running feud with the professor of English, so she'd get no help there: she needed friends in History and, especially, in Post-colonial Studies. It was time to talk to Ankie and Pieternelle again.

Remembering Ankie's caustic reaction to her last appeal for help, she decided to go about things a little less crassly, since Ankie was just about the only person she regarded as completely trustworthy. Their sexual relationship was ancient history; they had drifted apart quite amicably due to their mutual recognition that Corinne found men more sexually interesting than women (a perversion which Ankie affected to find incomprehensible), but it had left an abiding sense of mutual connection. There had been a great deal of sarcasm at times, and periods of coolness, but they had never really quarrelled, and after Ankie had met Pieternelle, the relationship had re-established itself as a steady friendship which was one of the most stable elements of her life. Rather than asking for assistance directly, therefore, she put together Theodoor's handwritten notes on Pelagius's book and typed them up as a document. She then simply sent it to Ankie attached to an email, which was a considerably more careful composition than it looked:

> Ankie, hi – remember aphra behn etc.? little mr oxford is getting on really well & says it's about a black king getting revenge on the guy who enslaved him, sounds exciting, yes?? Weird thing is we found a manuscript AB owned which really seems to be BY a black king, god knows how she got it. You know Th. v. Waesberghe? he took a look for me (its in Latin), and heres some notes he gave me. Thought Pieternelle wd want to know about this??? love & kisses xxx ☺

She then attached Pelagius.doc to the email, and sent it off with some complacency. That would fetch them. She was not in the least surprised to find the phone ringing little more than an hour later.

'Corinne Hoyers?'

'Hallo, Ankie! Did you get my email?'

'Rina, this is fantastic. I have to talk to you. We're very busy the next few days, Pieternelle's got some relatives over from Suriname, but they'll be going down to Amsterdam at the weekend – can you come to dinner on Saturday?'

'I hoped you'd be interested,' said Corinne humbly.

Ankie failed to recognise this as a manoeuvre, an indication in itself that she was genuinely excited. 'Can you bring what you've got on disk? You don't actually have spare microfilm or print-out, do you?'

'Theodoor's got the microfilms of the Pelagius books. You know him, don't you?'

'Oh, yes. We've met at gay things once in a while. I think his partner's outside the university – they don't socialise, but I see him on the university committee for affirmative action, you know?

I'll talk to him, and I'll lean on History to make a copy from his copy for me. Come early – we can talk, and then you can help us make dinner. It might be special. Nelle's aunt brought us some fresh goodies.'

'Sounds great. I always learn something from Pieternelle.'

This was true, and when Saturday came round and Corinne jumped off the bus at Ankie and Pieternelle's stop, it was in a mood of pleasant anticipation. Whereas she herself lived as cheaply as possible in the dreary streets out beyond the station, Ankie and Pieternelle were established far more elegantly in the Museumskwartier. It was a modern flat, but it was within sight of the Domkerk and the eccentric spire of the Catherijne convent, one of the nicest bits of town. As she kissed Ankie at the door a few minutes later, she looked around approvingly. Ankie had little visual sense of her own, so she had given Pieternelle a free hand with the décor, which, in consequence, had a strong Afro-Caribbean flavour. The hall was painted a vivid blue and hung with framed panels of West African kente cloth in fulvous yellows and oranges. The sitting-room, like the living-quarters of all academics, was dominated by shelving and books, but a lovely Nola Hatterman street scene glowed above the sleek steel fireplace, and paintings by Frank Creton, Eddy Goedhart and other Suriname artists hung wherever there was room.

Pieternelle was sitting at the computer. She stopped whatever she was doing as they came in, and turned to greet the guest. She was a large young woman, tall and unselfconsciously heavy, with a serene oval face and milk-chocolate skin, who habitually dressed in a tunic and drawstring trousers, for convenience, rather than for religious reasons.

'Hallo, Corinne,' she said, padding gracefully across to give her a hug.

Corinne returned the squeeze with interest, enjoying the soft lips and the resilient cushiony texture of Pieternelle's body.

Though she considered it on the whole unlikely that she would ever settle down with a female partner, she remained sensitive to the physical charm of women. As they all sorted themselves out and settled down with Ankie, as usual, sitting on the floor, she remembered how much she enjoyed the easy give and take of their conversation.

'I've been looking at your "Pelagius" document again,' said Pieternelle. 'It's a real find.'

'Theodoor and I were wondering where he was king of,' said Corinne. 'Have you any idea?'

'It's going to be very difficult to find out. Just because I work on the Caribbean doesn't mean I know that much about Africa. But broadly, early modern Africa was full of small kingdoms, and the sixteenth-to-seventeenth century's an important time for state formation. Since practically all our evidence is eighteenth-century or later, we can't even be sure his "Hoiones" even got into the historical record. Someone might have flattened them before 1700. He says he was captured by the Nubians, so that's a clue. Nubia's what's south of Egypt, so that would put him somewhere in East Africa.'

'There again,' added Ankie, 'he's a man with a classical education. We can't be sure he wasn't just using a classical name and not worrying too much about the fit, just because he was African himself and knew better. He's like one of those mammy-dolls – hold him one way up and you get an African, the other way up, and he's an early modern Protestant humanist. It's hard to make even basic assumptions about the way he thinks.'

'I like him, though,' said Pieternelle. 'He may have been brainwashed by Western culture, but there's something honest about him, even if you wouldn't really guess he was black if he hadn't said so – I mean, in this outline, it's hard to see anything but a good Dutch Calvinist. There's going to have to be a full translation, as soon as possible. All kinds of people will be interested, and with a full text, we might see more about what motivates him, what he knew.'

'I've been looking at the Latin, whenever I've had a bit of time,' said Ankie. 'My Latin's nothing like as good as Theodoor's, but I'm starting to make sense of some of it. I've been skipping the theology and looking for bits where he gets onto personal matters. So far, the most African thing I can find about him is the way he cares about family. He seems to have one child, and of course, if he'd been a king in Africa, he'd have probably had dozens. Although he talks about God all the time, it's clear that in his heart of hearts, he thinks his real immortality is in children. There's an interesting bit I was working on this morning, where he's talking about his son. It's something like, he is a child of promise, or maybe a child of the promise, which is the same thing in Latin; he is the one who was foreordained before the foundation of the world and will come forward in the last days. The last bit's out of the first letter of St Peter. I'm not sure if he's speaking literally or metaphorically. He may just mean he's had him baptised.'

'It sounds like a bit more than that, surely?'

'Mmm. You could well be right. In the Bible the passage refers to Christ. I've got a feeling he may have some kind of idea about his son as the Just King. It was an idea which was around at the time – there's a whole lot of prophetic literature saying there's going to be one great monarchy before the end of the world. The Rosicrucians thought the Elector Frederick might be the one, which is basically why he went on that crazy Protestant crusade in Bohemia.'

'It's come round again,' added Pieternelle. 'Some American fundamentalists reckon the founding of Israel is a fulfilment of God's prophecy, so it's a sign that the Last Days are coming.'

'That's true,' said Ankie. 'I don't know who they've got in mind for the Messiah, but I suppose they think Bin Laden's the Antichrist. Anyway, the point is, Pelagius could've picked the idea up just about anywhere, but I'm not clear why he should think it's personally relevant.'

'We don't know anything about where he's from, remember,' warned Pieternelle. 'He wasn't just some kind of empty box to be filled up with European ideas, and he may be connecting up this Christian stuff with something from his own background. When we know more about his culture, we might get a better sense of all this. What I'd really like to know is what happened to the son.'

'Oh, he probably died,' said Ankie at once. 'Dutch infant mortality rates were very good by early modern standards, but it wasn't easy to rear a child. Anyway, if he did live to grow up, he's part of the generation that was hit by the plague, so the odds were really stacked against him. If you can ever spare a day to go to Middelburg, Corinne, you should maybe look under van Overmeer in the card-catalogue, just to see if there's anything on either of them. All that can wait, though.'

'Pieternelle,' said Corinne, 'why Middelburg?'

She shrugged. 'Dumb chance? There was a VOC station there, so he may have been brought over by the East India Company, been freed, found some work, and just stayed. Your document says there's evidence he was a botanist? He may have practised as a herbalist. Actually, what I've started to ask myself is whether there was a black community in Middelburg.'

'Why should there be?' asked Corinne, intrigued.

'There's an interesting story from just before when Dutch colonialism really gets going. A Middelburg captain captured a Portuguese vessel, I think it was in 1596, and brought the cargo home, which happened to be a shipload of slaves. The *burgomeester* ruled that they had to be freed, because the Dutch didn't traffic in slaves. The incident's often quoted because it shows the Dutch in a good light, before they learned to put their consciences in their pockets. But what nobody's asked is what happened to these people. I wonder if they stayed in Middelburg? Later on, there's strong connections between Middelburg and Suriname. Paramaribo's even called New Middelburg in some early texts.'

'Wow. I see what you mean. He might even have been part of that group. There's the other document, of course, the "African Sibyl" text. I wonder if it's something which belonged in the Afro-Dutch community? This is all going to have to be researched. Some of these books for the English market are supposed to be printed by a guy called "Simon the African" – I've seen one, on Charles II's mistresses. I'd assumed this was just another of the lies printers tell, but maybe there really was a black printer. It's starting to add up, isn't it? And of course, all this stuff about black people in Middleburg's going to have to be integrated with the Aphra Behn story, because of the play, so we might get it in as part of this funding initiative.'

'Tell me about the African Sibyl text,' said Pieternelle. 'There isn't anything about it here.'

'That's because we don't know what to do with it. It's just waiting for you, really. The Behn press made a translation, probably not a very good one, to judge by what I've seen of their work generally, but you could take a look at it. There's a copy in the KB in The Hague – I found it through the new union-catalogue. It's called *The Thirteenth Sibyl* – I'll give you a note of the full title.'

'I'll go and look at it, the next time I have a research day,' said Pieternelle. 'I was wondering why nobody in black studies picked it up, but with a title like that, I'm not surprised. There's any number of almanacs and prophecy-books, nobody could look at them all. Let's go through now, I want to get dinner started. Tantie Marie brought me some groceries from Suriname.'

'What do you want me to do?' asked Corinne, washing her hands at the sink.

'Can you grate that coconut, while I do the cassava? Ankie, can you peel two plantains?'

'I hate peeling plantains,' grumbled Ankie.

'I'll do them,' said Corinne quickly. 'Ankie can do the coconut. What are you making?'

'It's called metagee. And Tantie Marie brought some conquintay flour, so I'm making conquintay porridge on the side.'

Corinne turned her attention to getting the skins off raw plantains. Pieternelle had taught her to do them in a basin of salt water, and it certainly seemed to help. Apart from the plantains, things were going very well. It was clear from what Pieternelle was saying that she saw distinct areas of interest for post-colonial studies; that made yet another buttress for the funding argument, a very fashionable and potentially high-profile one. 'Thinking of Middelburg,' she said, 'I wonder if any of this archive's going to have anything to tell us about the black community in the seventeenth century.'

'H'm. Sounds as if it might. It would certainly be something to be alert to.' Another little hook, thought Corinne, another bait taken. She felt a tiny bit bad about manipulating her friends like this, but there was no doubt it would be good for all of them in the long run. 'Ankie,' she said, as Pieternelle turned her attention to frying meat and onions, 'one thing I meant to ask you. Do you think Aphra Behn really went to Suriname? That's another thing which might help to link all this together.'

Ankie rinsed some clinging fragments off her fingers and poured boiling water over the grated coconut, prodding it with a wooden spoon to extract the goodness. 'I think there's some actual evidence that she did. At least, a woman called "Astrea" was there at the right time, a couple of years before we took Suriname off the English. Astrea's the name Behn used as a spy, and Suriname was riddled with them. It's hard to think of anyone else it could have been, really. But that novel of hers is written about twenty-five years later, and I don't think she could really remember what it was like. *Oroonoko*'s the earliest narrative account of Suriname, so

I brought it along when Pieternelle took me that first time, and once we were actually there, I realised it's completely vague, and there's no real sense of place. Part of the problem is she's representing herself as some sort of young noblewoman who just happened to drop in, when she was actually a secret agent. So she's had to muddle over the bits she probably remembered best, where she stayed, and who with, and what she was doing. The main plot about the "royal slave" and the slave revolt at the end are complete fiction. If there'd been anything of the sort, the English Colonial Office papers would've reported it. All the African background, the king's harem and so on, is straight out of travel-books and romances. My guess is she never spoke to an African in her life.'

'But the funny thing is, there was a slave revolt in Barbados in 1675, which focused on trying to make a slave the king of Barbados, because he'd been a king in Africa. Cuffee's Revolt,' said Pieternelle. She put the plantains and cassava in a casserole, and arranged the meat mixture, sliced vegetables and saltfish on top. Then she poured in the coconut milk, and put the whole thing on the stove-top to simmer. 'We looked into this, because I'm always interested in slave revolts. It would actually have been quite strange to have the sort of uprising she describes in Suriname, because people could run away into the interior and become maroons. Quite a few of them did. Barbados is a tiny little island, so it was like a pressure cooker, if she'd set her story there, it would've made more sense. It's hard to think how she'd have known about Cuffee, though, by 1675 she'd been out of the Indies for about fifteen years.'

'But she might have heard, all the same,' said Corinne. 'You know, even today, if you've been somewhere exotic, you go on taking an interest. For instance, when my father asked me out to Australia for his wedding, I stopped off in Malaysia for a few days to break the journey. I don't suppose I'll ever go back, but if someone mentions Kuala Lumpur, my ears prick up. It was quite a thing to visit the Antilles in the seventeenth century, and a spy who wrote plays must have got a lot of news one way or another. Important people went to the theatre, she'd hear all the gossip.'

'That's a good point, Rina,' said Ankie, opening the kitchen window and lighting a cigarette. 'Especially since English ships nearly always called at Barbados before they went anywhere else in the Americas. I don't suppose she spent long in the place, but she'd almost certainly been there, on the way out or the way back, if not both.' She leaned out of the window with practised ease, and directed a stream of smoke into the evening sky.

It was not until after dinner when Pieternelle was pouring tea and Ankie was rolling them each a joint that the conversation came round to practicalities.

'I've been thinking of this archive of yours, Rina,' said Ankie, handing the spliffs round. 'It's very rich. I'm seeing all kinds of possibilities. The Gemeente Middelburg's keen to develop it, aren't they?'

Corinne took a long, soothing drag, holding the smoke in her lungs for a few seconds, then letting it trickle luxuriously out of her nostrils. She was not a regular user; cannabis gave her a feeling of mild, spacey detachment with occasional overtones of paranoia. Something, therefore, she greatly enjoyed among assured friends, and found a little frightening among strangers or alone. Here with Ankie and Pieternelle, she felt mellow and safe. 'They seem to think there's some serious hope of government money to develop the website. That's why they came to me, after *Published in Middelburg*, which did everything they wanted. Obviously, they can't pick up the purely academic end off local government money, but they can see they need that work to be done before they can make anything of it. To be honest, I don't think they realised I couldn't do a thing on my own.'

'Well, if you sort something out, Derksen will be happy enough just being a figurehead,' observed Ankie. 'I've known him for a long time. He's not a bad scholar, but he's very lazy. I don't know how he got up the energy to start this "Book History" initiative, but you know better than I do that he hasn't really put much in to develop it. Just make him a deal, and he'll go along with it.'

'Do you really think so, Ankie? I've been worrying about this a lot. You know, I'm not exactly a favourite.'

'Well, no,' said Ankie judiciously. 'But he's not completely unjust, and he's faithful to that awful wife of his. I don't think there's anything sexual confusing the picture. You've not been so very bad. You're overdue, of course, but so are half the grad students in Utrecht. The only person I know who finished on time's Pieternelle.'

Pieternelle shrugged. 'I couldn't afford not to.'

'It was still amazing. It used up a lifetime's supply of punctuality, what's more. You've never been on time for anything since.'

'It's very bourgeois, counting the seconds,' retorted Pieternelle, tucking her feet up on the sofa.

'Phooey. But Rina, seriously. I don't think Derksen'd put out a hand to help you, but I don't think he's holding a grudge. Some supervisors would be a bit fed up with you by now, but he doesn't really care. Let me talk to Jacqueline.'

'She was your supervisor, wasn't she, Pieternelle?' asked Corinne.

'Yes. Very different from Derksen. She's the real reason I got my thesis in on time, she just insisted I kept writing. I think Ankie's right. Jacqueline may be an Indonesian specialist, but she's very well connected in black and African studies and the whole colonial history world, and she's a full professor.'

'We can't ask her to lead the project,' added Ankie. 'It might make sense intellectually, but it's not fair on you, Rina. In the end, it's Derksen who controls whether you get a job or not, and if we whisk all this out from under his nose and give it to someone else, then you really will have an enemy. Jacqueline will see that, of course. She's not any kind of a fool. But if I can get her to make a statement about how important she thinks all this is, and you've got Theodoor speaking for you as well, who after all just counts as a professor too, I think – he's got one of those one-sixth honorary professorships in Amsterdam, hasn't he, as well as his proper job? Anyway, with the two of them speaking for the project, Derksen will see a majority, and he's the sort of man who'll always go with the crowd. As long as he's clear he doesn't have to do any work, and he can just sit on his fat bottom and take the prestige, you'll have no trouble with him at all.'

Corinne leaned back against the sofa – she was sitting on the floor with Ankie – and closed her eyes. The dope was beginning to hit home, but her sense of unwinding was due to more than cannabis. Ankie and Pieternelle had behaved perfectly. They were on her side, a warm and happy thought. Ankie could be cross-grained, but with no more than legitimate manipulation, she had been put in a position where she was prepared to set her experience, knowledge and considerable political talent directly at Corinne's disposal . . . which was marvellous. Wonderful.

Someone waggled her foot. She opened her eyes to find Ankie holding her big toe, looking dourly amused.

'Rina, you're going to sleep.'

A few days later, Corinne was striding along the Oude Gracht when she heard someone call her name from the other side of the canal. She was not surprised to see Pieternelle was standing there waving – the Oude Gracht was not far from their flat. She waved back, and they met at the bridge.

'Corinne, are you in a hurry?' asked Pieternelle, once they had kissed.

'–Ish,' she replied, glancing at her watch. 'Look, I've got about twenty minutes. If we nipped in to the Graf Floris, we'd just have time for a cup of tea.'

'Come on, then. I've got something to tell you.' The two women hastened down the Gracht, and turned into the café, an old-fashioned sort of place with a heavily beamed ceiling, cosy, comfortable, and scented with cinnamon from the apple dumplings which were the house speciality. There were two seats free at the long oaken table in the middle, so they took them: Pieternelle made a tidy pile of the tumbled newspapers which had been left there, while Corinne gave their order to the waitress.

'I've been down to The Hague,' said Pieternelle, coming straight to the point. 'I wanted to find out more about the book of prophecies. When I saw it, I thought it looked very odd, because there's nothing in the book about how to work it. There's a collection of 256 paragraphs, you see, numbered, so it seems to be begging for some kind of instructions. I suppose if anyone actually used it, they'd just open it at random with their eyes shut, put a finger on a page and see what they'd got. So I was thinking about all that, and I'd got about half-way through, when I suddenly realised what I was actually looking at was the Ifà *odu.*'

'I'm sorry?'

'Ifà's a Yoruba system of divination, a bit like the I Ching,' she explained. 'It was certainly around in the seventeenth century – some monk or other visited West Africa then, and he says that the people there consulted with the Devil through casting lots. I know a bit about Yoruba religion because of Candomblé, you see. Yoruba ideas are a major influence on Afro-Caribbean culture. Even the idea of cool seems to start with them, it's one of the three main pillars of their philosophy of how to get along.'

'What?' said Corinne, side-tracked.

'*Itutu, ashe, iwa.* Cool, command and character. It's an ideal of self-mastery, or self-control if you like. Anyway, as I was saying, I was looking at this text, and after a while I recognised the structure, and then of course, I remembered there are 256 *odu.*'

'I've never heard of Ifà,' confessed Corinne.

'I'm not surprised. Everyone gets told about the wisdom of the East, but nobody talks about African wisdom unless they're black themselves, and not usually then. It just upsets people's world-views to think about black knowledge. But it's fascinating Ifà got to the Netherlands so early.'

'How do you work it?' asked Corinne, aware she was running off at a tangent again, but genuinely curious.

'You hold sixteen palm nuts in the right hand, then you hit your left palm with the hand full of nuts. This generally shakes some nuts into the left hand, and you note how many. You do this eight times, and make a calculation based on the eight results to find out which *odu* you want. We must get the Latin version trans-lated; there's no point in working from a Dutch text which you say is probably careless, and it must be the earliest surviving version of Ifà, which is important too. Anyway, Rina, I thought you'd be interested, but the important thing is, I've worked out roughly who your man must have been.'

'Pieternelle, that's wonderful. How come?'

'Well, I thought that if he knew Ifà, he was almost certainly a Yoruba, or from somewhere very close to Yoruba territory, so I looked up some stuff on the culture. You remember he said his people were the "Hoiones"? It just so happens there was a major kingdom in what's now northern Nigeria, called Oyo. It got swal-lowed up by the Ashanti later on. But I think Pelagius was the son of a king of Oyo.'

'Of course. That's got to be right. It doesn't explain being captured by the Nubians, though.'

Pieternelle waved a hand dismissively. 'It doesn't have to. Ankie's probably right, he's just using a classical word. But the whole story makes much more sense if he's West African. The Dutch held Elmina, which is near the mouth of the Niger, it was one of the principal centres of the West Coast slave-trade. It's very much easier to see how you might get from Nigeria to Batavia and the Netherlands than how you'd get over from Eritrea or thereabouts.'

'Thanks,' said Corinne to the waitress, who had just brought their tea. 'I'm glad something's making sense.'

'It's a good step forward,' said Pieternelle, reaching for the sugar. 'Now we're looking in the right place, I'm sure all kinds of things will come clear. There's a man in England who's written an awful lot about Oyo. If Jacqueline doesn't know anyone useful over here, we can always bring him in. The British controlled Nigeria for quite a while, so most of the writing about Oyo will be in English. Jacqueline might know someone at Kano or Ibadan, of course.'

'That's really helpful, and you've no idea how well timed. Suddenly I sound as if I know what I'm talking about – who needs the Web when you've got a network?' Corinne caught sight, upside-down, of Pieternelle's watch as she raised her cup to her lips. 'Oh, God. Is that the time. I'm sorry, Nelle, I've got to go.' She fished in her pocket for some Euros, put them on the table, kissed Pieternelle, and ran for it, leaving her tea half-drunk. As she wrestled with the door, she saw Pieternelle composedly picking up the *Utrechtse Nieuwsblad*, looking as if she had all the time in the world.

Once Corinne reached the university precincts, she slowed down, and assumed an air of casualness. She had made a study of Derksen's movements. It took a certain amount of discreet manoeuvring on her part, but as she had hoped, she just happened to be walking along a corridor in time to find him coming the other way, returning to his room with, almost certainly, an hour or two to spare. He stopped, and as usual, looked at her as if he had forgotten who she was; a glassy stare, before recognition kicked in.

'Ah, Corinne. Good to see you. How are you getting on? Work going well?'

'Pretty well. Actually, Professor, I'd like a word, if you can spare a few minutes.'

'Of course. Your time is precious now. I don't forget that.'

Corinne followed him back up the corridor to his room, mulling over the last remark. It was uncharacteristic of Derksen to be pleasant; was he warning her that this was absolutely her last year, or merely reminding her of it?

Derksen let them into his room, and she sat in the chair opposite the desk, where she had sat so often before. It was a notably impersonal space; while there was of course a sizeable collection of books on Dutch and Spanish history, bristling with dog-eared markers, there were no pictures or keepsakes, unless you counted the silver-framed photograph of Yvonne Derksen, a heavy, high-coloured woman with wiry black hair and round, button eyes, and a few more economically framed photos of the four Derksen children, graduation photos mostly, a wedding picture. She wondered vaguely what Yvonne did with herself, now they'd all left home.

Derksen finished fiddling about in a filing cabinet and settled in the desk chair, opening the familiar manila folder which contained his notes on her progress. She looked at him critically as he flipped over the pages, ignoring her. She was just about sure that the sandy hair was several shades greyer than when she had first known him, and he was certainly heavier. He did not look particularly well, and the folds around his mouth had a petulant droop. He was disappointed, she thought; he did not like the modern world. It was her private opinion that he had no right whatsoever to expect anything better than he had; he had got a long way on very much less than someone of her own generation would have to achieve, and he lived in a tall house on the Gracht of a kind which she would never be able to afford, with Yvonne looking after him hand and foot. Yet it was clear that he felt ill-used and poorly rewarded. Well, if she contrived to play the next few minutes correctly, she might yet turn this to her advantage.

'I've been meaning to speak to you for a while, Professor. I know you've been very busy, and I've been having quite a difficult time with my job.'

'Mmm.' Derksen disliked her talking about computers; he persisted in the belief that anything with a keyboard was properly the province of a secretary.

'I had an approach a few weeks ago, completely out of the blue, from Middelburg. They got in touch with me because of the website, as they wanted something else of the kind.'

'I hope you told them you had no time for any more of this nonsense,' said Derksen.

'Well, of course, I told them I absolutely had to finish the thesis before I could think of anything else, but I promised to mention it to you, because they really seem to have something interesting, and they want to get an academic involved. It's just that they came to me because they knew me, you see, and a website's part of what they want,' she concluded meekly, looking as girlish as she could manage.

'What have they found?'

'Basically, it's a collection of manuscripts and printed texts belonging to a printer's workshop. Some accounts, business correspondence and so on, and various material to do with the actual books, loose gatherings and so on. Of course, it's on nothing like the scale of the Plantijn collection in Antwerp, but it's in some ways comparable.' As she well knew, it was the Plantijn-Moretus material which had given Derksen the initial impetus to involve himself with book history. 'It might throw up some interesting issues,' she continued. 'Plantijn of course was a top international printer working for major clients like the King of Spain, but this man Behn's an international printer too, at the bottom end of the scale, producing pornography and political comment for anonymous clients. Maybe not so anonymous, actually, once we got a bit further into it.'

'Yes. I can see that might be interesting. Have you any indications that he dealt with the Spanish Netherlands, at all?'

'Well, Professor, I've hardly scratched the surface. You understand, I had to go down to Middelburg and take a quick look out of courtesy, since they asked me, but after I'd given them a day, I had to get back to my own concerns. I really haven't forgotten what you said last time, about letting myself get side-tracked.'

'Humph.' Derksen was not altogether pleased; not now he was interested himself.

'Off the cuff, I'd say not. The real link's with England. Most of the material's in Dutch, but there's quite a bit in English, comparable with the sort of stuff I've been working on for the thesis, so I knew what I was looking at. There's a little bit of Latin as well, but I haven't actually seen any French or Spanish.'

'Pity.' Derksen tapped his pen on the desk, a symptom of irritation; French and Spanish were his foreign languages. The riskiest phase was passing, he had been successfully got interested, he saw the point, but she had just seen off the possibility that he might make the tedious journey to Middelburg and take a look himself. The two changes of train and general inconvenience insulated her from the possibility that he would think it worth his while.

'The archive people think there's a very real possibility that they can get local political funding, but they need academic support. They want a nice website which will work with the archive, the library and the Tourist Board sites, but before they can get what they want, everything'll need to be catalogued, and it's obvious that the Gemeente will come straight back and say that's an academic research funding issue. So a joint application, with a strong academic aspect, stands more chance than just an application from the archive. I promised to put it to you.'

Derksen frowned. 'What are the academic arguments? I take the point about the Plantijn-Moretus, and it might be possible to argue that it was desirable to have something of the kind here in the Netherlands, but in today's economic climate, I doubt that'll be seen as strong enough. Do you think there's anything interesting in the actual material that was being printed?'

'Well, yes. There are two very promising lines of development, which have some real significance outside book history. We seem to be getting some kind of insight into the black community in seventeenth-century Zeeland.'

Derksen snuffled a little, as if at a private joke. 'Was Behn employing real blacks as printers' devils, then?'

Corinne fought down the temptation to call him a racist jerk, and reminded herself sternly of all that was at stake. 'Nothing like that. But the Behn press was publishing material by at least one black writer. There's a Latin text of a Yoruba system of divination in the collection, and they published a Dutch translation. And there was an established black community in Middelburg, and a black printer, Simon the African.' Well, there might be, anyway. This was no moment for being too scrupulous. 'Professor Smits-Kervesee thinks this is very significant for black studies in the Netherlands,' she added for good measure.

'Jacqueline? Well, she's got a keen nose for what's fashionable,' said Derksen dismissively.

It was absolutely typical of Derksen, she felt; he would never be able to be charitable about a woman who was more successful than he was. But there was no point in riding to Jacqueline's rescue, she was quite big enough to look after herself. 'There's also another Latin text by the same man who wrote the divination text, a spiritual diary. I don't yet know if it was published – as I said, I've really been trying not to waste time on this. But I sent it to Professor van Waesberghe, and he thinks it's very interesting.'

'Theodoor's a very fine scholar,' conceded Derksen. 'He's not the fellow to be seduced by the interests of the moment. Well, I can see that with the way things are now, all this strengthens our hand.'

Corinne lowered her eyes modestly, to conceal her satisfaction at his use of the word 'our'. 'There's another aspect to all this as well. The spiritual diary states that the writer had been a king in Africa before he became a slave, and the divination text suggests that he was also a magician of some kind. Another thing which turned up is a manuscript draft of a play, in English. It's by the first woman playwright in England, Aphra Behn, who seems to have been married to this publisher, and it's about a black ex-king who's also a magician. So there's a clear connection between the publishing house, the black community in Middelburg, and this unknown work by a famous English writer. That gives a clear area of interest for women's history and English studies as well.'

'This play is something which is not published?'

'Yes, Professor. There's someone editing it now, Dr Foxwist, in Oxford.'

'Did you tell him about it?' asked Derksen sharply.

'Yes, Professor.'

'That was extremely foolish of you. You girls have no political sense whatsoever. It's high time this project was in safe hands. I hope you have given nothing else away.'

'I'm sorry, Professor. I didn't know what it was, you see,' said Corinne pathetically. 'He's someone I know slightly, so I asked him if he could identify it. I didn't know it was important till he told me, and then of course, I could hardly stop him from working on it. Of course, I do see I should have come to you.' As if Derksen would have had any chance of identifying a play in English . . . but as she fully expected, he was happy to accept the myth of his own omniscience.

'Well, perhaps no real harm is done,' said Derksen magnanimously. 'Oxford is a name which will carry some weight with funding bodies. Corinne, you are right to be thinking first of your thesis, but I must just ask you to make me some notes on all this, and I will take it from there.'

Corinne got herself out of the office, restraining herself, just, from skipping down the corridor. 'Triumph, Triumph, Triumph,' her mind was yodelling, like the ladies who turn up in *The Magic Flute* to congratulate Tamino. It was how she felt. For the mere temporary sacrifice of a little dignity, and the grim prospect of writing the grant application – which was what Derksen meant by 'a few notes' – she had got away with it. Derksen had grasped that the website was a key element in the whole proposal; that it involved black studies, where she had friends, women's studies, where she had friends, and a scholar in England who was a personal contact of her own. Cees had no relevant knowledge, expertise, languages, or associates. Even if Derksen thought the sun shone out of his bottom, the proposal would have to go up with her name, not his, on it as chief project officer.

V

To say the truth, there is scarce a Prophet or Man of any Nation
in Europe, who had been indued with Prophetick Spirit but he in
some part of his works, or other, hath hinted at such a Person,
Emperor or King, nay some have not been wanting to affirme his
name.

Anonymous pamphlet of 1651

'This is really the bit where the story breaks down,' complained
Piers. 'I mean, you've got some attempt at characterisation up to
that point, but as soon as Sir Percivale meets the Fisher King, you
find you're in some kind of fairy-tale. Everything hangs on whether
he asks the right question or not, and there's no psychological
motivation for asking the wrong one.'

'That's a fair point,' said Michael, 'but medieval writers are much
more interested in what you do, than why.' A belated flash of suspicion roused him from his torpor: this particular infant Master of
the Universe was plausible, idle, and, he remembered suddenly,
relentlessly musical. 'But I think you'll find that in Malory, Sir
Percivale doesn't ask any questions at all, and it's that which causes
all the trouble. I'm afraid you've got a crossed wire, and you're
thinking of *Parsifal.*' The boy Piers flushed, and looked at him
with undiluted hatred, while the rest of the group rippled a little,
resentful that they had become so anaesthetised by boredom that
they had missed a chance to score a point.

It's the blind leading the blind, he thought to himself. He was
sitting with a cohort of the college's second-year English students,

dutifully chewing over the Middle Ages. The students were conscripts, doing a paper in which none of them was really interested, and nor was he. He was fully convinced of the intellectual value of introducing them to pre-modern literature, but all the same, there was no getting away from the fact that they were all bored to tears, including him. There must be better ways to get the stuff over, but trying to push through a modification to the syllabus was like trying to alter the course of the stars, and he had one fight on his hands already. He looked at his watch surreptitiously; they were coming up to the hour, thank God. 'The other thing I wanted to say, though,' he continued, 'is that even if you aren't enjoying it, it's worth knowing about this stuff. It's our national myth, so it keeps coming round one way or another. Wagner aside' – he glanced at Piers – 'if you're interested in the Victorians, you'll find there's an Arthurian nineteenth century, particularly with Tennyson, and then it surfaces again in the twentieth century with high modernism, Eliot and so on. Remember, even the Kennedys thought Camelot was still an idea with some mileage.'

'Didn't someone try to prove that the Holy Grail was really the blood of Jesus Christ?' asked Lydia brightly. Michael groaned inwardly. You could rely on Lydia to have heard of a surprising number of things, without having ever acquired the slightest ability to judge whether they were worth dragging in.

'Oh, yes. That crap about the Sangrail and the Sang Réal,' said Marcus dismissively. He was possibly the brightest of the group, and undoubtedly the one with the best opinion of himself. 'The Merovingian Kings of France were descended from Jesus Christ and Mary Magdalene, and therefore someone or other's the rightful king of the world. And the Templars had something to do with it.'

He was showing off; Michael was not displeased when his rival Piers took the wind out of his sails. 'I see you read it, then.'

Marcus glared at him, and Michael took advantage of his momentary deflation. 'We've got a long way from Malory, chaps,' he cut in smoothly. '*Gawain and the Green Knight* next time, remember. Look up the words, don't just guess. I want a lot more than eighty-five per cent this time, you'll find it's harder.' They all screwed up their faces childishly, and moaned; they were a clever group, but lazy. 'Oh, come on. You're supposed to be grown-ups. And remember, you're coming on the Friday, not the Wednesday next week. You'll have an extra couple of days to get to grips with it. Go on now, off you go. I can hear the next lot outside.'

They trooped off; as Michael put away his Malory and reached for *Middlemarch*, he could hear them exchanging civilities with the incomers, still on the landing. The last tute of the morning would be *Hamlet*, which he could teach in his sleep, but there was still the nineteenth-century novel to get through. The students were coming up to their exams, and even the second year were more on edge than they liked to pretend. Sometimes, especially with the finalists, he felt that they were actually trying to suck him dry, leaving nothing but a husk, desperate for the edge that would secure a first. He arranged his face, as far as possible, into a pleasant and receptive expression, and tried to think of something cogent to say about Dorothea Brooke.

Once the Shakespeare group had been successfully pushed out of the door, Michael had two hours to himself. He felt completely drained, so he decided to go and take a look at the papers, since he had not yet seen that week's job advertisements in the *Guardian*, and then nip across to the library to check the new journals.

When he pushed open the door of the Senior Common Room, he found three colleagues grouped by the table with the day's papers; the senior English Fellow, Robert Edzell, who was his principal ally in the English faculty, the senior tutor, Charles Ashton, who was looking particularly grim, and a young computer scientist called Royston Ellis, whom he did not know: however, he was instantly recognisable, because he was the only black person at all likely to be in the SCR. He was new that year, and their paths had not crossed: they had barely exchanged a word.

'How are things?' he enquired, and was not surprised when Ashton snapped,

'Barely tolerable. Admissions are difficult enough in themselves without knowing that any errors of judgement will end up in the papers. And on top of all that, I have Mr Singh on the phone from morning to night.'

'Mr Singh?'

'I've heard of this,' put in Royston Ellis. 'This is your eleven-year-old genius, right?'

'He's not my genius, Royston, and I hope he never will be. I wish we'd never heard of the wretched child. Duleep took a superb set of mathematical A levels in the spring session, at a time of life when he ought to have been playing with trains, and his father is laying siege to us. Of course, he wants the whole family to come up. The boy can't be expected to manage on his own, we haven't anywhere at all suitable for them, and they certainly can't afford Oxford house-prices.'

'Ruth Lawrence got her degree quite successfully, didn't she?' enquired Robert Edzell. 'I presume it's another case of the same kind? And we've got that other boy now, Ganesh something. I met him once, and I didn't understand a word he was saying, but the child seems to have all his buttons.'

'I believe so, Robert,' said the senior tutor impatiently. 'But from the college point of view, the important thing about infant geniuses is that the university always has an enormous amount of trouble from the parent, or parents. I've always hoped we could avoid anything of the kind at Balliol. In any case, what on earth is the point of his being here when he can't mix socially with the other students? Colleges are for developing the student as an individual, but with child students, all you can develop is a set of skills, so he may as well be at London, where they've got mathematicians quite as good as ours. We haven't been equipped to deal with children since the sixteenth century, and in any case, it's quite unnecessary.'

'You think it's the parent who creates the situation, then?' Royston asked.

'Of course. Obviously, there are children who show signs of unusual giftedness at a very early age, but they don't turn into Duleeps unless the parents manage to build on that and endow them with an unchildlike level of concentration and attention to detail. Surprising though it may seem, there are people who can persuade their children to live for an idea. I don't know if you follow chess at all? There's a fellow called Polgar in Hungary who decided he wanted his daughter to be a genius. He's coached her since before she could walk, and she's just beaten Gary Kasparov.'

'It seems to work with sport as well,' observed Royston. 'I'm thinking of Venus and Serena Williams. Their dad wanted tennis stars, he got 'em.'

The senior tutor sighed. 'So one hears. Well, I had better go back to the office. I will hope for an afternoon free from interruptions by Mr Singh, but frankly, I am not expecting it.'

Charles Ashton wandered out, heading back towards his rooms, and Robert Edzell smiled at the two younger men. 'Charles does take this kind of thing to heart, poor dear. I live in dread of the day he retires. When we've finally lost the last of the last generation that lived for the college, the rest of us are going to have to work an awful lot harder. Michael, this is not the moment, but we must have a word about the Campaign for Real Fiction. I think we're about ready to send the draft proposal up to faculty board.'

'Of course, Robert. Any time that suits you.' Michael turned apologetically to Royston, who was looking perplexed. 'Sorry, it's our nickname for a new course we're trying to get past the faculty. It's actually called "The Roots of the Novel".'

Robert Edzell, meanwhile, had nodded impartially to them both, picked up his letters and gone away. Royston turned to Michael conversationally. 'You're Michael Foxwist, and you're in English, aren't you? Listening to Charles just now, I was wondering about these stories, and what happens if the dad wants a genius and the kid isn't up to it. But I was also thinking, it's only a matter of degree. I don't suppose any of us got where we did without some pretty serious pushing from behind.'

'That's true enough,' said Michael. 'No one thought I was a genius, but I still had people standing over me to make sure I did my prep.'

'I owe it all to my Mum, really,' pursued Royston. 'I was brought up in Brixton, and school treated us like jungle bunnies, but she kept me under heavy manners, and she never gave up. I can hear her now – we came to this Godforsaken place to get you an education, you sit here with your book where I can see you or you feel the weight of my hand! – thank God for computers. I had a mathematical streak, you see, and it was nearly cool to be a geek, so long as you didn't look too geeky, 'cause you had skills, so I got through school and got a place at London, and just went on from there.'

'I didn't have that sort of peer-pressure,' said Michael. 'I was at a little public school, the sort of place where parents pay to insulate you from reality. But my father was the headmaster, and he wasn't well. I knew he was struggling to stay on till I was through school and he could retire, so I felt I had to keep my head down, or it would've killed him.'

'That's a lot worse, when they get you with guilt,' observed Royston soberly. 'You sound as if you regret it. But here we are, with jobs at Oxford. Mum nearly burst when I told her, and I'm sure your dad looped the loop.'

'Sometimes I just wish I'd had a bit more of a life. When I was fifteen or so, I'd've given anything for the chance to hang out in

Brixton, instead of sitting in an upstairs room in Cartmel.'

'Me too. I'd've liked to be on the streets, and it hurts when the cool dudes are calling you "batty-boy" and "coconut" and all that shit. But, you know, they're still playing today, and they're not looking so pretty.'

'How do you find the social side here?' asked Michael tentatively. 'They don't mean to be nasty, but some of the older Fellows are like people who've spent their lives in plastic tents. They can be incredibly impertinent, without even noticing. I just wanted to say, if you're having some grief, it's not just because you're black. It's also to do with being less than forty.'

Royston shrugged. 'It's OK. Like I say, I think of the alternatives. I want to get to the States if I can, and it's a great jumping-off place. They may not rate it, but it's one of the places they've heard of.'

'If it's not a rude question, I was wondering whether you think your parents think it was worth struggling on here? I can see you must've done all they can have hoped for, but have they had a life?'

'It's not been easy for them,' admitted Royston. 'Dad came over on the *Windrush*, which is sort of like the black British *Mayflower*, where it all started. Mum came a lot later – we're Jamaicans, by the way, if you haven't realised. It must've been hell for the first ten years, they tell stories – London was, like, "no Irish, no blacks" in the 1950s and 1960s. But we built a new world in the old world, you know. Where I grew up, all the white kids were grooving to Jamaica sound, trying to walk the walk, talk the talk.'

'That's true,' said Michael. 'Even in Cartmel, we'd heard of Bob Marley and Peter Tosh.'

'You can live in something like a real world now, in Brixton,' Royston said. 'There's church, of course, and now there's proper shops. They cuss the winter up and down, but they're not unhappy. Worried about the kids, of course; Mum did well with me and my sisters, but they can see if we've got problems as a community, it reflects on all of us. All the same, they'll never go home now. They're Londoners.'

'So you're not left feeling they did it all for you?'

'Exactly. I can thank them, and get on with it. You've got it a bit harder, I think.' Royston looked at his watch. 'You don't lunch in college, do you?'

'No, I've hardly ever got time, and anyway, I'm dining this evening for once, and two college meals in one day's more than anyone can stand. I was just going to nip over to the Bod. and look at some bits and bobs before the afternoon mob start coming in. I've got a lot of teaching stacked up at the moment, because I'm trying to get three days clear to go to London; I've had to shuffle them up a bit.'

'It's not easy to get away during term,' agreed Royston. 'I haven't been home since Christmas. I was in Stanford over Easter, meeting some of the guys, checking out what they're doing, so I didn't get down. Well, nice to meet you properly. I'll go in – I have my big meal now, because I'm in the lab all evening.'

Royston smiled amicably and went through to the SCR dining-room, while Michael wandered out into the street. The conversation stayed with him as he walked towards the Bodleian Library. Talking to Royston had increased his sensitivity towards Oxford. The man seemed amiably self-absorbed, content to pursue his own esoteric ends and unaware of social nuances, an obtuseness which, on reflection, was probably the only sane attitude he could have adopted. His own feelings were much more ambivalent. From his father's perspective, getting to Oxford had represented the summit of possible human ambition, an attitude which had naturally worn off on him. And by his third year, after two years in undistin-guished modern accommodation here and there in the town, he had finally achieved the dignity of a proper room in College, on a staircase, with an oak which could be sported, ogee windows, and a shared sitting-room overlooking the gardens; the Oxford of the imagination, which his mother had just not lived to see and enjoy. He had kept a bottle of port on the mantelpiece, worn white trousers and striped ties in the summer, tried to live out the dream.

Now, hurrying down Broad Street towards the library, he wondered what had happened to it all. It seemed to him as if the spires no longer dreamed, but posed self-consciously in an attitude of slumber, waiting to be photographed. The light still shone on the golden stone, the cartoonish busts of the emperors still glowered cretinously across Broad Street, images of men who in their day had been feared by half the world, now victims of the massive condescension of posterity. Wren's elegant Sheldonian rose behind them, with its elaborate, beautiful doorcase and swagged stone garlands, and high above, the Muses on the roof of the Clarendon Building were outlined against the sky; an uniquely odd, beautiful and interesting group of buildings. All around them books were being written and clever young people were being educated, but the introverted, familial life which had given rise to all this glory had gone for ever.

An open-topped tour bus was passing, the guide mechanically booming out the names of the colleges and some well-worn clichés of description. Groups of tourists, Japanese, American, German, jostled one another politely as each individual tried to take photographs without including all the others; anybody rash enough to appear on the street in an academic gown was pursued by the clicking of cameras. Far more obtrusive and tiresome, herds of Continental teenagers from the booming language schools traipsed about incuriously, ignoring the traffic, dropping litter and chattering amongst themselves in the language of their place of origin, quite manifestly learning almost nothing. Half the shops he could see were catering to the needs of visitors rather than residents. It occurred to him, as he tried to sort out his own feelings about what he saw, that although his schooldays had been miserable, they had at least taught him what it was really like to live in a close community, the notion which the university evoked, but no longer attempted to realise.

At least the library was still real, he thought, pushing open the glass doors tucked unobtrusively behind the life-sized statue which stood in a little cage of railings in front of the entrance, no gowned and otherworldly scholar, but a solid, stout old gentleman wearing a full suit of armour as if he felt comfortable in it. The front hall was accessible to visitors, and given over to the selling of rather expensive, vaguely book-related souvenirs, a guided tour clumped periodically up the worn oaken stairs to peer in at the readers in Duke Humphrey's Library, but that was the entire extent to which the place was implicated in the heritage business. Bodley remained a precious refuge, an Oxford experience, authentic and not for sale.

He had managed to clear Monday, Tuesday and Wednesday of the following week. His time was planned with care; there was an article on *Robinson Crusoe* he needed to finish for a forthcoming essay collection, and there was work he could usefully do on *The Female Rosicrucian*. But above all, he wanted to see Balthasar's book. With a little advance preparation in Bodley, he would certainly be able to take the time, and still get done all that he was supposed to be doing. It would be a long, tiring three days of catching the eight o'clock coach in the morning and another back to Oxford at eight or nine each evening, but he was looking forward to it.

On the Monday, therefore, he got off the coach at Victoria, brief-case in hand, and battled through the crowds of the busy, confused, mendicant, drunk, and insane who form the human landscape of a major bus terminal, and took the Tube to King's Cross. He intended to start his day by ordering books in the British Library, then once the orders were placed, he would read for a while in the open shelf collection, walk the few hundred yards down the road to the Wellcome, look at the book, and walk back. He knew from his advance reconnaissance that the Wellcome rather bloody-mindedly only fetched books twice a day, but with careful planning, he would waste almost no time. By the time he returned to his seat, the enormously efficient staff of the Rare Books Room in the British Library would have his other books waiting, a level of service sufficiently in contrast with that of Bodley to give him pleasure every time he used it.

A little over an hour later, therefore, Michael left the British Library and walked down Euston Road, a lone pedestrian amid the roaring traffic. Euston Road was unfamiliar territory to him beyond the library, and he was struck by the way that the streetscape was dominated by buildings that looked like something other than what they were. Juxtaposed with the blue-striped utilitarian box of a Travel Inn, there was a grimy Greek temple, complete with glum caryatids, St Pancras's Church. Euston Station, on his right, boasted a splendid pair of neo-classical gate-lodges which seemed to imply a mile or so of elm-lined carriage drive and a substantial Adamesque country house; the actual black steel station hulking behind these memorials of past grandeur looked like a geological intrusion from a different world. He was nearly there. The Post Office Tower lofted before him, framed by white-painted cranes – there had been a building site at the top of Gower Street for as long as he had been visiting London, and nothing ever seemed to come of it. And beside the vast gap, protected by hoardings, from which the cranes emerged like the skeletal necks of brontosauruses, stood a pretentious, 1930s neo-neo-classical building of vaguely Greek inspiration with a frontage of gigantic pillars, which looked as if it belonged in Munich: the Wellcome Library.

As he had on the whole expected, with the Wellcome Institute's money behind it, the library was remarkably well appointed. The collection, he discovered in the course of his conversation with the librarian, focused on medical books, but interpreted the concept very broadly to include recipe books and all sorts of miscellaneous treatises of vaguely medical tendencies. Once he had explained his business and presented some credentials, he was graciously allowed to see his book.

'I must ask you to take extra care,' said the librarian, handing him a pair of white cotton gloves. 'Please use these when you're turning the pages, and use a perspex sheet. It's one of our rarities. The first book ever published in Barbados was printed in 1741, and this book's only two years later. It's the unique copy, so of course, we have to treat it very conservatively.'

He sat down to wait, immediately under the librarian's eye, and within ten minutes his book had appeared, housed in a protective box. He pulled on his gloves, opened the box, and saw that it was not an impressive object. A slender little volume, with flaking grey card covers. He positioned it carefully on a book-rest and opened it with circumspection.

The title-page, *A Caribbean Flora, with a Guide to the Uses of Plants*, was as he expected, the author was given as Balthasar Stuart, Doctor of Medicine of the University of Leiden. So it was his Balthasar, he thought; excellent. Opening it at random, he could see why the Wellcome's buyers had swept it up. The text was divided into short chapters, and he was looking at 'Papaya, or Pappaw':

the fruit is esculent, sweet and like a Tree-mellon to the palate, and is not harmful if a little cordial is taken with it to counter the chill. Taken green, it is a specific for ague and cold in the stomach. The leaves may be applied green as a poultice for ulcers of the leg. The Milk which comes forth from the leaves, stems, and roots when they are cut is a vermifuge, and may be used against the tetter, eruptions, and warts upon the skin. It is said that the seeds, eaten raw, will restore the Menses in women, but few will venture the experiment for fear of their life.

117

The next page was on something called an Anchovy-Pear, he seemed to be in a section on fruit trees. Opening it again further on, he found Balthasar was dealing with plants.

> The Aloe is a plant of many uses and virtues. Applied internally, the mucilaginous Juice thereof is purgative and carminative, and used externally, it is a sovereign specific for wounds and burns of all kinds, promoting good healing. The Negroes use the juice also as a wash for the hair, and it is kindly as a lotion for skin scorched by the sun. A decoction, boiled, is used against megrim and the head-ache.

The principle of organisation, as far as he worked it out, paging cautiously back and forth under the librarian's watchful eye, seemed to be that trees were covered first, then plants of which the fruits were in some way useful, plants with useful leaves, then plants with useful roots or bark. It was pre-Linnaeus, he realised; Balthasar had no sense at all that plants divided into genera.

He went back to the beginning, and was delighted to find something he had hardly dared to hope for, 'Editor's Preface, with an Account of the Life of Dr Stuart'. It began thus:

> The Editor has availed himself of the new Resource of the Press, to lay before the Public the work of his respected Father. He respectfully begs the Attention of all well-disposed Citizens to this Work, the fruit of the Leisure-hours of a Licenciate of the University of Leiden, and for some years, Doctor to the Governor, and a resident of this Island. Going with true and impartial Charity about his business up and down the Parishes of Barbados, on many occasions, the poor Negroes and Indians made grateful return for his humane Attentions with some Accompt of the herbs and simples which the Island affords. Thus for the outlay of a mere five shillings, the householder has, in the knowledge contained in this Book, a

perpetual resource; he may gather from the natural bounty of the fields and hedgerows all that is necessary to tend to the ills of his Servants, securing thus, both their gratitude, and their Capacity.

Michael began to make notes. Balthasar had been physician to the governor, it was a pity that his son had not said which one. Never mind, the book might reveal something more by way of dating criteria. He was becoming powerfully curious what the son would tell him about the life.

He put his pencil down, lifted off the perspex, and turned the page. The gloves made his fingers rather clumsy, and he fumbled the turn; as he tried to rectify it, he found that he had opened the book on a dedication page he had not realised was there.

To the Sacred Memory of
THEODORE PALAEOLOGUE,
Emperor of the Christian Greeks,
Champion of Liberty,
and Native of this Island.
His Hero's Death was in the Fleet-Action at Corunna
in the year '92.

Why? And who was Theodore Palaeologue? It would probably not be all that difficult to find out. Corunna did ring a bell, but the wrong one; due to his father's somewhat old-fashioned views of what poetry made suitable pabulum for public-schoolboys, 'The Burial of Sir John Moore at Corunna' was a poem with which he had made a close and early acquaintance; 'Not a drum was heard, not a funeral note', was unscrolling in his mind unstoppably as he sat and tried to think. Sir John Moore had met his end in the early nineteenth century, so he clearly had nothing to do with it; but whom had England been at war with in 1692? The absence of any information about Palaeologue's rank caused Michael cynically to suppose that he had not exactly been a vice-admiral, but it was unlikely that a man generally known as the last emperor of Byzantium had been a mere able seaman. There would certainly be something about the man in the various records connected with the Royal Navy. He made another note, and returned to the preface.

The Life was all that he hoped for in the way of confirmation. Balthasar had been educated at Leiden, but had removed to London; his son was vague about when. He had married 'a lady of good family' – and how, thought Michael parenthetically to himself, had a lady reconciled herself to marrying a mulatto? Aha. Balthasar had been established in London for some years, when he made the acquaintance of Theodore Palaeologue, 'a name', the preface assured him, 'which will be familiar to all Readers resident in the Parish of St John, where his Family held for many years, a Plantation, atop Hackleton's Cliff, and his father, Ferdinando Palaeologue, enjoyed the dignity of Churchwarden of the Parish'. Invited by Palaeologue, Balthasar had come out to Barbados, and worked there for a while, then he had gone back to London. After the death of Theodore at Corunna, 'with the active Kindness which marks the Christian Gentleman', Balthasar had taken in his orphan daughter. The families, then, must have been close friends; the mother was presumably dead, at any rate, she went unmentioned. 'This lady, brought up in the place of a Sister, I now have the Honour to call my wife; uniting thus the blood of the Caesars with a Lineage which, though obscure in its present Possessor, has no reason to blush at such an association.' Interesting, thought Michael. He knows he's royal.

'In sum, I beg leave to commend this book to the Reader. Copies may be purchased at the Gazette printing-office in Bull-Head-Alley, or enquiry may be made of the Editor, Theodore Stuart, Esq., of Roebuck Street, Bridge-Town, Barbados.'

The British Library shuts at eight in the evening on a Monday; Michael, half-dozing on the nine o'clock coach after a long, hard day, was well contented with what he had achieved. The figure of Balthasar was becoming far more real to him, for all the vague pomposity of the son's narrative; he was active, conscientious, observant, charitable. The son's name was Theodore, he remembered suddenly. Therefore almost certainly a godson of Theodore Palaeologue's, another indication that the families were closely connected.

Once the coach left behind the flickering lights of London and turned onto the M40, Michael found his head drooping against the window. He rolled up his raincoat, wedged it under his ear as an impromptu pillow, and went to sleep; and as he slept, he dreamed.

He was in Silloth, standing on one of the immensely wide concrete steps which went down from the esplanade to the brown, muddy sand with the groynes that projected out to sea; a dreary, sad-coloured prospect of concrete and breakwaters. A few yards ahead of him stood another person; he was aware that the man was looking at him, but as he himself looked up, the other turned his face away and began to walk; Michael was just aware that he was black. Michael quickened his pace to catch up with him, but somehow the man seemed to be getting further and further away, so he began to walk faster and faster, slogging along with immense effort, his heart nearly bursting with anxiety and stress, but he somehow seemed not to be moving at all, while the stranger receded effortlessly into the distance.

Not exactly hard to interpret, he thought, waking as the coach negotiated the Oxford roundabout. The man had had a look of Royston, to whom he had been talking the previous week; Michael's sense of the elusiveness of the historical past was strong. QED. But all the same, it was disquieting, as if for that one moment when the man was looking at him, he had received some kind of contact, or warning.

Once he was back in his flat, he turned on the computer before going to bed. He was rather tempted to pursue the Palaeologue connection: somewhere there must be a naval library. He checked his email before making his search, and was pleased to find a message from Theodoor.

'Dear Michael': Theodoor was obviously one of the rare people who wrote emails as if they were letters.

> I will be coming to Oxford in two weeks' time; there is a Neo-Latin seminar at Keble which I wish to attend, and I will take the opportunity to work for a few days in Bodley. Is it possible do you think that you could reserve me a college room for four days? The Keble guest-rooms have all been reserved for some college event, and I need to find alternative accommodation. If not it does not matter, I will ask advice of the organiser.

How nice, thought Michael. It would be interesting to see a bit more of Theodoor. Well, it would have to keep; he would need to be up well before seven the next day, and it was getting late. At that time of year, there was unlikely to be any difficulty in getting a college guest-room. He fired off a brief reply promising action in a day or so, picked a search engine off his favourites list, and tried 'naval library' on Google.

After a certain amount of redefinition caused by the need to screen out US Navy sites, he came up with the answer: the National Maritime Museum at Greenwich seemed to hold the principal collection of manuscript records to do with the navy. Given the strong association of Greenwich with the Royal Navy, if he had thought for a minute, he might have remembered about it; but it was, from his point of view, well off the beaten track. The museum welcomed enquirers; it was in a beautiful neo-classical building, it all sounded rather nice. While it was not necessarily the most productive use of most of a day in London, it would certainly be interesting. He went and got a Tube map from his jacket pocket, and pored over it. The trip would involve the Docklands Light Railway, a new experience. But you could get it from Bank. If he kept the visit pretty brisk and went straight to the British Library afterwards and worked till closing time, he would still get a good deal out of his day. Pleased with himself, he shut down the computer, stumbled through a quick shower, and went to bed.

Putting this programme into practice the next day, Michael realised that it was the first he had actually seen of Mrs Thatcher's new London, not so very new any more. It was disorienting for someone who thought he knew his way around quite well to be discovering a whole new quarter, to leave the familiar precincts of the City for a series of stations with curious and alien-sounding names like Mudchute. There was hardly anybody about at the still new-looking station, or on the train. At other times of the day it was presumably packed solid with yuppies, but in mid-morning, he seemed just about to have the system to himself. The train took him on what seemed to be a contrived, touristic path through the miniature Manhattan of Docklands. The impression of contrivance was, as he realised, basically created by the fact that most of the track was considerably above ground level, but it produced a surprisingly stagy effect.

Docklands itself intrigued him; a panorama of mirror-faced office blocks, complete, or half-finished and hung about with cranes as if no sort of recession could be imagined. Presumably the idea was to hammer home the message that new Britain was up for anything, though given the relatively modest scale, he wondered how impressive it looked to hardfaced suits from Manhattan or the Loop. While a district intended simply for making money in had obvious built-in limitations as a social environment, the development was spectacular, and had a bit of zip. At least it suggested that the City had some notion of trading with the future rather than trading on the past.

He suddenly caught a glimpse of the ill-fated Millennium Dome, like a white jellyfish dropped from a height, a structure so much scoffed at that its actual existence came as something of a surprise. The site did it no favours, he thought; though rumour had it that the Dome was gigantic, seen in the distance beyond that macho reach of skyscrapers it looked lowly and unimpressive.

However self-consciously scenic, the DLR was at least efficient. It was not long before it brought him to Greenwich, where he was spat out by a series of escalators and emerged blinking onto some kind of high street. It was very clear to him, plodding up towards the Maritime Museum, that Greenwich had until fairly recently been a place entirely of itself, a microcosm exclusively centred on the Royal Navy. In the twentieth century, it had of course been engulfed by greater London, but more recently, it had succumbed to a far greater danger than mere absorption, by becoming a World Heritage site. The result was that, like Docklands, it was playing at being itself, but whereas in Docklands the posturing was purposeful, part of the constant mutual I've-got-a-bigger-one competitiveness of serious money-makers, Greenwich was, as it were, spray-coated with transparent plastic. Approaching the Maritime Museum, he was intensely irritated to find it broadcasting the sound of the sea from hidden speakers; well yes, he thought to himself, that's what it's fundamentally about, but what kind of an idiot needs to be reminded so literally?

Whoever was responsible for revamping the place had roofed over the central atrium of the grand baroque square, so it was bathed in cool, controlled grey light. The new-painted walls looked self-conscious and unnaturally clean, as architectural surfaces do when they were meant to be outside and are so no longer. There seemed to be almost no actual exhibits, as he threaded his way through chattering flocks of schoolchildren, except for a stupendous royal barge, with elegant gilt mermaids on the end, proffering a vast shield emblazoned with the royal arms. He turned away from their winsome golden bosoms, and went up the corner stairs to the library.

As he had half-expected from his initial approach, the library staff were all that was friendly and helpful, to an extent which he found almost embarrassing. But it was clear, looking around, that unlike the fetchers in Oxford, they were not exactly overburdened. A handful of elderly figures who all looked like retired admirals pottered to and fro with bundles of papers, there were a few graduate students to be seen, but not the purposeful hordes he was used to. Still, it was nice to feel welcome. He explained himself, and the librarian pointed him towards the catalogues of miscellaneous documents and private papers which, she suggested, were the most likely to yield the kind of information he wanted; so he settled himself in one of the rather clublike leather armchairs and began to read. It took less than half an hour's worth of practised flicking before he found something useful: a petition, addressed to the Lords of the Admiralty, from Theodore Stuart, Esq., in respect of his wife, Godscall Palaeologue, dated 1757. There was nothing relating directly to Theodore Palaeologue, but at least the trip had not been a total waste. He went back to the desk and asked for the manuscript, and then returned to the catalogue, which produced nothing more of interest. Before long, he found a librarian standing over him asking him politely to move to one of the tables within sight of the central desk, where his order was brought to him, one grubby sheet of eighteenth-century laid paper from a box of many such, written in a round copperplate hand in brownish ink.

I come to your Lordships as an humble petitioner being brought to very great necessaty through some very unfortunate circumstances that I have Lain under for some time following on the wreck of disappointments and the unforseen misfortunes of this world. My lords, I am a gentleman and not able to get a livelihood for the support of my wife and our hopeful Posterity. She is greatly deserving of your Lordships patronage Both in that she is the daughter of a Hero – who by falling in his Countreys defence at Corunna, deprived her alike of the support of an affectionate Parent, and of a Patrimony –, and because in her poor Person she is the last remnant of the Kings of Rome, the stout Bulkward of christendom against the Mahometans. I may say with the steward in the gospell, work I cannot and to beg I am ashamed, but mere necessaty forces me to give your Lordships this trouble, hoping your charity would consider us, for I have heard a very great and good character of what charity you have done and do dayly, so that I hope for your pitty on our unhappy state. If your Lordships will please to admit further solicittation, I will give you a very just account of our cercumstances which is too Long to do here.

Your Lps humble servant to command,
   Theodore Stuart

Roebuck Street, Bridgetown, Barbados

The page had been folded, a clerkly hand had written on the back, 'No Reply'. He was not in the least surprised. Michael had seen a good many eighteenth-century begging letters, they were something of a cottage industry of the time, but even within the general constraints of the genre, this was a curiously depressing document. Whereas it was clear that Balthasar had been a man of considerable character, observant and enquiring, the son seemed a pretty poor specimen, and it was obvious that he had made a hopeless mess of whatever project had taken him back to Barbados. He had achieved a quiverful of children with the strangely named Godscall (possibly a translation of a Greek name beginning Theo——? he asked himself, he must remember to try it on a classicist). There was something soggy about Theodore Stuart; the letter, put together with the preface to the book in the

Wellcome, somehow hinted at a picture of a man more interested in his ancestors than his descendants. A very English vice. Time to go; there was work to be done.

The rest of the week produced nothing relevant to Pelagius or his descendants, though from the point of view of his various projects, it was successful enough. He spent an afternoon with Robert Edzell, making the new course as faculty-board-proof as their joint ingenuity could contrive, and he booked a college room for Theodoor and emailed him to tell him so.

When Theodoor actually arrived, the following week, his first day was taken up with the colloquium, and, of course, he wanted to spend the second day in the library – Michael would have been hard put to it to accommodate him if this had not been the case. The first he saw of him, therefore, was on the second evening of the visit, fortunately one of the college's guest nights, when he had signed Theodoor in as his guest at High Table, an experience which he hoped that a Netherlander would find picturesque, if not exactly gastronomic.

At precisely seven o'clock, Theodoor knocked, by arrangement, on the door of Michael's college room, where he was waiting with a bottle of Tio Pepe and a bowl of olives.

'How are you enjoying Oxford?' Michael asked, once the preliminaries were over.

'Not very much. The colloquium was a disappointment: there is an English tendency to confuse speculation with argument, an absence of thorough preparation, which is not appropriate to a scientific subject. Also, I find Oxford very expensive. There are so many beggars.'

'You shouldn't really give them anything, you know,' said Michael, irritated. He had forgotten the Dutch addiction to candour even when circumstances seemed to an Englishman to demand social fibs. 'The police tell us not to, it just encourages them. Anyway, I've heard quite a lot of them are organised.'

'Well, that is a problem for their own consciences, and not a concern of yours. It is very bad for you as a citizen to learn to look through fellow persons as if they were furniture. It is not a lesson I wish to learn.'

Michael drained his sherry in silence; it was a sufficiently un-Oxfordian comment that he feared that the evening was not going to be quite the success he had hoped for.

'Theodoor, if you've finished your drink, I think we'd better go,' he said. 'Don't expect too much. If you want serious food, you have to make friends in Merton or Lincoln.' He held the door for Theodoor, and led the way across the quadrangle, pulling on his gown as he went.

In the event, the evening was not disastrous. As the diners gathered in the Senior Common Room, Michael was deeply relieved to see the new History Fellow, who was clever and sensible, and a chemist who was at least entertaining. The Master was dining, so Michael introduced his guest. The Master made a little speech of welcome with the ease of long practice, marred only by an awkward moment when it became clear that his mind had been elsewhere at a crucial moment, and he had formed the impression that Theodoor was from Leiden, Oxford's twin-town in the Netherlands. Fortunately, just as Theodoor politely but firmly repeated that he was from Utrecht, the butler banged the gong, and it was possible to relinquish the conversation. The Master strode off in a flourish of robes to lead the procession, and Michael annexed Catherine Sinclair, the History Fellow, to sit on Theodoor's other side.

Theodoor, as he ate his way through four courses of heavy, old-fashioned food and drank a very little of the quite good wine, maintained an impenetrable reserve. Michael wondered what he was thinking. He had hoped that the antique pageantry of Hall would exert its charm, or, at the very least, interest his guest, but it seemed not to be working. Michael looked down the length of the hall at the long tables and benches where the undergraduates sat; just a few of them on a midweek night, only those who were both well off and strongly invested in being Oxonian, or who, like himself, were entertaining outsiders.

It was all rather hard to justify, considered rationally, he thought, trying to see it through foreign eyes. The diehards of the nineteenth century had been quite right; allowing Fellows to marry had been the beginning of the end, because it spelled death to a life centred on the college. The system had coasted along for a while: in the early days of the oldest Fellows, everyone, dons, undergraduates and all, had eaten in as a matter of course. They would therefore all have known each other, and been aware of one another in the way that he remembered from school. But since Hall was now purely voluntary, it had ceased to perform any real function; it was, like foxhunting, merely an inordinately expensive relic of a way of life now actually obsolete. In some moods, the community aspect of the college seemed to him like the shell of a structure eaten by termites, apparently sound, but possibly liable to collapse suddenly, pouring out dust and maggots.

Meanwhile, the light from silver candelabra gleamed on dark portraits of college worthies; the butler went round with claret; the Fellows made general conversation, mostly, as far he could hear, about cricket. Fortunately, the excellent Catherine had sized up the situation correctly and had accordingly ditched the theoretically iron-clad rule about 'no shop at dinner'. She was asking intelligent questions about Spanhemius, and it became clear that she knew the man at Keble who had organised Theodoor's colloquium, and was reasonably well informed. The evening went off quite agreeably, but Michael was left with a strong feeling that Theodoor had privately considered the High Table ritual a very poor use of time and resources. Yet it was clear as they said their goodbyes outside Theodoor's guest-room, that whatever he felt about Oxford, his friendly feelings towards Michael himself were undiminished; the desire to give pleasure had been appreciated, even if pleasure had not, in fact, resulted.

The following day, as he was coming out of the Bodleian into Catte Street in order to pick up a lunchtime sandwich at the King's Arms, Michael passed the noticeboard which carries advertisements of university concerts and his eye was caught by a familiar name on the bill for a recital at the Sheldonian: 'The English Voice', a programme of Elizabethan and Jacobean songs to be sung by a man called Robin Parslowe, whom he knew slightly. It was scheduled for the following night, Theodoor's last night in Oxford, and Michael paused to consider. Robin, a gentle and likeable fellow, was also good-looking in a sweet-faced, blond English style, and though he was in fact a thoroughly competent musician, his pure, ingenuous tenor voice seemed as much a product of nature as that of a choirboy. A perfect voice for that sort of material; he sang the words with beautiful precision and as if he understood them, so that the meaning came through effortlessly. The Sheldonian, lit for a concert, was beautiful, and come to that, Robin himself was beautiful in his way: if Theodoor cherished any sentimental feelings about golden-haired youth, he would certainly enjoy him as an object of contemplation. All things considered, it seemed a perfect evening to send him off with; if the experience did not leave him with a more favourable impression of Oxford, it was hard to think what would.

He abandoned his original intention of getting some lunch, doubled back to the library, and ran Theodoor down, as he had expected to, in Duke Humphrey. When he made his invitation, Theodoor's face showed his genuine interest. 'I know very little of English music,' he said. 'I would be pleased to learn.' Michael dashed off again in order to get back to Balliol in time for the afternoon's tutorials, and later in the day, bought tickets. He fetched Theodoor from his room in good time the following evening, and they walked up Broad Street to the Sheldonian. He was gratified to see that God had thoughtfully provided the clichéd slanting, golden light which shows Oxford off at its best, and as they settled themselves on the intensely uncomfortable wooden chairs beneath the painted ceiling depicting Religion, Arts and Science triumphing over Envy, Hatred and Malice, he was also pleased to observe that Theodoor seemed at his most relaxed, even jovial, and prepared to enjoy himself. The concert began, and Michael was sure of success after the first ten minutes. Robin was in excellent voice, the clement weather had reduced the incidence of chronic coughers and sneezers endemic to concerts in the upper Thames valley, and the audience was intelligently appreciative. Theodoor was a silent and concentrated listener, but it was clear that he was moved.

They were most of the way through the first half before there was trouble. Robin began on one of Michael's favourite Dowland songs, Sir Henry Lee's farewell to Queen Elizabeth. He leaned back to let it wash over him, enjoying its resigned melancholy, the noble acceptance of ageing and change, the tricky timing which Robin was negotiating so gracefully that it seemed merely conversational, and glanced at Theodoor to see if he was appreciating how well Robin was putting it over. He was shocked to see that his guest was sitting bolt upright, his hands clasped between his knees, weeping uncontrollably. Michael reviewed the words then being sung, in painful bewilderment.

> His golden locks Time hath to silver turn'd,
> O Time too swift, O swiftness never ceasing!
> His youth 'gainst Time and Age hath ever spurn'd,
> But spurn'd in vain; youth waneth by increasing.
> Beauty, strength, youth, are flow'rs but fading seen;
> Duty, faith, love, are roots and ever green.

Poignant, yes, but enough to bring a man to tears? Yet this was obviously the case. Theodoor endured to the end of the song, shuddering a little, then under the cover of the final applause, he gave a huge, childish sniff, and hissed, in a voice hoarsened by emotion, 'I am sorry, I must go.' And he was off, stumbling along the row regardless of offended stares and trodden feet, fleeing for the exit with the tears still wet on his cheeks, leaving his host baffled, uneasy, and feeling obscurely in the wrong.

If he were English, thought Michael, trying to regain his concentration as Robin launched into 'My sweetest Lesbia', I'd know I'd never hear from him again, he'd be too embarrassed. But he can't possibly hold it against me, so maybe some day I'll find out what the hell this was all about. His curiosity seemed unlikely to be satisfied. He received an email from Theodoor three days later, thanking him for his hospitality but offering no explanation, no apology, no reassurance. And a few days after that, a copy of Jan van Dorsten's *The Anglo-Dutch Renaissance* arrived, which he was pleased to have since there seemed not to be a copy in Bodley, and there the matter rested.

VI

One day I meet an old woman selling, and I wanted something
    to eat
I thought I could put a little bit in she way, but I take back
    when I did meet.
I thought she had bananas, orange or pear, nothing that I need,
I asked the old woman what she was selling, she said she was
    selling weed.

She had de Pap-bush, Elder-bush, de Black-pepper bush,
    French-to-you and de Cure-for-all
Sapodilla, Tamarind leaf, Monkey-bush, and de Soldier-parsley,
Pumpkin blossom, with the Double-do-me, and Congo-pumps in
    galore,
Physic-nut, and even de Lily-root is the list of her every day soup.
                          Anonymous Barbadian calypso

The summer term was drifting, or from the point of view of the
students, racing, towards its end – even faster than usual, since
the exams had to be fitted in before the Queen's Jubilee celebrations. Michael found, as usual in the third term, that a strategic-
ally placed box of tissues was an essential adjunct to his teaching
sessions. He could remember only too well how it felt to be
approaching one's finals; most of the students he taught were
virtually certain two-ones, but many of them dreaded a Desmond
(the still-fashionable, defensively jocular euphemism, named after
Archbishop Tutu), and others, or the same ones in different moods,

were desperate to get a Patty. It all came out when he saw them on their own; before one another they were almost all determined to keep up appearances as favoured children of the gods, beings for whom success should be a matter neither of effort nor of anxiety. It was depressing; he longed to tell them not to.

One small chore he did manage to achieve; after talking to a medievalist colleague, he managed to identify the 'Prophecies of Gildas' that interested his great-uncle as a longish poem in Rawlinson *c.* 813, an early sixteenth-century manuscript, which, on inspection, turned out to be written in a snarly Gothic script which was completely beyond him. However, a graduate student called Erica Moore, also recommended by the medievalist, had no problems with it, and was delighted with the prospect of transcribing it for £10 an hour: as she said at once when he made the proposal, it touched on her own work, so she might well have transcribed it anyway, for nothing. Harold was deeply gratified, and sent one of his six-page letters, as well as, in due course, a cheque for Miss Moore. Michael read the first and last paragraphs of the letter, skimmed the rest in case of nasty surprises, gave the student her money, and felt that he had made two people happier than they had been, a rare outcome in life, and one to be cherished.

Meanwhile, as the senior tutor had predicted, Mr Singh involved the *Daily Mail* in his campaign, and the college found itself besieged by reporters. Dr Ashton did his best to explain why he thought Oxford was not the right place for an eleven-year-old, and was shouted down by the indignant Singhs. The crisis blew over, as things do. Duleep was offered a place at Imperial College, which, for a pure mathematician, was hardly a second best. Since the family lived in London anyway, Mr Singh, who had given up work when Duleep was two in order to devote himself full-time to the marvellous child, could simply take him back and forth on the Tube. It was a rational solution to Duleep's particular problem, which did not prevent the *Mail* from working itself into a fine flow of indignation about the arrogance which rejected undoubted genius on specious, and probably racist, grounds.

Meanwhile in Oxford, once the students had actually entered the meat-grinder of the examinations system, they were on their own. From Michael's viewpoint, apart from occasional invigilation, the pressure was off, and he was finally able to crack on with Aphra Behn. The Oxford system appoints specific examiners in a rota going over several years rather than spreading the load across the entire faculty, and that year, Michael had not drawn the short straw, so he was pretty well free to get on with his research.

Editing a work existing only in one manuscript was a reasonably straightforward task. There were difficulties, of course, since the text was in draft, but corrections and second thoughts were almost invariably written above or beside her first attempt, and it was usually possible to work out what Behn had wanted the final version of a line to look like. What she meant by it was sometimes another matter, and one or two hopeless messes remained, but that was to be expected, as were ambiguities; when she made Clarina describe Bianca as 'meat for Convent walls', had Behn meant 'meet', meaning 'suitable', or 'meat', in the sense of 'fodder'? One interesting aspect of it, as far as he was concerned, lay in working out what the play was meant to look like, and, indeed, if she had intended it to be staged. In her later life, Aphra had been a complete mistress of the technical resources of the Restoration theatre, using its inner and outer stage, balconies and other resources to great effect. But this, he strongly suspected, was a first play, the work of an enthusiastic amateur who had not yet mastered professional stagecraft, or, quite possibly, even seen a professional play. The plot was exuberant, but her command of technicalities was shaky, and there would have been some awkward moments.

Act Two was particularly difficult: the one in which the full intricacy of the plot mechanism was set up. The play's chief fixer, the untrustworthy maid Ismena, who was in league with Ali Puli since she recognised him as her natural king, was, in classic comedic fashion, happy to do a little business on the side. Accordingly, she persuaded Ali Puli to let the juvenile lead, Philander, who had seen Bianca leaving church and fallen in love with her, come with him to Lorenzo's house in the guise of a servant called Zarrack. Once admitted to the house, Ali Puli identified Lorenzo's daughter Bianca as an angelic spirit, the White Rose of the Rosy Cross, and persuaded her to scry for him, an episode which left Michael wondering if Aphra could possibly have been familiar with John Dee's *Angelic Conversations* in some form or another. The scrying scene was ornamented with a song; a marginal note identified it as 'duetto – Ali Puli & Zarrack – Mr P?'. Zarrack was the name of Ali Puli's servant, i.e. Philander in disguise, but 'Mr P' was a problem he could not solve; his best guess was that he was the person she hoped to approach about setting her lyric to music.

> From Earth's subtil veines distill
> This our *Stone Mercuriall;*
> Let the ardent *Roses* burne
> *Snow* and *Scarlett* in their turne;
> Crowne 'em with the *Moone* & *Sunne,*
> Thus our *Worke* is halfe-way-done.
>
> Let the *White-Rose* blush with *Red,*
> Blanch the *Red-Rose* in her stead;
> Let the *Black-Rose* in the darke
> Growe as the *Elixirs* worke;
> Crowne 'em with the *Moone* & *Sunne,*
> Thus our *Worke,* our *Worke* is done.

It was quite high-quality impressive mystic nonsense, and left Michael wishing he knew more about Rosicrucians. He had dutifully taken a look at the real Ali Puli's *Centrum naturae concentratum*, which some enthusiast had translated into English in 1682, and it did not seem to be a likely starting-point for this strong focus on symbolical roses. He was most reluctant to tap the vast knowledge of his great-uncle, since the result would be a deluge of information easier to start than to stop, so he'd have to do it himself.

Making a note to read *The Rosicrucian Enlightenment*, and returning to the immediate problems of Act Two, Michael tried to work out what was going on. Greatly impressed by Ali Puli's mystical abilities and general force of character, Bianca was duly persuaded to enter a trance state and told her enraptured father, who was in paroxysms of mercantile greed which reminded Michael of *Volpone*, exactly where all his vessels were and what they were doing, together with some forecasts of the price of Rhine wine and Italian silk. Once out of her trance, Bianca, who up to that point had been characterised as interested only in scholarship and the life of the mind, confided in her sister Clarina that she was deeply impressed with Ali Puli because he seemed to her a more than mortal figure of pure intellect.

It was unsurprising to find, therefore, that Philander, who was taking every opportunity to woo her energetically, was doing so to no effect, though Clarina herself found him most attractive. The situation was a straightforward romantic tangle, with everyone after the wrong person, but the problem in terms of stagecraft was working out where everyone was supposed to be. Wherever the father was, he must not overhear Philander making love to his daughter Bianca, Clarina revealing her state of mind, or Ismena taking bribes and talking to Ali Puli, so where was he? Michael was reduced to making a diagram of the Duke's Theatre, where Aphra had worked in the 1670s, and moving little blobs of Blu-Tak about on it to represent the actors. Aphra seemed not to have decided when she wanted Lorenzo to leave the stage: on Michael's first read-through, he had assumed Lorenzo simply left after the scrying scene, but he popped up again later: where was he meanwhile?

The character who interested him most was Lady Bianca; Behn seemed to have been in two minds about her. In some ways, she seemed set up from the beginning as a set of misogynist clichés; the idea of a woman scholar who, once sexually initiated, becomes a nymphomaniac was surely the stuff of after-dinner jokes, especially when it was a black man who seduced her. She seemed a figure of fun, but she also had some of the best lines, could one be sure? Near the beginning of Act Three, there was an angry exchange which interested him:

<u>Bianca</u> —— My lord, do you forget?

~~When day was done~~ the following night I sought my maiden bed

Nor was it long ere all the house was still.

I heard your gentle steps approach my door,

Undressed you came, and with resistless force

Entwined me in your arms; I called you Lord!

My dear lov'd Lord! and in return you breath'd

Into my bosom soft and gentle whispers,

My queen! my angel! Beauteous Bianca!

And at that word – I blush to tell the rest.

<u>Ali Puli</u> Ay, you did fume and fret, like greenwood laid i'th' fire;

Where now you blaze hot, a well-season'd tree

Rejoicing in the flame. Ay, now your blood rises,

Beyond my pow'r to cool it, you would have me

Make an extraction even of my soul,

Decay my youth, only to feed thy Lust!

<u>Bianca</u> And if 'tis so? The fault lies at thy door.

'Tis your dark art that taught me such delight.

It was hard to see where the sympathy was meant to lie. Was she expecting the audience to feel some sort of masculine solidarity with Ali Puli, since he was royal and, of course, male? Any woman reduced to pleading for sex was, needless to say, ludicrous in seventeenth-century eyes; there was plenty of evidence to support the notion that a woman unwise enough to lose her virginity became an immediate object of contempt. On the other hand, what did people in the seventeenth century think about black men having sex with white women? After some scratching around in Bodley, he came up with a lampoon on Charles II's mistress the Duchess of Mazarin and the Countess of Sussex, who both, it was alleged, had sex with the same 'loathsome filthy Black', suggesting that the concept aroused strong negative feelings; similarly *The Moderate Intelligencer*, an early newspaper, complained of 'Negers making sport with our English women'. On the whole, it was hard to believe that Ali Puli's conquest of Bianca would be received sympathetically. The solution, perhaps, lay in the notion that, as in Jonson's *Volpone*, which has an anti-hero as lead character, Ali Puli and Bianca were anti-hero and anti-heroine, with sympathy, if there was any, resolved for the relatively conventional Philander and Clarina.

All the same, the conclusion of the play was curiously ambiguous. At the end of Act Three, Ali Puli succeeded in persuading Lorenzo to part with a casket of jewels worth a prince's ransom (a phrase which, in that context, Ali Puli's vengeance for his own enslavement, went far beyond cliché), in return for an 'Elixir of Invulnerability' to be applied to his precious ships. This 'Great Work of Alchemy', according to Ali Puli, would take a month to prepare, in which it would have to be watched day and night, a month in which Ali Puli and his assistant were necessarily guests of the house, and thus able to pursue their various agendas of seduction and betrayal. In the course of the month in question, Ali Puli, heartily sick of Bianca's sexual insatiability, evolved an ingenious twist on his original scheme of vengeance. Bianca was easily persuaded to elope with him, taking with her yet more of her father's possessions, but unlike Shakespeare's Jessica in *The Merchant of Venice*, she would not find her lover waiting outside. The house the servant Zarrack would take her to, which she believed to be her lover's, she would in fact discover to be a brothel, and the future he had actually arranged for her was as a high-class courtesan. But did Aphra in fact intend this as vicious dismissal, as it seemed at first? The play was set in Venice, and she was presumably thinking of women such as the great Venetian courtesan Veronica Franco, poet, intellectual, wit and famous beauty, painted by Titian, visited by kings. From one point of view, Aphra had contrived an ending which gave the sexually aggressive woman the come-uppance which Restoration England would feel she deserved, from another, she had given her the nearest possible thing to a happy ending one could imagine, a life of freedom, in which scholarship and sex could be combined.

It was possible, and perhaps legitimate, Michael mused, to imagine young Aphra, only in her twenties when she was writing this play, dreaming of such a life. Perhaps she had thought to herself: if I had been born in Venice, talented, witty and attractive, there would have been a place for a woman like me. She said several times in later life that she 'desired fame'. As things were, in a London with no place for a woman who was artist and lover, she had had to make one by sheer force of character, and had died, worn out, in her late forties. She had certainly returned to the figure of the successful courtesan later, with her Angellica Bianca (was the name significant?) in *The Rover*. In the later play, that of a sadder and wiser woman, perhaps, Angellica compromised her success and independence by falling in love and being rejected, but it was far from clear to Michael that Aphra thought the courtesan's life an entirely negative one, or any more morally suspect than that of a wife. Later, as a woman of the theatre, she was friendly with women like Nell Gwynn and Peggy Hughes, after all. Michael found himself coming round to the view that the play's ambiguities were entirely deliberate; she was being cynically populist, to keep her audience, but with some private mental reservations.

As he read through the play again and again, it seemed to him that in some ways, the play was more risky than anything she had actually attempted to stage later on, because of the cross-race sex. Though she had returned to the theme in *Abdelazar*, in the later play the affair was basically over, and Abdelazar, when he appeared, was thoroughly sick of his royal mistress; in his own text, on the other hand, when Ali Puli left the stage at the end of Act Two of *The Female Rosicrucian*, he was explicitly going off to seduce Bianca. In other ways, though, the play seemed conventional, even old-fashioned. There were elements in it which could be seen as life-long themes or interests of Aphra Behn's, sympathy for the woman who asked more of life than the seventeenth century was prepared to give her, sympathy (qualified in this case) for the figure of the royal slave which came round again in *Oroonoko*. The plot, and still more the atmosphere, seemed to him to be quite strongly influenced by Shakespeare and, to some extent, Ben Jonson: it seemed as if she had prepared herself to write, naturally enough, by borrowing freely from acknowledged, if antique, masters of the playwright's art.

It was important, he reflected, to put the play's flaws in the proper context, to remember that when Aphra was growing up, the theatres had all been closed; they were shut down in 1642, two years after her birth, and the first new theatre of Charles II's London opened only in 1663, by which time she was probably in Holland. No wonder the plotting and characterisation looked a bit old-fashioned; she had not been in London to see the way Killigrew and Etheredge were transforming the drama. Instead, she must have been drawing on memories of her reading, or perhaps she had got hold of a Shakespeare quarto in Middelburg. As a result, apart from the most un-Shakespearean Philander, who was persuaded to switch his affections from one sister to the other as if he thought one rich Venetian was much like another, the characters seemed on the whole to care about each other, the basic concept of romantic love was not derided.

It was all very interesting, and gave him plenty to say. He intended to unveil the play at the next 'Perdita', the long-running seminar at Nottingham for discussing early modern women's work, by far the best way of making it known to the people who mattered most. At the same time, he hoped to place an account of the play and its discovery in the *TLS* or perhaps the *London Review of Books*, which would do him no harm at all professionally.

Another loose end which he tied up during this period of relatively uninterrupted work was Theodore Palaeologue. Since he was descended from the 'last emperor', the obvious next step was to find out about the last emperors and the fall of Constantinople. Theodore's family, he discovered, claimed descent from Thomas, brother of Constantine XI Palaeologus, last Emperor of the Roman Empire in the East, who had been killed in battle when Constantinople fell to the Turks in 1453. A descendant, Theodore, was established at Pesaro in the late sixteenth century. He married Eudocia Comnena, also the bearer of an imperial Byzantine name, and served the House of Orange as a soldier of fortune in the Low Countries. Later he moved to England, got married again, to an English lady called Mary Balls, and ended his days in Cornwall. His son Ferdinando fought for Charles I at the Battle of Naseby, emigrated to Barbados, and settled with his wife on a small pineapple plantation. His grandson, the Palaeologue Michael was interested in, returned to England, settled in Stepney, and served in Charles II's navy. He died at Corunna in 1692, leaving a posthumous daughter, baptised Godscall, who disappeared from history – though of course, now Michael knew what had happened to her.

The catastrophic decline of the family was only too obvious from the outline history; from the purple silk dalmatics and pearl diadems of fifteenth-century Byzantium, to the buff-coat of a cavalier soldier, and, to look only at Theodore and his daughter, from a plantation in Barbados to circumstances which, from Theodore Stuart's pathetic letter, sounded like unrespectable poverty on the downward slide.

Had anything more become of them? The books were no help; his glimpse into the life of Theodore and Godscall had come from sources unknown to Sir Steven Runciman and the historians who had followed him. It might be worth trying the Public Record Office some time when he next had a free day in London, but meanwhile, he would try the Web.

He was not wholly surprised to find that Google had a fair amount to say about 'Palaeologue', even more fascinatingly heterogeneous than usual. Genealogy; the gift of a famous ikon by Emperor Andronicus Palaeologue, dendrochronology dates within a period of Palaeologue revival, 240,000 people connected to royalty, the Patrick O'Brian discussion list, but nothing about the seventeenth century. His eye was caught by the only listing to relate to the present day, the electronically published proceedings of an international colloquium on tropical horticulture and environmental management, held in Barbados. Since the Palaeologue connection seemed as obscure as that of the Patrick O'Brian discussion list, if not more so, he clicked on the link, and found the reason at once: the colloquium had included a paper by one M. Palaeologue on 'Aloe barbadiensis: a cash crop for the new millennium'. It sounded pretty dull, but it was interesting that there were still Palaeologues in Barbados: he wondered if this botanist knew anything of the luckless Stuarts in Roebuck Street. Probably not, but someone with so unusual a name might just have an interest in genealogy. He scrolled down to the list of contributors, and found that M. Palaeologue was at the University of the West

Indies. Universities almost always make staff emails available; so Michael's next port of call was the UWI website, where he found 'mpalae@uwi.bb' without any difficulty, and left a polite message explaining his interest, and asking if, by any chance, his corres-pondent had information about the family. There would be a certain personal satisfaction in knowing the end of the story, and if he involved himself with editing the *Notatiunculae*, as he hoped, then whatever turned out to have happened to them would be useful to know. Meanwhile, he had done all he could, so it was back to Aphra Behn.

Eights Week, the period between the end of exams and the posting of results, is traditionally an Oxford Saturnalia, important to the students, particularly the finalists, but a bit of a chore to longer-term residents. It was further complicated in this particu-lar year by the queen's Jubilee, which Michael personally consid-ered a right royal nuisance. Though his great-uncle's enthusiasm for the Jacobite cause had failed actually to convert him, Harold's view of the current incumbents as a group of dull Germans cata-pulted by luck and chicanery onto the throne of England seemed to him not unreasonable in itself. If the country merely needed some kind of an alpha couple to provide grist for the mills of the media, he was inclined to think that there was a great deal to be said for electing one by popular acclaim. David and Victoria Beckham, for example, seemed to fit the bill nicely; they were good-looking, quite well behaved, and appeared to be devoted spouses and model parents, none of which was true of the Windsors, while the boy David at least was a person of consider-able talent. If they became tedious, they would vanish into oblivion without costing the country a mint of money, and some other starry couple, just as good-looking and successful, could be substi-tuted without the need for any sort of investiture.

Meanwhile, they were stuck with Mrs Battenburg and her fifty glorious years. Like many of the people he spoke to, Michael was

struck by the muted response of his fellow-Britons, and the obstin-
ate refusal of the country generally to see the Jubilee as any sort
of occasion for national celebration. He was old enough to remember
the street-parties and junketings of twenty-five years previously,
compared with which this Jubilee seemed to be being met with
almost universal apathy. He was puzzled to know what to make of
it. It was possible that the majority of Britons had ceased to care
about the monarchy, but it was also possible that the Jubilee had
flopped due to unfortunate timing. Millennium celebrations and the
building of millennial monuments must have exhausted civic spirit
in many a community; and if his father's reactions were anything
to go by, the recent death of the Queen Mother had provided a true
moment of closure for those older Britons who had lived through
the last war, and still felt strongly about the royal family.

However, the college had decided it was their patriotic duty to
mark the Jubilee with a gigantic garden party, scheduled to go on
well into the evening and end with fireworks. This turned out to
be, like most such events, fun up to a point. It had been an unusually good summer, so the heat of the night made it treacherously
easy to keep on drinking, but Michael paced himself with care, as
did all the old and experienced, though most of the young were
glassy-eyed and incoherent after the first hour. He wandered about
with the other Fellows and their guests – he himself had not had
anyone he wanted to bring – sipping Australian near-champagne
and making polite conversation, while resolutely ignoring indications of vomiting or attempted sexual activity from the more
secluded reaches of the shrubbery.

He had been milling about politely for around half an hour
when, after a couple of absolutely forgettable encounters, he
detoured round a group of physicists vehemently discussing football and probability theory only to find himself nose to nose with
Ellen Lorimer, a very senior member of his faculty, and one of the
people he least wanted, or expected, to see. She had made an effort,

he observed; her hair had been cut within living memory, and she was wearing the double row of yellowish pearls which invariably constituted her festive uniform. For the rest, she was a mountainous, grey-haired gentlewoman, built like a battleship, her formidable bulk decently shrouded in navy georgette.

She greeted him with marked lack of warmth. 'Good evening, Michael.'

'Ellen. Hallo.' He was wondering who could have brought her. 'How nice to see you. I didn't know you had friends here.'

'Kenelm invited me, of course,' she said crisply.

'Of course,' he echoed. Yuk, he thought. Kenelm Hayes was a retired professor of Engineering, right-wing to the point of near fascism; and like Ellen, conspicuously Anglo-Catholic; both of them were great writers of letters to the *Oxford Mail* protesting against just about everything which savoured of modernity. 'They've done us quite well, don't you think? This is the nicest sham cham I've had in ages.'

She looked at him without answering, and he realised that she was holding a glass of orange juice. 'Michael, I wanted to talk to you,' she said severely. 'You're supporting Robert in putting forward this idiotic course. It's really not going to do you the slightest good.'

'It's not idiotic,' he said, nettled. 'It's been extremely carefully thought through.'

'Nonsense. There's a perfectly good early-modern prose paper already.'

'Look, Ellen,' he protested. 'It's just Richardson and Fielding. There's masses of interesting stuff the kids aren't allowed to tackle. It's high time it was all opened up for them.'

'Oh, for heaven's sake. Richardson and Fielding are the only early novelists of any real importance.' As a response to suggestions of change to the sacred syllabus, it was entirely characteristic of her, and it reminded him horribly of his father.

'Defoe?' he enquired. 'And what about Aphra Behn?'

'What about her?' Ellen demanded. 'She's an entirely minor figure, and if she were not a woman, she would never even be mentioned. There are no women writers before Jane Austen who are worth studying.'

Michael opened his mouth, and shut it again. It was obvious she believed passionately in what she was saying. Goodness, she bought the package, he thought sourly to himself. When the patriarchy is finally assassinated, Ellen Lorimer will have no further reason to exist, so she will immolate herself on the grave.

'Do you really not know the difference between literature and penny-dreadfuls?' she demanded, her pendulous cheeks shaking and mottling with the strength of her feelings. 'Don't you see that what you're teaching is complete lack of discrimination? You're trying to destroy everything that Oxford English stands for.'

He pinched the bridge of his nose, wishing that a waiter would come by with a top-up. 'What I'm teaching is the idea that literature's got some kind of context, Ellen.' It would have been wise to leave things there, but he was sufficiently narked by her to carry the war into the enemy's camp. 'We need that very badly. Look at your Spenser edition. It's wonderful, of course. It's a masterpiece of old-fashioned scholarship, and you've noticed every last piece of inverted type in every single witness to every poem. But there's not a word in there to tell you that Spenser was rampaging round Ireland as an agent of systematic cultural genocide, hanging every Irish poet he could catch. He writes utterly movingly about this beautiful deserted country. But the reason he sees Ireland as empty is that he's imagining it on the other side of ethnic cleansing in which he is personally implicated. It gets into the text, Ellen, so you can't say it's irrelevant.'

'Don't be ridiculous,' she snapped. 'That is a completely frivolous response to one of the greatest poets ever to write in English. Of course he was a man of his time. It is not merely absurd to judge him by the standards of "p.c.", it's a crime against literature.'

Michael sighed. 'I'd buy that for Shakespeare, Ellen. I mean, it's obviously futile to be shocked that Shakespeare thought slavery was natural. But at the same time, he wasn't personally out slaving, was he? I think Spenser's in a different moral position, because he's directly the propagandist of one of the least defensible episodes in English history. If you take a good look at *The Faerie Queene*, it's actually a story about England's destiny as a master-race, so if you context it with what he was actually doing, I think it's got to be problematic. I mean, if Goebbels had happened to be a great poet, would that justify teaching him as "literature" without looking at what he'd chosen to do with his life?' For a moment, he wondered whether she was actually going to throw her orange juice in his face. 'I'm not saying we shouldn't teach Spenser,' he added, realising that he had gone a bit far. 'All I'm saying is that if you look at the context as well as the verse, you get something much more complex, and it tells you an awful lot about late Elizabethan England. Good and bad.'

She looked at him, and it was nearly a full minute before she replied. 'Michael, you have no business teaching at Oxford,' she said, her voice clanging with the overtones of a final judgment.

'There are times when I'm inclined to agree with you.' But she had already turned her back on him, and disappeared into the crowd. A servitor came by, and he held out his glass gratefully. He was furious about the squabble, and wished he had managed to hold his tongue. He in no way underestimated Ellen's ability to make herself unpleasant, or the amount of energy she was prepared to devote to a cause. Since she was now positively his enemy, she would lobby all her allies to split the faculty vote and capsize 'The Roots of the Novel'. It needed a marked degree of consensus to get a new paper onto the syllabus; within the Oxford system, innovation was hard to make, and easy to prevent. How completely stupid of him to jeopardise all that work for the sake of a momentary victory. He could have kicked himself.

'Michael. A penny for your thoughts.' Dusk was descending around them as he stood brooding on the lawn, and the senior tutor's wife was smiling at him: a shrewd, likeable woman who seemed to regard the college and its shibboleths with a species of restrained irony which reminded him a little of his own mother and her attitude to Cartmel. 'Isn't this nice,' she went on. 'I do hope HM's getting something out of her party, poor thing. It struck me when I saw the programme that she was absolutely the last person they'd thought about entertaining. Mr Blair's so keen to make us look modern, he forgets she was forty-odd when the Beatles happened, never mind this awful shouty stuff the children like. She's used to keeping the stiff upper lip, but it's rather hard on her.'

'She must be about the same age as my father,' he said. It was a strange thought; he was so used to thinking of the queen as an icon he had not made the connection. 'I've no idea what he listened to when he was young.'

'There was much less for teenagers then, but if you went out dancing, it'd be to people like Glenn Miller, and if you were desperately with-it, there was a bit of jazz about, and blues. It was all very tame. I was the Beatles generation, and we despised wrinklies' music.'

'I imagine she's having a horrible time, then. One of many. I was a bit surprised she didn't make this her farewell gig. Fifty years in any job's long enough, surely?'

'But she can't retire, Michael. Being the queen's not a job,' said Rosemary firmly. 'It's more like being a mother. She's embodying an idea, so she's got to go on doing it till she dies. I think that's terribly important. Everything's very "me"-orientated now, but getting on with things whether you want to or not is an essential social virtue. There's nobody else you can point to in public life who stands for just doggedly doing your duty. I admire her tremendously.'

He could not think how to respond to this, it was so alien to his own thinking, and when he did not immediately reply, she took a sip of her wine, and changed the subject. 'What are you doing this summer?' she asked.

'I'm not sure, Rosemary. I'll have to spend some time with my father, but after that, I might just come back to Oxford. I've got a very interesting project on the go, and I maybe ought to stay within reach of the library.'

She looked him up and down, her eyes bright and intelligent. 'I think you should go away if you can, Michael. I know you young people all feel you're on a sort of treadmill these days, but you can take it from me, if you don't have a break, it'll do you no good in the long run. Oxford is very tiresome and annoying, you know, and if you don't get away once in a while, you'll lose sight of what's still splendid.'

He took an inadvertently deep swig from his glass, surprised. He knew her for a perceptive woman, but he hadn't realised that she saw quite so clearly. 'I was looking a bit flattened when you saw me, because I've just had a tiff with Ellen Lorimer,' he confessed. 'But I've been feeling very down, generally. This Duleep Singh business hasn't helped. It wasn't just the being under siege that depressed me, it was the way it was reported, the way they were sneering and envious at the same time.'

'These things don't matter really,' she said. 'People forget.'

'That's not quite what I'm trying to say, Rosemary. The thing is, the next time they remember about us they'll say the same things all over again. What really worried me was the way the media assumed Oxford was some kind of tremendously value-added experience. I've found myself thinking about this, and I'm not sure it's still true. We're standing on a sandcastle, watching the tide come in, pretending everything essential's still the same, when it just isn't. On the one hand, we've doubled the numbers even since I was an undergraduate, which completely changes what we're able to offer the individual, and on the other, you can't actually say we're the best any more. Look at English. We've got some good people, of course, but if I was asked where the best English department in the country is, I'd have to say it was University College London.'

When she did not answer, he wondered if he had offended against her sense of loyalty. 'That's hardly an argument against privilege, Michael,' she said after a while. 'Quite the opposite. But tell me, how is your father?'

Two generations, two worlds, he thought. Beatles or no Beatles, she's just not hearing what I'm saying. 'You're saying the problem's with me, and you're probably right,' he said, hoping to smooth the moment over. 'He's not very good, I'm afraid. Just managing, but there's nowhere to go but down.'

'I do sympathise. It's a very difficult phase in one's life – I don't mean for your father, though of course we will all come to it in time, but for the mopper-upper, if I can put it like that. You mean he really needs to go into a home, and he'll hate it?'

'Yes, Rosemary. He's always been the one in control, you see.'

'How well I know it, my dear. My father had been in the army, and when it came to the last years, he gave us unmitigated hell. You must be under a great deal of strain. Do promise me one thing. If it comes to having rows with the local authority or anything of the kind, give me a buzz. There are ways of making these things just a little easier, you know, and I've had a good deal of practice.'

She was a magistrate, he remembered. It was a very kind offer, and possibly a very useful one. The thought of having someone on his side was warming, and the offer was quite obviously genuine. 'It's extremely good of you, Rosemary. I do realise you're very busy.'

'That means you're not going to pick up the phone. Don't worry about me. If you need me, call.'

'I will,' he promised, and felt a lightening of the heart. He couldn't see even Auntie May or the director of social services standing up to twenty minutes of Rosemary Ashton's vowels. While it was unfashionable to see any sort of virtue in her 'Mother of the Regiment' attitudes, he was aware that it could make all the difference to have a woman like that on one's side.

'Do,' she said. 'Now I must talk to dear little Catherine Sinclair. She's been frightening the pants off the old boys, and I want to congratulate her. It's very good for them.'

She strode off purposefully over the grass to where Catherine stood rather obviously not enjoying a conversation with a law don notorious for his lack of social talents, and split them efficiently, taking Catherine by the arm and piloting her off to admire the delphiniums.

He watched her go, half-admiring, half-bemused by the effort she, like her husband, was prepared to put into any sort of college event. He set off himself in the opposite direction, looking for some relief from the press of bodies, and keeping a wary eye out for Ellen Lorimer, whom he had no desire to meet again. The central area of the gardens was lit by floodlights, but the more distant reaches were falling under the mantle of dusk, and he was only too aware that to stray too far into the darkest parts of the grounds might involve him in considerable embarrassment.

'Hi,' said a voice from under a great chestnut tree on the back lawn, making him jump, since he had not noticed anyone was there. Royston was leaning against the trunk, hard to see in the twilight, enveloped as he was in a black academic gown. As he turned towards Michael, the gown fell open, revealing a flash of white shirt-front, and the sultry evening air brought with it a sweet and familiar odour. 'I thought I'd take a little time out,' he said. 'Want one?'

'Royston, is this wise?' he said.

The other man chuckled. 'This isn't the only herb in the garden, man. You walk around back here, and you'll smell it. You want to be discreet, of course, not set a bad example, but there's nobody under this here tree but us. I got a little tired of the old guys, that's all, and I'm not much of a drinker. I'd go home, but I have a thing about fireworks.'

'Can I just have a toke?' he asked. He had very little experience of cannabis, since alcohol had been the preferred recreational drug of his own undergraduate social circle, but he had an impulse towards solidarity. Also, he felt, the sooner the thing was finished and extinguished, the better.

'Sure,' said Royston.

Michael put his empty glass into his pocket, and took the spliff which the other man held out to him. He drew the smoke deep into his lungs, which made him momentarily dizzy, but it seemed to have no other effect. 'Thanks.' He handed it back to Royston, who finished it at his leisure, pinched it out carefully, and dropped the dog-end on the ground. 'What does it do for you?' he asked. 'I've never found it had much effect.'

'It doesn't suit everyone. But if it's your friend, it helps you stay cool. Just calm, you see. Not a serious high, like the hard shit.'

'It's a big Jamaican thing, isn't it?'

Royston laughed. 'And all over the Caribbean. But you're thinking of the Rastafarians, aren't you?'

'Yes. By the way, what do they actually believe? I mean, I used to listen to the music, but I never got much sense of Rasta theology, or even if they've got one. I know they think ganja's a sort of sacrament, but what do they do apart from smoke weed?'

'It basically starts with Marcus Garvey. He's, like, the Rastas' John the Baptist. He said, "Look to Africa, when a black king shall be crowned, for the day of deliverance is at hand." Then in 1930, Ras Tafari was crowned as Emperor Haile Selassie, the Lion of

Judah. The Rastas are people who thought the prophecy was fulfilled.'

'Oh, God. Another cult of the apocalypse.'

'Yeah. The Rastas reckon these are the last days. You sound pretty disgusted, though. What've you got against apocalypses?'

'Oops. I haven't dropped anything serious, I hope?'

'Don't you worry. I'm a Babylon man. The way the Rastas tell it, there's no computers in Zion.'

'It's nothing to do with you,' Michael apologised. 'It's just that I've got this great-uncle who's a darling but a total fruitbat. He believes in just about everything from Jacobites to the end of the world, and if he'd heard of Marcus Garvey I'm sure he'd believe in him too. I've had signs and portents dinned into my ears ever since I was old enough to notice.'

'So? Maybe they're all right. It's not my kind of thing, I have to say. I just smoke a little herb once in a while. But people have to believe something, and the thing about Rastafari is, it's ours. It comes out of the black world, nobody brought it, or made us do it. It's good for a people to have something of their own.'

'I suppose so,' he said doubtfully. He suddenly felt immensely tired, and somehow estranged from himself; in a sudden moment of lucidity, he realised that the wine and the cannabis were interacting, pushing him into an odd state of mind.

Royston somehow divined what was happening. 'Hey, man,' he said, and reached out and caught him by the hand. Michael clung to the warm fingers as if to a lifeline; profoundly aware of Royston's whole physical being, the quiet breathing he could just hear, the dimly discernible pulse. It was not a sexual moment, but an apprehension of another person's bodily existence of a kind normally associated with sex, a perception of the whole lovely, fragile structure, so close and yet so distant. It had been a long time since he had touched anybody seriously, or been touched: something in him was starved for contact.

Time passed, he could not tell how long. 'Sorry,' he said, releasing Royston's hand. 'It got on top of me for a minute.'

'That's OK,' said Royston equably. There was a bang and a whoosh; above them, the sky erupted in a fountain of red, white and blue stars. 'Let's go and watch the show.'

Together, they strolled towards the main lawn, where they could hear clapping, and see people beginning to gather.

Michael found the garden-party hangover no worse than usual, but he vowed to avoid cannabis in future. The experience had rather frightened him, though he kept in touch with Royston, and one Saturday, went out to Folly Bridge with him for a pub lunch, an occasion which would have been even more agreeable had the pub held half the number of people it actually did.

He was also pleased, and a little surprised, to find a message in his inbox one day, from distant Dr Palaeologue. It contained a copy of his original, with under his final question – 'Do you by any chance have any information about the Stuart family who lived in Roebuck Street, Bridgetown, in the mid-seventeenth century, who I believe may be relatives of yours?' – the laconic answer, 'Yes. I believe I'm a direct descendant.' The message was unsigned, and it seemed fair to deduce that Dr Palaeologue was either busy or not interested. Michael wanted to know more, but decided to let it rest, while he meditated a tactful approach.

Quite soon after term was over, he went up to Silloth to check on the older generation, where he found things no better, but apparently no worse. He spent an amicable couple of days with his father. There were some odd jobs which needed doing; he had always rather enjoyed messing about with screwdrivers and so forth, a streak of practical ability he had inherited from his mother – he strongly suspected that his father was unable to wire a plug without looking at the diagram. Neville was always genuinely grateful for such help, and it allowed them to spend time together without having to find something to talk about, which was a good thing in itself. Once his father's practical problems had been sorted out, he went to see Harold Boumphrey, whom he found in excellent health and spirits.

'I am very grateful both to you and to that clever young lady,' he announced, once they were sat down by the empty grate with cups of tea. The just-audible chimes of a distant ice-cream van tinkled through the summer air, playing 'Yesterday', Michael noticed irrelevantly. 'The Prophecies have been extraordinarily useful and revealing. As I was inclined to suspect, the son of Mordred was none other than Urien, King of Rheged, the great hero of our own Cumbria, as you will recall. This opens up all kinds of possibilities, including, of course, a connection with the line of the Emperor Constantine, whose mother, as you may recall, was a British princess, known to the Welsh as Elen *lluydag*, that is, Helena of the Hosts. This connection is most important. I discovered recently that Constantine himself declared, "God sought my service, and judged it fitting for the achievement of His purpose. Starting from the British Isles, He chose me to shatter the powers of evil, so that the human race might be recalled to the worship of the Supreme Law." That is from a papyrus in the British Museum, and it shows quite clearly that he was an essential link in the Great Chain.'

'I'm glad you're happy, Uncle,' said Michael.

Harold Boumphrey looked at him shrewdly, cocking his head a little. 'You are a kind boy. I'm not a fool, you know. I am perfectly well aware that you have some intellectual doubts about the soundness of my methods. It is my hope that with increasing maturity, the value of my work will become clear to you. But whether you doubted or no, you have been most helpful, and I may say, you have shown an intellectual humility which is not always found in Oxford men.'

Michael was touched. It was always disconcerting to be

reminded that the old darling was bonkers rather than stupid, he thought, smiling at him affectionately. 'I don't know what I know any more, Uncle,' he said. 'I've a lot more questions than answers at the moment. And actually, there's something you might be able to help me with, if you fancied doing a favour in return. Do your Jacobite contacts know anything about a second, clandestine marriage for Elizabeth of Bohemia?'

Boumphrey stiffened to attention. 'Indeed they do not. Do you have evidence of one?'

'Oh, yes. The best possible. I've seen the marriage certificate. It's in Middelburg, wedged in the binding of an old book.'

'And were there children of this union?'

'There was certainly one, and I know a bit about him. He was called Balthasar van Overmeer, and he was a doctor.'

'And after that? Do you know if he married?'

Michael looked at his great-uncle in some surprise; this cross-questioning was quite unlike the old man's usual gentle and leisurely manner. 'There's a son. Again, it's rather your sort of thing. He married Godscall Palaeologue.'

'How extraordinary. The last heiress of Byzantium. We were just speaking of the Emperor Constantine and his British mother. So the wheel came full circle.'

'That's right. I might've known you'd know.'

'Give me a moment. I have some information on the Palaeologues.' Boumphrey rose laboriously to his feet and shuffled over to a distant bookcase, where he spent some time browsing among the shelves. 'Last heard of in Wapping. You have some later history, I gather?'

'Well, it looks as if she went back to Barbados. The family had connections with the place.'

'Her grandfather went there after the Battle of Naseby,' said Boumphrey, deep in a book.

'Yes – that's Donald Nicol you've got there, is it? But the thing really I wanted to tell you is something I found out myself, after I looked up "Palaeologue" on the World Wide Web. I don't know if you've caught up with the idea of the Web, but the point about it is, information comes up pretty much at random. I found all kinds of stuff, but I also found there was a real live Palaeologue at the University of the West Indies. It's not hard to get a university person's email, so I got in touch, and asked him if he knew anything about a connection with Godscall Palaeologue. He got back to me the other day and said, "I think I'm a direct descendant."'

'The certificate you found,' said Boumphrey sharply, 'was it for a marriage properly conducted by a Protestant clergyman?'

Michael looked at him, at a loss; it seemed a typically tangential approach. 'Oh, yes. He was Elizabeth's chaplain, one of Laud's men, absolutely definitely Anglican, and Pelagius himself was as Protestant as anything. He had a theology degree from Leiden.'

'Well, then, you must go to Barbados.'

'What?'

'My dear Michael, I do not think you understand the significance of your tale! The Princess Elizabeth was the daughter of James VI. She was therefore a Stuart and of the senior line. The Catholic faith has, as you know, been held a bar to the enjoyment of the throne of England, but the product of a clandestine marriage is not under any such ban, as long as the marriage was Protestant. Both Queen Mary II and Queen Anne came to the throne as the daughters of James II by his clandestine marriage with Anne Hyde. Your Palaeologue carries in his veins the Sang Réal, the Blood Royal of the house and lineage of David, of Our Lord by His sacred marriage with the Magdalene, and of the House of Stuart. He also carries the blood of Constantine and the Caesars, and he is the rightful King of England by every possible means of calculation.'

'I suppose he is,' said Michael slowly. 'Yes, that would work, wouldn't it?'

'The descendant of a legitimate, Protestant son of Elizabeth of Bohemia would have had a claim even after Charles II, and certainly after James II,' said Boumphrey with authority. 'Perhaps this is the Hidden Line, of which we have heard much, from the Rosicrucians and others. And of course, the link with Constantine greatly strengthens the case.'

'If any of it can be authenticated,' objected Michael.

'Well then, you must authenticate it. I am not wholly without sense, Michael. It is perfectly clear to me that whatever the justice of his claim *sub specie aeternitatis*, Prince Michael of Albany would not be acceptable as King of England. But if the facts are as you state them, your Palaeologue answers all the criteria so painfully established for the definition of the English monarchy in the seventeenth century; and though he was not born in England, he is at least a child of the English colonies. They will have to recognise him. This is a very great moment, my dear boy. I may yet live to see a Stuart on the throne! *Nunc dimittis*, Michael. O Lord, thou lettest now thy servant depart in peace. You have made me very happy.'

'But Uncle Harold! I can't just drop everything and go to Barbados. Apart from anything else, I can't afford it.'

Boumphrey put the book back on the shelf, went to his desk, and sat down. After a few moments' scribbling, he got up again, waddled over to Michael's chair, and put something in his hands. It was a personal cheque made out for £5,000.

'I can't take this,' Michael protested.

'Michael,' said Boumphrey firmly, 'to bring this man to the throne of his fathers, I would spend money like water. I would give all that I have. This is no time for false shame. Take it.'

VII

O happy sight to see great Britainnes King
One day ascending from Mount Olivet!
O happy song to hear the Hebrewes sing!
For joy of heart James to congratulate:
Blest be the king that comes in Jesus name
To christen Jewes and Crowne Jerusalem.
Alexander Maxwell, *The Laudable Life and Deplorable
Death of our Late Peerlesse Prince Henry* (1612)

As he worked upstairs in his bedroom, pottered about Silloth, and
shared his father's dreary meals, Michael struggled with the
dilemma which Harold had inadvertently created. He was deeply
unhappy at the idea of taking his great-uncle's money. But there
was no doubt that the old man could afford it, and nothing would
make him happier than for his great-nephew to cash the cheque.
Rosemary Ashton's words were in his mind as well. On the one
hand, he had become very depressed with Oxford. On the other,
while he had spent periods of time elsewhere, he had taken no
holiday, as such, for something like three or four years. A mistake,
in all kinds of ways. For one thing, if he had not insisted on staying
home to finish his Defoe book while Eimer waltzed off to Skiathos
by herself, a lot of things might now be very different. Eimer aside,
Rosemary had made him ask himself whether his present mood
of revulsion from Oxford meant that he had acquired perspective
on his life or lost it. But the idea of going to Barbados . . . the
associations it evoked for him were of sun, sand, sex, vulgar

weddings, rum, minor-league pop-stars, palm-trees . . . of all the places on the globe where the trail might have led, it was hard to think of anywhere that he was less likely to find congenial.

There was one person he knew who might help him make up his mind. 'Father,' he said, after they had lunched together on waterlogged ham and salad, 'do you mind if I connect up the modem?'

'By all means,' said his father graciously. The modem had been a source of considerable tension when Michael had first tried to explain it: his father had been convinced that it was a diabolical device for making trunk or possibly even international phone calls an hour or more in length. But for once, he had refused to let the old man have his own way. If he were not able to work effectively in Silloth, he would go out of his mind. The deadlock had been resolved only by making a number of timed calls, noting down the duration, and waiting for the next quarter's bill, which he had offered to pay if it seemed in any way excessive. Though he was not an easy man to convince, Neville was amenable to direct evidence, and he was prepared to accept the phone bill as such. But having capitulated on this issue, he had since come to regard the modem as a symptom of up-to-dateness, and even to be, apparently, quietly proud of having it in the house.

Michael emailed Royston: 'Do you know if there's anywhere to stay in Barbados that isn't some sort of tropical Disneyland & doesn't cost a fortune? M.'

There was a reply that evening. 'If youre taking time out why not Jamaica? Dont know about Bdos, will find out.' This was followed the next day by another message. 'Got onto Bajan friends of Mums: stay on the east coast, and hire a car. That's where Bajans go to take a break. You'll like it.' Further investigation revealed that Royston's lack of specificity had been less unhelpful than it had seemed, there were almost no hotels of any kind on the east coast, as opposed to hundreds on the west, a fact which obviously had some kind of tale to tell – possibly that the east coast was, in some not immediately apparent way, unpleasant. Royston's Mum's friends' advice suggested otherwise, but in any case, with the amount of money he had at his disposal, if there turned out to be hidden horrors in the way of rampaging insect life or terrible weather, he could simply cut his losses and remove to the other side of the island.

For the rest of the week, things contrived to a surprising extent to make him think of the West Indies. There was cricket of course, a subject dear to his father and hence one of their safest topics for discussion, but when he gave himself a day out, and took a bus down the coast to Whitehaven, following his Aunt May's observation that it had been smartened up considerably, he found there, amid other evidence for gentrification, the Rum Story, a tourist-trap trading on an alleged long connection, news to him, between Whitehaven and Antigua. On another trip out of Silloth, he came across Encona pepper-sauce in the long-established delicatessen in Station Street in Cockermouth, where he had gone to buy some decent cheese, unobtainable more locally. He was surprised and sorry to see as he emerged that a Sainsbury's had opened at the top of the road, since it probably meant that No. XVII's days were numbered, along with those of the local bakers, butchers and greengrocers. All part of the unstoppable process of everywhere becoming just like everywhere else. He bought a bottle of the sauce, out of curiosity, and it turned out to be a great mitigation for the sort of food his father ate.

On Friday, he and his father left the house together at six o'clock. His father was on his way to the Balmoral Hotel, where a small group of retired professional men and fellow-Masons met regularly once a week for an evening of dominoes and a light supper. Michael had been invited to join them, as he always was, but as usual, could not face it. They were all men who had done reasonably well in life, who would certainly have responded to enquiry of any kind with 'mustn't grumble'. They did not seem unhappy. Yet Michael, whenever he was forced into their company, found them strangely horrible, even frightening, in their blank, indifferent acceptance of the second- or even third-rate in everything they touched, or that touched them. So he and his father parted company, Neville to make his slow way down Criffel Street, while Michael cut diagonally across the grass, making for the embankment which protected the town from the Solway.

He climbed up to the Japanese-looking belvedere hidden among the Scots pines which overlooked the firth, and was glad to find it empty, since he was aware it served from time to time as a cruising-spot for gay Silloth, such as it was. He settled himself to watch the sunset, a good one, with violent pink and tangerine streaks of cloud against transparent blue, and found himself recalling the smoke-poisoned skies of the previous summer. At the worst, it had been possible to see nine burning-grounds from the vantage-point of the belvedere, either across the water, or along the coast. The funeral pyres of thousands upon thousands of slaughtered sheep and cattle, innocent victims of the desperate attempt to contain foot-and-mouth disease.

The sight and smell of burning had been impossible to ignore, and it had been equally hard not to see the huge lorries that lumbered up and down the twisting country lanes, laden with the dead, but everyone had done their best to hide their eyes. He remembered a moment when his bus had surprised a white-coated MAFF team going into a farm, and he and everyone else had looked the other way, passive, uneasily complicit. Partly it was the sense of an obscene waste of flesh which had rendered the whole thing so distressing, the difference between killing for food and wholesale destruction. There was also the knowledge that an incalculable amount of human knowledge and effort, expressed through the harmless persons of Herdwick sheep, had been wantonly destroyed. Whole strains and bloodlines, decades of careful and conscientious breeding for particular qualities, and with them, not only livelihoods, but lives, hopes and dreams.

Since Cumbria had been the epicentre of the outbreak, by its end the Lake District had been empty alike of animals and walkers. Michael remembered the strange, empty hills, the riot of butter-cups, more than in any other year; the glimpses of heaped, grey-white corpses in the corner of a field or under a hedge as the bus went past. A year later, it was not spoken of, as if even to mention it was somehow ill-omened, but the tale was told mutely by notices of farms for sale and the collateral damage of shops that had ceased trading, people 'gone South', or even dead. Now, of course, the *Times & Star* was full of ill-tempered tales of farmers using their compensation-money for purposes other than restocking, as if chronic anxiety, heartbreak and the destruction of a lifetime's work could not possibly account for wanting to get the hell out and do something else. There were known to have been suicides.

In his most extreme moments of disaffection with university life in the twenty-first century, Michael had occasionally entertained a fantasy of returning to somewhere like Cockermouth and opening a secondhand bookshop, or even an ironmonger's: as a little boy, he had thought ironmongers' shops the most interesting places in the world, and they still held a certain charm for him. The foot-and-mouth episode put paid to that particular dream, by revealing with terrible clarity the fragility of life in the remote country.

Now, all was peace. The thin voices of children floated up from somewhere not immediately visible; and Michael remembered there was a paddling pool sheltered in the lee of the embankment. It was good to hear children, in this town dominated by the respectably retired, and he wondered if any of them were Elaine's. He stared out across the cold Solway, lying puddled like mercury in its muddy bed on this fine summer evening, and reflecting the blue of the sky . . . an infinite distance from the turquoise sea and white sand he knew only from pictures. Yet the world was connected, by the massive, unlikely coincidences of history. His father's family were Welsh by ancestry, but his mother's, the Boumphreys, were Cumbrian. Probably ancestors of his had sailed from Whitehaven to Antigua and returned with rum for the rum butter, the ginger and allspice which flavoured the traditional cakes of Cumbria, and the massive, castellated white conch shells still sometimes seen by the doors of unimproved cottages.

Long ago, a man called Pelagius van Overmeer had gone from Africa to the Dutch West Indies, and from there on to The Hague, where he had met and married the eclipse and glory of her kind, Elizabeth of Bohemia, lost princess of the Reformation. In the following century, it was perfectly possible that some Lieutenant or Midshipman Boumphrey of the mid-eighteenth century had met the grandson of this unlikely pair while on shore-leave in Barbados, rollicking down Roebuck Street in search of rum, and dark and smiling ladies. The light was going, and he was getting cold, but he had finally made up his mind. He would go to the West Indies.

Having made his decision, it was the end of July before Michael got around to implementing it. The minute he had definitely decided to go away, in the usual way of things, little bits of business of one kind or another conspired to keep him in place. But they did not deflect him from his purpose, and nor did the unexpectedly vehement objections of his father. As headmasterly rage crashed over his head, it became clear to Michael that although his father's automatic respect for wealth normally led him to condone Harold Boumphrey's vagaries, however peculiar, he was mortified that his son should have taken money from him. Michael could see only too clearly that to Neville, the issue was one of essential self-respect, but for once he refused to be coerced. He dug his heels in, and after a day of futile argument, curtailed his visit and went angrily back to Oxford before either of them said anything unforgivable.

Once back in his flat, he dealt with the various chores which the college and the university had thrown him, and booked a ticket to Barbados. Eventually, he was able to take his place in the red-eye coach to Gatwick, and after the usual interminable processing, he finally found himself shuffling aboard a plane, trapped in a long crocodile of four hundred or so people, most of them tense and anxious, though a few extroverts were already depressing everybody else by insisting, in defiance of probability, that the fun was starting already.

It was the first long-haul flight he had taken since September the Eleventh, and he had not taken the luxury option; he wanted to return as much of Harold's largess to him as possible. Strapping in and trying to find an easy position for his long legs, it was hard to avoid dark thoughts; as he tried not to think about hijackers, the diagram of the jet on the safety card and the relentless pressure of humanity round him brought into his mind the famous engraving of the hold of a slave-ship showing black bodies packed together like logs. Then, as his liberal intelligence tried to avoid the comparison, recognising its fundamentally trivialising nature, he found his mind skittering back to the hijacks. Like the unfortunate Africans on the slave-ships, the passengers on those planes had had their lives suddenly seized and taken away. Several of them, he recalled, had rung out on their mobile phones, with nothing to say but the Lord's Prayer or 'I love you'. If this plane were hijacked, he found himself wondering, and you realised you'd be dead in the next ten minutes, who would you ring? The Porter's Lodge? Even *in extremis*, he could not imagine ringing his father, especially since they had parted in anger. 'What? What? Who's there? State your business.' 'It's Michael, Daddy. I think I'm about to die . . .' No. If he had been there, he would not have said, or done, anything. He would have died in silence, unable to experience an authentically unambiguous emotion, even in the privacy of his own heart. With the exception of bowel-loosening terror, naturally.

Well, looking on the bright side, he had a window seat, and he seemed not to have anyone next to him. The next eight hours or so were not going to be fun, but with an empty seat, he might be able to wriggle himself around to some extent and ease the inevitable cramps.

He was gazing out of the window at the other planes, trying to identify the carriers, when at the last possible minute, to his immense irritation, he heard a voice saying 'Excuse me?' Huffily, he removed his book and his lightweight jacket from the seat beside him, and wedged them under the seat in front, before looking up to see who was taking his territory. A tall, slim black man was looking down at him, a rather dapper figure with wire-rimmed spectacles, wearing well-cut trousers and a loose pale cotton sweater with the sleeves pushed up to the elbow. 'Hi,' he said, smiling, as Michael made room for him. 'Sorry to disturb you.'

'That's all right,' said Michael. 'We're all selfish bastards on long-haul flights, I'm afraid.'

'That's true. It's crazy, anyway,' said the other man, forcing a bag into the overhead locker and easing himself into the seat. 'What's average height these days? Five-eight, five-ten? But they design these seats for blasted midgets. I swear, one day I'm going to end up walking out of one of these damn planes six inches shorter than I went in.'

The crew had started the safety–and–orientation spiel; it was hard to make oneself heard. Michael smiled back politely, and let the conversation lapse. Once they were actually in the air and heading out over the Channel, with the screens showing a discouragingly vast distance between current position and destination, he scrabbled under the seat in front of him, and got out his book, a collection of recent West Indian short stories called *All the Devils are Here*, which he had bought in the hopes that it would help to orient him with local cultural patterns. After an hour of quiet reading, just after he had come to the end of a story, he heard a voice from his right.

'You enjoying it?'

'There's some interesting writing.'

'Glad to hear it.' He could not but be aware of the other man's desire to talk. Oh, God, he thought to himself. I'm landed with some sort of chattering lunatic. There were still at least seven hours to go . . . he wondered how he was going to cope.

'Do you know the collection?' he said, reluctantly.

'Well, I'm Nathaniel Polgreen. Natty. Is this your first visit to Barbados?'

Michael turned a little in his seat to look at him properly. No, the question was all right, or at least comprehensible. Polgreen was the author of the story he had just finished reading; fortunately, by the grace of God, he had rather enjoyed it. 'Pleased to meet you,' he said, turning round more fully and holding out his hand. 'I'm Michael Foxwist. This is the first piece of yours I've seen. Do you publish in England?'

'Yes,' said Natty, shaking hands. 'I'm usually with Macmillan, but that collection came out with Peepal. I'm glad you were able to find it. Small presses, it's distribution that's the problem, so I'm pleased to see someone managed to pick up on it.'

'I have to admit, it wasn't all that easy to get, and I'd asked a friend for suggestions.'

Natty sighed. 'That's the world today. An information gap between books and readers.'

'Not a problem I'd ever see being solved,' commented Michael. 'Probably Amazon's the way forward for bookselling, but it's extraordinarily difficult to cue people to know what to ask for.'

'Anyway, it's not easy being a West Indian writer just now, 'cause we've got two Nobel prize-winners alive, V.S. for prose, and Walcott for poetry. Outside our own community, that's just about all the West Indians anyone's got time for. Course, you try just to be a writer, but publicity like to put you in a category.' He was interrupted by an announcement from the cabin staff, the film was starting. 'Are you watching?' he asked.

'No. I'll read this, and then try and rest.'

'I think I will. I missed this one when it came out.' Natty reached for his earphones, and Michael returned to his book.

Some unconscionable amount of time later, three-quarters of the way across the Atlantic, Michael woke with a start, realising that his right leg had, without his knowledge or permission, escaped into Natty's space and entwined itself with the other man's.

'Sorry,' he said, stiffly trying to reposition himself.

'That's all right', said Natty. He looked rather grey.

'How was the film?'

'Crap. You didn't miss anything.'

'I don't often go to the cinema. Oxford's not well serviced. One thing Cambridge does better, actually.'

'You an Oxford don, then?' said Natty. He seemed amused by the idea. 'I don't think I ever met one of those. What's it like?'

'Tell me what you think it's like.'

'English. Gothic buildings, the jolly old coll, boats on the river. I had some of the Billy Bunter books when I was a kid, and I have to admit they're probably the basis of my picture. Do you still wear gowns and mortarboards and all that shit?'

'Not mortarboards. We do still wear gowns on formal occasions, but the nineteenth-centuryness is strictly superficial. The university's changed out of all recognition in the last century.'

'What d'you think it's like being West Indian?' asked Natty in his turn.

'I don't know I've ever thought about it. Tropical beauty and violence. Drugs. Reggae and calypso. Yardies. And cricket, I suppose.'

'Graham-Greene-land. Sorrow in sunlight. No one outside the islands ever thinks about West Indians being middle-class. If you believe the journalists, we're all taking drugs and carving each other up with machetes, and if you trust the brochures, we're singin' calypsos under de coco-nut tree. My parents sent me to

Harrison College. It's a good school. The exams we took were set by the Cambridge exam board.'

'We've all got to navigate by cliché,' apologised Michael. 'The world's just so complicated.'

'Too true. Talking of clichés, why Barbados? There's a lot of reasons these good people here are going to Barbados, but you don't fit any of them. If you had a girl with you, or you were maybe twenty years older, I'd think "holiday of a lifetime", but no. And from what you've said, you don't work in post-colonial lit – as a writer, you get to recognise the symptoms.'

Michael laughed. 'No. I'm an English Fellow, but I work on the late seventeenth and eighteenth centuries. Oxford doesn't teach living authors, and West Indian writing hasn't been around long enough to creep onto the syllabus. You don't have to be male, and I don't think you have to be white, but you do have to be dead. It's an awful thing to say, but it's a pity Walcott's holding out so long. I'd love to see us teaching him. Why I'm here . . . well, it's a long story.'

'That's fine. I need something to take my mind off all this.'

'It all starts with a lost play by Aphra Behn, which turned up in the Netherlands. She's the first woman playwright in England, born 1640. One of the things we found with it was a manuscript by a black man written at about the same time, i.e. the 1660s, sort of meditations on his life and what it meant. He'd been a king in Africa, and then a slave, but at the time he was writing, he was a free man living in Middelburg.'

'Interesting. I'd really like to see that. It needs to be published.'

'That's just the start. I was looking at this thing, and I found two documents hidden in the binding. One's the certificate of a marriage between this man, who called himself Pelagius van Overmeer, and Elizabeth of Bohemia, who was the oldest daughter of King James I of England.'

'Jesus.'

Michael held up his hand. 'There's more. The other document was the baptismal certificate for their son, Balthasar van Overmeer, in 1640, the year after they married. He was baptised a Protestant, which is important. I did some digging around to see if I could find out more, and I was able to establish that Balthasar lived to grow up. He became a doctor and moved to London. He had a son called Theodore, and a foster-daughter called Godscall Palaeologue.'

'Now, Palaeologue's a name I know,' said Natty. 'The last of the Palaeologues is buried up at St John. You know, magic realism was invented there?'

'What?'

'By a Cuban writer, Alejo Carpentier. He was looking at that tomb, and when he started thinking about the way a Byzantine emperor ended up buried in Barbados, he decided life's weirder than people think it is.'

'Really? He'd like this. Godscall's that Palaeologue's grand-daughter. She and Theodore married – the family were calling themselves Stuart by then – and went back to Barbados. By the mid-eighteenth century, they were living in Roebuck Street in Bridgetown.'

'Poor people, then. Roebuck Street's pretty downmarket, and always was.'

'It's obviously named after a pub, so I thought it might be. Anyway, to the best of my knowledge, their direct descendant's alive and well, calling himself Palaeologue, and teaching in the University of the West Indies. That's what I'm here to find out about.'

'If it's the seventeenth-eighteenth centuries you're interested in, you've come a long way just for that,' Natty observed.

'Ah. But the thing is, if all the links in the second half of the chain are sound, this character's the rightful King of England.'

Natty burst into delighted laughter. 'No shit? Out of some

poor-great family from Roebuck Street? You have got to be kidding.'

'No, I'm not. If the family went on marrying legitimately through the nineteenth century, and I do realise that's a big if, then the son of Elizabeth of Bohemia herself, even by a clandestine marriage, ought to take precedence over the son of her youngest daughter by an official marriage, and that's where the Hanoverians come from. It gets even worse after that. The Hanoverian line really comes to an end with Princess Charlotte, who died in the early nineteenth century. Victoria was only George IV's niece, not his daughter.'

'You really think you can prove there's a Bajan long-lost heir?'

'No, of course not. And I don't think it matters, really. But the Stuarts are my great-uncle's obsession, and he gave me the money to come and find out. I have to say, I was fascinated, and of course, I was glad to get out of England.'

'I'll bet you were. What a crazy idea.' Natty stretched himself, in so far as this was possible. 'We're just an hour or so off landing. It won't be long before you find out.'

When, later, Michael joined the foreign passport holders' queue at Grantley Adams and they said their goodbyes, Natty gave him his card, saying, 'Keep in touch. I'd like to know what happened.'

Once through the formalities, Michael walked out of the airport into humid heat and found himself a taxi. He peered out of its window at Barbados, full of curiosity, as the driver left the airport precincts. As the plane banked over the little island, he had seen what must be Bridgetown and its environs, a solid fringe of building along the white sand and turquoise sea which he was delighted to see were quite real and not merely a figment of Kodak Ektachrome. But his taxi was taking him away from all that into impenetrable rurality, winding through what must be canefields. The plants reminded him of bamboo.

The terrain they were negotiating was hilly, and once in a while revealed wonderful vistas of undulating green fields and distant hills, their silhouettes fringed with palm-trees. The road was punctuated by bus stops, most of them carrying advertisements for paint, and occasional hamlets of small, veranda'd wooden houses which seemed from the arrangement of doors and windows to follow the ground plan of an eighteenth-century English cottage, though they were painted in the brightest of colours, azure, tangerine, candy pink, picked out with contrasting trims. Each was perched high on a substrate of rocks and breeze-blocks, and had a yard behind it, sided with corrugated iron. Then amid the strangeness, there was a shock of familiarity – enormous scarlet poinsettias, huge versions of the ones his mother had bought every Christmas in cold Cartmel and cherished till they died. They flaunted here, enormous and common as floribunda roses, by every other house.

'They're called chattel-houses,' said the driver helpfully, mistaking his interest. 'People own the house, see, but rent the land, so you can move 'em if you need to.' It was evident from the state of some of them that without constant work, the sun blowtorched the paint back to bare, silvery wood in no time, which at least explained the advertisements. Uniformed schoolchildren trudged sturdily up the slopes, children of an age that no English mother known to him would have expected or even allowed to walk unaccompanied, let alone for considerable distances. From time to time, they passed roadside rum-shops. Groups of men sat or leaned on the verandas, watching impassively; but when the driver hooted, they would wave, sometimes smile.

The hotel, when they eventually reached it, turned out to be a small white concrete structure, rather shabby, perched on a little bluff just above the rocky beach. The view, looking out over a long, curving bay, was extraordinarily beautiful.

'Tell me,' he said to the manager, as he was signing himself in, 'why are nearly all the hotels on the other side of the island?'

'It's 'cause of the sea. The other side's sheltered, so people can bathe, but don't you try bathing here, 'less you're a strong swimmer. We don't advise it. That's the Atlantic out there. We've a hundred feet of reef between us and the open ocean, but there's still a hell of a current. There's a surfers' beach just down the way, they call it the Soup Bowl. We don't get the height of waves they get in Maui and places, but the world champions come here to chill out, 'cause it's tricksy. And if champion surfers think it's tricksy, then you want to watch yourself all along here. The only safe bathing-spot on this side's Bath beach, a ways along the coast. Are you hiring a car?'

'Yes, I will.'

'Just a little runabout?'

'That's right.'

'Leave it with me. I'll have someone come along after breakfast tomorrow. Dinner's at seven. Enjoy your stay.'

Michael went up to his room, a white concrete box with, as he found when he opened the french windows, a blue-painted balcony. The effect was delightful; from where he stood in the doorway, it made a strong, cobalt-blue frame for a view of the beach, a couple of palms, and brilliant Atlantic. He stood looking out, and the wind ruffled his hair, blowing steadily and refreshingly off the sea. The trade winds, of course. He'd forgotten about trade winds, which had last crossed his consciousness in Geography at the age of eleven. He remembered drawing big arrows in red pencil all over a map of the tropic zone, and if his memory served him well, they would blow all the time, taking the edge off the heat. He unpacked, and hung a few things up. Everything in the room itself was faintly sticky with salt, but it was quiet and pleasant. The décor had a feel of the 1950s, dark-stained wooden utility furniture, and incongruous chintzy curtains. Incongruous? There was no earthly reason why Barbados should conform to an English interior designer's palette of tropical clichés.

Dinner seemed strangely early, though welcome enough on that day when he had lost track of time, but he began to see why when the night seemed to slam down pretty well as he was going down the stairs. He remembered Coleridge's note in *The Ancient Mariner*, 'no twilight within the courts of the sun'. Now he knew it for himself.

He went to bed early, after a dinner of pea soup, spicy chicken, steamed vegetables, not all of which he recognised, and coconut pie. Wholesome food, but again, not what he had vaguely expected; he had envisaged salad, and something involving pineapple and perhaps shellfish. To his surprise, he slept well, and woke to a bright morning.

When he went out onto the balcony, he saw that there were men on the beach below the hotel, locals. Three of them were working at a little concrete station, apparently gutting or preparing fish, while one stood on the beach, patiently hand-casting a long line into the surf. He stood watching, wondering what the fisherman was after. After several minutes, he was thrilled to see the fisherman's body tense: the man had a bite. He brought the line in hand over hand, while Michael craned over the edge of the balcony. The fisherman hauled in the last few feet, and a big, whitish creature emerged from the foaming surf, flapping on the hook, perhaps eighteen inches long. The man tossed it onto the shingle behind him, and Michael was taken aback to see the thing inflate like a football. It was a puffer-fish, covered in spines, frantically deploying its last defence as it drowned in the air. After a little while it deflated again, twitching. The fisherman had gone back to work, so Michael went down to breakfast, which turned out to be fruit and fried flying-fish. Sitting on in the dining-room after his meal, waiting for the car-hire man and watching the hotel staff at work, he was intrigued by their attitude: they were not uncivil, but rather than laying themselves out to pamper the guests with laid-back tropical charm, they suggested by their body-language an abiding faint surprise that an able-bodied adult was not getting up and fetching things for himself. They made the college servitors seem obsequious by comparison.

Before too long, the promised car arrived, a little Japanese model, almost new. A map of the island was thrown in with the deal, and Michael, sitting behind the wheel and studying it carefully, became fairly sure that he could find his way to St John's Church. It was not very far, and looked like a good morning's excursion. He moved off with care, remembering from his arrival that the road down to the hotel was at an angle which felt like forty-five degrees. Low gear and caution would see him through, with any luck.

The country roads were not crowded, which was fortunate, since he was disconcerted and made nervous by being hooted at repeatedly, and even got out at one point to walk round the car in case there was something wrong with it. But he came to realise after a time that a blast of the horn was sometimes simply a greeting – the numberplate identified the car as hired – and also that people automatically hooted when overtaking, an extrovert style of driving, un-English.

Having zigzagged up the eastern cliff to the plateau which was central Barbados, he turned left, following a sign for Codrington College and St John's Church. He was winding deep into the country again, and at one point, he was startled to see a group of elderly women in a canefield, wearing print overalls and thick leggings and wielding formidable heavy hoes, who looked like figures from another time. After the first sign, things were not made so easy for him, and he went wrong repeatedly, but at last, he picked up another direction to the church.

When he swung into the car-park, he saw a low, very English-looking building, poised somewhere between eighteenth-century Gothick and nineteenth-century Gothic Revival. Quite a number of vehicles were there already, and when he slipped the car into the welcome shade of giant mahogany trees (helpfully labelled as such) and opened the door, he realised a service was in progress. He could hear the singing from where he stood, and on approaching the church, he saw that the west door was standing wide open for coolness. He intended to go quietly round to the churchyard, but out of interest, paused as he passed the door to look in. The spectacle before him, apart from everyone's being black, looked like a churchgoing scene from an Ealing film; hats were being worn. Suddenly, to his embarrassment, he realised that a large woman in a species of lilac academic gown was smiling and beckoning; he was being invited in.

It seemed rude simply to flee, so, rather shyly, he went in and shuffled into a pew as near the back as possible; three people budged up to make room for him. The interior was Gilbert Scott-influenced high Victorian, all dark wood and painted fretwork. He realised the lilac lady was hovering at his elbow; in her kindness, she had brought him a hymn-book.

'It's all right, I know them,' he whispered, and was rewarded with a beam of seraphic approval which he hardly felt he had earned.

But, he thought, as he joined in with 'Breathe on me, Breath of God', he could hardly have explained to her that he simply knew them from school, where he had sung in the choir. The treacherous ability of songs to evoke whole scenes and moods overwhelmed him. The world of arbitrary tyranny which had left *Hymns Ancient and Modern* his for ever was powerfully present, overlying the hot, strange place where he now stood; Father in a greening academic gown, cricket practice, the smell of sweat and old socks. In the present, though, as the only white person in a large group of blacks, he felt awkward and conspicuous. It was a useful experience, it made him think of Royston, and wonder again how he coped.

Despite his self-consciousness, he found himself being caught up by the sober enthusiasm of the congregation. Unlike the boys at St Ninian's, they all sang at the tops of their voices: he was particularly aware of the tiny old lady on his immediate left, who had a soprano which seemed bigger than she was, a little quavery, but perfectly true. She was so carried away that he saw that she was rhythmically beating the back of the pew in front of her with the heel of her small, white-gloved hand, and she was using a peculiar sanctified pronunciation, quite unlike the gently Cockney rhythm of Bajan, which was beginning to be familiar to him – 'Bree' on meee, Bray-y-yth of Gaaad', which threatened to tip the whole experience into the ludicrous. No, Michael told himself firmly, you can be inside this or outside it. Accept it on its own terms. He took a deep breath, and began to sing wholeheartedly, head up and spitting out the words, as his choirmaster had taught him.

The service was about half-way along; the flavour was something more like American Episcopalian than public-school Anglican; the priest led his people in prayer with an un-English slickness and flourish which made Michael uneasy. It must be association with American telly-evangelists and politicians that makes any prayer made fluently sound insincere, he thought to himself, dutifully kneeling and rising with the others. But why not? What's the English confusion of sincerity with inarticulacy done but empty the churches?

To his secret delight, the final hymn was the Old Hundredth, one of the first poems ever to have moved him, when he was a little boy of twelve or so. It seemed to have the local vote as well; when the congregation launched into 'All people that on earth do dwell', the building seemed actually to vibrate as it absorbed the noise. He realised with a corner of his mind that he had completely forgotten that singing really loudly is a physical pleasure; he could not think when he had last done it. The ineffable seventeenth-century logic of the hymn built itself anew, step by step, and absorbed him in its structure, the words falling neatly into his mind one after the other. 'Praise, laud and bless his name always, for it is seemly so to do.' Emerging at the far end of the doxology, he felt as shaky and exhilarated as if he had been on a long run.

Once the service was over, he shook hands with the old lady, but managed to make his escape before the priest was able to catch him – he caught a glimpse of the man bearing down on him, wearing a relentless clerical smile, and pretended he hadn't. Under cover of the leisurely, chattering groups standing about in the car-park, he slipped round the side of the church to look for Palaeologue's tomb. The church and its churchyard were built on the top of a cliff. There was a stupendous drop to his left, and he could see flat coastal land far below. Walking on, he realised that the same was true on the other side as well; he was standing on the tip of an escarpment like the prow of a great ocean liner. The site embodied in itself the central contradiction of Barbados. If he looked back, he saw an unmistakably Anglican church and rectory embosomed in trees, an entirely English-seeming view. If he faced the other way, he was looking at an immense tropical vista, framed with palms.

The wind from the sea carried away the sounds of cars and conversation, so that he seemed entirely alone in this landscape of trees and strange, low-built, prehistoric-looking tombs. The stone for Ferdinando Palaeologue was so unpretentious that it took him a while to find it. It was pink and stood in the perfumed shade of a frangipani, and it was inscribed:

> Here lyeth the body of
> Ferdinando Palaeologue,
> descended from ye imperiall lyne
> of the Last Christian Emperors of Greece.

The stone and the ground around it were starred with fragrant flowers, incense for a dead emperor. Michael heard a rapid patter of rain and looked up, startled, to see where it was falling, but it was not rain. Another tree, above and behind the frangipani, carried bundles of dry, pea-like pods; it was their rattling that he had heard. Otherwise, all was silent, and suddenly he realised why he had felt so disoriented ever since he had first stood on the balcony looking out at the sea. No gulls. It was completely unnatural to be within sight of a coast without their harsh mewing, the white wings slicing the sky.

This is another start, he told himself. One trail had begun in the archive in Middelburg, with Pelagius and his secret marriage. The other began here, under the frangipani. He was winding through a labyrinth like Theseus, trusting to the threads he held, and at the heart of the labyrinth there stood the shadow of a king, for they met, or would meet, in the person of Dr Palaeologue, whose first name he still did not know. In one of the emails they had exchanged while Michael was still in Oxford planning his visit, Palaeologue had agreed to meet him at his home next Sunday, 4 Casuarina Court, Desert Rose Drive, off Wanstead Heights, somewhere near the university, doubtless a far cry from the romantic place where he now stood between two worlds. He was no longer certain that he was motivated by his own will; he felt that he was walking a path laid down for him by Pelagius, towards a person whom he could not yet see.

In the meantime, he explored the island. He went to Bridgetown, and found it much less pleasant than the east coast. It was, though in a different key, rather distressingly like Oxford without the tour-buses. There were no beggars, but every few feet along Broad Street, the main shopping drag, someone tried to persuade him to take a taxi. The vista was rendered scenic up to a point by occa-sional older buildings decorated with ornate, white-painted wrought iron, as well as by the sporadic visibility of the sea down gaps between the blocks, but the overall impression was of concrete and glass; impersonal modernity. The street's life seemed oriented almost entirely towards tourists, and a good half of the people wandering about were white.

'Would you mind telling me where to find Roebuck Street?' he asked the next taxi-tout to accost him. The man looked astonished, but directed him with courtesy into the interior of the town. Roebuck Street turned out to be something far more distinctive and alien than Broad Street, a long, dusty road of unpainted buildings faced with ruinous plaster and roofed with corrugated iron: there were shabby markets, cheap clothes outlets and shops where almost anything could be repaired. A hairdresser's had hung out a sign which said 'My God is a proper God', as if that was the most significant thing to worry about when you went for a trim. Most of the buildings had decaying wooden balconies with closed shutters on the first floor, which gave them a secretive air, and the disrepair of the pavements together with the deep gullies for rain run-off made it difficult for two people to pass one another.

At intervals along the street, it was also necessary to negotiate stout women in cotton print dresses who sat guarding small collections of vegetables, familiar carrots and onions side by side with yams and plantains and knobbly tubers he could not identify. They did not call out, but merely watched him as he passed; in general, though people were moving about, the street was surprisingly quiet. He had expected pounding reggae, or the local equivalent, soca (which to his ear, sounded much the same, though he was not planning to say so in public).

Michael paused at a convenient corner, and thought about what he saw. He did not feel particularly unsafe, but he knew that here in the back streets, he was on sufferance. The likes of him were supposed to stay on Broad Street, but he was glad he had come. Even allowing for the ageing effects of the sun, some of the structures he was looking at were quite probably old enough to have been there in Theodore and Godscall's time. Whatever hopes or intentions may have brought them to Barbados must have died there in the soft, sandy dust.

In the afternoon, he went to the Barbados National Archive. He had no very clear idea of what he was looking for, but his instinct was to try and get under the surface. It seemed the wrong place to be doing it. Compared with the highly idiosyncratic eastern coast, the west was a wholly undistinguished tropical wasteland. His car was speeding towards Black Rock, where the Archive was, down a modern highway, with palm-trees and the sea popping in and out of view on his left, among nondescript white concrete buildings standing amid scrub, new building projects which were holes in the ground with piles of white gravel and breeze-blocks standing ready, hotels, hotels, hotels.

But when he finally located the Archive, it turned out to inhabit a handsome set of old buildings, out towards where he knew the university to be, very secluded and rather difficult to find: the complex had once been the island's lazaretto, and still had a hospital-like air. Once he had presented his credentials to the archivist, he asked her, 'Can you tell me anything about poor whites in Barbados in the eighteenth century? I'm completely ignorant, I'm afraid, and I'd be grateful for some orientation.'

'Come across to the catalogue,' she said, walking over with him. 'There are some books you'll find useful. But what you basically need to know is, things were very difficult for anyone white who wasn't a planter. So much of the actual work was done by slaves, there wasn't much economic opportunity for free men. White men could serve in the militia, since coloured people weren't allowed to bear arms, and some of them were craftsmen, but they mostly didn't do very well. Excuse me.' She vanished into the back quarters, and returned with a couple of books. 'They seem to have been a very demoralised group,' she commented, putting down the books she had brought, and leafing through one. 'Listen to this. John Steele notes in 1789, "Free Negres and Mulattoes are never seen begging. The island in general is pestered with white beggars of both sexes, covered only with filthy rags." This is about the time-frame you're interested in, isn't it?'

'That's right. I'll look at these, if I may. But it sounds as if things were a bit hopeless.'

'Nothing's hopeless', she retorted, 'if a person's got a bit of back-bone. Things were really much more weighted against the free coloureds, but the trouble with the whites was, they lost their pride. They thought if they weren't on top, they were nobody. I'll leave you to look at these. The subject-index is in that card catalogue behind you, and the order forms are on that table, if you want anything else. I've made a note that you've got these two. Try the catalogue under "redlegs" and maybe "poor whites" and "backra Johnny".'

She went away to get on with whatever she had been doing, and Michael sat reading for the rest of the afternoon. He came away with a bleak picture of the kind of life which vague, pompous, pretentious Theodore might have led, and returned to his hotel in thoughtful mood.

On Sunday morning, he returned to the west coast and went in search of Wanstead Heights. Following the directions he had been given in an email, he found himself driving into an enclave of newish concrete apartment blocks and houses built up the high ground overlooking the campus. He found Desert Rose Drive without difficulty, and parked the car outside Casuarina Court, a block of six or eight flatlets, pink with mint-green detailing. His first impression was that they looked like holiday flats, and he realised on a second glance that this was both because they were painted in sweet-pea colours, and because they were tiny. He got out, and rang the bell of Number 4.

The door opened, and he found himself confronting a shortish, sturdy, round-faced young woman with very dark skin and her hair in a short Afro, wearing severe gold-framed glasses. She was staring at him with a faintly truculent air, as if whatever he planned to say had better be interesting.

Michael recovered himself with an effort. How completely stupid of him not to consider the possibility that his correspondent might be a woman. There were relatively few women in the sciences in

Oxford, but that was no real excuse. 'Dr Palaeologue? I'm Michael, Michael Foxwist.'

'Hi.' The initial frosty impression dissolved as her stern face melted into a smile, in a way which he had begun to find characteristic of Barbadians. 'You'd better come in.'

It was a bare, somewhat conventual little room that he was ushered into: there was a bookcase, of course, and a table with a laptop, humming to itself, and simple rattan chairs. The principal decorations were framed photographs of, he assumed, bits of plant seen through a microscope; they formed rather beautiful abstract patterns.

'Can I get you something? Coffee? Coke?'

'Thanks – just water would be nice.'

When she returned with two glasses, one of which she handed to him, she asked, 'How did you get on to me?'

'Via the Web, Dr Palaeologue. I found your name in an electronically published conference *Proceedings*. I was very surprised, I didn't think there were any Palaeologues left in Barbados. Do you know much about your family?'

'Quite a lot, actually. We weren't always called Palaeologue. It was my grandpapa who changed the name back. He was the one who was interested.'

'Why was that?'

'If you're interested in the Palaeologues, you maybe know that in the 1820s, the Greeks were having some kind of war and wanted a figurehead king – they sent people to Barbados to see if there were any Palaeologues still around?'

He nodded. 'I read about that.'

'Well, my grandpapa's great-great-grandfather paid a call on these people, and they just laughed at him.'

'He was black, I take it?'

She looked at him with faint irony. 'Yes. As you see, I'm pretty black myself. Sorry. That's not fair, he could have been white, of course, but the fact is, I don't have any white ancestors I can put a name to till you get back to Godscall Paleologue, as far as we can work out, they're all free blacks and coloureds. Anyway, the Greeks told him to go away, but it was a tale in the family, you can imagine. He was only a young fellow when this happened, but he was a man could tell a story, and his son grew up to be a journalist on the free-coloured paper. There's been this radical, own-way-ish streak in us from way back. With my grandpapa, it came out in pride. He was a schoolmaster, and he dug into the history whenever he had the time. When he traced us back to Godscall Palaeologue, he changed his name. He called my daddy Constantine, and I'm actually Melpomene on my baptism certificate, though Mama calls me Pomme, and my friends call me Melita.'

'Why Melpomene?' One of the Muses, he was fairly sure, though he could not remember which one.

She shrugged. 'They liked the sound? The old man was heavy about wanting something Greek, and he just kept suggesting things till Mama came round to one of them.'

'What was the family name before it turned into Palaeologue?'

'Stewart.'

He sipped his water, wondering what to say.

'Michael, why are you interested in this stuff? None of it matters.'

'Dr Palaeologue, can you prove any of this?'

'Call me Melita. I don't know what you mean by "prove", but I've got my grandfather's notes. My daddy was a disappointment to him, he left us and went to England after I was born and then he died there, so Grandpapa gave them to me.'

'Melita, if you can prove you're the direct descendant of Godscall Palaeologue, I think you may be the rightful Queen of England.'

She stared at him. 'Michael, you are going to have to explain.'

VIII

Of all the classes of people who inhabit Bridgetown, the poor whites
are the lowest and most degraded: residing in the meanest hovels, they
pay no attention either to neatness in their dwellings or cleanliness in
their persons; and they subsist too often, to their shame let it be spoken,
on the kindness and charity of slaves. I have never seen a more sallow,
dirty, ill looking and unhappy race; the men lazy, the women disgusting;
and the children neglected: all without any notion of principle, morality,
or religion; forming a melancholy picture of living misery; and a strong
contrast with the general appearance of happiness depicted on the coun-
tenances of the free black, and coloured people of the same class.'

Description of Barbados, 1820s

'What I really need to know is, how important is Pelagius?' Corinne
and Theodoor were sitting together in his office, working over
the fine details of the grant proposal. 'I think it's vitally important all the texts are keyed in and not just scanned, because if you
do that, people can search them properly. Only that's going to take
ten or twenty times as long, and we'll need to hire someone expensive with a PhD or they'll make a mess of it. A lot of this stuff is
really hard to read. But that means the budget is getting bigger
and bigger, and I need to think where we can shave costs, just in
case they get frightened.'

Theodoor shrugged. 'It's hard to quantify these things, Corinne.
You will know from your friend Pieternelle that there is a great
deal of interest in early slave narratives, justifiably so. Pelagius
would be important for that reason alone, but this thesis which

186

Michael has found is more interesting still. And I think that if Pelagius could know what we were doing, he would be pleased to think that we were concerned with his work and not just his life.'

'But it's only the life which makes the work interesting,' she protested. 'Nobody reads theology. It must be just about the most boring subject there is. That's why I'm asking if the thesis can wait.'

Theodoor laughed. 'You are a child of your time, Corinne. Theology has evoked more passion than any other intellectual construct in the history of humanity.'

Corinne wrinkled her nose. 'I know, I know. When I was looking at the big picture of what's published in the seventeenth century for my thesis, there was more theology than anything else. But the point is, nobody cares now. Is there any reason why we should be treating this as something special?'

'Because it is a theology of being African, which gives it a unique value. I'll try to put this as simply as possible. The Dutch Reformed Church is Calvinist. Do you actually know what that means?'

'Not really. My family isn't religious. Basically, the Calvinists didn't believe in having priests, so they were anti-Catholic. That's why William I revolted against the Spaniards.'

'Yes,' said Theodoor impatiently, 'but that's relatively superficial. The core of Calvinist thinking is the concept of salvation by grace. Grace can only come through Christ, and it only comes to those in whom God has awakened a corresponding desire for salvation – that's what they mean by the term. It may all seem very abstract to you, but think of this from Pelagius's point of view. In effect, he was being taught by his professors that he was the only man from his whole people, his whole civilisation, and very nearly his whole continent, who would be received into Heaven, because he had had a chance to become a Calvinist, and had taken it. This theology was formulated by Europeans, of course, so they had no psychological difficulty with the notion that, up to that point in the history of the world, almost the only people to be saved would be members of their own race. But think what a painful idea this would have been for Pelagius. He had been alone, apart from his people, for nearly all his life, and he would not, I think, have rejoiced to hear that he would also be alone into eternity. Check this with Pieternelle, but I believe early modern Africans set great store by the idea of rejoining their ancestors. Also, he was being told that everyone he had cared about, even venerated, as he grew up in Africa, his mother, let's say, or some wise old priest, was rejected by God in the same way as a thief or a murderer.'

'But that doesn't make sense. There weren't any missionaries, so they didn't have a chance not to be pagans,' objected Corinne.

'It is a cruel position, but trust me, it is logical in its own terms. If you want to understand how it works, go and read the proceedings of the Synod of Dordrecht, where it's spelled out. Anyway, whatever you may think of it, this was certainly what Pelagius was taught, and the reason why he is so important is that he was too proud to accept it. He argues in this thesis that the degree of knowledge of God, and reverence for God, in his own Yoruba people, show that they did experience divine mercy. They did not know Christ, of course, but their reverent, religious disposition showed that God was merciful towards them and disposed to accept them as sons of the covenant, rather than rejects from grace. I do realise that this may not seem very wonderful to you, Corinne, but it is. In its own time and its own context, it is profoundly radical and moving. By comparison, the diary is of only anecdotal interest.'

'I think I see. He's saying something about equality?'

'Yes. He is saying that it is not necessarily a handicap to be African. He cannot go so far as to assert that there will be many Africans in heaven, because as a Calvinist, he must believe that men can only be saved through Christ – if he did, you see, his work would be rejected as heresy. But he piles up the evidence in such a way that it is ambiguous whether he means to demonstrate that God's mercy already extends to Africa, or whether he thinks that, in the future, Africans will be ready converts to Christianity. This is courageous and original writing, and I would go so far as to say it is a work of genius. I am afraid it was too original to be a success in its own time. It passed, so it was deemed acceptable, but I fear that it strayed too near to Arminianism to make an impact, since I have yet to find anybody using it or quoting it. Perhaps now its time has come. I should like to think so.'

'Thanks for telling me,' said Corinne. 'It's going to have to be very carefully presented to make people understand, but from what you say, this'll have to be up-front. The trouble is, I can't go into too much detail.'

'There is something else you need to know,' said Theodoor. Corinne looked at him sharply; he was not smiling, but his tone held nuances of a private joke. 'Pelagius's thesis is extremely difficult, and you will need a very able neo-Latinist to edit it. I have found the perfect person for you.'

'Yes?'

'His name is Lucas Peeters. He was one of the late Professor Ijsewijn's last students at Leuven. I met him at one or two neo-Latin symposia, and he got in touch with me after Ijsewijn died to see if I could help him find appropriate work. He has all the skills you need for this project, and I am sure you will like him personally. He is from Brabant, and he is very charming.'

Corinne tried to think of the most tactful way of asking the next obvious question, but Theodoor took pity on her before she had achieved a form of words.

'Not, I think, homosexual,' he said, looking at her benignly. 'And he is handsome, and unattached.'

Michael and Melita sat at her worktable surrounded by bits of paper, her grandfather's notes on family history.

'Let me get this straight,' he said. 'Theodore Stuart and Godscall had a son called Ferdinando, named after his grandfather, who married Marribah Grannum.'

'Almost certainly coloured, with a name like that. Something which happened a lot in the old days was free-coloured women taking up with poor white men who were drifting down in the world. They'd take a white man on, you see, and look after him, and in return, they'd get the protection of his name, and his status. You couldn't be a freeholder unless you were white. And of course, if there were children, they'd be light, which was an advantage.'

'Right. I was reading about this in the archives. Of course, it would give the white man problems with white society from that point on, but I suppose if he wasn't staying afloat anyway, he reckoned it was worth it. Though we need to remember Ferdinando was actually one-eighth black anyway, since his great-grandfather was Pelagius. D'you think that would have influenced him?'

'I doubt it. If he could pass, he'd not've thought about it for a second.'

'I'm sure you're right. So; Ferdinando and Marribah have a son, another Theodore, who married a woman called Amaryllis Cumberbatch. Then their son Ferdinand Stewart married Phoebe Kippins – he's the one who approached the Greek government. Then Ferdinand's son Andrew married Mimbo Catwell.'

'That's the one who worked for Samuel Jackson Prescod's free-coloured paper. *The Liberal.*'

'Yes. So his son's called James Prescod Stewart, which tells us how he felt about his editor, and James married Delphine Haines. In the next generation, Frederick Stewart married Dorothy Puckerin, and they had Lincoln Stewart, who married Eunice Babb. Their son's your grandfather, another James, who married Lerilla Padmore, and changed his name to Palaeologue. So then he called your father Constantine Palaeologue, and that's it. We've got to the twenty-first century. I love these names.'

'They're just ordinary,' she said. 'Mimbo's African for sure, and fancy ones like Amaryllis and Phoebe are slave names.'

'Sorry. I didn't mean to sound patronising. It's just that to me, they're exotic. Delphine's charming, it must be French.'

Melita sat back and stretched herself, then looked at her watch. 'I think we'd better get some lunch.'

'Let me take you out,' he said, 'you're being extremely helpful'.

'OK. There's a good café by the roundabout. You know, the blue building on the corner?'

'Yes, I noticed it.'

They got into Michael's car, and drove down to the café, which was cool and quiet, not crowded.

'It's mostly an evening place,' she explained, as they were waiting for their food, 'they're hardly ever busy at lunchtime out of term, so I thought we'd be able to talk.'

A waitress appeared with their orders, chicken stuffed into the chewy, flavoursome rolls locally known as cutters, salad, and soft drinks. The chicken had been freshly pan-fried; it was a nicer meal than it would have been in an equivalent place in Oxford.

Once they began to eat, Michael found Melita a rather silent companion, she seemed to be brooding about something. Half-way through her cutter, she laid it down, and began to speak. 'I've been thinking, Michael. We spent the whole morning on my family history, but I don't think you know what it means.'

'It means you're the rightful Queen of England, Melita. The bits fit together.'

'No, that's not what I'm trying to say. I mean, I don't think you understand what it means in my terms. You know I'm a botanist, but actually, my PhD's in plant genetics, so I teach a first-year bio science course on genetics. Have you taken basic science courses?'

He shook his head. 'We tend to be either/or in Britain.'

'The point is, if you're approaching from that perspective, which is what I know about, this whole idea's almost like an insult. In terms of genetics, you can't say one bloodline's important and none of the others count. I mean, if you do the math, Elizabeth of Bohemia's maybe ten or eleven generations back. If you look at the population of your ancestors ten generations ago, you find you're dealing with just over a thousand individuals. Eleven generations, it's two thousand. The story you're telling me says we're supposed to worry about just two out of all those people, but it only makes sense to look at the whole picture, if you want to understand about ancestry. If you forget about humans and think about breeding sheep or peas, then it's easier to see that each cross counts for just as much as any other. When it comes down to it, I'm nothing but a pure-bred Bajan mongrel, and genetically, I should guess I'm ninety per cent African and maybe more. My features and my general somatotype say Africa. I've got absolutely nothing to do with England. I've never even visited.'

'I'm not saying it makes sense either, Melita. But it's still true. I haven't invented the rules. It's the system Europe's been using for a thousand years, and in its own terms, you're the one. Come to that, Pelagius was a king in Africa, and then there's the Palaeologues, the ones your grandfather knew about. You're a very royal person.'

'Oh, this is completely crazy. When it comes to the last emperor of Byzantium, my little drop of Roman blood, he's back seventeen generations! And what about everyone else? You're forgetting about Marribah Grannum and Mimbo Catwell and all these other women with the names you liked. They're a damn sight nearer to me than Godscall Palaeologue. Grandpapa edited them out, because he was interested in the Palaeologues, and you're doing the same, because you're interested in Stuarts. But they were people too, and if you had any way of knowing what happened to them, who's to say they were less interesting than this queen? They must've fought for their children – it wasn't easy for blacks and coloureds to get an education, but my family weren't cane-cutters.

Most of them were skilled people, they were cabinet-makers, or tailors, or musicians. Andrew Stewart was even a journalist. I've always been proud of my family, but not because of Byzantium. What I've prided myself on is having a heritage of people who made the best of what society let them be. The stuff you're talking about isn't nearly as important.'

'Well, yes,' he argued. 'Personally I agree with you, in fact, and I think it's clear that Theodore Stuart was pretty much of a loser. But all the same, he was the only male great-grandchild of King James I, who was also a Protestant born in wedlock, so that gives his line a serious claim to the throne. Primogeniture, you see, plus the rule of preferring a male heir over an older female one, makes you the descendant of a senior royal line. Of course it's not fair, but it wasn't fair either that Ferdinando could be a freeholder just because he was white. We're talking about arbitrary social rules here. All this heritage stuff is empowering and interesting and whatever you want it to be, but it doesn't have anything to do with you being royal, one way or the other.'

'Maybe that's what worries me. I just don't like the basic principle. And anyway, this island's mine and I belong here. I don't care about Europe. It can get along without me.'

'I'm surprised you're not more impressed by the notion,' confessed Michael. 'It may just be because I'm English, but frankly, I'd be thrilled if someone told me I was the rightful Queen of England. King, I mean.'

Melita chuckled. She seemed to be thawing, his mistake had tickled her, but her amusement was kindly rather than scornful. 'The thing is, you've found yourself absolutely the wrong person to be impressed,' she explained. 'I've been brought up all my life with Grandpapa's crazy stories about being the last empress, so I'm used to the idea I'm some kind of descendant, and I know it just makes you out of place. He talked plenty, and Barbados is so small, it's like growing up in a goldfish bowl. I've been called "poor-great" all my life. It wasn't easy, growing up here with people all around trying to keep me down where I belonged.' She dropped into a country accent, mimicking some voice from the past, '"You puttin' on airs, you t'ink you white?" Bajans don't like people acting up, you know,' she continued, reverting to her ordinary mode of speech. 'I suppose if I wasn't called Palaeologue, I'd have more of a feeling about it, but as it is it's, like, Oh no, not again.'

'Oh, dear. No, I do see that.' They had finished their modest lunch, and the waitress mooched over with the bill. Melita was reaching for her purse, but he whisked it away before she could pick it up, then wondered if he should have. Mores differed, and he already had cause to realise that she was strong-willed. It was hard to know on so short an acquaintance what would offend her. But he wanted to keep her talking, and hoped that a tiny debt would help.

'Melita, I'm very grateful to you for giving me so much of your time,' he began diffidently, once they were paid up and ready to go. 'Are you very busy just at the moment? I'd love to go on exploring all these questions, and I don't have a clue about Barbados, as you'll have gathered. If you could bear it, I'd really like to have you show me around. Anything you think's interesting.'

She looked at him, he felt weighed and measured. Her face was a difficult one to read; it seemed, in repose, as impenetrably reserved as one of the Yoruba bronzes he had looked at when he started researching into Pelagius. The small island effect, he thought. It was a village mentality. He had imagined the West Indies as a place where people lived their lives on their front porches, relaxed and open, but Barbados was not like that. The little chattel-houses all had yards with twelve-foot fences of corrugated iron; you had less idea of how people were living their lives than you did in Silloth or Oxford. And people's faces were as secret as their gardens.

'I've got a bit of time – it's outside term here. I've got a paper to finish, but it's not due for a while. I'm trying to decide what you'd like. I don't see you as a plantation houses type,' she said finally.

Michael shook his head. 'I'm sure they're attractive, but it's the white underclass that I need to think about.'

'Well, what I'd like to do is show you a bit of the Barbados I care about, to try and help you understand. I'm thinking of taking you to Turner's Hall Woods. If you think it's dull, we can go on to Welchman Hall Gully which is much more spectacular, it's got most of what you'd think of as tropical, ginger, sandalwood, bamboo, you name it, but it's really a botanic garden pretending to be wilderness. The woods aren't so pretty, but they really are something like primeval Barbados, so it's got something to tell you about what the island's really like. It's remote, and you've got to be scared walking around on your own in the country, so I haven't been there in a while.'

'It sounds perfect. Come on then, let's go.' There wasn't a boyfriend, then, Michael thought as he got to his feet. He might have guessed, she had a solitary, self-sufficient air. The trenchant stare, he realised, must have been at least partly about whether she felt she could trust herself walking about in the wilds with a strange man.

'What's it like being a woman on your own here?' he asked as they got into the car.

'Not easy. You get a lot of rudeness. Some of the men at Cave Hill act like they've got rights, specially the professors. This is still a country where men rule on the streets.'

'You surprise me. From what I've read, I thought this was a country of tough women.'

'Oh, they're tough. But they stay at home, or they get hassled – we swing right here.'

Melita piloted them efficiently into the depths of the country, past endless fields of sugar-cane, varied by occasional patches of bananas or guavas. Something dark and swift dashed across the road.

'My God, what was that?' he said, swerving to avoid it.

'Mongoose. They were imported to keep the rats down, and now they're a pest. Biocontrol's not as easy as people used to think.'

'Well, I'd certainly not have got here without you,' he observed some time later. They had turned off the road some time back, and the little car had toiled up a narrow, barely navigable track which had just petered out in the middle of nowhere. They were in the highlands, in a region of densely wooded alternating hills and ravines. There was a piteous little hamlet of three or four sunblasted, almost paintless chattel-houses by the last bend of the track, but nobody seemed to be about.

'This is the sort of place where the Rastas have their gardens,' said Melita. 'There's no real cultivation up here because the terrain's too broken – that's why it's been left unspoiled. The dreads grow their ganja in clearings up here in the hills, with just old slave-trails for paths. It's not actually legal in Barbados, you know. So you want to be careful not to go where you've got no business, if you see what I mean.'

'Yes,' he said. ' "Watch the wall, my darling, while the gentlemen go by." ' As Melita made the first move to get out, he reached over to the back seat, and retrieved a folder. 'I've just remembered,' he said. 'I've been carrying this about with me. It's a xerox from microfilm of a book which Pelagius's son Balthasar wrote, about Barbadian plants and their uses. From what you've said, it's his Barbados we're looking at.'

'Oh, I'd like to see that,' she said, and he slid the pages out of the folder and handed them over. She glanced through the pages, frowning. 'It's not in botanical order.'

'Pre-Linnaeus.'

''Course. I'd forgotten. I don't look at old books. Can we take it with us?'

'If you like. I've got a microfilm, so if this copy gets damaged I can easily make another.' She was already walking away, so he locked the car and followed as she vanished into the green shade.

It looks like an English wood in high summer, he thought, as they walked down a path formed by a dry stream-bed. 'I was expecting a rain forest,' he complained.

'We have a long dry period, and Barbados is well drained, so we don't support humid jungle. Welchman Hall Gully's one of the few spots on the island where we can grow rain-forest plants. This is what's actually characteristic – technically, it's called tropical mesophytic forest.'

Looking more closely at his surroundings, he realised every single tree was unfamiliar, and that the branches high above them were laced together with lianas. The gully they were walking down gave a misleading impression of European openness to the structure of the wood, but when he looked more closely, a few yards to either side, he was looking at, not into, vegetation impenetrably tangled like a giant hank of green knitting. He also became belatedly aware of the alien quietness; English birds were a noisy bunch, by comparison; woods, in his experience, meant wood-pigeons going roo-coo-coo, blackbirds shouting their alarm, a sudden kak-kak from a pheasant. Just as the thought formed, there was a sudden crash from somewhere up in the canopy, but no call of any kind followed.

'What was that?' he asked.

'Monkey, probably,' said Melita. 'We have green monkeys here, brought from West Africa with the slaves. Look. Those are bearded figs. The island's named after them, so they must have been the dominant forest tree once. Now they're mostly in botanic gardens, Welchman Hall, and here. Most of the forest cover's gone in the rest of the island, and we've got Australian casuarinas all along

197

the coastline instead of indigenous mangrove. We're a classic colonial society here. Practically the whole biomass is imported, not just the people, but the vegetation and the wildlife as well. If you want to see Balthasar's landscape, this is just about the only spot.'

'What's that?' Michael was looking at a curious trunk with bark as white as silver birch, decorated with close-set little black barbs or spines. He reached out and touched one; it was sharp.

'Sandbox tree.' She bent and picked up a piece of something that looked like a carved wooden petal and handed it to him. 'This is part of the fruit – when they're whole, they're like a pretty wooden box. Let's see what Balthasar says, he's got a section on trees.' She riffled through the pages, biting her lower lip in concentration. 'Here we go. He says, take the leaves, and lay them in a vessel with fair white salt. When the vessel is full, set a weight on the top and put it aside for no less than a month. They may be used for a poultice on all swellings and–' She broke off, her eyebrows rising, and held out the book wordlessly.

'Imposthumes,' he said. 'Means boils, I think.'

'–And they alleviate the symptoms of Barbados leg when the case is not too severe. He means filariasis, what they used to call elephantiasis. It used to be a big problem here till they found out what caused it. My grandpa used sandbox leaves for rheumatism, pressed in oil.'

They walked together along the bed of the stream, or when the track did not permit it, in single file, with Melita pointing out Macaw palms, ferns, and unusual aroids as they went, apparently unaware that he was looking as much at her as he was at the plantlife. He had seen Bajan girls as thin as whips, but Melita had a type of figure which was considerably commoner in the island, athletic but chunky, long-waisted, with narrow hips and a jutting, muscular behind. She walked beautifully, and her movements were dignified and self-contained. As she showed him, or so it began to feel, every fertile inch o' the island, she seemed an Amazonian

Caliban, the Caliban of the happy time remembered in the play, when he introduced Prospero to his beloved land, before he was enslaved.

Michael let the words flow over him; the technicalities of botany did not interest him, but he was fascinated by the way she was talking, her awareness of interrelations, her sense of the ecosystem as something precious. He began to see that Turner's Hall, in its deep authenticity, was a touchstone for her, and to understand something of the depth of her knowledge and commitment, why she had said 'This island's mine'. He tried to convey this.

'It's not the individual plants that matter,' she replied, 'it's the system. It's pretty much in balance at the moment, but if you throw something else in here because you want to achieve some particular benefit, you're taking a risk that the whole thing may change in unpredictable ways. There's been a huge amount of change in the last three hundred years, but we know how to work with what's here now, just about, so we're trying to put the brakes on. We do a lot of work on environmental management in the university, looking at the impact of changing land-use on the whole ecosystem. This is such a small island it's near the limit of its capacity, and we can't afford to make mistakes. Water's a primary issue for us — we've got no rivers in Barbados, and that's a key problem for industrial development. I don't like what tourism's doing to the culture, but we have to develop somehow, and in a lot of ways it's less damaging than the alternatives.'

He sat down on a rock, having first cautiously inspected the immediately surrounding area. A couple of enormous millipedes were flowing smoothly through the leaf-litter on the rippling fringes that served them as legs, but they seemed unaggressive creatures, and no other insect life was to be seen.

'Since the place is so small, can you get people to see there's a problem?' he asked. 'It seems to be very difficult to shift public opinion in England.'

'No, it's very difficult here too,' she said. 'The trouble is, we're an ex-slave-country, and that gives us a whole extra set of issues with balancing out human and environmental factors. For instance, there's a completely ecologically sound way of growing sugar-cane, you put the plants in four-foot-square pits. Cane-holes collect the rain, you see, so there's no run-off. Trouble is, you can't make free men do it. Even in slavery times, holing was a punishment job. Quite a lot of people here actually like the idea of mechanised, chemical farming, because it looks like getting away from the bad old days. We're trying to educate the people and the politicians about green issues, but there's a lot of resistance, and of course, it's always hard to get politicians to see beyond the short term. The only thing which is on our side really is that tourism's so important to us here there's always an argument we can make about not destroying natural beauty.'

'I can see why you feel so committed to all this,' he said. 'It's the feeling that if people like you don't keep monitoring and nagging, some pinheaded politician will make a decision based on doing a favour for a friend and you'll end up with some disastrous secondary consequence. I'm no scientist, but in the last couple of years, I've seen Britain's entire livestock industry devastated, at a cost of billions, and they seem to think it all started because one or two individuals bent the rules about feeding pigs. But the other thing I've been thinking, listening to you, is that it's very strange. Back in the seventeenth century, Pelagius van Overmeer was interested in botany. As far as we can work out, he contributed the plates to a book on the plant-life of Java which was published in Holland in 1638. And you know about Balthasar and plants, you're holding the evidence. Now, all these years later, I meet you, and it turns out you're a botanist as well.'

'Coincidence,' said Melita, who had also sat down on a rock. 'In a way, the story's actually the opposite of what you're imagining. It's reacting against Grandpapa Palaeologue that made me a

botanist. The other kids picked on me on account of his foolish-
ness, so my Grandpa Walrond used to take me up and down the
island from when I was a little girl and talk to me about plants.
He knows a lot about bush-teas. It's an old tradition in the country,
medicine's expensive, and not everyone could afford it.'

Conversation lapsed for a while; they sat in friendly silence,
staring at the green wall of vegetation before them.

'Melita, have you ever lived outside Barbados?' he asked, after
some minutes had passed.

'The University of the West Indies has campuses on several
islands, so I studied up in Mona in Jamaica. Then I went to Canada
for my PhD. It was good training and interesting, but I wasn't
happy. I don't know how people survive those winters. Since then
I haven't been off the island. Our taxes are high here, and the cost
of living is high too, and young staff aren't paid very much. I have
to run a car, because you can get into trouble if you go around on
foot, and the flat takes the rest of my money.' She looked at her
watch. 'We'd maybe better start heading back. The afternoon's
getting on.'

'Could I take you to dinner? There's quite a nice-looking place
I spotted not far from my hotel. It's called the Round House, or
something?'

'Oh, yes. I've heard of it, but I've never been. I don't get out
much. It's not easy going out with men here, they're not too good
at taking no for an answer, and the trouble with going out with
the girls is you get involved with local politics. The university's
riddled with factions. I don't like being made to take sides, but
some people think I'm too big for my boots anyway, so if I'm in
a group, I can't hold myself above what's going on. It's easier just
to stay clear.'

'Just for the record, I wasn't planning to make a pest of myself,'
he said, a little huffily. He realised as he said it that some deeply
un-p.c. part of his psyche was hoping that the fact she felt safe

with him did not imply that she had written him off as some sort of sad half-man. A Fisher King, wounded in the thigh.

'I can see that. I'd like to come, and I wasn't thinking I needed to drop hints,' she apologised. 'I was only trying to explain. You're like some of the boys I knew in Canada, not bothered with all that macho shit. I do appreciate it. I like to talk when I get the chance, but you've got to be so careful. I see my mum once a week, so I get to lime with my family and play with their kids, but that's about it for my social life, mostly.'

'Well, I'm very pleased I can do something in return for all this,' he said, gesturing at the vista before them.

Melita got to her feet. 'Tell you what. If you let me navigate, we can just drive about for an hour, and I can show you some beauty spots and nice views, generally introduce you to the island, then we'll be in good time for dinner before it gets too crowded. How about it?'

'Perfect.'

'Did you like Bridgetown?'

'No, I'm afraid not.'

'I'll take you to Speightstown, which is a ways up the west coast. It hasn't really been developed yet. If you're interested in the eighteenth century, it's the place that'll give you the best idea. Then we can go up Chalky Mount for the view, and then down again and along the coast to Bathsheba.'

She directed him out of the labyrinth of country roads and back onto what was recognisably a highway, and before long, they were dropping down to the western plain.

'It used to be called Little Bristol,' she said as they entered the town, 'but nothing much goes on here now.'

'My God,' he said, looking at the merchants' houses, the shape of the street, as they parked. 'It looks like Whitehaven.' They got out of the car, and he turned to her to try and explain. 'I come from Cumbria, you see. Whitehaven's a fishing port just up the coast from where we are. Of course, it's not as colourful as this, but the houses are basically similar.'

'I thought you were from Oxford?'

'Oxford's just where I work.'

'Cumbria's Lakeland, isn't it?' she said. 'Hills and lakes, sort of like parts of Quebec?'

'Sort of. But there's also a coastline, and that's the bit I'm from. The coastal towns are basically shaped by fishing and maritime trade. It looks as if it's the same here.'

'Yes. And there used to be whaling, I think.' They walked down the street together, past a barber's pumping out high-decibel gospel. People were moving about, doing their shopping now the noonday heat was past, or sitting in groups, watching the world go by. 'That's an old merchant's house,' she said, pointing, when they could hear themselves speak. 'You see those windows? Those are what they call Demerara shutters. They let the air circulate.' There was a pause, then she suddenly said, '"I wandered lonely as a cloud." That's supposed to be the Lake District, isn't it?'

'That's right. Wordsworth's "Daffodils".'

'I just remembered we did it at school. None of us had ever seen a daffodil, of course. Do you want to stop for a drink or an ice-cream, or shall we go on?'

'Let's go on. I can always come back here and take photos to show my father, in case he's interested – it's on Highway One, so I know I can find it. I'd rather spend time in the country, where I need a navigator.'

They got back into the car, and wound through the mountain ridges of the Scotland district, a tremendous panorama of shaggy green slopes with the coastal plain of Bathsheba dimly visible beyond, then they came down again to pick up the east coast road. They stopped at Barclay's Park, and strolled for a while under the coconut palms and casuarinas, watching the incessant thundering of the surf on the beach. There were people about, but they were packing up to go home, and the light was beginning to fade into glorious Tiepolo clouds of grey and Naples yellow.

'I've got some cousins not too far from here,' she said, 'down towards Bathsheba, just around where you're staying, mostly Haggats and Walronds. A lot of them are fishermen. My grandpapa Palaeologue had a house at Cattlewash – he taught in St Joseph's parish school.'

'How wonderful to live somewhere this beautiful.'

'Mmm. The trouble is, there's not a lot to do, and land's very expensive.'

'Like home,' said Michael. 'The locals are priced out of anywhere desirable, the youngsters go away because there's nothing for them, and London gets bigger and bigger. There doesn't seem to be any way of stopping it. Let's get on to the Round House, it'll be dark soon.'

The restaurant was, to his relief, easy to find, and had a good view out over the strange sea-haggled rocks of Bathsheba in the last of the light. He was glad they had waited no longer; the place was beginning to fill up, mostly with visitors: the flavour was tropical-international, and the prices were high, which probably kept the locals away, but it was pleasant enough and, he was glad to see, not too smart. Melita was wearing jeans and a short-sleeved white jumper, neat but not exactly dressy, while his chinos and polo shirt had suffered from a long hot day in the car.

'I'm trying to think what would happen if we told people,' he said, once they were sitting waiting. 'It's a tremendous story, you know. I hope you don't think it's vulgar to say so, but you'd almost certainly make serious money.' Their food arrived; blackened dolphin steaks with salad and French fries. It smelt delicious.

'Wouldn't people just say I was crazy?' she asked, picking up her fork.

'Hardly. I'm an Oxford don, and I have documentary proof of the first half of the story. I've got one or two contacts in the media, and anyway, because I'm where I am, I can get a hearing. You've got an excellent account of the second half, thanks to your grandfather: I don't know if we can produce actual hard evidence for every single link in the chain, but it's a bloody good, sound narrative. People will be fascinated. If anything, the fact that you're black is probably a plus point. The royals stand for everything that's backward-looking in today's Britain, class, privilege, arrogance, the *ancien régime*. If you came along and said "I've got a better right than they have", looking the way you do, a lot of people would respond to that.'

'But the queen isn't going to say, "Here's my crown, girl, and here's the key of the palace",' she objected. 'Why should she?'

'Of course not. What'd actually happen, I'm pretty sure, is that after it'd all been looked into, there'd be an Act of Parliament confirming Elizabeth II and her designated heirs as monarchs of Great Britain.'

'So nothing would change.'

'It would and it wouldn't.' Michael was thinking it out. 'The point is, at the moment, the queen's supposed to be "I Elizabeth by the grace of God", etcetera etcetera. That's to say, her title's based on the notion that the royal family are somehow divinely ordained to their position, and of course, on primogeniture, all the stuff you don't approve of. You'd punch a beautiful hole in that just by existing. But once Parliament had ridden to the rescue, she'd be queen by the grace of Tony Blair, and Tony's a lot less trustworthy than God, from the Windsors' point of view. You see, if the monarchy's based on nothing more fundamental than a Royal Succession Bill, then Parliament can mess around with it, and of course, another Parliament can change its mind and decide the whole thing's too expensive or past its time. On the surface, it would look as if everything was the same, but in fact, the implications would be tremendous. I've told you about Pelagius van Overmeer's journal. He wrote that he had a great hope that his son would be the Just King who was to reign at the end of the world. By being the Just Queen, I mean, the person who'd be queen if the system was just even by its own weird rules, then you'd call the whole thing into question, and strengthen the democratic process, which is actually a way of fulfilling Pelagius's dream. I agree with you, the world's outlived kings and queens, but it still needs symbols. You'd be a symbol, all right. You'd stand for justice.'

Melita frowned. 'And how would I get on with my life? I've got work to do. Things are difficult enough for me. Can you imagine, if I was working here, and people kept ringing the department, wanting interviews and God knows what? I told you, there are people who think I put on airs just because of the Palaeologue stuff. Can you imagine what it'd be like if there were stories in the magazines calling me Queen Melita?'

Michael sipped his lager, and thought about it. 'I can see it would be hard,' he admitted. 'I'm still left wondering if it's important. Not that I mean to imply your work isn't important. But what about the race thing? Britain's a multi-race society, but we aren't doing that well with coming to terms with it. There aren't a lot of visible black people, except sportsmen and pop-stars. The odd politician, now.'

'I know. So if I was running around saying I was the queen, I'd be treated like a freak, wouldn't I? I mean, if I even visited in England, people would see me first and foremost as someone they'd expect to be scrubbing their floors. Barbados is a lot more race-conscious than it should be, but at least you can't look at a person here and say "He's black, so I assume he's dumb, uneducated, and poor," but that goes down all the time in England. My father lived up there, you know. He didn't get very far. People diss me here because they think I'm poor-great, not because of my colour.'

'Yes. The question is, should you be doing something about it?'

'I'd end up sacrificing my career for something I didn't even believe in,' she pointed out.

'I can't help feeling you could do some good, if only by high-lighting the monstrous absurdity of the whole notion,' he argued. 'We've got such a problem at home with a culture of low expecta-tions. I've got a black colleague at Balliol, just the one of course, and he told me that his school pretty well wrote him off, though it's obvious in retrospect he must have been very bright. It was his mum who kept pushing him. But I can see it's difficult to convince children to keep their heads down if they haven't any role-models. Look at you, Melita. You're clever, educated, articu-late, good-looking, and black. You're just the sort of person who'd do some good if you were famous.'

'You sound like Booker T. Washington,' she said drily.

'Who?'

'American. He believed in improving the race.'

'Maybe he had a point. If it wasn't that black people are natur-ally better athletes, I shudder to think how we'd socialise the kids at all.'

He realised as the words left his mouth he had made a mistake. Melita sat up a little straighter, looking furious. 'That sort of pseudo-Darwinism just makes me tired,' she snapped.

'Don't you approve of Darwin?'

She sighed impatiently. 'Of course I approve of Darwin. I just don't like the way racists use him, even liberal racists just miss the point.'

'I'm sorry,' said Michael, hurt. 'What have I said?'

'We're back to genetics again. I wish people would get to grips with genetics, I have to explain this every year. The basic point is that it doesn't really make sense to consider Africans as a single population at all. They're incredibly variable. Some are good athletes, yes: for instance, if your ancestors came from the Kenyan highlands, you've probably got long legs and a great cardiovas-cular system, but Kenya's not exactly the whole of Africa. Actually, you can probably make fewer assumptions about the natural endowments of a person of African ancestry than you can about any other type of human.'

'I think I'm beginning to see why you got ticked off,' he said.

'Well, when you've got a huge variability, you've inevitably got a wider base to the distribution curve, whatever you're measuring, you see?' she persisted. It was something she seemed anxious that he should understand, and he gave her his full attention. 'Worst'll be worse, best'll be better. Athletic competitions sort for skills which are pretty easy to identify, so with a global culture, blacks start coming out on top, just so long as the sport's not too expensive to get into. I mean, people are talent-spotting because there's money in it, and the kids themselves can see that's potentially a way out for them, so if they're good runners or boxers or whatever, they work on it. That doesn't necessarily mean the average black person's more athletic. It's perfectly possible that the worst athletes in the world're black too, but who's ever going to bother finding out?'

'Point taken. But you have to remember, nobody's ever talked to me about any of this. I'm just an English don, so I've done about as much science as your average gerbil. Logically then,' said Michael, 'Harvard and Yale ought to be crammed with black Americans?'

'I can't see why not. The principle's exactly the same. Only there are tremendous cultural pressures on black kids which keep them from developing their potential, some from the school system, and I have to say, some from inside the black community. The world's full of young brothers kicking footballs for hours every day. No wonder some of them are good. If you can imagine the same numbers putting that much effort into math, don't you think we'd find by college age some of them were clearly gifted?'

'But outside Africa, would really brilliant black people have survived to breed? I mean, they wouldn't exactly have made themselves popular in the days of slavery?' he objected.

Melita gave him a bleak look. 'Intelligence doesn't come out of an on/off gene like the one for blue or brown eyes. Which is just as well, look at Europe. I mean, I was taught in History that for more than a thousand years, all the academic types were priests or nuns. That means they didn't have babies, and they sorted themselves out of the gene-pool. If intelligence was heritable in a simple way, you-all ought to be going around with your knuckles dragging on the ground. Intelligence turns up everywhere.'

'But Melita, if you're right about this, don't you think you should take the chance to make your views known? You might really be able to make a difference.'

'Oh, my grandfathers! All I want is just to get on with my life. What do you think'd happen? I'd get to go on Oprah in a sparkly dress trying to explain genetics in one and a half minutes? Anyway, if I was famous for being a queen, do you think anyone'd listen to me if I was talking about anything serious? I'd just have to deal with endless shit. And I don't say I couldn't do with a bit more money, but what would I want with ninety-three bedrooms if I hadn't a single one I could sleep in without being seen as a God-damned symbol of something?'

'Stalemate,' said Michael.

The waitress came over, and cleared their plates. 'You-all want any dessert? Coffee?'

'I'd like something,' said Michael. 'Ice-cream, maybe. How about you?'

They sorted out their order, and when the girl had gone, he returned to their previous conversation. 'I'm nagging you, Melita. I'm sorry. The trouble is, to me, there's a kind of narrative logic implicit in the whole situation. Back in Holland, in the mid-seventeenth century, Pelagius van Overmeer, who's your ancestor whether you like it or not, dreamed of fathering a just king. Now, three hundred years later, I've come along and put the bits together, so from my perspective, it's as if Pelagius has programmed me to want to find a just king. That's how stories are supposed to work, d'you see? If the prince waltzes in holding a glass slipper and finds Cinderella sitting in the kitchen, she's not supposed to tell him to bugger off because she's started studying for the Open University.'

'It sounds like you believe more in Pelagius than you do in me,' she said.

'I'm afraid that's true. I've known him a lot longer. And I teach English. Being open to narrative's what I do for a living.'

'You're a story person. I'm not, you see,' she said. 'I'm a scientist. I deal with what you can demonstrate.'

Michael regarded her, half-admiring and half-exasperated. He had thought momentarily of Caliban, when they were at Turner's Hall, and it struck him now that he seemed to be making a remarkably poor go of being Prospero.

IX

I believe those tests were worth what the war cost . . . if they served
to show clearly to our people the lack of intelligence in our country,
and the degrees of intelligence in different races . . . We have learned
once and for all that the negro is not like us.

Henry Fairfield Osborn, president of the American Museum
of Natural History, 1923

It was rather late when Michael got back to the hotel, having
taken Melita back to her flat and then driven himself across the
island again. No more than fifteen or sixteen miles, but intensely
stressful once he was on his own on country roads in the velvet
dark of the tropical night. He was barely able to make himself
stand under the shower before dropping exhausted into bed, but
when he closed his eyes, he found he had fallen through sleep into
a vivid dream.

He walked in through the french windows of their old house in
Cartmel, out of the summer garden. His father was in his usual
chair behind the *Sunday Times*, at his ease in his Sunday pullover
and slacks. Since he could see almost nothing else of him, Michael
was strongly aware of his father's feet, crossed at the ankle, clad
in grey hand-knitted socks and old red leather slippers. He could
hear his mother singing in the kitchen; at any moment she might
come through. He was gripped by panic; within the logic of the
dream, he knew with part of his mind that he was in the past, and
that if his mother came through and failed to recognise him as an
adult, he would be wounded beyond toleration. But as he stood

dithering, his father lowered the paper to peer at him over the top, and he found himself confronted by the wrong face. There in his father's chair, wearing his father's clothes, was a strong-featured black man with high cheekbones and a severe, sculpted mouth, looking hard at him from large, somewhat bloodshot eyes. Please don't speak, he thought, willing the thought towards the man as hard as he could. He did not want Mum to come in and find a room full of strangers; let her go on making gravy, ignorant and happy. Please, please, do not speak. The singing in the kitchen stopped; and he feared that his mother was about to come through. He tried with all his will to run away, and woke.

It was still completely dark, he had no idea of the time. The incessant roaring of the surf pounding the reef outside was soothing and reminded him of the Solway on winter nights, which possibly accounted for his dreaming about Cumbria. He pulled a coverlet over himself, for the night had grown cooler, and drifted back to sleep. This time he dreamed of Melita, walking in the woods. She turned to him as they walked, and smiled, the smile which illuminated her dark face, and he reached out to kiss her. As they touched, suddenly they both seemed to be naked, rolling together on soft leaf-mould, while a frangipani tree rained down a soft confetti of pink blossoms, and she was sweet and welcoming beneath him.

Well, no trouble interpreting that one, he thought when he woke up again properly, reaching for a hanky to mop his sticky thighs and stomach. He felt more drawn towards Melita, for all her stern-ness, than towards any woman he had met in the last year. Chance would be a fine thing, but he was far from displeased his libido had indulged him with a sexy dream. He looked at his watch: it was still forty minutes to breakfast time, so he decided it was high time to experiment with the sea. So far, though he was doing a certain amount of walking, he was not getting much real exer-cise, and he felt the lack of it.

Picking his way across the pebbles, trying to avoid both sharp fragments of coral and an occasional fish-head – flying-fish, they must be, from the enormous fins, he would doubtless be meeting them again, fried, in about half an hour – he found that the surf looked a great deal more formidable than it did when viewed from the hotel. Even after coming over a hundred feet of reef, the breakers were a good three feet high. He looked round dubiously, and one of the fishermen gave him a friendly hail, which was reassuring, since at least someone knew he was there. He stepped into the vast energy of the waves, and found that the current was sucking and pulling at his legs like something living – he had not waded very far before it twitched his feet from under him and dumped him on his backside, where a wave crashed over his head. Spluttering, he righted himself, and began to swim. It was an alarming, exhilarating experience in water just cool enough to be refreshing. He kept an eye on a couple of landmarks on the shore, and realised quite soon that the current was carrying him to the south and onto jagged rocks: so swiftly that if he set himself against it, it was easy to swim reasonably hard without actually moving relative to the shore at all. A good thing, since he had not the slightest intention of getting far out of his depth, and going any great distance parallel with the shore would run him onto the reef. He swam happily for some time, bounced up and down by the swell, until his stomach told him it was breakfast time. Stumbling out of the sea, he bounded up the steps to the hotel, becoming aware as he did so that blood was running down his legs in pale-red streaks from childish scrapes on his knees and shins.

After breakfast, he rummaged in the pockets of his jacket, unworn since the day of his arrival, till he found Natty Polgreen's card, and gave him a ring.

'Hallo, Natty? It's Michael. Michael Foxwist.'

'Oh, yes.' Natty sounded a little muzzy. 'How're you doing?'

'I'm having a wonderful time.' It was with a little jolt of private surprise that Michael realised, as he uttered the words, that they were true. 'I've met Dr Palaeologue.'

'No shit?' Natty was pulling himself together; a faint click and fizz from the other end of the line suggested that he had just opened a can of Coke or something of the sort. 'Oh, I remember now. How did that go?'

'Fascinating. She's a very interesting person.'

'She? You didn't say that. A babe?'

'I only found out when I met her. It depends what you mean by babe. She's a very good-looking woman, but she's not exactly a model type.'

'Oh, well. Would she look good in a crown?'

'She would, actually.'

Natty laughed. 'Move over, Lizzie.'

'Natty, could we meet?'

'I've got to see some TV people today. This evening, maybe? We could lime a while in Bridgetown. Or tell you what. You been to St John's? We were talking about the churchyard?'

'Yes, I have.'

'Bascombe's bar, Four Cross Roads, St John's. Easier for you to find. Bridgetown can be pretty confusing if you don't know it. You'll've passed Bascombe's, going to the church, everything goes through Four Cross. Opposite the post office, next up to the gas station. It's a real old-fashioned rum-shop. Meet you there at five?'

'Excellent. See you there.'

He remembered seeing the rum-shop, because he had marked down the Texaco station for future reference, since petrol outlets were not that common in the island. Pulling up beside it, he thought that it looked a little like a trailer, painted in bold stripes of yellow, red and white; the interior was dark and uninviting. He walked in, and the habitués fell silent. Coming in out of the sun, he found he could hardly see their faces, other than a flash of eyes as they registered his presence. He took off his sunglasses and stuffed them in his pocket.

'Hallo,' he said, going up to the counter with an assurance he did not feel.

'Hi,' said one or two voices from the gloom. The babble of conversation rose again, and he began to relax.

'You staying round here?' asked the girl behind the bar. 'What can I get you?'

'Have you got fizzy water?'

She looked at him in silence, and he felt rebuked. 'There's Coke, Fanta, Lilt, Sprite, and Tango, sir.'

'Lilt, thanks,' he said, on the grounds that it was the only one he didn't know for certain he disliked.

'You have a li'l taste with that,' advised one of a group of men sitting round a table in the corner – playing dominoes, he realised, noticing the little white counters among the bottles and glasses.

'I can't, really. I'm driving, you see,' he said apologetically.

'They not too severe,' said the voice of the tempter. 'And you a touriss, they not bother they selfs too much.'

Which possibly explained something about the more interesting moments he had experienced on Barbadian roads, he thought to himself. It irked him a little to be so readily identifiable as an outsider. He took a swig of his Lilt, and found it revolting.

'Actually, I'll change my mind. Can I have a beer, please?' he asked, and one of the men laughed, a friendly chuckle.

'Way to go, man. It not the same, but it good.'

The girl gave him a cold bottle of lager, Banks's, the beer of the country.

'Thanks.' It was good, and it went down very gratefully. Sipping it, he leaned on the bar and took stock of what was around him as his eyes adjusted to the dark. The bar mostly carried rum, in various brands, and a surprising variety of sizes. The habitués, he noticed, mostly had a bottle apiece, though not a full-sized one.

There was a glass cabinet on the counter with a variety of uniden-
tifiable foodstuffs in it – the only things he recognised were the
tasty rolls known as cutters – and the walls were lined with advertisements. Over in the corner, the domino players had returned to
their game, which was clearly a serious matter: it seemed incongruous to Michael, since he associated dominoes with Neville and
his friends. But they did not play like that, not with such brio and
bursts of laughter. He could hear the tiles slapping down in a
steady patter from where he stood. Elsewhere in the room, men
were chatting quietly, and the bargirl was polishing glasses. They
left him to himself, but he did not feel he was unwelcome.

A plump young woman in pink cycling-shorts stopped a moment
and put her head in at the door, apparently looking for someone,
which provoked an outburst of chirrups, whistles, and comment.
'Hey, Gina, sugar cakes, you looking good'; 'Sweet thing, you comin'
to sit with we?'

'Not in this age of the world,' she retorted, and withdrew.

Michael heard a car drawing up outside, the squeak of the hand-
brake, and a moment later, Natty Polgreen walked in. He was
wearing a khaki garment half-way between a shirt and a short-
sleeved jacket, cotton chinos and penny loafers, and looked altogether smarter and more citified than the domino-players in their
shorts and vests. It seemed to Michael, watching Natty's entrance,
that the reaction of the locals was no less wary towards this man,
one of their own, than it had been towards himself.

Natty got himself a rum and coke, and they settled down at a
vacant table in the corner. Once they had done so, Michael asked
the most recent question to have come into his mind. 'Natty, why
dominoes?'

'It came in from the US, with Bajans who served in World War
Two. Before then, people played warri. They still play it in
Speightstown, I'm told, but in the rest of the island, dominoes
took over. It's a shame we lost warri, they played it in ancient

Egypt, and it must've come over with the slaves, but that's Barbados for you. We like America. How'd you get on with little Ms P? Did she mash your balls? Everyone says she's a dyke.'

'She's a perfectly pleasant woman, Natty,' said Michael, irritated. 'What on earth makes you think she's a lesbian? Anyway, I didn't think you knew her.'

'It's a small island. I just asked around. The word is, nobody ever got into her panties all the time she's been working at Cave Hill, which is two-three years now, so either she a matty, or she maybe has some sweet-man back in Canada.'

'Mightn't she just be single and happy with it?' he demanded.

Natty looked at him in astonishment. 'It's not the way we do things round here. This ain't no cold climate. But it's a thought, anyway – I've seen the Rightful Queen, and she's a black lesbian!'

Michael was beginning to regret having ever arranged the meeting. 'I'd hate to think of Dr Palaeologue just becoming a joke,' he said. 'She's a lovely person.'

Natty looked at him, and stopped clowning. 'Well, OK then. What did she tell you?'

'I couldn't have asked for more. It turned out her grandfather was a schoolmaster, and an antiquarian on the side. He did the family history back as far as he could go, and it's the other end of the same story. All the links are there: Melita Palaeologue's the direct descendant of James I by the most senior Protestant line, so she ought by rights to be the Queen of England.'

Natty whistled softly. 'No shit.'

'The thing is, she's not at all interested in it herself. It's a position I have to respect.'

'What's her problem?'

'Partly it's intellectual. She doesn't believe in the principle. And she doesn't want to be made a fool of by the media, which I completely understand.'

'But that's not the whole picture. You can't keep it quiet just to spare one little wicka some hassle when it's something so import- ant to us. We're descended from slaves, remember, the bottom of the heap. Just think about it. A black Bajan dyke with a PhD, and she's the Queen of England, the Empress of Byzantium – the Queen of bloody Nigeria as well, I suppose. She must be just about the most royal person in the whole history of the world. People are going to care about this.'

'They shouldn't.'

'They should. You Brits told us it all mattered for three hundred years. Every time a black dude tried to get somewhere in life, he was told he wasn't a member of the master race. You ever read any Kipling? Or *Prester John*? Well, you can't get any more like a member of a master race than the Queen of England. You can't go off the idea just because a black person ends up top of the pile.'

'That's not why I've gone off it.'

'I know that, Michael. But you have to think how people are going to feel about all this.'

'Natty,' he pleaded, 'I beg you, don't spread this around. It all needs a lot more thought.'

'I suppose so. But it's a powerful idea.'

'Melita said I was a story person. She's not, you see, she's a scientist, so she's just interested in what happens. You're another. Narrative matters more to you than people.'

'I'm a writer. It goes with the territory. And you need to think some more about the politics of storytelling, brother. You're acting like you're the one can decide what's a story and what isn't, but who d'you think you are? Prospero?'

'You're being bloody cold-hearted, Natty. It's a black woman's life and her personal dignity we're talking about. Or are moral scruples something else which goes with a cold climate?'

'You gone too far, man.'

'You're right. That was rude, but I'm seriously bothered about this.'

'Really?' said Natty ironically.

Michael drank off the last of his beer, and tried to marshal his thoughts. Natty signalled for another round, which Michael did not resist, in the interests of mending relations. 'I think it's important not to go off at half-cock,' he said at last. 'There are major issues here. You've raised some of them, and I raised them too when I was talking to Melita. There's also the fact that the present Queen of England's just celebrated her fiftieth year on the throne, and on the whole, a nation yawned. People seem to have lost interest in the whole idea.'

'Melita could be Queen of Scotland,' said Natty suddenly. 'They wanted a Stuart, didn't they?'

'Yes they did, but Melita's not going to help. She's about 250 years too late. I love the thought of Bonny Prince Ferdinando storming out of Roebuck Street in 1745 and taking Scotland at cutlass point –'

'– Machete –'

'– But the fact is, he didn't. Scotland's getting more republican by the minute, and the only people who'd welcome an authentic Stuart would be the Tourist Board. But of course they wouldn't welcome Melita. The heritage industry wants its history a lot simpler than the actual facts.'

'That's true here too. You should see the shit people talk about pirates. History's what people want to remember. In fact, these days, I'd say history's what people need. There isn't one single thing called history now.'

'Right. So we're talking about stories again. I think, frankly, this particular set of facts needs to cool for a while before we come to any sudden conclusions about what they add up to. Personally, I hate the thought of Dr Palaeologue becoming a victim of narrative, but I'm even more worried about her becoming the victim of stupid narrative. That's what she's afraid of. I'm happy to admit that I wanted to use you as a sounding-board,

Natty, but I'm alarmed by the way you've reacted.'

Natty drank off some of his rum and coke, looking uncharac-
teristically serious. 'It's a game to you,' he said. 'I mean, it's all
abstract, except maybe you're carrying a torch for Melita. But
you're white, you're from Oxford. How are you going to understand if this is important or not? Who are you to say it doesn't
matter any more, when you're still benefiting from all the time
when it did matter?'

'Ouch. I deserved that one, Natty. But can you build a fairer
society on a lie?'

'Can you build a society on anything else? The *Aeneid*'s a lie.
It's a story the Romans told themselves, then they went and made
it happen. Melita's wrong to toss out stories. You can't get away
from them.'

The light was beginning to fade as they sat; Michael could see
little more than an occasional flash from Natty's glasses in the
gloom of the bar. He looked at his watch.

'Oops, I'm going to have to go,' he said. 'Dinner-time's not flex-
ible, and I said I'd be in tonight. I'm sorry if I've been offensive.'

'Nothing to worry about. I got some licks in myself. You do
some Oxford thinking, Michael, I'll do some Bajan thinking. We'll
talk again before you go home.'

Home. A curious prospect, thought Michael, making his best
possible speed on the country roads. He had been in Barbados for
just under a week, and it already felt like months. But the fact was,
the days were ticking away. In England, he would have left it for
at least a week before contacting Melita again, but time was
pressing, and he very much wanted to see her. He decided to ring
her after supper.

To his great relief, her voice was friendly; in fact, he belatedly
realised, collecting his scattered wits, she was asking him over.
'. . . I've taken lunch and dinner off you, would you like to come
by?'

'I'd love to.' He thought for a moment about the difficulties of the journey back, then thought, to hell with it, I made it the last time. If I stick to soft drinks, I'll be fine.

He spent the following day driving about the island, trying to see it through early modern eyes. How had Balthasar felt, coming here? he asked himself. How had Theodore and Godscall felt? In some ways, they must have seen this place as Paradise, since it was a land of perpetual summer. Yet as their experience deepened, they would have thought it a poisoned paradise, perhaps even diabolical. They would have found the insects much more trying than they now were, without modern mosquito-repellents; they built not with concrete but in wood and coral limestone, so they would have had trouble with termites as well. Children of the Little Ice Age, they were habituated to extreme cold, but not to extreme heat: they had had no refrigerators, no air-conditioning, and according to Richard Ligon, their houses were stifling because they retained an English suspicion of letting in the night air. They refused to wear sensible clothes. Aphra Behn had, or so she claimed, paid a ceremonial visit to Suriname Indians in the full panoply of a European lady, from taffeta cap down to shoes, stockings and garters. She must have been drowning in her own sweat.

Balthasar, like the Barbadian settlers Ligon wrote about, would surely have been alarmed by the speed at which everything grew, the inexplicable failure of familiar wheat, grapes and apples, the way precious seedlings from Europe were overwhelmed by local weeds, as if the land had a mind of its own – how could they have said, in the Lord's Prayer, 'Give us each day our daily bread', when there was no bread? He remembered the moment in *Robinson Crusoe* when Crusoe found wheat and barley growing, having forgotten that he had shaken out the remains of some hen-food from a sack months before, and thought for a moment that 'God had miraculously caus'd this Grain to grow'. It was the moment where Crusoe began to realise that he could re-create his identity as an Englishman, an eater of bread and drinker of beer, a turning-point of the narrative. But Defoe had been wrong. Tropical colonists had not been able to grow wheat and barley for their bread and their beer; they had lived off imports from Virginia. The seventeenth century had made strong links between diet and character as well as diet and well-being: a place such as Barbados must have left them in perpetual fear of a fluxy leaching of identity, a *Tempest*-like melting and dissolving of everything they believed themselves to be. Perhaps they were right to fear; even protected as he was by the global culture of the third millennium, he had a sense that aspects of his personality were being transmuted in the crucible of Barbados.

He dropped into a supermarket on the way back; an odd little place perched half-way up a hill memorably precipitous even by local standards, with chickens scratching about outside and a Salvator Rosa-ish view of banana- and palm-clad slopes where the ground dropped away to the front. It turned out to sell quantities of pharmaceuticals, some of them archaic and unexpected – he had heard of, but had never before seen, gentian violet, coal tar, or flowers of sulphur – a good deal of miscellaneous ironmongery, and relatively little food. He browsed around, interested; there was rice in ten-kilo sacks, tinned vegetables, no fresh fish, but marble-like white slabs of saltfish, red herrings, which had previously come his way only as a metaphor, and by way of fresh meat, packs of particularly horrid-looking pigs' tails together with other curious bits and pieces: pigs' ears, chicken wings and gizzards. Fortunately, it also had what he was looking for, which was a bottle of wine: the choice was not extensive, but he found a reasonable-looking Californian zinfandel, for approximately double what a bottle of rum would have cost him. Pleased with himself, he went back to the hotel to shower and change.

When Melita opened the door and welcomed him in, he was gratified to observe that she had gone to some trouble, as he had himself. She was not, he suspected, a makeup sort of person, and she was wearing a simple cotton blouse and trousers, but she had put on pearl earrings and a little pearl pendant, which flattered her smooth dark skin, and as she stood back to let him pass, he caught a whiff of a fresh, flowery cologne. He handed over the bottle of wine; which was received with smiles and thanks.

'Would you like some?' she asked, setting the bottle down.

'Maybe a glass with supper? But I'd better start with something soft. Just water will do. Or anything that isn't very sweet.'

'Would you like to try mauby? It's kind of old-fashioned, but I like it.'

'Certainly.' Mauby turned out to be something of a ritual. Melita poured some heavy, dark syrup into a jug and added water, then poured it out into a glass, holding the jug as high as she could, and poured it back again, repeating the manoeuvre several times before dropping ice into the glass and handing it to him. After all that, it turned out to taste a bit like cold, stewed sweet tea, though admittedly nicer; there was a pleasantly aromatic quality, and an attractive bitterness. Melita mixed a glass for herself, and came and sat down.

'What's it made of?' he asked.

'The bark of a tree, *Colubrina elliptica*, boiled up with spices. And sugar of course.'

'Is it in Balthasar's book? Ligon mentions "mobby", but to him, it's a fermented drink made out of sweet potatoes.'

'No, or at least, I can't identify it. Some of the names for plants are the same as the ones Grandpa Walrond used, but not all of them, and if mauby meant something else in his day, it's no wonder he doesn't give it. The book's really interesting. Quite a lot of our flora came over from West Africa with the slaves, and he knows what those plants were used for, so he must've been talking to slaves. For instance, he mentions man-piabba – he uses it for fevers and as a vermifuge. It's native to Africa, but it's grown here since slavery times. My grandpa still uses it for worms. And Balthasar knew some Caribs too – he mentions that you can make arrow-poison from the root of the Barbados lily, which is a real give-away, because the Caribs hunted with poisoned arrows.'

'This is fascinating,' said Michael. 'So you can reconstruct who he was talking to from what he knew.'

'Just about. Anyway, if you'll excuse me, I'll just go and deal with the rice.'

Dinner consisted of a chicken and vegetable stir-fry, and a fruit salad, much the sort of food which Michael might have cooked himself. As they ate, they talked about their lives, and Melita shed some of her reserve.

'This isn't an easy country to come back to,' she confessed, serving him with fruit salad. 'People see it as you thinking the place isn't good enough for you. I grew up loving the country, but when I was with other people, I felt I wasn't allowed to belong, and I always had to watch my mouth. When I had the chance of going to school somewhere else, I had to take it, though I knew it would make my social problem even worse. I realised I needed to get away and get some perspective.'

'It was much the same for me,' he said. 'My father ran a public school. That sounds very grand, I suppose, but it wasn't. People think you mean somewhere like Eton, but St Ninian's was deeply minor-league. The thing about public schools is they're supposed to teach you how to live collectively and be part of a team, but I was the headmaster's son, so I went home at night, which meant I was always an outsider. Then of course, outside term, the other boys went away and I was just stuck there with Mum and my father. We didn't go away much; I don't know what he actually earned, but he hated spending money, and anyway, he wasn't very fit. He just wanted to stay at home. When I got to Oxford, it was like the Great Escape.'

'Did you have brothers and sisters?' she asked.

'No. I'm an only child. So are you, aren't you?'

'I'm the only child of my parents, but Dad had a couple of kids by a woman in London before he died, and Mama had four more by Papa Eustace, who's my stepfather. Most of them are grown and gone now, and two of them have kids of their own. I'm in touch with my London brothers, though we haven't met, and of course I was brought up with Mama's children.'

'Gosh. So you've got six half-siblings.'

'Seven, actually. There's an outside child of Papa Eustace's who was brought up with us.'

'How do you keep track of it all?'

'It's not always easy. But family's important here. You must've been lonely. And you didn't know any girls, is that right? School was just boys?'

'That's right. It must sound very strange. Father was very down on my getting to know local girls. It was partly that he wanted me to concentrate on my work, but also, he argued that if I got involved with someone in Cartmel, the girl would be the one to suffer, because I was going off to a different kind of life. He thought it wasn't fair, and I saw the point, even if I didn't like it. It wasn't as if there were that many girls in Cartmel anyway. But I didn't have female friends, let alone girlfriends, till I went to university.'

'That maybe explains why you act like women are human beings,' commented Melita. 'Boys are pretty dreadful, and they make each other worse. Because you weren't running around with a gang, you never learned to treat us like doll-babies.'

'That's looking on the bright side. But thanks.'

'We all got our problems. People think I'm too fussy. I was brought up to take a pride in myself, and I was out of the island for long enough I feel I don't have to settle for badness if I can't get good. Don't worry about yourself.' She pushed back her chair. 'Would you like a cup of tea, or anything else?'

'Tea would be lovely.' He stacked the dishes neatly and carried them through to her tiny kitchen while she boiled the kettle.

'Thanks,' she said, looking rather surprised.

'Melita, I've been thinking about this business of your being the rightful queen,' he said, once they were sitting down again. 'I think I understand your intellectual objections to the basic principle. "Long-lost-prince" stories assume that there's a sort of gold thread of royalness which goes through the generations, like apostolic succession or something. You've explained quite clearly why that doesn't make sense scientifically, but you see, it doesn't have to, because it's actually magical, or religious, if you like. It's the idea that God singled out a particular bloodline as the rulers of the world. Do you remember the beginning of St Matthew's gospel, where you get about a page and a half of x begat y, and it all goes to prove that Jesus Christ was of the house and lineage of David?'

'I've never understood that bit,' said Melita. 'All that fuss about genealogy, then it turns out it's the genealogy of Joseph, who's not supposed to have fathered the Christ Child anyway.'

'You're right, aren't you! I'd forgotten that. But the point is, because this bit of Matthew defines one particular bloodline as special, it gives a sanction to the idea of monarchy, and that means medieval Europe took the idea seriously. Solomon had hundreds of wives and concubines, as I recall, so he presumably had hundreds of children. David certainly had quite a few. So by the time of Christ, there must have been thousands of people in Palestine who had David for an ancestor, but the way the story's shaped, God decreed that this one lineage was something different from all others. You've got the idea of David's kingliness sort of bubbling underground for thirty generations, then bursting out again.'

'It's interesting to see where the concept comes from,' she observed. 'I never thought about it before. I just set my face against it when I was young, because Grandpapa was dinning it in my ear and everyone else was laughing. I took science to get away from it. It sounds like you've been studying about this for a while, though?'

'You're not the only one with mad relatives,' he said with feeling. 'I haven't told you about my mother's uncle yet. Harold's devoted his whole life to the idea of this ultimate royal line. As far as he's concerned, it starts with King David, and goes through Christ, who secretly married Mary Magdalene and became the ancestor of the early kings of France. He's just managed to get King Arthur worked into it all, which he's very pleased about, and then it somehow all ends up with the Stuarts. I'll spare you the details. Anyway, when Father retired, my parents moved to Silloth, which is where my mother's family comes from. Harold's lived there all his life, and Mum wanted to be near him. She was fond of him, I think, but it's also relevant that he's very wealthy. His father owned a lot of the land around Silloth, and sold it for development when the town started expanding in the 1920s. Personally, I've always told myself he'll leave his money to the Rosicrucians, which he probably will, but I have to admit that my parents wanted to stay in his line of sight. And the result of that is that in the last fifteen years I've heard more than any reasonable person could stand about royal genealogy.'

'Oh, that explains why you know so much about it all. You aren't exactly a fanatic yourself, though?'

'No. I thought he was barmy, and I still do. I don't suppose you've read anything about the bloodline of the Holy Grail, you wouldn't be interested, but I read the book which started it all when I was young, and even at eighteen or so I could see it was pants. Of course, I'd just won a place at Oxford, so I was feeling obnoxiously superior, and I tried to convince Uncle Harold he was basing his thinking on hopelessly unsatisfactory premises. I didn't even annoy him. He just smiled in his gentle, superior way and said, "Of course, my boy, you are very young." I could've throttled him.'

Melita was laughing. 'That's the one thing you can't counter, when you're just standing there, a snotty little brat full of education. Grandpapa used to say, "When you're my age, girl, you'll see the sense in it." I had to bottle up my smart remarks, or I'd have felt his hand.'

'I've mellowed since then. I even look up some of the weirdness sites on the net once in a while, so we'll have something to talk about, but I remember feeling very hurt when I was younger. I thought that because I was a baby intellectual, the world owed me some respect. There are public schools where being good at games counts for just about everything, but St Ninian's wasn't one of them. We were serious about exams, and the Oxbridge Entrance group felt we were being sort of groomed for stardom. I suppose it sounds ridiculous, but it was a very sheltered life, and in the world of school, everyone thought we really mattered. Uncle Harold was the first person who really showed me that people weren't going to let me adjust their ideas just because I knew better. Put like that, I must sound an evil little bastard, but I don't think I was.'

'I don't think you sound evil. You're just being honest. It's hard, being a clever kid. All those hours you spend with your head in your books, when the people you know are having a life. You've got to tell yourself it matters.'

'I'm beginning to wonder if it does, or if that's just another of the stories we tell children. My father used to think there was a sort of educated élite who ran things, and I was supposed to grow up and be part of it. But that's not what it feels like now I've actually done it. I love the research, and I like the teaching, but the rest is just awful. Most of the professional people I know are having a horrible time. I've sometimes thought of jacking in the whole thing and starting a company called Gadgets & Widgets. I mean, if you can create a multi-million pound empire based on socks, which God knows are boring, you ought to be able to make a living off ironmongery, which nearly everyone likes.'

'There's too many of us,' she said. 'Once you extend education to the masses, you need so many educators they just can't have the old status, because governments couldn't afford it. Anyway, education's not the same thing as intelligence. Only, the thing about white-collar types is that they're prepared to invest in their children. I don't know about England, but here and in Canada, you find schools are full of middle-class kids who've been taught how to stay inside the system.'

'It rings a bell,' he admitted. 'I read somewhere that there are more accountants in Britain now than miners. It's hard to believe that actually makes sense.'

'OK. So what we have now is colleges turning out legions of these people who are white-collar without really being all that bright, so they need jobs which are based on supervising or measuring or accounting for what someone else does. The justification is you can't be sure if a system's successful unless it's monitored, so now we're all in the power of clerks.'

'That's a very bleak way of looking at it,' he said. 'You're suggesting that the Tite Barnacles have won.'

'Tite Barnacles?'

'Sorry. I'm quoting again. Dickens's emblematic middle-class parasites on the social structure. So you think nothing's ever going to get any better?'

'How can it? Once a system's invested in accountability, either it's self-perpetuating, or it dissolves into anarchy. I wouldn't mind so much, if I thought it made any difference and the playing-field was actually level, but it doesn't, and it isn't.'

'Talking of level playing-fields,' said Michael with some hesitation, 'it's maybe a bit heavy for after dinner, but when we were talking the other day, I got the impression you didn't think racial difference really exists. Or did I misunderstand? You were also saying you were African, so you obviously do think it matters to some extent?' His conversation with Natty Polgreen, and Natty's reaction to his story, were uppermost in his mind, but he was not particularly keen to discuss it with her directly – he hesitated at the thought of explaining that he had been discussing her private affairs with another Barbadian, given that, as he was rapidly discovering, the place was about as gossip-ridden as his old school.

'Well, we were talking about monarchy too,' she said. 'And we're both quite sure that monarchy doesn't make sense, but that doesn't mean it doesn't exist in the real world. Race is like that, I think. It's one of the things people use to make sense of their world.'

'A story.'

'Yes, I think so. I mean, of course there are lots of distinct human types. There's a Bajan face, you've maybe noticed.'

'Yes, I have. Dark skin and African-type hair, but a rather European shape of face, with a short nose and a square jaw?'

'That's right. If I saw someone who looked like that in Canada, ten to one, if I had a chance to get chatting, they turned out to be Bajans, or have Bajan parents. And if you said someone looked typically Irish or typically Italian, it would mean something. But that's what animal breeders would call strains. People act as if race is something fundamental, connected with huge issues like temperament and IQ, but when you get down to the genetic level, it just dissolves. The average genetic difference between whites and blacks as two populations is smaller than the difference between any two individuals, even if they're brother and sister. We're a very uniform species.'

'Then why do people think it matters so much?'

'Because if you pretend social facts are biological facts, it gives them authority. I've spent this whole evening saying Bajans think like this, Bajans look like that, and Bajans don't like you getting above yourself, but that's not anything to do with race, it's just the local culture. The thing is, there isn't ever enough well-paid, interesting work to go around. So if the majority culture decides in advance their minorities are uneducable on account of race, there's no need to invest in education programmes, they save on taxes, and the good jobs go to their own kids. It's win-win, from their point of view.'

'It all seems so unfair. Melita, do you think there's anything to be done about any of this?'

She did not answer. Instead, she took her glasses off and polished them, and he wondered anxiously if in his desire to show he was taking her seriously, he was boring her stupid. He glanced at his watch, and received a severe shock. 'Oh, God. Is that the time? I'm terribly sorry.'

'That's all right,' she said. 'I wasn't noticing.' She looked at him directly, then away; a softer look than the challenging stare he was becoming accustomed to. He could feel his heart banging against his ribs. He reached out and took the glasses from her gently, putting them out of harm's way on a bookcase. She made no move to stop him.

'I was looking at Ligon's *History of Barbados*,' he said. 'Another of my old books. He met a black woman in the Cape Verdes, on his way over here, and he couldn't get over how beautiful her eyes were. "The largest and most oriental I have ever seen."'

'Do you have a quote for every occasion, Michael?'

'Sorry. If you teach English, you get into the habit.'

'Well, it's better than "God, you're lovely without your glasses".'

'But you are. Lovely, I mean. Glasses and all.'

Her full mouth twisted down at the corners. 'Don't they tell you about clichés in Oxford?'

'Melita, you're bloody well bright enough to pick up subtexts. I like quotations. They're good for hiding behind.'

She smiled at him, the smile he remembered from his dream, and he stood up.

'Do you want me to go?' he demanded.

Melita stood up in her turn and came over to him. Now she

was standing so close, he realised she only came up to his chin; because of her good posture, he had thought she was taller. 'You don't have to,' she said, provokingly calm.

'I thought you were choosy,' he said. 'Do you make a habit of this?' He was powerfully aroused and longed to touch her, but he was terrified. Had he misread her completely? It seemed unlikely, but on such a short acquaintance, could he be sure?

She stepped back a little, when he did not reach out to her, and looked him in the eye, with her hands on her hips. 'No. But that doesn't mean I'm never going to choose.'

'Melita, you've got to realise I'm falling for you.'

'Is that a warning?'

'Probably. I'm asking you if you're messing me about? I'm not a casual person.'

She gave a little nod, as if something had been confirmed. 'Neither am I. I'm not fast, I do like to take my time, but I know you're only here for another couple of weeks, and to me, that changes the rules. I've had you on my mind all day. The way you've let me have my space, listened to what I was saying. What you've said just now, even. If we took to friendsing, we'd hate to have wasted a week just courting, don't you think? I sort of like you, and I've been lonely.' She stepped forward and tilted her face up to kiss him lightly on the cheek. 'Give it a go?'

X

O what an easie thing is to descry
The gentle bloud, how ever it be wrapt
In sad misfortunes foul deformity
And wretched sorrowes, which have often hapt.
For howsoever it may grow mis-shapt
Like this wyld man being undisciplyned
That to all virtue it may seem unapt
Yet will it shew some sparks of gentle mynd
And at the last breake forth in his own proper kynd.

Edmund Spenser, *The Faerie Queene*, VI.v.1

Since she had handed in her thesis at last, Corinne was temporarily liberated from the university. Half her time was still spent on her paid work for 'Logistik', but the preliminary sorting-out she was doing towards the Middelburg project could just as easily be done at home on her own computer, so although it was only a week or so since her emancipation, the overcrowded university office and its scratchy relationships already felt like part of the past. She had spoken to a couple of her neighbours for the first time in months, she had time to go to a café once in a while, or even a film, and pick up threads with various acquaintances; generally, she felt as if she was beginning to get a life again.

Coming out of work one day, thinking about nothing but the groceries she intended to buy on her way home, she was disagreeably surprised by a familiar voice.

'Corinne!'

Startled, she looked up. Cees was walking towards her, inter-
cepting her from a stake-out position under a chestnut-tree. He
looked somehow different from her memory of him; and as he
came nearer, she realised he had lost the air of smugness which
had been driving her mad.

'Oh, hi,' she said without enthusiasm. 'What do you want?'

'Corinne, I have to talk to you.'

She glanced at him dubiously. Close to, he was looking ill and
slightly crazy. It had to come, she supposed, and she began thinking
furiously how best to manage him. She kept moving, and he fell
into step beside her. 'I haven't a lot of time, but we'd better find
somewhere we can sit down,' she said. 'There's quite a nice café
just along the Gracht. They've got some tables down by the water,
so it's quiet, and we can talk.'

'Fine,' he said shortly, and fell silent; he did not speak again
until they were seated, and the waiter had gone off with their
order for tea and coffee. 'Corinne,' he began abruptly, 'what the
hell is going on?'

'I'm sorry?'

'Don't play the innocent. You know what I mean. I hardly saw
Derksen all summer.'

'But he was always like that with me,' said Corinne, and wished
she hadn't. Fortunately it made no difference; he was too upset to
be listening.

'I started to get the impression he was actually avoiding me.
Then you remember my *promotie*?'

'Yes, of course,' said Corinne, with a cold feeling that she did
not want to know what might be coming next. In accordance with
one of the ironclad rules of Dutch academic life, Cees had invited
her to the formal public defence of his thesis (a similar event lay
in her own future) and to the drinks-party afterwards, though not
to the subsequent dinner. It would have been unforgivably rude
not to turn up, but having sat through the viva, she had given

Cees a token present, and slipped away from his party after one drink. Anything could have happened after that.

'It was awful. And what was worse was I thought it was going to be the high point of my life.'

'You did a really good defence,' said Corinne, hoping to distract him. 'I thought your response to that man from Leiden was brilliant.'

He looked at her, and she fell silent. 'It was at the dinner afterwards. Dad was talking to Derksen, and said something about my future, being pleasant, you know? And Derksen went brick-red, he just changed colour like a traffic light, and said it was too soon to be talking about all that. Then afterwards he couldn't get away fast enough. Dad was devastated. He felt he'd made a fool of himself because I'd given him a completely different impression of the relationship. He was wondering if I'd been lying to them, I could see it in his face.'

Corinne could see only too well, and she felt a bit sick. Yes, he had been graceless and pushy, but he hadn't deserved that. Nobody did.

'Derksen was acting as if I'd done something terrible,' pursued Cees wretchedly. 'But I knew I hadn't, so I started doing some digging around. I've got friends in Admin., you know. And you know what I found. This massive grant proposal going forward, with Derksen's name on it, and the university's end of the commitment will use the whole of the allocation for Book History. He hadn't even told me about it, so it's obvious he's dropped me flat. But this new project can't've been his idea. He hasn't the energy for anything new, we both know that, so it's got to be you that's behind it all. How the hell did you talk him into it? Are you screwing him or something?'

'Don't be grotesque,' snapped Corinne. The waiter arrived with their order, and they suspended hostilities, glaring, until he went away.

'It's nothing to do with sex, and it's nothing to do with you,

Cees,' she said, shaking a little inside, and thankful for having been given a moment to think out her response. 'The fact is, the Middelburg project needs some specific kinds of expertise. IT experience, English, and post-colonial. It's just not your world. Don't blame me if Derksen's been too embarrassed to tell you. You know what he's like. You've watched him giving me the cold shoulder for two solid years, ever since he decided he couldn't be bothered to try and scare up money to keep me.'

'Don't give me that. Just why does the new project need this set of skills, you conniving cow? You must've drafted the proposal, and I'm sure you hand-crafted the project to suit you. I should've known something was up when I saw you with those microfilms. You said you weren't working on the stuff, but you must've been lying your head off.'

'You don't know anything about it,' she snapped, losing her temper. 'You haven't seen the documents. You didn't offer to help. Not bloody likely. You were too busy with all that important stuff you do, and you sneered at me for getting interested in things.'

Cees did not reply directly. After a short silence, he said with the impressiveness of complete sincerity, 'Corinne, you have ruined my life.'

'Oh, no. Not me. It was pure luck. Something came up which gave me an advantage, so of course I used it. I've got a life too, you know. Blame Derksen, if you like. He could've tried to build you a place, you know, and he hasn't. He's written you off because he can't be bothered any more, the way he wrote me off, till I fell over the Middelburg project. Now you know how I've felt for the last two years, with you smirking at me, rubbing my nose in it.'

Cees picked absently at a spot on his chin, and Corinne, at once sympathetic and revolted, realised that he was not far from tears. 'That's not fair,' he protested. 'It's completely different for me, because it's all I've ever wanted to do. You've got other skills.'

She was sympathetic, but she was also exasperated. That was

too much. 'Don't pretend you were thinking about me. You just went for what you wanted. Well, so have I, but I've made a better job of it.' Distractedly, she wondered why she felt so bad. If Cees had eased her out, and he was making no secret that he would have if he could, he wouldn't have wasted a minute's thought on her. Yet somehow, his absolute sense that it wasn't the same was something she couldn't wave away.

'Crap. I've been effective,' he argued, a little of his old aggressiveness coming back. 'I've organised my time well, while you've been swanning around, picking up something here and something there as if you thought it was some kind of game. How was I to know you were serious?'

'You don't know anything about me.'

'Yes I do. You're the bitch who's stolen my future.'

'Cees, it wasn't yours. You just thought it was.'

But the tears had come; first a huge, childish sob; then suddenly he was quivering in blind grief, pouring tears and snot and mopping frantically at his face, while she sat frozen with embarrassment. She looked at her cooling tea; it would be unkind to start drinking it while he was in such a state, but she longed for a little stimulation.

'Cees, you can find another professor,' she said, proffering what comfort she could, once he had got himself under control. 'There must be someone somewhere who's interested in the Eighty Years War. You've done lots of good work, and it's a major area.'

'Don't be so stupid,' he spat, rejecting consolation. 'You know perfectly well that everything I've done's aimed at extending Derksen's work in the next generation. He owes me his loyalty because he knows I'm his natural successor. That's what really hurts – it's not just me he's betrayed, it's himself. You don't care about his work, and you're not loyal. If all this goes ahead you'll just drop everything we've done with the Antwerp trade, and he'll never finish it on his own.'

'I never knew you cared like that,' said Corinne in surprise. 'I thought you were just ambitious.'

Cees blew his nose and stared at her with angry, red-rimmed eyes. 'Of course I care. It's my life.' The thought threatened to set him off again, but he got himself under control.

'I'm sure you'll find a project you can join,' said Corinne again. 'You're very talented.'

'But I'll have to start all over again. And if I find someone, he'll already have people of his own. And my girlfriend's here.'

'Yes, well, that's what the system's like. But you can beat it, you know. People sometimes do.'

Cees scrubbed his swollen face with his hands. 'I'm going to end up teaching in a school.'

Corinne took a long swallow of tea, her own eyes pricking at the blank despair in his voice. 'I'm truly sorry, Cees. I think Derksen's been vile. It's not right of him to drop you like that.'

'I thought he liked me,' said Cees, sounding like a hurt child.

'I think he does in his way. But he's lost interest really, he's just living for his pension. This project's going to be something prestigious to keep him busy till he retires, and that's all he cares about. He could've been asking for more money to look at a comparison with Antwerp, you know, to give you something. No guarantee he'd've got it, but he didn't even try.'

'He's not been well lately,' said Cees, with automatic defensiveness.

'Cees,' said Corinne urgently, 'it's time you stopped believing in him. The truth is, you're more interested in his work than he is. He knows he's behaved badly, and that's why he doesn't want to see you, you just make him feel guilty. I don't want to give you advice when you're angry with me, but I have to say, be careful not to remind him he owes you, or he'll turn on you. Try and stay away from him till you can go to him with some kind of positive proposal.'

'He was a fine scholar,' said Cees.

Corinne picked up the elegiac tone. Cees was letting go of Daddy, and about time too. She hesitated; wondering if she should say that there would be money for someone to input texts, at least part-time. It was highly skilled work: she'd be doing some of it herself. But whoever took the job would have to be working under her direction . . . she decided that at that moment, it would be throwing petrol on the flames. He'd see the job when it was advert-ised, and if he thought he could put his pride in his pocket, he'd apply for it. If not, not.

'Yes, he was,' she said. 'But his last real book was fifteen years ago, and he's a disappointed, lazy man. He's had his best times, like last week's milk.'

Cees almost smiled. 'Curdled, you mean? You're maybe right.'

'I'm truly sorry we've been set against each other like this,' she said, and realised it was true. In another world, they might even have been friends.

'Melita,' said Michael, squinting in the sun. She was smiling down at him, standing naked beside the bed: she had just opened the blinds and the light was pouring in around her. 'Good morning.' He reached out and caught her round the knees, tugging gently, not hard enough to overbalance her. 'You wouldn't care to come back to bed, would you?'

'Could be. But you might want to go and freshen up?'

'What a tactful soul you are. Back in a minute.'

When he came back, she was lying at full length, her arms behind her head, looking at him. He liked her solidity and strength, the long sleek lines of her body, adorned with round, high breasts. Though her lips and skin were miraculously soft, she did not seem even slightly fragile . . . Melita smiled and reached out to him, and he abandoned any further attempt to analyse her individual appeal.

Later, when they were drinking tea companionably, he aired a question which was troubling him a little. 'Melita, was that OK for you? I mean . . . Look, I'm trying to think of the best way to put this. Urban legend has it that black men are a lot sexier. I hope I didn't disappoint you.'

She put out her tongue at him saucily, just the pink tip. 'Boy talk. You're just looking for flattery.'

'I'm not, actually.'

'You're fine. You want to trust yourself.'

'I do want to trust myself, darling, but I don't find it easy. I'd like to make you happy.'

Melita sighed, looking a little concerned. 'You're a very nice person, Michael. What's hurt you so much?'

'I've told you. My father. My mother. The usual stuff.' He was still privately astonished by himself.

She sipped her tea and took her time before replying. He looked at her profile as she sat beside him; her blunt nose and firm lips made him think of a serious little cat. 'Don't worry,' she said eventually. 'I think you're just what I need. I've been thinking for a while it might be easier for me to go out with a foreigner. Partly because you're an outside man, and you don't know anyone here but me, so there's no one going to be running their mouths about us, and partly 'cause I know you won't make so many assumptions. It's people making assumptions that kills your heart.'

'I know what you mean. That feeling you get when you're dealing with someone who acts as if they know the rules and you don't.' Her comment made an unexpectedly deep impression on him. He thought of Eimer, Corinne, and still earlier girlfriends, Rebecca and Marie-Claude . . . because Melita was black, he realised suddenly, he had been surprised to find himself so drawn towards her, but now that he thought about it, he could see that the attraction was part of a pattern. Looking back, all the women he had ever really fancied had been, in some definable way, exotic, there had been some major difference in nationality, background, or religion. Interesting; and she had just given him a reason why.

Meanwhile, they would have to get up soon. As he had been relieved to discover the previous night, Melita, with the down-to-earth practicality which seemed characteristic of her, had provided herself with a pack of vending-machine condoms. There had only been three, so more must certainly be acquired. In any case, he was dying for a shower. The opened window had let in the sun, but no cooling breezes. It was a lot hotter in Cave Hill than it was under the trade winds on the east coast, and Melita's tiny flat had no air-conditioning. Sweat was running down his chest; the morning's lovemaking had been a slippery, salty affair.

'What's the shape of your day, Melita?' he asked.

'I need to do some shopping, and then I've got a little work to do in the lab. How would you feel about coming into the university? There won't be a lot of people around at this time of year, so I don't think anyone will see us. Or do you want to go back to your hotel?'

'Could I use a networked computer? I can't connect up my modem at the hotel, because there's just a public phone, and I hate to think what my inbox looks like.'

'Sure. There's one in my office. If you want to do email and all that stuff, you're welcome.'

'Yes. I'd like to do that, if you think I'm presentable.'

She glanced at his discarded clothes. 'I'll get the iron out, and freshen those a little.'

'Bless you. I think I'd better go and wash.' He got up and went back into the tiny bathroom. There were bras and panties hung about the shower-cabinet, and he wondered where to put them while he used it.

'Sorry about that,' said Melita, coming through and whisking them away. 'There's a clothes-line down in the yard, but we've been having trouble with theft, I don't like to leave stuff down there.'

'Do people steal used clothes? Or are you talking about some kind of knicker-bandit?'

'People will steal anything that isn't nailed down. This is a poor country.'

He stepped under the shower, in thoughtful mood. When he emerged, wishing he had a toothbrush, Melita came back in to shower in her turn. 'Is that why people's yards have those huge iron fences?' he asked.

'Of course.'

It set Barbadian reserve and privacy in a starker light. There were plenty of poor people in Oxford, but to the best of his knowledge, they were hardly likely to nip over walls to steal second-hand underwear, let alone onions. Certainly in Silloth, though theft from allotments was an endemic irritation, no one would actually invade your back garden, not just for that. For a moment, he felt very foreign.

Melita had ironed his shirt and trousers and sprinkled them with some kind of floral freshener; the effect was a bit girly, though he appreciated the effort, but at least it was an advance on yesterday's sweat. In the course of the day, he must get back to the east coast for fresh clothes, though unless he got strong signals to the contrary, he had every intention of spending the night in Desert Rose Drive. The intensely respectable hotel, he was certain, would take a dim view of his turning up with a woman, and in any case, form so far suggested that if he did, someone on the staff would know someone who knew one of Melita's relatives in Bathsheba, who would know all about it by the time breakfast was over.

He stepped into the little kitchen, and took a look round. There were some vegetables in a basket on the counter, so he took a carrot to chew in lieu of brushing his teeth. She did not keep much in the house; there were tins of rather bleak staples such as corned beef and tuna, a large bin of rice, some flour and so forth, with very

little except milk, canned drinks, and the inevitable hot-sauce in the
fridge. It was all very neat, much tidier than his own flat, and everything perishable was stored in labelled, sealed, plastic containers.

He heard a footstep and turned. Melita was standing there
wearing white Bermuda shorts and a blue-and-white top, she
looked fresh and pretty. 'Thank you for doing my clothes,' he said.
'Will I do?'

She came over and squeezed his bottom in a friendly fashion.
'You'll do fine.'

The Cave Hill campus turned out to be very much what he had
been expecting, rather American in overall feel, scruffy and utilitarian. The oddest thing about it was that, though it was a stone's
throw from the coast, it contrived to turn its back on the sea.
They parked the car, walked past some deserted sports fields and
then Melita led them through a breeze-block labyrinth, from which
they emerged to cross a little courtyard and enter a very smart
new building, freshly painted in bright colours, and with a plant-
filled atrium which looked as if it belonged to a hotel.

'Biology's quite high profile here,' she explained. 'Our head
professor's the vice-principal, and he's good at getting resources
for us. He's in marine biology, but the whole faculty gets to benefit.'

He followed her up the stairs and into an office, shared, he
observed, though there was nobody else about. She pulled up a
chair, activated her computer and connected it to the Web.

'There you are,' she said. 'I'm going across to the lab. Are you
OK here for a couple of hours?'

'Absolutely fine,' he said. 'There's plenty I can do. Is there
anything I can use for rough notes?'

She found him some paper, kissed him, and went about her business. He got into his email, the first essential, before his mailbox
overflowed with useless information. Deleting right and left
without compunction, he was pleased to find messages from
Theodoor and Corinne lurking amid the spam.

Corinne. It was strange to think about her, here in Barbados, sitting in Melita's chair. In his newfound happiness he felt more kindly disposed towards her than he had for a long time, but it was Theodoor he really wanted to talk to, so he opened his email first. 'We are all through with examinations, you also, I think,' Theodoor began abruptly:

I have been looking at Pelagius's thesis, which is remarkably interesting. With immense intellectual daring, the work sets out to integrate the spiritual life of his own people with Christian revelation. It is deeply learned and complex, and in future years, I think this may come to seem the most important of all the works which have been uncovered by this study. I have certainly not got time to edit it as it deserves, so I have spoken to Corinne and warned her that the oeuvre of Pelagius (i.e. the thesis, the diary, the botany, the divinations) now form a substantial and very important research project in themselves, which she must bear in mind when she is looking for funding. This would also 'kill two birds', as I think you say in England, because I have been trying to find a post for a very talented young man who has no sponsor through no fault of his own. Meanwhile, I have returned to working on the *Notatiunculae*, and I have found a passage which I thought might possibly bear on Behn's play, and another which puzzles me. I have translated them both and now send them to you:

'Is not the journey of the Israelites a type of our pilgrimage? Is not their journey from Egypt to Canaan, a sign of our passage from bondage to liberty, from darkness to light, from a vale of tears to the joys of heaven? The lord sent a precursor, that Joseph who was sold for a servant, whose feet they hurt with fetters, who was laid in iron. Until the time that his word came: the word of the Lord tried him. The king sent and loosed him, even the ruler of the people, and let him go free. He made him lord of his house, and ruler of all his substance, to bind his princes at their pleasure, and teach his senators wisdom. Thus the way is made straight for the Lord's appointed one.'

Much of this is from Psalm 105, by the way. Pelagius seems here to allude to his status as a prince, and his belief that he is awaiting a great reversal of fortune.

My second passage is this: 'as in the painting of Quercitanus, I stand before the Lord, doubting/uncertain whether my offering will be accepted.'

'Quercitanus' is a name which was used by the French alchemist Du Chesne, it means, of course, 'the man of the oak'. I can think of no seventeenth-century painter of any country with a name which has to do with oak-trees, and I do not know what he means.

How are things with you? Here in the Netherlands we are still trying to understand the country's shift to the right following the assassination of that reckless man Fortuyn. We are not, I hope, falling into simple xenophobia: I think we must understand Fortuyn's legacy as an appeal for us to maintain our cultural consensus, the true spirit of Dutchness. We must make our Muslim immigrants into Netherlanders, able to cherish our values along-side their own, and not let them form a community of resistance within our society, so we must listen before we talk. I wish we saw more Muslim students in the humanities; they are common enough in the sciences, but we see very few in our faculty, and without Muslim humanists, we cannot reach common ground.

We heard very little about your Royal Jubilee over here, but I think it was not a great moment of sentiment for many people? I feared it might encourage your countrymen to look backwards, which is a tendency everywhere in Europe at the moment. There is a nostalgia for a simpler world, I fear, which holds many dangers. Meanwhile, we must do the task which is nearest – it serves as a reminder that even three hundred years ago, the world was already very complex.

Hartelijke groeten, Theodoor.

Michael sat looking at the screen, and wondered where to start. As far as Theodoor knew, he was merely editing *The Female Rosicrucian*. Just how was he going to tell him that, as a result of Aphra Behn's appearance in his life, he was now in Barbados, and in love with the rightful Queen of England? He was interested in all the points which Theodoor made, part of the long-running conversation they seemed to have fallen into, and above all, he was interested in Pelagius. The marriage- and birth-certificates he had found in Middelburg cast a different light on Pelagius's hopes, which seemed to him to centre on the idea of himself as a precursor whose sufferings would be rewarded not in his own lifetime, but in that of his son, or his descendant. The passage before him seemed to confirm this reading, which delighted him. But more than anything, he longed to confide. He hit the reply button, and began to type.

Dear Theodoor, I never thought I'd find myself saying I was looking forward to reading a tome on Reformation theology, but it sounds gripping. I ought to answer you properly, but I'll do that another time. When I saw your name in my inbox, I realised you were the one person I wanted to tell (it does have to do with Pelagius in a way): I'm sending you this email from Barbados, where I've fallen in love with Pelagius's great-great-great-great-great-great-great-great-great-granddaughter. So now I've told somebody, I know it's true. As to how it happened . . . I'm beginning to feel very guilty about not sharing my finds but honestly one thing has led to another. I went back to Middelburg that last time I was over, and turned up another couple of documents – Corinne hasn't seen them unless she's been back. Pelagius married Elizabeth Stuart, the Winter Queen. I didn't tell you at the time, because I wanted to find out what happened next, but this amazing marriage explains quite a lot about Pelagius's narrative, I think – you can see how he might have come to feel specially marked out by fate. They had a son, which we guessed from *Notatiunculae*, but what I've found out since then is that he survived and went to London, his grandson went to Barbados, and the last descendant's still here. I've been working out the story in fits and starts, and I kept putting off telling you till I got to the end of the story which I did last Sunday: Melita was able to take it from the 18th to the 20th century, thanks to an antiquarian grandfather. I have to say she's not in the least interested in being a descendant, but I can see Pelagius in her. She's very honest, she thinks things through, and she's stubborn. I'm sure you'd like her.

Barbados has shaken me up a lot. Theodoor, I'm sorry if I'm being a bore. I've looked over this email, and it's all me, me, me – I'm not feeling very coherent. I'll try and pull myself together in a day or so, but just for now, I'm living in the present and utterly happy. Love, M.

PS. I'll think about Quercitanus.

He opened Corinne's mail next, and found that she had sent him an account of progress which, as he recalled the state of affairs when they had last been in touch, must represent something of a personal triumph. The PhD was finally in, which in itself must be a huge weight off her mind, but still more importantly, she had written a grant proposal and persuaded Derksen to put it forward. Nothing was absolutely in the bag, but the liaison she had achieved between the Middelburg archive people and the university made for a very strong case, and she was getting positive signals from everyone with a say in the matter. She sounded infinitely more cheerful than she had done when he had last seen her — it was clear that she did not seriously imagine that the project would fail to go ahead. She ended by asking, how was he? How was work going on the play?

Michael considered for a while, and began his answer.

Wonderful news about the grant application, I'll be crossing my fingers for you. Aphra's coming along — and I'm involved in a spin-off which may strengthen your hand in the sense of attracting attention, though not directly relevant: Pelagius was secretly married to Elizabeth of Bohemia later in her life — the marriage record turned up in Middelburg when I went up for another look. I don't think you had time when you were in Middelburg to look up the persons index, but there's some evidence for the son which I've been chasing — in fact there's a clear chain of descent going down to the present day. All sort of issues here but it certainly makes things more interesting.

He looked at the message. It got the main point over, with any luck neither she nor Theodoor should be huffy about him sitting on facts which they needed. Anyway a gentle little reminder to Corinne that he'd got as far as he had by being thorough was maybe not out of place.

The third actual message he found among the spam was a brief and discouraging note from Professor Edzell.

Michael, we have problems. Ellen's taken a thing about the Campaign for Real Fiction, and you know what happens when she gets a bee in her bonnet. She's doing a lot of work talking us down, so my guess is, miracles aside, we're dead in the water. I think the best thing is to put it to one side & wait a couple of years. A lot of things are going to be easier when she retires, poor woman. Over & out, R.

He had been half-expecting this, ever since the row he had had with Ellen Lorimer during the queen's Jubilee garden-party, but it was still intensely annoying. It was also disturbing; he was so disconcerted by the sheer energy the woman was prepared to put into negativity that he found himself thinking of her as the Goddess of Dulness. There was certainly something beyond ordinary dissent in her inveterate malignacy towards the idea of change and development in the Oxford English faculty.

He sat back, and gave the notion some thought. She had never married, she had no life that anyone knew of outside her college. Basic chronology suggested that she must have been a child of the early 1960s, just before the years of student revolt, and her current behaviour made it clear that she must have arrived at Oxford and looked at its powerful, privileged professors with the eyes of an idolater and not a sceptic. It was sheer hard luck on her that by the time she had joined the ranks of these godlike beings, professorial status no longer meant anything like what it had, either financially or in terms of social prestige. No wonder the poor silly cow clung like fury to the rags and tatters of obsolete glory. He hit the 'reply' button and began to type: Robert had done a certain amount of work on Pope, though he mostly worked on the nineteenth century, and he would appreciate the message.

> She comes! she comes! the sable Throne behold
> Of Night Primaeval, and of Chaos old!
> Before her, Fancy's gilded clouds decay,
> And all its varying rainbows die away.
> Nor public flame nor private dares to shine,
> Nor human spark is left, nor glimpse divine.

Lo! thy dread empire, Chaos, is restored

Light dies before thy uncreating word.

Just about says it all, don't you think? It's not as if the Campaign
for RF was exactly cutting edge . . . we were only trying to edge
the faculty gently into the 1980s or thereabouts. Did you know it
was Aphra Behn who coined the phrase 'sick as a parrot'? True.
Well as Aphra nearly said, I'm as bilious as a bloody budgie and I
bet you are too. I'm away at the moment: I'll see you when I get
back.

He felt a little better after that, so he dealt with a few minor
matters, and since Melita had still not returned, began messing
around on the Net, trawling for valuable old books being sold by
gullible American antique-dealers: he had scored an occasional
triumph in that context just often enough to make the game worth
playing. After a while, Melita put her head round the door.

'How're you doing?' she asked.

'Ready when you are. I'm just pissing about with Ebay.'

'I've actually got a bit more to do,' said Melita apologetically,
'but perhaps I could come back later?'

'Tell you what, love. If it's not a nuisance, I'll take you back
home, drop you off so you can pick up your own car, and go on
to the east coast. Then you can come back here under your own
steam, and you won't have to think about me. I'll come back to
Desert Rose Drive at sixish, in time to take you out to dinner.'

'You thinking of spending the night, then?'

'If you're asking.' He stood up, and she came fully into the room,
shutting the door carefully behind her.

'I'm asking,' she said, as he put his hands on her hips and pulled
her gently towards him.

'Then I'm staying.'

Some time later, he dropped Melita off in Wanstead Heights
and headed across the island, singing loudly and quite tunefully

to himself; 'Where'er you walk', an old school-choir favourite. Surely when every other car boomed with recorded music, nobody would mind. Perhaps all the botany he had been exposed to had brought it into his mind, or perhaps it was because he had been thinking about Pope . . . 'Trees whe-here you sit shall crowd into a sha-ha-hade, ha-ha-ha-ha-ha-hade . . .' He felt ridiculously pleased with himself; though sex with Melita leaned up against her desk had been successful only up to a point, the adolescentness of it had been strangely appealing. Perhaps he was belatedly making up for the unnatural virtue of his teens.

He was slightly relieved to find that there was nobody visibly about at the hotel, though he could hear voices from the kitchen. Doubtless conclusions had already been drawn from his night's absence, well, let them be. He showered again meticulously, took a couple of hours' nap (Melita's single bed was desperately uncomfortable for two, in the muggy heat of Bridgetown), packed his sponge-bag and a few clean clothes in his briefcase, then wrote a note for the manager to say that he did not expect to be in for meals unless he specifically said that he would be. He left it in the office on his way out, embarrassed, but feeling that he had done right. It was a very small place, after all, and it was clear from their general attitude that they would have views about waste.

For the rest of the week, he spent as much time with Melita as possible, blessing Harold Boumphrey for the fact that he did not need to worry about dining out every night. She insisted on working during the day, so, conscious of his duty to give value for money, he put in long hours in the archives, which, anyway, put him conveniently near Desert Rose Drive. He prowled the UWI bookstore, and caught up on some local reading; he found a couple of novels by Natty, which he quite enjoyed.

As soon as Melita finished with work, he came to join her and discovered her lighter side; together they larked about in the sea on her favourite beaches, sampled their way round the little cookshops of Baxter's Road and Oistins Market, where they ate cutters, rotis, conkies, flying-fish sandwiches, sugar-cakes and ice-cream, and above all, drove endlessly around the island, talking and talking, trying to explain their lives to one another, trying to pretend that time was not rushing by. On Friday afternoon, they were sitting on the sand in Cove Bay watching a group of little boys flying kites with great *élan*: beautiful kites, made to look like hawks, dragons and butterflies, when Melita suddenly came out with something which sounded like a prepared speech, as if she was raising a subject which had been on her mind for a while.

'Michael, I generally go to my mum's on Sunday. I didn't go last week because she was busy with a funeral.'

'Dear God,' he said. 'I've known you less than a week. What a thought. So you've got to go this Sunday?'

'You do understand,' said Melita, sounding very surprised.

'I think so. Remember, I come from a little place too. Let's see. It's much easier to go than not go because she'll only worry. And if you take me, she'll want to know everything down to my social security number and quite possibly how you're planning to dress the bridesmaids. Am I about there?'

Melita laughed. 'That's about it. Maybe not the bridesmaids, but she's been sucking her teeth over my lack of boyfriends since I got back from Canada. And then there's the rest of the family. It'd be like having lunch in a piranha tank.'

'Oh, yes. I know. My father isn't the sort to say anything, but his sister's been dropping hints about Miss Right for the last decade. She didn't have kids, you see, and Father only had me, so they're keen to see me settled. I've never had the bottle to actu-ally drag anyone home.' Another aspect of the situation occurred to him as he was speaking, and he hesitated, wondering how best to voice it. 'Melita, will your mother mind me being white?'

She chewed her lip, frowning slightly. 'She'd be a little thrown, I think. Maybe not so much because you're white, but because you're so English. She wouldn't know how to talk to you, and she'd be shy. But basically she'd approve, because if it came to something, it would be good for the children.'

'I haven't got around to the idea of children, I have to say,' he confessed. 'I'm still at the stage of thinking they're basically tiny highwaymen. I mean, they just come along and want your money or your life. I know people change on this one, but that's where I am at the moment. Why would it be good, though? I don't think I'm with you.'

'Well, it doesn't hurt here to have clear skin and good hair.'

'But you've got clear skin and good hair,' he objected. 'Your skin's perfect. You look as if you've never had a spot in your life.' It was true; since she was sitting cross-legged on the sand wearing nothing but a raspberry-red swimsuit, he was in a position to be definite on this one.

'That's not what I mean. The way people use the words over here, they mean light skin, and hair that's not too kinky. I'm not exactly Miss Barbados.'

'Is the same true on all the islands?'

'Probably. The only reason anyone started saying "black is beautiful" is because people thought it wasn't.'

'It seems very unfair.' Melita's hair was a soft, springy cloud, resilient to the hand; he had learned to appreciate it.

Melita snorted. 'Oh, boy,' she said. 'Where've you been?'

'England,' he said, irritated. 'Look, Melita. This is a tropical island with a mostly black population. If I assumed it was just like home, you'd jump on me for thinking English rules apply everywhere. Why shouldn't I start out by guessing it's different? It sodding well ought to be. Anyway, for what it's worth, I think you're beautiful.'

Melita took his hand and squeezed it. Her fingers were gritty with sand. 'Sorry I pissed you off, sweetheart. You should have lunch at the hotel,' she advised. 'You missed it last week, coming

to see me, but it's famous all over the island. Half Barbados goes
– you need to tell them you'll be there.'

Michael took her advice; moreover, he rang up Natty and asked
him over. In his first days in Barbados, he had begun to make
friends with some of the other guests at the hotel, but these fragile
connections had been broken by his own neglect. If he was going
to have anyone to talk to, he needed to invite a guest.

Theodoor's 'Quercitanus' puzzle nagged at his mind. Pelagius
had clearly been thinking of a particular painting, one known to
him. Since there were no public picture galleries in the seventeenth
century, as far as he knew, it seemed a good guess that it might
be one owned by Elizabeth of Bohemia, though it was also possible
that it was one in Middelburg – Theodoor would have thought of
all that. But what was it a painting of? He explained the problem
to Melita on Saturday, to see if she had any ideas.

'I don't know about art,' she said. 'But what he seems to be
saying is he sees himself in this picture, right? Are there any
pictures of black men from the seventeenth century?'

'There can't be a lot,' he said. 'I've seen one by Rembrandt,
though, in Utrecht, St Philip baptising the Ethiopian eunuch. The
only place you usually find black men—' he broke off abruptly.
'Melita, you've got it, you genius. The visit of the Three Kings.
One of them's almost always black. That explains why he's hoping
his offering will be accepted. He's seeing himself the black king
in a picture, carrying gold, waiting to present his gift. There's
hundreds of Dutch Epiphany pictures, unfortunately, but I bet
that's the answer.'

On Sunday morning, Michael and Melita said a temporary
farewell, and he drove back east to his hotel. The buffet was all
that had been promised, and as Melita had forecast, the place was
packed with Bajans in their churchgoing best, looking *en masse* like
a cheerful if not particularly tasteful flower-bed, and making so
much noise that, for the first time in his experience of the place,

he could not even hear the surf on the shore. There was an array of cold dishes and beyond it, a hot table; as Natty advised, they joined the line to sample the cold food, which included salads of chicken, saltfish and breadfruit, and some perfectly revolting-looking greyish-white pork in a clear pickle, which Natty fell on with enthusiasm.

'The best souse on the island,' he explained, helping himself lavishly. 'Hardly anyone makes it now, too much trouble, but it's Bajan soul-food. Goes right back to slavery days. The old lady who used to run this place was a famous cook, and they still use her recipes.' Michael took a little out of politeness; once they had sat down with their plates, it turned out, as he had rather feared, to be vinegary and reminiscent of the worst excesses of school salad, though Natty was wolfing it with every sign of enjoyment. He hid it tactfully under a lettuce-leaf and concentrated on the breadfruit and saltfish mixture, which was piquant and interest-ingly textured. The hot-table offerings which they had as a second course were by and large far more appetising; there was pepperpot, a strange black stew lurking beneath a good inch of golden fat, but there was also pork, chicken, fish, vegetables, and delicious deepfried cakes of spinach, plantain and saltfish. He piled his plate with a little of this, a little of that, heeding Natty's warning to leave room for dessert.

They ate slowly, and with enjoyment; Michael promised himself a long walk after lunch, if he could still move.

'You done anything more with your research?' asked Natty.

'Well, yes and no.'

'I hear you got it on with Ms Palaeologue.'

'What?'

'She not the only university person lives up Wanstead Heights, and someone did say, there was a hire-car parked up at Casuarina Court, and it was still there in the morning.'

Michael stared at him, momentarily at a loss for words; in that moment, the oppressive parochiality of Barbados came thundering home to him. 'Oh, God. This island. Natty, I absolutely do not want to discuss it. I care about Melita very much, and I am not going to say anything at all. Just keep your mouth off her.'

Natty raised his hands in token of peace. 'OK, OK. Well, is there anything to talk about that isn't taboo?'

'How about Pelagius, the man it all started with? You know I've got friends in Holland working on the beginning of this story?'

'This is the guy who married the queen?'

'Yes. My Dutch friends have sent me a puzzle. In this Latin diary I told you about, he identifies himself with the black king in a picture of the visit of the Magi. He says it's a picture by Quercitanus, which means "oak", and if we can only work out who Quercitanus was, we'll have an idea of how he saw himself.'

Natty ate a spinach ball, and took his time before replying 'Or you could start from the other end, and look for pictures of the Three Kings. There's two I know of with a really dramatic black king, one's by Breughel and one's by Bosch. I looked into this once, because I was thinking about cover art for a book.'

'Bosch. That's a thought – the name means wood, in Dutch. He came from 'sHertogensbosch in the south. But you'd expect that to be Latinised as Sylvius, I think, from *silva*. Hang on a minute, though. We call him Hieronymus Bosch, but that wasn't his name. He was really Jerome van Aken, from Bosch.'

'And is that by any chance Jerome Oak?'

'Actually I don't think it is. I suspect it means his family started off in Aachen, but Pelagius knew a lot about trees, and maybe not all that much about European geography. He could very well have thought it meant oak. Anyway, since there doesn't seem to be anyone else coming to mind, it's a good guess.'

'So all you need to do is find an image of Bosch's *Visit of the Magi* and you'll know what he looked like.'

'Possibly. We'd need to know if it was in Holland at the time.

I don't think I can find out from here, but I'll ask Theodoor –
that's my friend in Utrecht.'

'I'm very attracted to this idea,' said Natty. 'I've been thinking
about Pelagius, after all you've said. Even after experiencing
slavery, he persuades the white world to treat him like a king, and
he marries a white queen. He must be the coolest dude in the
whole of the seventeenth century. I'd love to think we could see
his face. If he was like the king in the picture I'm thinking of, he
was a handsome fellow.'

'I know what you mean. I've dreamed about Pelagius more than
once. And don't forget the thesis. Theodoor thinks it's very important. If I've understood him properly, Pelagius was actually
demanding that the Christian world should recognise African
spirituality. It's as if he wasn't afraid of anything, physically or
intellectually.'

'He's the one person in all this who makes his own story,' said
Natty. 'The rest of us are just reacting. I was thinking, though.
In his day, people must've worried about money and illness, serious
stuff, but now what we worry about half the time is who owns
stories, like, who's got the right to make their version count as
real.'

'Natty, it's not that simple. What about reputation? Honour?
Credit-worthiness? They're all stories, in the sense you mean, and
they're part of what people used to worry about when Pelagius
was alive, that's for sure. The thing is, in retrospect, all you see
are the versions which won. You don't see the competition.'

The conversation lapsed; already over-fed, they pushed the last
of the food around on their plates, nibbling a little here and there.

'What about the main issue, though?' asked Natty. 'Melpomene
being the Queen of England?'

'I've come to think you're right,' admitted Michael reluctantly.
'I think the story needs telling, but very carefully. I have to admit
I haven't talked to Melita about this, and I just hope I can bring

her round to my way of seeing things. The way most people would do it, I think, is to put the whole thing in the hands of a publicity agent. But Melita would hate it, and it'd make her look ridiculous. She'd become a celebrity, and probably make quite a bit of money, but she'd have to give up everything else. She's a serious scientist, Natty. If she ended up pulling swords out of stones on afternoon TV, she'd have a nervous breakdown.'

'I'd do it, if it had turned out to be me,' said Natty.

'Would you really? If you're honest?'

'I'm not sure,' he admitted. 'I'm shallow, Michael, not a scholartype like you and Melita. I'd like expensive cars and gorgeous girls, silk suits and alligator shoes, bling-bling on my fingers. I've done some TV presenting and stuff like that, I know how to handle myself in public. Actually, I think I'd enjoy it. But on the other hand, I like my privacy as much as the next guy, and you can't cool out in Baxter's Road if you arriving in a white stretch limo. Maybe it wouldn't be that much fun, and I can certainly see there's a difficulty if Melita's a little shy. So what are you thinking of?'

'Breaking the story through some channel which would let me have enough space to lay out the issues – the ones that worry Melita, the ones that worry you, and the actual evidence. A big story in one of the English Sunday papers might do it. Anywhere which was respectable, and let us have plenty of space. Also, before we went public, I'd like to run the whole thing past the College of Heralds. They're the people in London who keep track of peerages and so forth, so their authentication would be important. I don't think I'm going to find hard evidence for every single marriage, especially the early ones, so we'd need to know what the professionals thought about it. Also, once I found out how seriously the college was inclined to take the evidence, I'd want to know what the government made of it. Even if the college didn't quite think it worked, the story would generate enough interest that the Labour Party would have to take up an attitude. The point is, what they'd then do about it really depends on how keen Tony Blair is to discipline the Windsors – I think the answer is, "quite a lot", but it's also going to depend on how Melita behaves and whether she's making any money out of it. If everyone's looking at this pillar of integrity who's trying to explain that the concept of monarchy doesn't make scientific sense, she'll be very impressive. If they're looking at someone who's hired Max Clifford and keeps turning up on chat-shows, she'll lose credibility by the bucket. You can say what you like about the queen, but she's a dignified person, and if Melita did anything vulgar, she'd cop a huge amount of hostility from the right-wing press. If she goes on being thoughtful, she may attract a thoughtful response. Are you with me?'

'Yes. I can see that,' said Natty slowly.

'That's why I don't want you to do anything sudden.'

'OK. But I'm very taken with all this. I think I might just start working on some kind of fictional treatment. That would take a long time. I'm talking about serious writing, not some kind of airhead novelisation, so it would be a couple of years, maybe. That wouldn't get under your feet. I'd like to talk to some of your Dutch friends and pick up a bit of the history – they speak English?'

'Yes, of course.'

'I'm going back to England in the fall. I've picked up a creative-writing gig at the University of East Anglia for the autumn semester. While I'm on your side of the water, I'll maybe cross over to Holland, take a look at Middelburg, get a feel for it all.'

'Good idea,' said Michael. He was greatly relieved; Natty was – not precisely neutralised, that was not quite the word, but prevented from roaring around making trouble, and also, with any luck, he had been made to see that it was in his own interests to keep his mouth shut for the time being. It seemed perfectly possible that he would even write quite a good book; on the basis of what he had read, Michael thought him a talented writer, though a slightly lazy one; it had not been lost on him that, for all that Natty had had sharp words to say about Caribbean clichés and was, by his own admission, the product of a good school, his writing centred on poor but aspirant lads brought up in chattel-houses in the middle of nowhere. But all the same, he seemed genuinely moved by the idea of Pelagius, and perhaps the subject might call forth something more ambitious than he had yet attempted. 'Did you say something about desserts?'

'Oh, God, yes.' Natty craned his neck. 'It's OK. There's still some coconut pie. Let's go get it, before someone else does.'

Later on, they went for a walk, down the coast towards Bathsheba. Lunch had taken so long that the light was beginning to fade, and a surprisingly sizeable congregation was pouring out of St Aidan's Church, a little Victorian building only yards from the sea: men in suits, ladies in lace bodices and georgette skirts, little girls so overdressed they looked like fuchsias or carnations, with touchingly skinny legs emerging beneath full petticoats. Looking out to sea, once the tide of worshippers had flowed past them, his eye was caught by a human head bobbing where the waves began to break, behaving rather strangely. He squinted, shading his eyes, to see if the swimmer was in difficulties, and realised that it was a boy with a surfboard – they had reached the Soup Bowl, the surfers' beach – and he was trying to catch a wave. They watched for a while as he aimed at a wave, missed his moment, recovered, waited for another, and missed that too.

'You forget people have to learn to surf,' said Michael. 'It's a pretty public way to make a fool of yourself. No wonder he's out in the dark.'

'Yeah. He's not looking too cool,' Natty replied, watching as a big wave rolled in, formed its crest, and was missed once more. Some small waves came by, then at last, another beauty. 'Maybe he'll get this one . . . hey.' The boy caught the swell of the wave, and for a perfect moment, his board balanced on the crest. Natty chuckled as the surfer got to his feet on the board, and after a dizzy second of verticality, pitched headfirst into the boiling foam. A few seconds later, the little black head emerged again, and after a brief struggle, the boy conquered his board and paddled doggedly back out to sea. 'You can see him thinking, can't you? I'm going to get this right one day, then the girls will just fall over themselfs. Some rich touriss, with blonde hair and a gold ring in she belly-button – she'll see me riding on the sea, the coolest thing there is, and she'll just carry me away, buy me a watch and a car, and love me up.'

'Is that what young men think here?'

'That's what beach-boys think. There's a good few brothers spend their days on the beaches, chatting up the little rich girls.'

'Do they get what they want?'

'Not usually. They can get the girls to put out, no problem, but what they really want's a ticket to the States, a life, small change like that. The tourisses don't understand it ain't no holiday romance, they're buying sex. And mostly they don't like being told.'

'It all sounds rather sad.'

'You've got to understand, Michael. You think you're middle-class, but to most people here, you're rich. So it's like you're prey, see? That's what a tourism industry's about, redistributing wealth from rich folks to poor folks. It's just that here in the Caribbean, you get free-lance operatives as well as the hotels and businesses.'

Shortly after that, they turned round and headed back towards the hotel, since night was coming down. They shook hands and said goodbye, and Michael went up to his room. On Monday morning, he woke in the pellucid light of the Atlantic dawn, seized with a sudden and inescapable perception. A week . . . he would be gone in a week. The curdling anxiety which filled him at that thought was only too familiar, but no school term, however dreaded, had ever been so unwelcome as the thought of getting on a plane and flying back to England. He had enjoyed Barbados hugely but that was not the point. The thought of being without Melita was desolating. As he lay on his back staring at the shifting patterns of light on the ceiling, the depth of his own feeling began to make itself clear to him.

After breakfast, he got in the car and drove to Bridgetown, mildly surprised by his own decisiveness. Barbados seemed to be bringing out aspects of his character which he had barely known were there. He had a goal in mind: he remembered that somewhere on Broad Street, between assaults by taxi-touts, he had vaguely observed a shrieking advertisement for Colombian emeralds. He had noticed it because he liked the thought of emeralds, which had always seemed to him a beautiful colour. It did not take him very long to find the place.

He entered with some diffidence, since he had never bought an item of jewellery in his life. The salesgirl took charge of him efficiently, and showed him tray after tray of rings, a bewildering variety of stones, settings and of course prices, and after a great deal of discussion, he finally settled on a ring which pleased him, a fine deep-green stone with a little diamond on either side, which looked to him as if it would suit Melita's small, strong hand. While he had no real way of gauging if it represented value for money, it was at least tax-free.

'You keep this receipt, now,' warned the salesgirl, as he signed the credit slip, 'then if it don' suit the lady, there's no problem with an exchange. And we can resize, if you guess the finger wrong.'

'Thank you,' he said, putting the little box in his inside breast pocket.

They met at Desert Rose Drive, at six. Melita opened the door, freshly showered and changed after her day's work.

'Darling, I've made us a reservation at Josef's,' he said. 'Are you ready to go?'

Melita raised her eyebrows. 'You pushing the boat out, sweetheart. I hope you know that's expensive!'

262

'Yes, but I haven't seen you for nearly thirty-six hours,' he pointed out.

'H'm,' said Melita, 'will I do like this?'

'Of course. You look wonderful.'

Melita ignored him and ducked into her bedroom, coming back a minute or two later having changed her T-shirt for a silk camisole, and slipped a gold chain round her neck. 'Ready to go,' she said, reaching for her white jacket.

He had made the booking for six-thirty. Barbados had accustomed him to eating ridiculously early, and as he hoped, the hour and the priceyness combined to ensure that the place was quiet. They had a nice table, inside but looking out onto the water, and the food was all that had been promised. Melita was cheerful; she told him about lunch with her mother, who had said she was looking less anxious, a bit more about her siblings, and about work in progress. In return, he told her about Natty, explaining that they had met on the plane: given the parochiality of island culture, he was not surprised to find that she had heard of him, or that he made occasional appearances on local television.

When they had got to dessert, an elegant array of tropical fruits, ice-creams and sorbets laid out fanwise on large white plates, he fished in his pocket, and handed her his present.

'I want you to have this,' he said.

Melita looked completely dumbfounded. Slowly she laid down her spoon, and opened the box.

'It's beautiful,' she said rather blankly. She put the box down on the table in the pool of candle-light, and looked carefully at the ring without touching it.

'Green for a botanist,' said Michael.

Melita smiled, a constrained smile. I ought to be panicking, he thought, registering her lack of enthusiasm, but he felt strangely at ease. He reached across the table and took the ring, flashing newly as it caught the light, and put it on her hand. Her right hand. 'It's a present, darling. But I do want to marry you.'

She smiled properly this time, the tender, luminous smile which he could not resist. 'Michael, you are so nice. I can't move this quickly. I'm not made like that. Not committing myself to someone I've known for a week.'

'Well, why did you sweep me off my feet, then?'

She looked a little impish. 'There you were, sitting on the shelf, just waiting for some sweet thing to carry you away.'

'Melita, you're just trying to wind me up. I've spent my entire life being cautious, you know. This is the first time I've ever been sure of anything.'

'That's a powerful thought,' she said. 'Well. For now, and not saying I won't change my mind.' She took the ring off her right hand, and slid it onto the left. 'It's a perfect fit.'

Suddenly, the *maître d'* was towering over them. Michael cursed silently as the man's expansive shadow fell across the table, realising too late that an efficient up-market restaurant would pick up on such byplay, and heartily wished he had picked somewhere more casual. 'Congratulations, sir and madam! A lil' glass of bubbly, maybe, to toast the occasion?'

Melita was laughing, so he left off being cross. 'Oh, shit. We might as well.'

A bottle of Veuve Cliquot arrived, together with a spray of orchids; the chef appeared to shake their hands and collect some compliments; Michael and Melita smiled foolishly over their melting dessert at a sequence of beaming faces, and drank their champagne.

'Have I said I think it's beautiful?' asked Melita, once they were left to themselves. 'I really like it.'

'It suits you.'

'I don't usually wear rings, I spend too much time with my hands dirty.'

'But you'll wear this one once in a while?'

'Oh, I think so. Michael, do you want to finish this bottle? It seems a waste to leave it.'

'Doesn't it just.' Especially at restaurant prices, he thought meanly. Melita wasn't a great drinker, but in the circumstances, a half-bottle would have been ridiculous. 'But I think we should. I still have to drive us back, and the traffic's going to be thickening up. Anyway, I'd rather be in bed, wouldn't you? Let's get the bill.' It would be exorbitant, but never mind. For all its silliness, he was pleased with the evening. It was the sort of thing which ought to happen, a story to look back on.

They had an idyllic night, having got home unscathed, but by the following evening, reality had interposed itself.

'It just wouldn't work,' said Melita. They were half an hour into an exhausting wrangle about practicalities. 'You think you like it here, but you wouldn't. You have to've been born here to stand it.'

'That's true of most places,' said Michael.

'No. It's worse than you think. People who come in really don't have a good time. Even people who come back. It's the eyes, watching whatever you do, the way they judge you. They don't like incomers telling them what to do. You'd start to hate it if you were really living here, and anyway, there's nothing for you. We haven't a lot of resourcing for academics, and there's never going to be a job for a white boy from Oxford.'

'Reverse racism?' asked Michael, misery lending sharpness to his tone.

'Well, not exactly, sweetheart. It would be OK if you were a white Bajan, maybe. The point is, you wouldn't understand where the students were coming from, so there'd be all kinds of trouble. You'd be a bad buy, you see? And you'd be unhappy, because they'd let you know you were out of place.'

'You could come to England', said Michael desperately.

'I don't want to. Look, Michael. I work on tropical plants.

Botany's not a well-resourced subject anywhere, so where d'you think I'd find a job? Anyway, if you're anything to go by, I wouldn't like England, all you-all do is sit on your botsies and talk about the past. Do you know, I haven't heard a single word out of you about the future?'

'I'm talking about the future now,' said Michael desperately.

'That's personal. That's different. But what you've been telling me all adds up to saying Europe's full of old stuff, and so's Africa. I mean, we've got bad history here. This was a slave society. But all the same, it's not going back that far. Some of us came, some of us were brought, but we've made each other, over the years. I don't really get on too well with Africans, or Europeans either. I'm the first to admit that Barbados isn't paradise, but it's where I belong.'

'Well, that's perfect, then,' snapped Michael. 'I'll send you a card at Christmas.'

'Oh, sweetheart . . .' Melita held out her arms, and he accepted her embrace, letting her hug and rock him in wordless apology.

'Canada?' he said after a while, then:

'The winter,' they said in unison.

'I think it's really hard to get a job in Canada if you're not Canadian,' said Melita. 'And there's the tropical question.'

'Well, you can hardly get less tropical than Canada,' said Michael. 'Look, love. We're just making ourselves unhappy. Let's try and make the most of our time. We can start making compromises and all that stuff when we're surviving on email. Just leave it. Who knows, you might suddenly go off me.'

'Oh, Michael,' said Melita miserably. 'I just don't think so.'

XI

Give the king thy judgments, O God, and thy righteousness unto the king's son.

He shall come down like rain upon the mown grass: as showers that water the earth.

In his days shall the righteous flourish; and abundance of peace so long as the moon endureth.

Psalm 72, 1, 6+7

Oxford was even worse than Michael had feared. He ached for Melita, and composed long maudlin emails, which he generally deleted without sending. Even with this self-imposed censorship they both got in touch at least once a day, but this contact, though greatly valued, barely mitigated his sense of loss.

Once he had recovered from his jet-lag sufficiently to be certain he was actually awake, he set about composing a long and careful letter to his great-uncle.

Dear Uncle Harold,

I don't know if you've got any of my postcards from Barbados, but now I'm back, it's time you had a proper report. I think the first thing you'll want to know is that I contacted Dr Melpomene Palaeologue – for that's who she turned out to be – and she was able to fill in the story from 1700. By great good luck, her grandfather was interested in family history, so he took the family tree back to Theodore Stuart and Godscall Palaeologue. Naturally, not knowing the significance of the name Stuart, his interest was tracing the senior line descended from the Palaeologues – but of course, that's the information you want too. Anyway, that's why she's called Palaeologue, which was puzzling me: the grandfather changed the name back to make the point that they were the authentic descendants of the last emperor. The key fact which I haven't mentioned yet is that Melpomene and her immediate family are black, which is why her grandfather was touchy about his illustrious lineage. I don't know if it makes any difference to the way you think about all this? As far as I can see, it shouldn't, but there may be factors I haven't considered.

Michael contemplated his computer screen, quite pleased with the delicacy of the last phrase. Old Harold was a pretty good class of raving loony, but was he a racist? Given the aplomb with which he contemplated a Stuart family tree which included King Solomon and Scota the daughter of Pharaoh, he probably wasn't, but the subject had never come up. Silloth had attracted few settlers from anywhere else in the British Isles, let alone further afield.

The trickiest problem with the new evidence, from your point of view, is the eighteenth century, which seems rather a shame since we've got such wonderful evidence for earlier on. The Pelagius = Elizabeth marriage is absolutely unchallengeable, and there's a note of Balthasar's marriage to Sibella Carteret, gentlewoman, in the records of the Dutch church at Austin Friars in London. Their son Theodore states in writing that he married Godscall, but I haven't run down actual confirmation (we don't know what parish they lived in, or even if they married in London). It's in Barbados that the trouble starts. The line looks like this (these are links from eldest surviving son to son, leaving out siblings, other marriages, etc.):

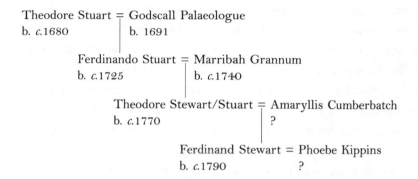

Theodore Stuart = Godscall Palaeologue
b. *c.*1680   b. 1691

    Ferdinando Stuart = Marribah Grannum
    b. *c.*1725   b. *c.*1740

        Theodore Stewart/Stuart = Amaryllis Cumberbatch
        b. *c.*1770   ?

            Ferdinand Stewart = Phoebe Kippins
            b. *c.*1790   ?

(NB: Melpomene tells me this Ferdinand approached the Greek govt when they came to Bdos to look for traces of the Palaeologues, and was treated very rudely because he was black: it's the family story of this rebuff which gets James Stewart (below) interested in tracing the line.)

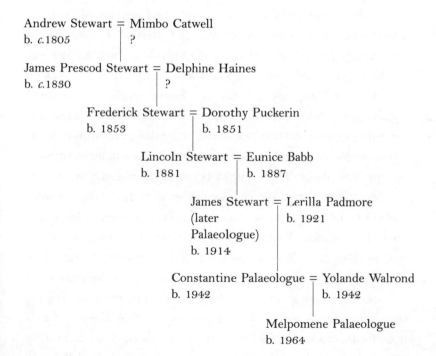

Andrew Stewart = Mimbo Catwell
b. *c.*1805   ?

James Prescod Stewart = Delphine Haines
b. *c.*1830   ?

    Frederick Stewart = Dorothy Puckerin
    b. 1853   b. 1851

        Lincoln Stewart = Eunice Babb
        b. 1881   b. 1887

            James Stewart = Lerilla Padmore
            (later   b. 1921
            Palaeologue)
            b. 1914

        Constantine Palaeologue = Yolande Walrond
        b. 1942   b. 1942

            Melpomene Palaeologue
            b. 1964

As you can see for yourself, the tree as such is very satisfactory, and we have all the names. The question-mark over the whole thing is the status of the eighteenth-century relationships: these people were 'free-coloured' in the vocabulary of the time, and they had limited social rights. I've successfully dealt with Ferdinando Stuart and Marribah Grannum. I spent a fair amount of time in the Bdos National Archives, and there are early parish registers for St Michael, the parish which includes Bridgetown, where the marriage is recorded in 1768. This is very, very unusual for Barbados, by the way: interracial marriages were legal there in the 18th century, but they hardly ever happened. There were plenty of relationships, of course, but they were generally extra-marital, 'respectable concubinage', so to speak. Perhaps the fact that Ferdinando knew he was one-eighth black influenced him? Anyway, the key fact is, he did marry his Marribah. It's the next three generations which are the headache; I haven't been able to find any actual evidence (due to hurricanes, termites, fires, etc., Barbadian records are dismayingly patchy). But however Ferdinando defined himself, the children would have been 'free-coloured', since Marribah was (it says so on the marriage certificate). Free-coloured people could legally marry among themselves, but they didn't, necessarily – it depends I suppose on how respectable the family considered themselves at that time, and that's something it's very difficult to make assumptions about. There might be some more to be got out of the Mormons' International Genealogical Index, which covers Barbados, and I'll get on to this when I can (as I've recently discovered, the Mormons have ended up the world's genealogy specialists, because they have a theory that if you can identify your ancestors you can baptise them retrospectively as Mormons – I can see this causing some gnashing of teeth at the Last Trump, can't you? But it's worth your knowing about this, you might find it useful for your research). Meanwhile I was thinking of putting the whole Palaeologue problem in front of the College of Heralds, who I suppose are the ultimate authority in this sort of question. Does that suit you?

The last thing you might want to know something about is what Melpomene is actually like.

He paused again, stared at the screen for a while, then got up to make a cup of tea. Where to start . . . ?

The first thing you need to know, I think, is that she is dignified, very polite, and quite charming. She is highly intelligent, of course (she is a botanist by training, and a serious scientist, with a proper university job), and I think you would find her most delightful.

It crossed Michael's mind, ignobly, that he could envisage some future point at which he might be able to enlist Harold Boumphrey on his side in the battle royal with his father which he could see looming on the horizon.

She is not unduly impressed by the idea of her Stuart ancestry – because of her grandfather's interest in the Palaeologues, she's had a lifetime to get used to the idea of being the 'last empress'. She also has some intellectual doubts about the whole business which stem from her scientific training. All the same, she has all the qualities you might hope or want to find in someone naturally royal.

Michael's conscience gave him a nasty twinge as he considered the last sentence and imagined what Melita would say if she ever saw it, but he let it stand.

I think that's about it. As you may have gathered, I am very taken with Melpomene ('Melita', as her friends call her). We spent a lot of time together, and became very close. I think you would like her very much. I still have a lot left over from your very generous gift, by the way, and I've kept track: do you want a proper account?

This has turned out a very interesting adventure. I'm so glad you made it possible, and I hope you are pleased with what I found. The enclosed photos are a snapshot I took of Melita at St John's Church, and a photograph of the Palaeologue tomb.

Michael read over his letter twice, decided it would do, and printed it out. It was only with a pang that he was prepared to part with any photograph of Melita at all, but the St John's one was a duplicate: he was not very used to the camera, a new one bought for the trip, and had somehow contrived to press the shutter-switch twice. It was quite a nice photo, a close-up of Melita's head and shoulders, with the view down towards Bathsheba dimly visible behind her. He had been greatly irritated to find when he got home that many of his efforts had reduced Melita to a silhouette; because he had not realised how much light her dark, matte complexion absorbed. But in this particular one, the sun had been on their left, and had illuminated the strong planes of her face. It showed the actual colour of her skin well too. She was smiling slightly, and looked a little quizzical, the expression she tended to have when she thought he was babbling . . . Michael realised that he had been mooning over the picture for some little while, and stuffed it resolutely into the envelope.

One of the pleasures of re-entry – there were not many – was a long message from Corinne. After his conversation with Natty, Michael had passed on the suggestion that Pelagius had been thinking of Bosch to Theodoor, who had found it persuasive and been delighted. A scanned picture of the black king in Bosch's *Epiphany* had followed almost immediately: in it, whereas the other two kings knelt at the Christ Child's feet, the black king stood at a slight distance, holding the orb which would be his gift somehow hesitantly, as if he thought it might be refused. The image therefore made perfect sense of Pelagius's analogy. But a day or so later, just before he had left Barbados, a rather downcast follow-up message arrived, briefly saying that Philip II of Spain had started collecting Bosch seriously in 1570, and had sent nine of his paintings to the Prado in 1574, probably including the *Epiphany*, since it was certainly there now. There was not the slightest indication that Pelagius had ever set foot in Spain.

That seemed to be that, unfortunately, but Theodoor had also told Corinne, who was well informed and well connected in the world of art history. Her email, sent both to him and to Theodoor, solved the puzzle conclusively. It was a cheerful communication generally: things were looking very good for the future of the Middelburg project. It thus now looked as if her story might have a happy ending, and Michael was genuinely pleased; though he had felt rather sour about her at times in the past, he was greatly inclined, in his newfound happiness, to forgive and forget. He had also been affected, more than he realised, by Theodoor's judgement of her. But apart from her personal news, she had good news about 'Quercitanus' for them. She had asked a couple of friends – i.e. Corinne exercising her undoubted talent for scamming hours and days of work out of unsuspecting victims, thought Michael tolerantly. It was a talent which would undoubtedly stand her in good stead if she really did end up running a research project – Anyway, what the 'couple of friends' had done was to remind her that there were copies and/or variant versions of several of Bosch's major works, including this one: there was an *Epiphany* in Anderlecht in Brussels, and two more in America. Most directly to the point, there was a version which had been sold by the Duke of Gelderland to Elizabeth of Bohemia: the transaction was mentioned in a letter quoted in the van der Ploeg/Vermeeren book on the art-collections of Stadhouder Fredrik Hendrik, Elizabeth's contemporary and friend. It was probable, though not certain, that the painting in question was the half-size version of the triptych now in Upton House in Warwickshire, where the son of the founder of Shell had fulfilled the natural destiny of second-generation oil barons by becoming an aesthete, falling under the spell of Bernard Berenson and collecting art. What lies behind that 'probable, though not certain'? thought Michael, half-amused and half-horrified. How long had this all taken someone? Well, however dubious her methods, Corinne had done them proud. They had found the Black King.

Michael opened the .jpg file Theodoor had sent him, and looked at the picture again. It was not a portrait, of course, at least not of Pelagius; and he reminded himself sternly that he must not think about it as if it were one. When Pelagius likened himself to this image, he may have been thinking only about the psychological distance which the figure seemed to express, and not about the features. Yet how tempting it was. It was a handsome, dignified face, shown in three-quarters profile; though it seemed oval at first, the depth of the jaw suggested that the face was actually quite wide, like Melita's, and like hers, neither prognathous nor weak-chinned. Above all, it was a face which questioned; it was as if Bosch were saying that this king longed to believe in the Christ Child, but was not certain that he did. He seemed lonely, very isolated from the other figures, even within that alienated canvas: the Christ Child was apparently looking at him, but no one else was. Was this what Pelagius was like? Michael wondered. It was easy to believe. It was even tempting to try and see Melita in the image, though she would pour scorn on such a notion, even if it had been an actual portrait, he could hear her saying, how would a face persist through twelve generations, unless the family kept intermarrying like the Hapsburgs.

Perhaps fortunately, he had a good deal of work on hand. The Perdita conference was coming up, so he had to finish his paper on *The Female Rosicrucian,* and the edition itself was due at his publisher's by the end of the year, so he would need to get all the actual library work fitted into the summer break. He was well aware that if he had thoughts of moving on, he must make the best possible use of Oxford's resources while he had them. There was no excuse not to; most of the Fellows had vanished abroad or into libraries, and the porters, enjoying the annual lull, sat about in their Lodge reading the *Daily Mail*. Royston, whom he would have rather liked to see, had gone to the States, and there was nobody about in Oxford who had any calls on his time.

A week later, he received a reply from Harold Boumphrey, which he opened with interest. It turned out to be a classic Boumphrey epistle, page after page of closely written copperplate script.

My dear Michael,

Thank you for your most informative letter. I was surprised in the first instance by the photograph of Her Most Sacred Majesty, but a moment's reflection told me that prejudice must be cast aside, and it was wholly appropriate and suitable that she should be a coloured lady. Her countenance is that of a most gracious and distinguished person, it is full of character and bespeaks both warmth and majesty. It is to be presumed that Tea Tephi, who is the ancestress of the Irish royal line which leads ultimately to the Stuarts, was the daughter of King Solomon and the Queen of Sheba – since the latter, as the Good Book says, was 'black but comely', so, doubtless, was Tea Tephi herself!

Her Majesty is of course Queen of England, but prompted by her appearance, I have come to think more seriously about how much else she is besides. As an Englishman and a patriot I have naturally been principally concerned with the Stuarts, but we must consider that as Our Lord spoke to all nations, so His royal line is a royal line in perpetuity and is also, by definition, supra-national. It has seemed hard to me, in the present state of World Politics, to understand how God might make the path of His favoured one manifest, so I have taken the view, up to this point, that it was the restoration of the Stuarts which was the task which seemed to be laid upon me.

However, Her Majesty also carries the blood of Constantine, the first Christian emperor (<u>nota</u> <u>bene</u>, we should not forget that Constantine's mother was a British princess). Since we are told in the Book of Daniel that the Romans were to be the last of the great World Empires, she may be therefore considered the titular ruler of Europe and Asia. Moreover, Pelagius, chosen spouse of Queen Elizabeth of Bohemia, if I understand what you have told me of him, was the rightful ruler of a great people in Africa, and certainly, his bride's ancestor, the Queen of Sheba, was such. We should not imagine that our darker brethren are outside the infinite mercy of Our Lord, quite the contrary: does the Bible not tell us, 'Ethiopia shall stretch forth her hands unto God'? Moreover, the Queen of Sheba, through Menyelek, her son by Solomon, was ancestress of the great Christian kings of Ethiopia, such as Ella-Asbeha. I would not be in the least surprised, therefore, to find that His Majesty Pelagius was descended from the Ethiopic strand of the Great Lineage. Thus by the mysterious providence of God, the Royal Line of David and Our Lord unites unto Itself the rule of the three great divisions of the Old World: we may assume that the fact that the lady who fulfils the prophecies is herself a daughter of the New World, is to be taken as an indication that the New World is also included in the benign rule of the Chosen One.

'O watch, I say unto you, Watch, that ye may not be surprised.' It is clear from the perfectly astonishing drawing-together of the Nations in the person of this lady, that we have come to the Last Days. I had attached no significance to the passing of the second millennium, but on reflection, I now think that I was wrong so to do. Young persons are sadly neglectful of the Good Book; let me remind you of the Revelation accorded to St John the Divine, and that of the blessed Joachim of Fiore. We have seen the Vessels of Wrath poured upon the land, the armies of Gog and Magog. We have not yet seen the Just King, the Lord's anointed, the Healer, whom we are promised. It is now my considered opinion that Her Sacred Majesty Melpomene is this Personage: the Empress of the Last Days.

'Shit,' said Michael, aloud. The old man had done him proud; even at his most (or least) optimistic, he had not expected anything quite so exotic.

You may be aware that there is a long-standing tradition to the effect that the last imperial monarchy is to be that of a descendant of the Stuarts; thus the Rose of England will be called upon to reform the world (a doctrine dimly perceived in the writings of the Brothers of the Rosy Cross). The prophecy that 'The Rose of England beareth the Cross of Christ to foreign lands' first appears in the time of Edward the Confessor. Furthermore, the learned Maxwell declared in 1615 that 'from the rose of England shall proceed or spring the reformation or purgation of the Church of Rome, like as the same city once received from the same country the first authorised profession of the Christian faith, by the blessed meanes of Constantine, a Briton born.' Note here the bringing-together of the Rose, that is, the Stuart line, and of Constantine, as they are in the Person of this lady!

Of course I do not wish to hear any more about the subvention which I was able to offer you. If it can be in any way applied to purposes indicated by Her Sacred Majesty, I would be only too pleased and honoured: should there be a need for a little more, do not hesitate to write. The College of Heralds is an excellent idea. They are prejudiced fools, of course, but the information you can bring them is weighty and substantial, and since their opinion will certainly be canvassed, it is as well to be forearmed. Another person who will need to be consulted is Lord St John of Fawsley, the erstwhile Norman St John Stevas. To the best of my knowledge, Lord

St John is the principal living historian of the British Constitution.
He will surely recognise the appearance of Her Sacred Majesty as
a second, and still more Glorious Revolution.

Michael began to feel that he had sailed into deep and uncharted
waters. It was one thing to try and wind up the establishment in
the interests, fundamentally, of calling attention to his own belief
that monarchy was a concept which had long passed its sell-by
date, discovering how widely shared this idea might be, and incid-
entally increasing his own saleability in the academic market-place.
Apocalypse Now was not quite what he had had in mind. In the
course of the afternoon, however, he wrote a brief and civil reply,
and dropped it in the post. All that would keep.

A couple of evenings later, the phone rang as he was sitting
over his computer. Picking it up, he was caught by a sense of *déjà
vu*, as a familiar voice chirruped, 'Michael, I'm so glad I've caught
you. I was wondering if you could do one tiny little thing for me?'

'Oh, no. Corinne, what are you after this time? Just tell me, and
I may even do it.'

'OK,' said Corinne agreeably. 'What have you been doing,
Michael? You sound so much more cheerful. It is just this. You
remember I have made a grant application? – well, officially it is
Professor Derksen's, but really it is me.'

'Yes, you told me. I was very pleased for you.'

'Well, the Middelburg people would like to have a little presentation on the academic interest. It's fair enough; they want to
understand a bit more about why we think this is exciting. It's
just to be an afternoon seminar in Middelburg, with really short
papers, fifteen, twenty minutes. Theodoor has said he will speak
about Pelagius, and I'll talk about Petrus Behn. I'd be so pleased
if you could speak about Aphra. You know we haven't any money,
but there are really cheap flights to Amsterdam now – I know
Easyjet do one, and I could find out some others if you like.'

Michael thought about being difficult, and charitably decided not to. 'It's all right, Corinne. I'm not actually that short of cash at the moment. I'm doing a paper on Aphra for Perdita anyway, so I can just take the introductory bit and twiddle it for you. Do they all speak English?'

'I'm not sure. If you could let me have it in advance I could make a one-page summary in Dutch, so they could look at it if they wanted. It'd be tactful.'

'I wouldn't mind saying a bit about something else, actually. As well, I mean.'

'My goodness. I thought it would be hard to persuade you, *schat*, and here you are volunteering. What do you mean?'

'Do you remember I found evidence that Pelagius was married to Elizabeth of Bohemia? I emailed you about a month ago. No, maybe more.'

'Oh, yes! I was very busy, and it went out of my head. It was a big surprise. She was some kind of royal person, wasn't she?'

'She was indeed. She was the daughter of James I, King of England.'

'That's fascinating. Yes, of course they'll be interested. I'll be interested too. I'm sorry, Michael, you did tell me, but the English royal family isn't really something I know about, and I didn't realise she was so important. The evidence is in Middelburg, is it?'

'Yes, it's in the archive. The record of his marriage, and Balthasar's certificate of baptism. Since then, I've put together a complete family tree for their descendants down to the present day.'

'That's great! If you can really be bothered, please do tell them. I'll make space in the programme. If you email me the call numbers of the documents, I'll make sure they're part of the display.'

'Please do that. I'm writing the story up anyway, for some other reasons, so it's no trouble to speak about it.' The significance of the marriage had passed completely over her head, unsurprisingly, given that it had passed over his; it took a genealogy nut like his great-uncle to spot why it really mattered.

'Michael, you are saving my life. We can have a lovely dinner, with Ankie and Pieternelle and Theodoor. It'll be great to see you.'

'You too, Corinne.' Rather to his surprise, he meant it. She was sounding on top of things again, not whiny or grabby, and he remembered why he had liked her in the first place. It was a great mistake to believe that suffering improved people's characters. With a job in prospect, Corinne was a cheerful and lovable pirate; similarly, with Melita to love him, he knew he had become more tolerant, less frightened, and almost certainly nicer to know; all kinds of people had made oblique comments on the improvement in his character.

The other agreeable event of August was an email from Natty, asking where he expected to be in the second week of September. Silloth, he replied; he intended to go up for a week and check that all was well with his father before term closed over his head: while he had not heard anything was worse, he had certainly not heard things were any better. Having assumed that Natty wanted to see Oxford, he was rather surprised by his response.

Cool. I've a gig with some kind of Glasgow lit festival just before I start at East Anglia. Jackie Kay's going to be there and some other homegrown black talent, so they're flying in a couple of not too expensive West Indians and someone from India so they can call it 'international'. So I'll be coming up north – how would you feel if I dropped by for a day or so? I'd like to catch up on how the story's going, and after all you've said about Cumbria, I'd like to see it.

There was both a best and a second-best spare bedroom at the Criffel Street house. There was certainly room for Natty, and as

Michael thought about the idea, he saw all kinds of positive aspects. Given that, if Melita was prepared to go through with it, he intended to present his father with a black daughter-in-law, there was something to be said for paving the way by introducing him to a black friend. At the very least, he might get some notion of where his father stood on the subject of race, which he had very little idea of: the old man had been heard to approve of Moira Stewart and Trevor Macdonald as newscasters, and his comments about black cricketers had been confined entirely to their ability to play cricket, so it seemed fair to guess that he had no very strong feelings. Also, it would be strange but interesting to show his horrid little town to a Barbadian; to be not the visitor, examining the quaint folkways of others, but the object of such vague anthropological condescension.

The most crucial aspect of August, work aside, was the series of emails in which he talked Melita round to a reluctant endorsement of his perspective on the queenship question. He kept Harold Boumphrey's new and improved version of her status to himself, fearing that it might provoke an explosion, but Melita's essential serious-mindedness was susceptible, he found, to cunningly reiterated variations on his argument that the public discovery of her royal heritage would more probably bring the idea of monarchy into disrepute than benefit her directly. He also put Melita and Natty in touch with one another, and after an initial frostiness, caused by Natty's difficulty in reaching conversational terms with a woman who was not interested in impressing him, they got along quite well. He was not surprised to find that Natty's sense of the issues had an effect on her; for all the strength of her views about race, she was in no way naïve about its significance in the real world.

'I've prayed about this,' she wrote eventually, in reluctant agreement, 'and I asked my mum's vicar what he thought I should do, and he reckoned God meant this to be. What I'm really hoping is that if you do it the way we've decided, I can pretty well keep out of it. You've got all the actual evidence, and you've checked everything Grandpapa did in the archives here. Natty says he can handle the photographs/interviews for me when we get to that stage, he knows all the media people here. He says the thing to remember is, even if people offer me money they can't make me take it. If they get too bad about it, there are people I can stay with. It's really crazy, though. Here I am talking about turning down money, when I'm eating rice and chicken backs and wondering if I can keep the car out of the scrapyard. You can call me Ms Stubborn, everyone else does sooner or later. But it's just not worth it to me.'

Here's hoping, thought Michael, reading her message. There was a terrifying innocence about Melita sometimes, which reminded him of the millipedes they had watched in Turner's Hall Woods; she was pootling harmlessly down her own little track, completely unaware of what might be going on around her. He wondered just how many fingers Natty had had crossed behind his back at the time. Quite apart from the media interest, which he suspected she had gravely underestimated, he was slowly beginning to realise the uncharted depths of lunacy that lapped about them. He had long been in the habit of playing around with the Web in idle moments to keep up with the topics that interested Harold; now, as he worked outwards to include sites relevant either to Afrocentrism or the end of the world, he was daunted by the sheer quantity of mythology in circulation. Moreover, by comparison with the stuff which the Sacerdotal Knights of National Security, W. Thor Zollinger, the Spirit of Truth, and many, many more were putting into circulation, Great-Uncle Harold's notions looked like a miracle of scholarly cogency; and he was not looking forward to what happened when the British National Party found out about Melita. Or the KMWR Scientific Consortium either.

He also wondered whether he should send her some of Harold's bounty. Her remark about the car worried him; while he had felt very safe in Barbados, he was not a young woman living alone, and from what she had told him of her life, he did not like the thought of her walking around Cave Hill at night. The old fellow would be only too delighted, but he suspected that she would refuse to take it from him. She had that sort of pride.

In the first week of September, when the light had turned dusty and elegiac, he went over to the Netherlands for two nights, as he had promised Corinne. He would arrive in the evening – Theodoor had invited him out that night – then they would all start for Middelburg at the crack of dawn on the second day, and the second night, once they were back in Utrecht, there was to be a party at Ankie and Pieternelle's house. Then after a couple of days to sort out himself and his laundry, he would go to Silloth.

Theodoor was taking him to a concert in the Domkerk; Mozart. Sitting in the lobby of the university hostel waiting to be picked up, he found he was looking forward to it, and still more to spending an evening with Theodoor himself.

Theodoor came in, bang on time, looming in the doorway with the awkward grace of a giraffe, and Michael scrambled to his feet. He was immensely pleased to see him, so pleased that, quite spontaneously, he put out his arms and hugged him. Theodoor returned the embrace, pecking him formally on both cheeks in Dutch style, then looked down at him curiously.

'Michael, you have changed. When I first knew you, you would not have done that.'

'It's Melita. She seems to have given me some kind of confidence.'

'*Seker*. You no longer look as if you hate that you live in a body. That is very good.'

Michael shrugged. The remark might have fazed him once, but no longer. 'English platonism's got a lot to answer for,' he said cheerfully. 'Shall we go?'

Theodoor looked at his watch. 'I think we should, if we are to get good seats.'

They walked off together into the old part of town, past book-shops, antique shops and shops selling domestic elegancies; witch-balls, expensive patchwork, eccentric chandeliers: a pleasant pottering-ground on a nice evening, which the citizenry were taking full advantage of, strolling in pairs or small groups, sitting on walls under the trees or in front of cafés. 'I like the way Dutch towns are used,' observed Michael. 'You've held onto a sense of civicness, which I'm not sure we've ever had in England. We're opening up a bit, though – have you walked on the South Bank in London at all recently?'

'Yes, and I have visited your excellent new Tate. I see what you mean, and I am glad you like it here. I think that the way we live here is precious, and it needs to be defended.' They had glimpsed the tremendous spire of the Domkerk repeatedly as they walked, since from the middle of town it appeared at the end of every vista: Utrecht's Dom was a late medieval church so gigantic and so ambi-tious that even though the nave had actually fallen in almost as soon as it was completed, what was left of it was quite big enough for any practical purposes. The spire stood rather eccentrically apart from the structure as it now was, at the opposite end of an extensive square adorned with a war memorial. Concert-goers were beginning to assemble as Theodoor and Michael walked up, so they went in and took their places.

After the concert, Theodoor took him to what passed locally for an Italian restaurant. 'We have come a long way since Corinne first went to Middelburg,' he observed, as the waiter brought them their food. 'One finding has led to another, and now we are all leading different lives. Me not so much, but it has touched me also.'

'You must have done a hell of a lot of work behind the scenes for Corinne,' said Michael. 'She's kept me posted from time to time, and I can't believe things would have gone so smoothly for her if you hadn't been discreetly pulling strings on her behalf.'

'That is so,' confirmed Theodoor. 'She does not know how much, of course. I confess I developed a secondary interest as time went on, which encouraged me to spend more time and energy on her problems than I might have done otherwise. A very able and very deserving young man, a Latinist, who has no sponsor because his supervisor died – by helping Corinne, I was also able to make a place for Lucas as the editor of Pelagius, which will be the making of him.'

'Well, that's legitimate,' said Michael. 'In a system like yours, you've got to try and help people who fall down the cracks. But I do find all this ironic.'

'Why so?'

'Well, just look at the story we've uncovered. Once upon a time, there was a grand romance of star-crossed royals, but they weren't just in love. They had a great idea, about ushering in the Reign of the Just King at the end of the world. If I've understood what you've been telling me, Elizabeth and Pelagius didn't exactly think their infant was a new Messiah, but they certainly had a notion that he had a major part to play in the great scheme of things. Then what actually happens? – he goes through life as a poor but honest doctor, and his descendants dribble downhill till they end up as a bunch of artisans on the east coast of Barbados. The story isn't rediscovered till the twenty-first century, by which time, even if their descendant is the rightful heir to the throne, the concept of the British monarchy's getting to be a bad joke. I tried to convince Melita she could be an embodiment of justice for the new millennium, and she said she had better things to do with her time. I think she's probably right. So in the end, the only result of this tremendous secret is that Melita and I have fallen in love, I've improved my career prospects, and Corinne and this bloke Lucas have got themselves sorted out. It's all good clever stuff, especially for me, but it's not exactly earth-shattering. By the way, what happened to the man Corinne was so sure would get all the gravy?'

'Cees? Well, Cees has been unlucky enough to find that the most important decision of his life so far has been a mistake. He set his hopes on following Derksen, and he has found that the man he trusted with his whole future has let him down. I am sure his story is not over; a person of his qualities, both positive and negative, will succeed in this Holland of ours one way or another. But at the moment, he is bitterly disappointed.'

'More of the same, in a way. All that human effort, the risk of discovery, whatever it took to bring Pelagius and Elizabeth together across half the known world, and it's done nothing more than create a game of snakes and ladders for young academics.'

'What did you want it to do?' asked Theodoor.

'I'm a romantic, you know. I'd have liked to see some justice. Does that sound completely stupid?'

'Not stupid, but perhaps – I am not sure how to say this in English. "Poetical"?'

'That's probably right enough. I think one of the reasons I don't work on the first half of the seventeenth century is I find it so depressing to look at the way the idealists get betrayed by events. I stick with post-Restoration cynics and pragmatists, because they're people who've realised you can buy and sell just about anything, so they're easier to cope with. I suppose that for once, I wanted to see a seventeenth-century ideal taking root and flowering.'

'That is not a small thing to ask,' observed Theodoor, 'and anyway, perhaps you are in error. You assume that because the story has come to light in your time, its resolution belongs in your time also, but that might not be so. Here is a possible future. You and Melita marry and go to the United States. You succeed in your professional lives, you take out citizenship, and you have children. Four or five generations from now, one of your descendants becomes the President, which is to say, the nearest thing to the Emperor of the World that there has ever been.'

'What a completely horrible idea,' he said.

'Would it have been horrible to Pelagius, do you think? Remember, the world of Pelagius was hierarchical and centred on God, and there is a streak in American political thinking which is godly and apocalyptic. Many Americans see political events in religious terms, as an ultimate battle between good and evil, and they also appear to believe that the spread of their way of life across the world must increase the sum of human happiness in just the same way that seventeenth-century idealists believed in the Rule of the Saints. Do you not think that Pelagius would have understood President Bush a great deal better than you do? But I am only teasing. You are a child of European humanism, as am I. If you are honest with yourself, you do not truly love idealists, unless their ideas are dead past hope of resurrection. Let's talk about something else.'

Their conversation moved to other topics, and after a while, Michael found himself talking about Melita, who was seldom far from his mind. 'I think it's the first relationship I've ever felt really happy in,' he said. 'School taught me to make myself agreeable, because I was always trying to get the other boys to like me, so as an adult, I tend to make friends easily, but it's not a good set of responses to base a relationship on. I used to envy Corinne, because she seemed to find it all so easy. What is it about Holland? We used to hear all sorts of rumours about Dutch sex education. Did you all get a practical in the gym at three o'clock on Wednesdays, and write essays on sexual hygiene?'

'Not quite,' said Theodoor. 'But we teach children not to be afraid of each other.'

'It sounds like heaven. It was ages after I left home before I found anyone. It's not that I didn't want to, it just all seemed so impossibly complicated.'

'It is.'

'Even in Holland? Well, I suppose it isn't a bed of roses growing up queer anywhere. Did you have a lot of trouble coming out?'

Theodoor sighed. 'My parents were understanding, my father more so than my mother, which surprised me. But I think she had known for a long time, and did not wish to know, if you understand me. Also, she is a Catholic, and she was worried about me. But there are other kinds of problem in life. My partner Diederic is HIV-positive. He is in good health for the moment, but we must be very careful. Even in Holland, there is a stigma, you know.'

'Oh, God,' said Michael, appalled. 'I mean, I'm sorry. Thanks for telling me. I really appreciate the confidence. Er – look, there's no tactful way to ask this, but you're all right in yourself, are you?'

'As far as we know. I get a regular test, of course.'

'What a thing to have to live with. Like living under a volcano.'

'Nothing so dramatic. But if I catch a cold, I stay with a friend, and if Diederic catches a cold, we worry a great deal until he is better. Corinne knows nothing of this, by the way, it is not part of university gossip.'

'No, of course. I shan't say anything to her.'

'It has changed my life, and not only in bad ways. I think it is Diederic's health which has made me think about the universities so much, and where we are all going. There is an urge to leave something behind which is strengthened when you know that life is frail. Even if I were not homosexual, I would find it difficult to attach a value to the notion of having children. Our world is evolving so fast that one generation's experience can no longer provide *grundrisse* for the next. It is the meeting of teacher and student which is the essential contact that allows our culture to survive and renew itself. Nothing is more important.'

Michael's mind flashed back to the concert in the Sheldonian, and Theodoor's inexplicable, atrocious grief. Looked at in the light of this new knowledge, he perceived the song anew, as essentially

about unwavering personal loyalty despite inevitable physical deteri-
oration, a farewell to desire, but not to love. No wonder Theodoor
had found it impossibly moving.

'I wish I thought like that about teaching,' he confessed. 'I'm
sure you're right, but half the time I just scramble through. Some
of them are hard work because they're bored, and the keen ones
are so bloody avid, you know? And mostly they're so focused on
their wretched exams, it's very hard to get them to actually think,
even if they're bright.'

Theodoor shrugged. 'It is the same here. A great battle of wits.
You cannot tell students that knowledge hardly matters, but it is
true. What we really need to teach is the ability to ask good questions and where to go to find relevant information, even though
the state is demanding that we impart quantifiable facts, and the
students are demanding that we teach only what will earn them
marks. We must try, somehow, to give them wisdom and judgement, which they resent, and the government despises. But this
has always been so. We are a pragmatic nation, but as I try to
tell them, pragmatism alone should tell them to lift up their heads
and look around. Erasmus of Rotterdam was a very practical
fellow.'

'I don't think it's any better anywhere else. I don't know about
America, maybe in the very best places, sheer wealth lets them
have a bit more vision. I've just about given up on Oxford. It's so
conservative it isn't true.'

'Is it?' asked Theodoor. 'Then what is it keeping? In one sense,
it is the duty of our profession to conserve, but we must always
be clear what we are guarding, and why. Oxford, as I experienced
it, seems to be taking the shadow for the solid thing. It is letting
go of the *respublica litterarum*, and what it is holding onto is tokens
and symbols of prestige. Why have you stayed so long?'

'It wasn't pure inertia. I thought there was a lot of room for
improvement when I was a research student, but that made me

want to hang on in there and try and make things better. It's easier to push over walls from the inside.'

Theodoor raised his eyebrows. 'True, but sometimes then the ceiling falls on your head.'

'It hasn't, in this case. The worst you can say is I haven't managed to change anything. But I'd be looking for another job anyway, now I've got together with Melita. I don't know what we're going to do. It looks as if I can't work in Barbados, and she doesn't really want to leave.'

'Though she could?'

'Oh, yes. I think so. I can't judge her work, because I don't really understand it, but she seems to be very talented. One thing Oxford does teach you is to spot when someone really knows what they're talking about. And of course, she's a black woman. She'd hate me to say this, but I have to say that in an English university the way things are at the moment, people would be absolutely delighted to hire her. We're forever being asked about how many women and ethnics we've got in senior positions, and the answer's always "nothing like enough". I think things are better in some of the sciences, but even so, I'm sure she'd be taken very seriously for all the wrong reasons. It's all very unfair, and of course it leaves her exposed to people saying that she was only hired *because* she was black, but Melita's good at making herself respected. I'm not sure she'd have that bad a time, actually, compared with what she's used to. The University of the West Indies sounds actively dreadful, from what she's told me. It's very generous to students, but it's horrible to its staff, because they've got a permanent cash-crisis. British universities are very badly treated, outside Oxbridge where we have a lot of our own money, but almost anywhere's still going to be better resourced than UWI.'

'I wish you luck,' said Theodoor. They had finished their meal, and he raised a hand to attract the waiter. 'Do you want dessert?'

'No thanks, Theodoor. That was nice, but it was as much as I could get through. Some coffee, perhaps?'

The waiter came over, and Theodoor ordered coffee for Michael and tea for himself. They talked no more of intimate matters, but Michael felt glad that he had both made and received confidences. One without the other would have unbalanced the relationship, but as it was, he felt confirmed in Theodoor's affection, and honoured that he had said so much.

Corinne did not see Michael until they were actually in Middelburg; she knew from Theodoor that he was definitely somewhere about, so she had not been greatly worried, but it was still nice to get him ticked off on her mental list. It was vitally important that everything should go well, and she had prepared for the afternoon very carefully, including scouring every shop in Utrecht which boasted a sale-rack in search of something to wear that would boost her credibility. She had eventually found a Max Mara suit, greatly reduced due to a torn seam and a missing button, which was exactly what she wanted. Pieternelle, who was a very skilful seamstress, despite her own preference for casual comfort, had sorted out the problems for her and reshaped the skirt slightly so that it was a perfect fit. She was wearing it for the first time in honour of the Gemeente committee, and it felt wonderful.

When she saw Michael walking in with Theodoor, she hardly recognised him. To her surprise, he was also wearing a suit rather than the English academics' uniform of scruffy jacket and trousers, an unexpectedly assertive one of chalk-striped navy blue, worn with a pink shirt and a college tie. His hair was blonder than she remembered and he was tanned, as if he had been spending a lot of time in the sun, his posture was better, and he walked with confidence. Remembering his diffident shuffle of earlier days, she wondered what had come over him. Whatever it was, his previous rather mousy good looks had gained definition to the point where he was positively handsome.

The group assembled, very much on time, a positive augury in itself. The meeting was being held at the archive building, in an upstairs committee room, so that they could have actual objects on display. Piet van der Velde was there, dapper in a blue blazer, as was the chief archivist herself, together with representatives from the municipal council, the regional council, the Zeeland museums services, the library, the Zeeland history society, and the Tourist Board. On a side-table, with a junior archivist hovering protectively over them, were the principal documents which she had asked for, Aphra Behn's play and Pelagius's two notebooks, specimens of Petrus Behn's correspondence and a couple of sample books from his press, together with three documents relating to Elizabeth of Bohemia: the marriage and baptism records, and one of the letters. The committee looked at the collection curiously, not quite daring to defy the archivist's glare and pick any of them up, clearly impressed, but largely uncomprehending. Corinne let them potter and make what they could of it all for a while, before calling the meeting to order. Even though it was very informal, mere information-gathering, a largely middle-aged, male group would not care greatly to be ordered about by a young woman, so she planned to speak first very briefly, then hand over to Theodoor, who at least had the title of professor, even if he was only a one-sixth one. They didn't know that, of course.

'Thank you very much for giving us your time,' she said, smiling engagingly at them all, 'we will try not to waste it. Now, as Heer van der Velde will remember very well, this meeting today is the latest stage in a long story which began early this spring . . .' She made her points as briefly as possible; the co-operation of the Middelburg Civic Trust, the helpfulness and professional skill of the archivist and her staff, the interest of the material. 'I will speak again a little later about Petrus Behn's printworks,' she concluded, 'but for now, I will hand over to Professor van Waesberghe, who will talk about the Latin books.'

Theodoor got to his feet, and began to explain Pelagius, which he did concisely, and with great lucidity. Corinne kept a wary eye on Michael; his spoken Dutch wasn't exactly wonderful, and she wondered if he was following. But if he wasn't, he at least had the social nous to sit there looking intelligent. Theodoor caused a susurrus of interest throughout the room when he concluded his remarks by putting an acetate on the overhead projector, and flashing up Bosch's black king, explaining Pelagius's 'Quercitanus' comment as he did so. 'So we see that many disciplines must work together,' he said. 'We have no art historians in this room, but it is thanks to them that we understand the relevance of this image.'

'This will be on the website?' asked someone, a councillor, Corinne thought.

'Yes of course. We can have hyperlinks to all kinds of relevant images. We will make it easy to see how these documents relate to actual people.'

Michael spoke next, in English, but she had given him a Dutch summary of his outline of what he intended to say, and he remembered to put it on the overhead projector. He was taking some trouble to be clear and to keep his sentences short, but she could see more than one of the working party glancing at the screen. Still, as long as he didn't go on for too long, she reckoned that he was definitely scoring points simply by being a foreign expert interested in their material.

'Apart from this very interesting play,' he went on, 'these Middelburg discoveries have made a permanent change in English history.' There was a rustle of interest round the room, and Corinne regarded him warily. He had come to the end of the points indicated in his summary, and she wondered where he was going. He returned Theodoor's Bosch image to the projector. 'This man', he said, as Bosch's king appeared again, 'married this woman.' He whisked it away, and replaced it with a Mytens portrait of Elizabeth of Bohemia, a long-nosed face with shrewd, heavy-lidded eyes, an opulent bosom hung with heavy ropes of pearl. This he replaced in turn with a pedigree of the English royal family, with Elizabeth's name underlined, and deliberately drew in the names of Pelagius and Balthasar with a felt-tip. They all stared fascinated at the screen as the shadow of his hand half-revealed what he was writing.

'Elizabeth of Bohemia is a very important person,' he went on, straightening up and looking soberly at the group in front of him. 'You could call her the mother of European monarchy. In the year 1939, every single ruling sovereign of Europe except the King of Albania traced his or her descent from this woman. Over there, on that table, there is evidence that exactly three hundred years earlier, Elizabeth secretly married Pelagius van Overmeer in her chapel in The Hague, in June 1639. There was nothing whatsoever to prevent her doing this, by the way. She was married by her own Anglican chaplain, and her chapel was what's technically called a "royal peculiar", that is, it wasn't subject to ecclesiastical supervision, English or Dutch. There were complaints more than once that she allowed irregular marriages to be contracted there. In the following year, 1640, Elizabeth had a son by this second marriage. The record of baptism is over there as well. His name was Balthasar, and I've traced his later career as a doctor in Leiden and London. This is all very interesting in itself, of course, and related to my Aphra Behn project, but it's still more interesting in its implications. Look at this pedigree of the kings of England. Catholics were debarred from the succession after James II, so when Queen Anne died, leaving no surviving child, they had to go back to her nearest relative who wasn't Catholic, who turned out to be the son of Elizabeth's youngest daughter, Sophia. Yet as we now know, Elizabeth also had a Protestant son, who married and had children in his turn. By the rules of the English succession, therefore, this son had a legitimate claim on the English throne, and there is a living descendant. Ladies and gentlemen, I don't claim that the world is about to turn upside-down, but I think quite a lot of people in England are going to be very interested in Middelburg.'

The audience sat stunned for a few seconds, absorbing and translating what had been said, then several people began to talk at once. Corinne cursed Michael silently but vehemently for not having told her explicitly how the bits fitted together. Along with his new looks, he had evidently developed a previously unsuspected theatrical streak. It was a sensation, a triumph, but she would have liked to be consulted. As things were, her little piece on Petrus Behn was about to fall as flat as a pancake, though it represented the absolute centre of the interface between the Gemeente and the various academic projects which had arisen out of the Middelburg documents. It was not at all easy to see how to salvage the situation; so she glanced at her watch.

'I think we should take a break here,' she announced, standing up. 'I think we all want to look at those documents, I know I do. And perhaps Michael will read off what they say, and I can translate?' It was the best she could manage; she would have to bring the meeting in on time because of the trains, and she was cutting into the space available for her own presentation, but it couldn't be helped.

By the time they had reached Ankie and Pieternelle's, after the long and tiresome journey north, she had forgiven him. The meeting had inevitably changed direction following his little bombshell, but it had not fallen apart. What was more, the most determinedly stuiver-counting of the local worthies had seen the attractive potential of the material; there was even talk of freeing up space in the Zeeuws Museum so as to make a possibly permanent display. Knowing the museum director as she did, she was well aware that particular turf-war would be fought as bitterly as the Battle of the Somme, but as an indication of commitment and interest from the Gemeente, it could hardly be better.

'Well, how did it all go?' asked Ankie, ushering them into the Catherijnestraat flat. She spoke in English, Corinne was pleased to note, suggesting that she had forgiven Michael for daring to work on Aphra Behn without being a lesbian.

'Hallo, Ankie,' said Michael. 'Nice to see you again. It went very well. Corinne was brilliant.'

'I'm glad to hear it. Come and have some drinks.'

Corinne introduced Michael to Pieternelle, and they got themselves sorted out. Suddenly extremely tired, she took some orange juice, and plumped down on the sofa, leaving it to Theodoor and Michael to recount the deeds of the day in a mixture of Dutch and English.

Ankie and Pieternelle, while properly appreciative of Corinne's political triumph, were intensely interested in the aftermath of the Pelagius story. 'So you have this family of free blacks in Barbados who know they're the rightful kings of England?' asked Pieternelle.

'Well, no, actually. The Stuart connection got forgotten – I suppose someone didn't get around to telling his son in time. What they really think they are is the emperors of Byzantium.'

Pieternelle laughed. 'Living on rice and saltfish.'

'Well, why not? It's not as if ancestry entitles you to anything. My friend Natty thinks people ought to be told about all this. He's quite seduced by the idea of Melita as a black queen, though of course that wouldn't happen. What Melita and I really want is to make the story public so as to question the whole idea of monarchy. She's very down on kings and queens.'

'I think you're all of you right,' said Pieternelle. 'Rationally speaking, I agree with you and Melita, but people like stories, especially old ones, and this is the story of Assepoester.'

'Cinderella,' Corinne put in from the sofa where she sat, since he looked completely confused.

'Thank you,' said Pieternelle. 'In so many of the old stories, becoming a king or a queen stands for everything good. In Cinderella, we have the tale of a despised girl who becomes a beautiful princess. It is a seducing idea, and it is possible to read the story of Melita in this way.'

'Yes, I can see that,' he said. 'Alternatively, you can read her as a long-lost princess who's reclaimed to her rightful position, like the Grimms' Goose Girl, or Perdita in *The Winter's Tale*. I'm afraid that sort of idea's still very attractive – the thing is, if people are going to be attracted by presenting Melita's heritage as a real-life version of an archetypal story, then we're going to have to try and use that interest to make them question the whole idea.'

'Difficult,' said Ankie. 'The last time I saw my young niece, she was glued to some idiotic books called *The Princess Diaries*, which seem to be about just this – a heroine who finds out she is really a princess. Giesela is a sensible girl, but she loves these stories.'

'I think everyone wants to be Cinderella,' he said, 'not just girls. She gets this enormous reward just for being her lovely self, and she gets a future on a plate. I mean, that has to be appealing, especially to teenagers. But surely you can separate that out from trying to see if British monarchy is a dinosaur that doesn't know it's dead? We might find that out by seeing how people react to Melita.'

'The trouble is, fairy-tale queens and kings are one thing. Third-millennium limited, constitutional monarchies are another, and your story crosses over between the two,' said Ankie.

'I think that's the point. We don't have a constitution, and we've got a monarchy with far too much mystique. Melita might help people to think about that.'

Theodoor glanced at his watch. 'Ankie, Pieternelle, my dears. I think I must go. It is getting late.'

'We'll see you to the door,' said Ankie.

Once their goodbyes had been said, Michael sat down beside Corinne on the sofa, as the other three moved into the hall.

'What a day,' he said.

'Mmm.' She was almost too tired to speak.

Michael fished for his wallet, and took out a photograph, which he put into her hand.

'Is this your Goose Girl? Melita?' she asked, registering that the image was that of a young black woman.

'Yes. I'm in love with her, Corinne. I want to marry her. God knows how we're going to manage our lives.'

She looked at him properly, astounded. He was obviously quite serious, and she surprised herself with a tiny pang of regret.

'Congratulations,' she said.

XII

How will it be to belong to a land whose history witnesses this hideous default, a land self-maddened, psychologically burnt-out, which quite understandably despairs of governing itself?

Thomas Mann, *Doctor Faustus*, ch. xlv

'I'm just going out for a walk,' announced Neville Foxwist after breakfast, on the second day of Michael's visit. Michael looked at his father, and worried. He had surprised a glance of furtive distrust on the evening of his arrival, which seemed to bespeak a further downturn in their relationship. He had been in touch periodically with his Aunt May over the summer, and she had mentioned that his father had taken up walking; not merely his familiar pottering to and fro in Criffel Street, but quite long excursions. Michael presumed that in response to his generally deteriorating state, Neville was taking active steps to maintain health, but although he was pleased to see the fighting spirit implicit in such activity, he worried whether his father was stopping to rest as often as he should. Certainly, the previous evening, he had looked very grey when he returned, and he had had no appetite for his supper.

'Father, be careful. You're not as young as you were. Remember you're not in a race.'

'I'm perfectly well aware of that, Michael. That's no reason a fellow shouldn't keep as fit as he can. I wish you'd keep up with your running, it'll pay dividends in the end, believe me. You haven't had your tracksuit on since you got here.'

Neville left the room, victorious, as Michael opened his mouth to retort that he had barely been in Cumbria for thirty-six hours, and a moment later, he heard the front door shutting.

Michael sat on for a while, envisaging his father's spare figure dotting jerkily down Criffel Street, and wondering why he felt so bothered; in a way, he was so used to the old man's invariability that any sort of change, however benign, was liable to cause anxiety. Later that day, he was due to go into Carlisle and pick up Natty from the train; he must go up and make the bed and find a couple of newish towels. He was not looking forward to the visit. However good an idea it had seemed in the abstract, in practice it had had to be laboriously explained over the phone, then laboriously explained all over again the previous night, and doubtless he would have laboriously to explain it for a third time over lunch.

Neville had been disconcerted at having a guest at all, rather than hostile towards the idea of entertaining a black man; when the subject was broached, he had responded by recalling every single one of the few St Ninian's boys who had come from 'the Colonies', who had all, it seemed, been reasonably creditable and jolly good at cricket. Michael thought parenthetically that he had better warn Natty that unless he had particularly vehement feelings about the matter, it would help the visit go more easily if he refrained from pointing out that Barbados was and had been for some time an independent country.

He made himself a little list on the back of an envelope. Bed, towels, food shopping; he would do a roast joint of some kind with roast potatoes and get in a couple of bottles of decent wine. They would have a pudding, for once. He had no talents in that direction, but perhaps he could get a bought apple pie, or failing that, some expensive ice-cream, since he remembered that Natty had a sweet tooth. He would have to set off for Carlisle at around three. At least the prospect was less dreadful than on previous visits; as part of the process of taking charge of his life which he had instituted on his return from Barbados, he had taken out a small loan, and bought a car: it was only a ten-year-old Renault Five, but it went, and he had driven up from Oxford in it. He had come off the motorway at Penrith, and then across the Lake District, and he was not looking forward to his first experience of the Carlisle one-way system, though after learning to cope with Bridgetown, he thought he could probably manage.

None of that need take very long, unless he went all the way to Cockermouth to get a fruit pie from Bryson's or some goodies from No. XVII. There was no denying he had a potential chunk of spare time, and he ought to go and see Harold Boumphrey, a thought which made his heart sink. The quarrel over Harold's cheque seemed to have permanently damaged his relationship with his father, and according to May, the occasional calls which Neville used to pay on his uncle by marriage had ceased: as far as he could discover, they were no longer on speaking terms. Apart from the domestic friction which contact might bring, he dreaded finding out where Harold had got to. The news of Melita seemed to have reconfigured the old man's obsessions, sending him off in yet another set of erratic directions.

Great-Uncle Harold was, inevitably, delighted to see him when he presented himself just after lunch; a meal which Michael and his father had, in fact, eaten in virtual silence.

'I am holding myself in readiness,' he announced, once he and Michael had sat down in their usual chairs by the study fireplace, and he had asked earnestly after Melita.

'What for?'

'The Last Days,' said Harold serenely. 'My dear Michael, what may we not see, with these our living eyes! It is hard to know what to do for the best, of course. The present state of affairs is not easy to interpret. The so-called scientists are saying, I gather, that we may expect something they call "the heat-death of the universe".'

'Global warming, Uncle Harold,' interjected Michael.

'Be that as it may. It is a mere matter of terminology. It seems to me probable that they perceive preliminary monitions of the wrath to come. Fire from heaven, Michael. Cleansing fire, to purge the dross of this world, and show forth the Lord's Elect, "like refinèd gold"!'

'Not immediately, surely?'

'Oh, by no means. The present world may continue for some time. Remember, we have yet to enjoy the rule of the Empress. Yet it seems to me that if she is to come over the great seas and enter into her glory, borne upon the wings of the wind, clothèd with the sun, terrible as an army with banners, yet companioned with justice and mercy, we may expect some degree of civic disruption. Since your last letter, I have been realising my various investments and turning them into gold, which I am storing in the wine-cellar.'

Michael sighed. The combination of prophetic vision with a species of perverse practicality left him searching rather cautiously for firm ground. The cynical thought occurred to him that as one behemoth of the global culture after another either fell to bits or confessed to telling its investors a pack of lies, there might be sillier things than investing in gold, whatever the rationale. And due to the foulness of the local weather, older Cumbrian houses were built to withstand just about anything short of fire from heaven, so the cellar was probably safe enough.

'What else have you been doing? Have you spoken to Prince Michael of Albany?' The Belgian Pretender, it occurred to him, might be a little miffed at his great-uncle's withdrawal of interest.

'Prince Michael's conduct was quite extraordinary,' said Harold coldly. 'He made a number of most regrettable remarks. I fear I may have been mistaken in that young man. He saw fit to take exception to Her Sacred Majesty, in terms which I considered quite unacceptable, and he seemed unable to understand that the colour distinction is of course one of degree and not of kind. I was forced to remind him that the Good Book does not direct our attention to distinction of race, other than, of course, the distinction between the Chosen and the Rejected. But the distinction between patrician and plebeian, both physical and mental, is natural and, of course, it is to be found in all colours of peoples. Still more so, naturally, in scions of the Royal Line. I have been looking into this question, and it is certainly significant that the greatest hero of the negroes of America was named King. Furthermore, I have discovered that the coloured peoples themselves recognised Haile Selassie, a direct descendant of Solomon and the Queen of Sheba through her son Menyelek, as the Lion of Judah.'

Oh God, thought Michael resignedly. He's got round to Rastafarianism. I might have known it. All the same, he was cheered by the thought of Harold's doing his bit against racism, even on the eccentric grounds of ultimate royalty; the old man had a fine flow of words when he was roused, and the ghastly Pretender had probably had the shock of his life. Moreover, if one could judge by appearances, the excitement of Melita's advent in their lives had given his uncle a new lease of life. He looked as if he was having a lovely time. 'Excellent,' he said vaguely. 'I've heard something about that. Look, Uncle, I'm going to have to go in a minute. I'm meeting someone off the train so I have to get over to Carlisle. I'll be here for the rest of the week, and I'll come and see you again.'

Michael was waiting on the platform when the London train came in. Natty was easy to spot amid the scuttling passengers; he was wearing a bright blue padded jacket which looked to Michael as if it had been intended to be worn for climbing in the Himalayas, and suggested that he was not disposed to be optimistic about northern weather. They shook hands warmly, and walked out towards the car.

'There's no good way to get out of Carlisle,' said Michael, once he had slung Natty's bag and laptop into the boot and they were strapping in. 'I take it you haven't been anywhere round here?'

'No. I've never been north of Birmingham. That's why I took Glasgow up on this one, I was curious.'

'Well, I can tell you now, there's not much in the town, and it's a foul place to drive through. What I was thinking was, instead of battling the one-way system to get across to the west, why don't we take the short hop to the motorway, and whizz down to Penrith? Then we can drive across the Lake District, via Keswick and Bassenthwaite, and home via Cockermouth and Aspatria. You'll laugh if I show you on the map, because it looks like a ridiculously long way for a short cut, but it will be much nicer, and you'll see the pretty bit. I came up that way myself a couple of days ago, and it really is a lovely drive. Cockermouth's where Wordsworth was born.'

'I'd like that,' said Natty agreeably.

'How long've you been in England?' asked Michael a bit later, when they were hammering down the M6.

'About a week. I've been staying with a friend in Coventry. I was thinking just now, when I was on the train, if you're black, your networks in this country are totally urban. That's one of the reasons I wanted to come and see you. You're the only country-type English person I've ever met. I've visited in quite a few bits of England, but when I stop to think about it, they've all been cities. It's like when most white people come to the Caribbean, they sit on the beaches. You get a very particular view.'

'Well,' said Michael, swinging off the motorway at junction forty, 'this is different.'

'Different?' said Natty, peering out. 'It's practically Switzerland.'

Michael stopped the car in the tourists' layby beside Bassenthwaite Lake, where several other cars were already parked, and they got out to admire the vista, which was having one of its picture-postcard moments. The water was very blue, and the vast bulk of Skiddaw loomed beyond, looking almost benign in the golden light. To right and left of them, people were taking photographs or peering through binoculars; the latter were looking, Michael knew, for the ospreys, which did live on the lake, but tended to make themselves visible with the discouraging infrequency of the Loch Ness Monster.

'Do people climb up there?' asked Natty, indicating Skiddaw.

'They do indeed. You've got to be quite careful, though. Weather conditions can change very quickly, and it's surprisingly easy to get into trouble.'

'I believe you. No way you'd get me up that thing.'

Some while later, coming out of Cockermouth, Natty said, 'I've been thinking about the English and the countryside. Is this the sort of place English people really want to live?'

'Oh, yes. If one of those lovely grey-stone farmhouses in the National Park comes up, you can get telephone-numbers for it. It makes a big difference if you're in the National Park, you see, because you're protected against future development.'

'And that's important?'

'Of course. You want to protect your view, your privacy. That's what you're really paying for.'

'Do you know, I find that completely alien? The houses are scenic, yes, but to me they look lonely, and maybe vulnerable. I even wondered if they might be some sort of wardens' houses you get paid for living in. We don't think like that in Barbados. If I was buying a place back home, I wouldn't think twice about the neighbours, 'less they were coming over the damn fence. You live inside your own four walls.'

'You can't afford to do anything else,' Michael pointed out. 'You could fit the whole of Barbados into the Lake District National Park with plenty of room left over. If you went over to Holland, which is another crowded country, you'd find people were more like Bajans about social distance.'

'I don't think that's the whole story,' said Natty. 'Other West

Indians aren't like that either, and there's some big islands. Jamaica, for instance. Isn't there some kind of quote about the English, that they look at desolation and call it peace?'

'Not exactly,' said Michael. ' "They made a desolation and called it peace." That's Tacitus talking about the Romans in Scotland, but you have a point.'

'It's beautiful here,' admitted Natty, 'but I wouldn't feel comfortable. Too visible.'

'How about Melita? Can you guess how she'd react?'

'Well, you wouldn't be trying to live half-way up a mountain, would you?'

'Certainly not, we couldn't possibly afford it.'

'Well, let's say that if you were settling down with her, I'd imagine she'd prefer to live in a town. I know she's an ecologist, but even scientists must want time out from work. I'm sure she'd like a yard, most Bajans like to garden, but that's maybe enough nature for daily life.'

'Here we are at last,' said Michael, as they swung onto the main street. 'I warn you, we've done the scenic bit. The only arty book to feature Silloth is *Boring Postcards*.'

'Oh, but this is a great little place,' said Natty. 'I love the colours.'

Surveying Criffel Street in the evening light, a streetscape which featured a cream house picked out with red adjacent to a yellow house picked out with pink, and other façades in the terrace painted in enterprising combinations of green, pink, white, blue, and black, Michael was forced to recognise that it had points in common with Barbadian decorative taste.

'It's quite cheerful,' he admitted, 'and you're seeing it on a good day. It can look a bit sad in bad light.'

'So can anything in this fair land,' said Natty.

Michael looked at his watch. 'Father's not expecting us till sixish,' he said. 'Do you want to go for a walk?'

'I'd like that.'

They parked the car and went down to look at the Solway, but after a minute, Michael realised that Natty was looking along the promenade rather than out to sea. 'What've you spotted?' he asked.

'Is that a big wheel?'

'Yes, it's the amusement park.'

'Hey, can we go?'

It was a very small amusement park, though bravely and recently repainted: its most notable feature, apart from the not-very-big wheel, a wheel of a mere dozen gondolas, was a central construction called 'Irvin's Ultra-Modern Juvenile Ride', dodgems, of course. Michael remembered it well, though it had not had any of his custom since he was an undergraduate. The familiar smell of hot-dogs, fried onions, petrol and popcorn came out to meet them as they went through, and hurled him back to the end of his teens. There were still mums and dads supervising young children on the swings, little boys underfoot, demanding a go at the shooting-gallery, teenagers blank-eyed with metropolitan ennui, emanating that they were there for the lack of anything better to do; he remembered being one such. Natty, he remembered, embraced the cult of cool, but he seemed to have taken a vacation from the need to be unimpressed; laughing with pleasure, he insisted on buying two tickets for the big wheel.

'What d'you think a Postmodern Juvenile Ride would be like?' asked Michael, as they were strapping themselves in. The gondolas were intended for couples, or perhaps a parent with a child; as their knees touched, he was reminded of their first meeting, hugger-mugger in economy. 'It hardly bears thinking about.'

'Oh, I don't know. You might have a Quantum Mechanical Twister? You'd never be certain where your stomach was. Or you could have a Spin Doctor, which would be a modernised waltzer.'

'A Railtrack Rollercoaster,' suggested Michael, 'or possibly it would have to be a Ghost Train.'

'I think the crucial thing would be introducing the principle of uncertainty. One person in five hundred randomly killed, maybe. That'd suit a Railtrack theme, for sure.'

'What a cheerful thought, as we're about to start,' said Michael drily.

'Ah, but this one's only ultra-modern. We're OK.'

The wheel began to move; they went once round, then went round again, stopping to let each couple enjoy the view from the top. Cumbria spun past them; in the distance, he could see the towering blue backs of the Lake District's fells rising from the relative flatness of the Solway Plain like a school of basking whales.

Michael swung gently in the air, looking at the fells and thinking about Melita, borne upon the wings of the wind in a wide-bodied Boeing 767, as she would be one day, not that year, but perhaps the year after. He was abruptly positive that somehow it would all work out.

Once they had come down again, Michael deflected Natty tactfully from the dodgems, and suggested that it was probably time to go home. He had bought a piece of lamb, and it would need time to cook.

When they got there, he left the bags in the hall, and took Natty up to meet his father.

'Michael tells me you're a writer,' said Neville, shaking hands. 'I have no dealings with the modern novel, but you're doing well, I trust?'

Michael looked at his father; he was in full headmaster mode. Oh, good. Well, he thought, he had perhaps been worrying unduly. It was easy to forget from day to day that his father was after all an experienced man in his own way.

'Not too badly,' said Natty, who was plainly adept at fielding that kind of question. 'It's hard to make a living as a serious novelist, you know. I do some journalism, a little TV work back home, and this semester, I'm teaching creative writing in UEA. It's creative writing which keeps a lot of us going.'

'And have you ever found any talent worth fostering?' enquired Neville, while Michael poured drinks.

'It's not quite like that, Mr Foxwist. You get some strange people signing up. Kids with dreams and no grammar. People who're good at telling stories and think they just have to start writing it down and they'll make a fortune. Ladies who wish they weren't married, the odd genuine crazy. The real trick is to sort out the people who want to write, 'cause you can teach them something. The rest is social work.'

'But surely they all want to write, or they would not be there?' objected Neville.

'No, not at all, Mr Foxwist. A surprising variety want to "be writers", I mean, they have an idea of themselves as an author, and they see the writing as just a necessary chore. Sometimes it's that they see themselves being interviewed on TV, or sometimes it's just, "If I published a book, my husband would realise I'm a human being", or "If I could make money out of a book, I could get out of this Godawful job". You can't help a person who thinks like that, but you can sometimes help a guy who's really and truly trying to communicate some sort of idea, even if he's never heard of apostrophes.'

'That is very illuminating,' said Neville. 'You are telling me that writing is disinterested?'

'Oh, no. I've never met a writer who didn't want to make money. But if you don't keep faith with the writing, you'll never make a damn cent.'

'I'll just go and put the lamb in,' said Michael, escaping. Things were going quite well, thank God. He got the dinner on – everything was prepared, it was simply a matter of shoving it in the oven and hoping for the best – nipped downstairs for Natty's stuff, and took it up to his room. Seeing Natty again, hearing the Barbadian accent, made him miss Melita acutely. His moment of mysterious confidence at the top of the big wheel had worn off again, and he was seized by despair at the inordinate difficulties in their way. He must remember to tell her that he had discovered via the Web that Newcastle University taught tropical coastal management studies, God alone knew why. If she could get a job at Newcastle, he could find something at Newcastle, or Durham, maybe even Edinburgh or York. It was not impossible. Or there was Kew, which would give him all the universities within reach of London, though he could not think how they could afford to live in the south. Shaking off his squirrelling thoughts, he went back downstairs to his father and Natty.

By the time he was able to rejoin them, they were talking about cricket, and it was at once apparent to him that Natty could make cricket conversation on automatic pilot. Michael wondered what he was actually thinking. He was certainly on a second gin and tonic, which perhaps accounted for his fluency; Neville's glass was also full, but, he suspected, untouched. Michael could see the whites of Natty's eyes moving behind his glasses, the way his gaze was flick-flicking round the room as if he were trying to memorise it. Perhaps he was. Michael could see very well that it was a situation he might want to make use of at some future point, a thought he found distasteful.

Dinner was a reasonable success; the lamb was at any rate cooked, even if the potatoes had got a bit hard while they waited for it, and he had remembered to buy a jar of mint-sauce. They were having frozen peas with it, in the interests of simplicity.

'Thank you, Michael,' said his father, accepting a laden plate. 'Bravo. This is quite a feast. Michael's mother, God rest her, was an excellent cook, and he has inherited her turn for it,' he explained to Natty. 'I can just about shift for myself, but I don't venture out of my depth, as it were.'

'I don't cook much,' said Natty.

'I imagine you eat a lot of cold food in the West Indies?'

'Not really. I tend to pick up some fried chicken or a roti from a Chefette, or grab a cutter in a rum-shop. It's not healthy, but it's quick.'

'I liked Barbadian food,' said Michael. 'The hotel I was staying in was famous for good, traditional cooking.'

His father's face closed down at once, and Michael cursed himself for mentioning his trip to Barbados; with Natty there, he had momentarily forgotten that it was a taboo subject. Natty leaped into the breach with an exhaustive description of the Sunday lunch they had eaten together, a well-intentioned gesture which only made things worse. Neville was sulking; he made barely a pretence of eating, and watching him, Michael felt his own stomach closing up with nervous irritation. He poured more wine; he and Natty were drinking too much, he thought, and Neville not enough. Please God, he thought, let this be over soon. By way of damage limitation, he could take Natty for a walk and drop in at a pub, returning only at eleven once Neville had gone to bed; with proper management, the three of them would only have to get through another hour together.

'Each to their own,' said Neville, when Natty ran out of things to say, in a tone which cancelled any further discussion. Michael stood up, his stomach curdling with rage at his father's rudeness, and collected up the plates, with their cold and mangled food.

They got through the rest of the meal somehow, chewing over the topics of the city of Glasgow, a subject on which they were all three almost equally ignorant, and the world of literary fest-ivals, on which Natty at least could speak with knowledge, along with their bought apple pie and ice-cream. As soon as possible after dinner, Michael announced his intention of taking Natty out for a walk.

'I've got my key,' he said, glaring at his father, settled once more in the sitting-room. 'Don't wait up.'

Neville fished down the side of his chair for the remote control, and turned on the television. 'Very well, Michael. I shall watch the news.' He did not bid Natty good-night; it was as if he no longer existed.

'I'm sorry, Natty,' said Michael, once they were outside the house. 'Let's go and get a drink. I hope you weren't too embarrassed.'

'Don't worry about it,' said Natty as they set off. 'What got into him? I thought things were going pretty well, then he turned sour.'

'It was mentioning the trip to Barbados that did it,' confessed Michael. 'The thing is, my mad great-uncle gave me the money to go – I told you that, I think – and father's mortally offended. He thinks I should've refused to take Harold's cheque, though he's rolling in money. I do understand his viewpoint, but I don't actually share it. It's one of those generational things.'

'Why?' asked Natty. 'He's your uncle. At home, we set a lot of store by family. If there was some old uncle comfortably off and he bought the kids their uniforms and schoolbooks, no one would think anything about it. If it was outside the family, maybe they'd suck their teeths.'

'I suppose Father might've accepted help with my education, though it would've gone against the grain. The trouble is, as he sees it, old Harold gave me the money because he was nuts, and I took advantage of him being doolally to get myself an expensive holiday. There's an element of truth in that, of course. Father thinks I should've refused to pander to his delusions, and torn up the cheque.'

'That's a real sea-green incorruptible attitude,' remarked Natty. 'I'm with you, though. I'd've taken the money.'

'Sometimes I wish I hadn't. Though if I hadn't, I wouldn't've met Melita. But I don't think he's ever going to forgive me.'

'Not the end of the world.'

'It's the end of something,' confessed Michael. They were pacing round the empty and silent streets of Silloth in the dark: they had already passed two different pubs, but he did not want to break up the moment by going into the light, the roar of voices and the smell of beer. 'What you have to understand is that I've been trained for my whole life to want his approval. Because he used to be my headmaster, he can't resist marking me out of ten, but there's always been at least one tick, as it were, or E for effort. Like with that bloody awful dinner. He tries to be encouraging. I know it just looks like the sulks, but it's not. He thinks I've done something which shows I'm fundamentally not officer material, and he's disappointed and ashamed. I've failed, and there's nothing I can do about it.'

Natty came to a halt under a street-lamp, and Michael stopped, facing him. A police-car, passing, slowed and nearly stopped; Michael raised his face to let the light fall on it properly, and recognised the constable at the wheel, Tom Asby, a contemporary, who nodded to him, and drove on.

'Let him go,' Natty advised soberly. 'You a man now.'

'If only it was that easy. He needs me, you see. I read somewhere that in the eighteenth century, someone who murdered someone else at sea used to be tied to the corpse and left to rot. It was in one of those ghastly books boys read, and I remember having nightmares about it, but I've forgotten if it was the Royal Navy or pirates or what. But that's what it's like, Natty. I'm tied to him.'

'How about that drink?'

'You're right. We need it.'

At about twenty past eleven, Michael let them into the dark and silent house, and they crept stocking-footed to the bathroom and to their beds. Michael lay awake half the night, staring angrily into the dark, and when the morning light came filtering through the blue curtains with the little white boats, he listened to his father's ablutions without affection, and then pulled on some clothes, and went downstairs to put the kettle on. There was no sign of Natty, who was either sleeping late or lying low, sensibly waiting till all the coughing and shuffling about was over with.

As soon as the kettle was on the stove, he went down to collect the post. It was always his job when he was at home, because it saved Neville a trip up and down the stairs. There was seldom anything for him, but once in a while, the most conscientious of the porters sent on anything which looked urgent. That morning, along with the flyers for replacement windows and Littlewoods catalogues, he could see an expensive, official-looking envelope lying on the mat. It was franked as from the university, which was doubtless why Mervyn had readdressed it; he recognised the chief porter's handwriting.

The contents turned out to be short and to the point. The English Faculty regretted that the proposed course on 'The Roots of the Novel' had not been acceptable to a majority of its members, they were his sincerely, etcetera etcetera. It was not unexpected, but he thought, with passion, That's it. I must go. Robert Edzell, who had spent his entire working life in Oxford and could not imagine living anywhere else, would doubtless choke down this victory for inertia, and come back in two years when Ellen had retired. Fine. In a way, he was glad that someone had that sort of stamina, but he could no longer envisage doing it himself. He had spent too many years of his life already teaching courses he did not quite believe in. It would be idiotic to flounce out when he did not yet know what Melita would be able to do, since she was the harder of the pair of them to place, but his decision was made. From that time on he was simply marking time till something came up. Meanwhile, he must make Neville's breakfast.

He had tea and toast waiting on the table by the time his father came down, a peace-offering, which was accepted up to a point. Neville looked rather grey; he had evidently not had a good night either.

'How are you?' Michael asked.

'Mustn't grumble,' said his father, buttering a piece of toast.

'You make a good cup of tea, Michael. It makes all the difference when you take the trouble to warm the pot.'

Neville drank two cups of tea, but after a couple of token nibbles, the toast and marmalade was laid uneaten on his plate, and he refused offers of an egg or porridge. They could hear Natty's footsteps creaking overhead as Neville stood up, rolling his napkin and returning it to its ring. 'It's a nice morning,' he said. 'I think I'll go out for a bit, leave you with your pal. You're taking him into Carlisle later on, aren't you? If I'm not back before you go, give him my regards.'

'Yes, Father,' said Michael. Neville went out, and moments later, Natty came in.

'Morning,' he said. 'Any chance of coffee?'

'I'll have to make it in a jug,' warned Michael, putting the kettle on.

'Anything,' said Natty.

The bright promise of the morning faded towards nine o'clock. Michael looked uneasily out of the window at the greying sky, an unease which deepened as a patter of rain hit the window like a handful of gravel, blown by some random gust.

'I hope Father's taking shelter somewhere,' he said.

'He's old enough to take care of himself,' said Natty. 'Don't worry.'

But the spatter of rain turned to a definite downpour, and by ten o'clock, when his father had not yet come home, Michael went to look for him, carrying two umbrellas. He wasn't in the Balmoral, the first and best idea, or taking shelter in the belvedere on the esplanade. But if he had got caught as the rain started, and knocked on a friend's door, surely he would have had the sense to ring? With an appalling sense of role-reversal, Michael rang the three most obvious cronies, and met blankness in response. He was acutely aware that time was running on, and Natty would need to be got to Carlisle.

'Look, Natty, I'm going out in the car to look for him. If I'm not back by eleven, here's a taxi number and twenty quid. I'm sorry, but I'm getting seriously bothered.'

'I'll come with you,' said Natty. 'I can jump ship and ring for a cab if I need to. I'll get my bags.'

They ran out in the rain, and piled into the Renault. Michael cast down by the amusement park, then past Boumphrey's house, up the little road to Skinburness. He visited the cramped and pebble-dashed back-streets of Silloth, hunted briefly up towards Causewayside, then took the road past the allotments, the football fields, and Carr's; how far could his father reasonably have got, in an hour and a half?

Half-way to Blitterlees turned out to be the answer. Michael and Natty were driving down the coast road, past endless mudflats, shining taupe and silver, marram grass on undulating dunes, gorse, and thorn-bushes blown by the wind into Bride of Frankenstein wigs, peering out anxiously to either side. The road jinked past a tiny isolated bungalow looking out over desolation. It was a nasty dangerous corner, a corner where cars would naturally swing out. If Michael had not been looking everywhere, he would hardly have spotted his father; Neville looked such a small thing by the side of the road.

They did not dare to lift him; he was still breathing, but sodden, flattened by the rain, and unconscious, so it was unclear whether he had been hit by a car, or had suffered one of his fainting-fits. If he had been hit, there might be something broken. Michael just prayed it was not his back, frantically dialling nine-nine-nine with shaking fingers. He did not carry a mobile, but Natty had one.

Natty, meanwhile, covered Neville with Michael's coat, and the blanket out of the back of the car, and propped an umbrella over him. They sat in the car together with the hazard lights on, watching the inert heap of coverings and waiting for the ambulance.

Michael was shaking with rage. 'The bastard. The old bastard. He's done this on purpose.' There were tears running down his face; Natty passed him a handkerchief in silence. 'He doesn't want to go into a home. I can see it now, he's been wantonly courting trouble.'

'Hasn't he the right?' asked Natty.

'Well, he's picked his bloody moment, hasn't he?' Michael snarled. He was hardly able to explain his feeling of complete betrayal; at that moment, looking at Neville lying there in the rain, he at once fervently wished him dead, and longed for him to come round. He was appalled by the thought that his father might contrive to die before they had talked things through.

He heard the distant wailing of an ambulance, and moved the car a yard or two up the road to give them easier access. Moments later, the van drew up, and a couple of men leaped out.

'You've done well, lad,' said the team-leader, surveying the scene. 'Folks often meddle, just wanting to help, but it's best left to us. We're taking him to the C.I. – the New Cumberland Infirmary, you know? D'you know the way? Good. Well, you just follow on when you're ready, and we'll have him sorted out in a brace of shakes.' Only seconds seemed to pass before Neville was transferred to a stretcher and lifted into the ambulance. 'See you in a minute,' the ambulanceman called cheerily, just as the doors closed.

Michael got back into his own car, and realised as he sat down that his hands were shaking uncontrollably. He felt about a hundred. 'I'm sorry, Natty. I don't think I can drive.'

'I'll drive,' said Natty, getting out.

Michael dully transferred to the passenger seat. In some corner of his mind was the thought that Natty would probably kill them, and was, in any case, almost certainly not insured. He was past caring.

But in fact, Natty, though using the horn in a way that caused consternation and even rage among his fellow road-users, drove very capably, and Michael relaxed blankly into the passenger seat, letting him get on with it, and speaking only when they came to a crossroads.

'Oh, God, Natty. Your train,' he said suddenly, about half an hour later, as they were making their way up the A596.

'There are other trains,' said Natty absently, his eyes on a caravan ahead of them. 'I don't need to be there for a while.' He pulled out to overtake, hooting in Barbadian style, and provoking a shaken fist from the elderly driver.

Natty left him at the infirmary, and took a taxi on to the station. Michael took his hand as they said their farewells, unable to find words to thank him.

'Hey,' said Natty, disengaging his fingers. He touched Michael briefly on the shoulder. 'Stay cool. Hope it all works out.' He folded himself into the back of the taxi, and was carried smoothly away.

Michael trudged into the glass palace of the C.I., which looked to him more like an award-winning airport than a place of healing, and started trying to find out what had happened to his father.

In the course of the hours that followed, Neville was admitted, X-rayed, and since geriatrics didn't quite count as proper emergencies even when found unconscious by the side of the road, was handed over to the 'elderly care' team for assessment. After some delay, Michael was told that he had been found a bed. It was hoped that a doctor might be available to see him.

Michael sat on, enquiring every half-hour or so where his father had got to, and retreating between-whiles into a sort of cafeteria, unwilling to leave until he had some sense of what the position was, and fortifying himself randomly with instant coffee and snacks; he felt he needed sugar badly. In this enforced interlude, he found himself mustering the case for the defence; he felt, quite irrationally, that if he had it straight in his mind, he might have a chance to deliver it.

318

The money. He could have taken out a loan to go to Barbados, as he had recently taken one to buy a car. But he had not perceived at the time that he had any need to go to Barbados. The reasons for going were Harold Boumphrey's reasons, they served his ends. The fact that he had found there Melita, who was so much more than merely the Empress of the Last Days, not because she was Stuart as well as Palaeologue, but because she was all that she was, Walrond, Padmore, Babb, Puckerin and all the rest . . . all that must be left out of the balance. His love for Melita was a pure gift from God, which nobody could have predicted when he decided to go.

The ethics of taking money from a man in a deluded state. Well, as Neville was busily demonstrating, somewhere in this hygienic ant-heap, a man not actually defined as mad in the sense of being committed to a mental hospital had some right to determine his own actions. Compared with attempting indirect suicide and thereby causing consternation, anguish and an unbelievable amount of trouble, giving someone £5,000 to do something which you wanted done seemed both rational and harmless.

His father's son shouldn't have done it. Well, and why the hell not? He was, after all, the only man for the job because he was the one in possession of the facts. It was not a holiday, it was a research trip. Who else could, or should, have tracked down Melpomene; who else could have matched up the two sets of information? It was real research, and, quite coincidentally, served a whole other set of legitimate concerns beside the manifestly nutty obsessions of Harold Boumphrey. Apart from running across Neville's archaic, straight-bat-keeping moral code, nothing but good had come of it, which was more than you could say for waltzing around Silloth trying to get run over.

As he got to that point, drinking the last of his cold and horrible coffee, Michael realised that somewhere in the indigestible stew of emotions he was harbouring there was a passionate conviction that Neville had put himself morally in the wrong with respect to him, and while two wrongs do not make a right, he felt obscurely fortified by the perception.

By four o'clock in the afternoon, they had news for him. 'There's some bruising, but no breakage,' said the doctor. 'Actually, I'm not at all sure he was hit by a car. People are usually quite decent about stopping, you know, unless they're drunk. I think he was probably taking things rather fast, and had a slight syncope. He's had a couple of these little cardiac episodes before, hasn't he?'

'Yes,' said Michael.

'We'd better keep an eye on him for tonight,' said the doctor. 'After that, I think he can probably go home, unless he's picked up something respiratory from getting so chilled. I think you'd better have a word with the GP, though. I'm not sure he should be managing on his own. You're in the south, aren't you? Any brothers and sisters?'

'I'm at Oxford,' said Michael, 'this is the vacation. And no, I'm an only child.'

'Talk to his doctor,' said the other man again. 'I'd advise your making arrangements to stick around for a good week, longer if necessary. I think you've reached the point where you need to make contact with the social services and sort this out.'

A brisk handshake, and he was gone. Another little job done. Michael looked at his watch. They would not let him see his father until actual visiting hours began; he would have to sit it out for another forty-five minutes, not long enough to get home and back. He realised belatedly that he should have gone an hour or so earlier, so as to to get his father's stuff for him. But he could do some shopping, at least; throwing away the last of his most recent cup of coffee, he went off to look for the hospital shop.

When they finally let him into the ward, the first thing he thought, advancing with a carrier bag containing orange-juice, plain biscuits, mints, a couple of detective stories, and everything else which he thought might be welcome, was that his father seemed to have shrunk to half his normal size.

'Thank you, Michael,' said Neville, as he stowed his offering in the bedside locker. His speech was oddly thick and he looked much older; Michael realised distastefully that for once he was seeing his father without his false teeth. He also looked feverish and unwell; it seemed virtually certain that he had caught a filthy cold. For all the hospital's determined policy of slinging the elderly back into the hands of 'community services', they would have to keep him a couple of nights, Michael reckoned. There would be time to talk to the GP and the social worker and do some research, then with any luck they'd send the old man home and he could use the leverage of the situation to get him to agree to consider some kind of sheltered environment. It seemed a shame, when his father was looking so frail, but he had better open the campaign.

'Do you have any memory of what happened?' he asked.

'No.' Neville evidently considered the subject closed.

'Well, do you *know* what happened?' persisted Michael, looking at his father's stony, denying face. 'We found you by the side of the road. You'd blacked out. Father, you've got to be more careful.'

'Don't worry about me, Michael. I've had a good innings.'

Michael almost opened his mouth to explode, but caught it back in time. It was hardly fair, when the old man had had such a dreadful day. 'I hope you're not telling me you're planning to curl up and die,' he said icily. 'I'd thought better of you.'

His father's eyes flew open, and he tried to hitch himself up. 'And who are you to judge, Michael?'

Michael thought of all he had done to make his father's life possible, the long, long years of pretending that the old man was fully in control of his affairs, and cold rage overwhelmed him. 'Don't you think I might've earned the right by now?'

Neville shut his eyes again, and did not reply; and to his horror,

Michael realised after a minute or so of angry waiting that his father was in tears.

'I'm sorry, Father. We're both a bit on edge. I'll come back tomorrow with a pair of your own pyjamas and your sponge-bag, in case they're hanging onto you for a bit. I should've gone home to pick your stuff up instead of sitting around here, but I kept thinking there'd be some news in a minute. I hope you can manage for tonight.'

He sat on for another few minutes, but Neville did not speak again. He would have felt awkward kissing him, since he could not remember ever having done so, so, after a while, he got up and left. When he turned up the next morning with pyjamas and other necessities, he was told that his father had contracted viral pneumonia; he was feverish, and too breathless to talk. Viral pneumonia was, the doctors explained, unpleasant but not dangerous, though it would need to be watched. However, by that evening, the viral pneumonia had opened a way for bacterial pneumonia, which was quite a different matter. His father was lying open-mouthed, barely conscious and blue in the face, with fluid rasping horribly in his lungs. The hospital started pumping him full of antibiotics, but there was no response.

Michael, visiting the next morning, saw no change in him, and began to be seriously worried. He had no access to his father's inner life, he never had had, but a slow dismay came upon him; had rage or grief played a part in driving Neville out on that too-long, too-fast walk? It was beginning to look ominously as if he would never know. By the evening, when things were still no better, he was not wholly surprised to find the ward sister taking him aside to tell him that he was welcome to stay after the end of visiting hours. He sat on beside Neville with the curtains drawn round them, mechanically counting the terrible breaths till he got to a hundred, then starting again. He found himself thinking he was sitting by a sort of breathing-machine. Periodically he reached forward and held the unresponsive hand, flaccid like a silk sock full of pebbles, but he was not at all sure that his father even knew he was there. And at ten past eleven, the rattling breaths finally drew out, and ceased.

Setting about all necessary arrangements, dealing with May and Harold, he found he was too bruised by conflicting feelings to be either glad or sorry, though he imagined that with the passage of time he might come to feel either one or the other. He deeply regretted that he and his father had not parted in charity, and he was grieved that he had never told Neville about Melita. It seemed a shame that due to the red-herring of the quarrel over Harold's money, he had never managed to share the most important thing that had ever happened to him. Materially, he was surprised to find that he was significantly better off; the house was worth something, though in that condition and in that part of the country not all that much. But there was also a surprisingly hefty insurance policy which must have been intended to cover his mother's anticipated widowhood. In retrospect, its existence explained much of the penny-pinching he remembered from his childhood. He remembered, also, the resentment and anger he had felt at the time. How typical, somehow, of his relationship with his father that Neville had managed to wrong-foot him even from beyond the grave.

Walking once more by the blue and peaceful Solway on the evening of the day after the day on which his father had died, he thought rather sadly that now he had got over the shock, his primary reaction to orphanhood was relief. There had been so much affection, almost none of it articulated, all of it wasted. And he was doubly bereft, since he felt much the same about Oxford. He felt weightless, without ties, except of course to Melita. Around him, the dog-owners of Silloth walked their pets in the autumnal light, the animals flickering in and out of the long shadows cast by the trees like the figures projected by a magic lantern. A young man was playing football on the green with his little son, who could barely kick as yet, but who ran about like a mechanical toy, laughing in delight. Possibly Elaine's Dean and their Tyler; he would not recognise Dean if he saw him. He could not remember ever having had fun with Neville; it would be nice to think that his father had once played beach-cricket with him, or scampered about with a football as this man was doing, but if they had ever played together, he had wiped it from his memory. There had been educational outings and games, yes, but no messing about. If he and Melita ever got to the point of having children, he would try to do better by them.

The life of the town had already healed over the tiny hole in its texture left by his father's death. The Masons and the domino-players had muttered 'great loss', 'sorely missed' and 'happy release', according to temperament, and would continue to do so for a few days as news got around, but with the careful stoicism of their kind, they would be no more effusive in mourning Neville's demise than in acknowledging his life. His friends had all reached a stage where they could no longer afford to react strongly to death; like a flock of hens, they greeted the sudden disappearance of one of their number with no more than perfunctory shuffling about. Meals-on-Wheels would be glad to be relieved of a customer, Mrs Denton would easily find other work. The Cartmel Old Boys' Association would send a wreath, as would the Masons, but would anyone actually mourn, apart from May?

For his own part, he found it saddening to think that his father had done more for him by dying than he could ever have done by staying alive. Crucially, Neville's death had not only freed him from Silloth, it had given him a hefty lump-sum to put down towards a house, so he was free to think of taking a job in the south. Thus, whatever the problems of the immediate future, he could finally define himself as an independent person. Great-Uncle Harold would need an eye kept on him, as would Auntie May, but Harold Boumphrey was sufficiently wealthy that his journey towards the grave would be a placid and easy coast downhill, and May had her husband's family to share the burden of her final years. Finally, there was an occasion of actual joy: Melita had agreed to accept being bought a ticket so that she could come over for the funeral, so he would see her again, and in the very near future, even though she could only stay for a week. May would have to lump it, or learn to like it. And, however grimly farcical the encounter, Her Sacred Majesty's most loyal subject would indeed behold with his own eyes the Empress of the Last Days.

'Darling, wake up. I'm sorry.'

'Hnnn?' Melita stirred in her cocoon of quilts, and raised herself on one elbow. She gave the impression that she hardly knew where she was, and Michael looked at her with compunction. She had arrived at Heathrow in the early morning, after little or no sleep, where Michael had met her and driven her up to Silloth, which had taken till two o'clock in the afternoon. He had made up the room Natty had used for her, with all three of the house's electric fires going full blast. The result was an unpleasant soupy atmosphere with faint undertones of mould, but at least it was warm. Where to put her had been a problem in itself. The household's only double bed was Neville's, and to Michael, there was something fundamentally repellent about the idea of sharing it with Melita and the crowding ghosts; his father in striped pyjamas as Michael remembered him from nursing him through his last bout of bronchitis, his mother, who had died there, lying stiff, grey and unrecognisable, his infant self, cuddling with Mummy after Father had got up, a younger Mummy with curly light-brown hair, her body soft and loose beneath a cosy flannel nightgown. He had only to sit on the bed for the memories to come swarming, the idea of sleeping in it was intolerable.

'It's half past six, love. You've been asleep for four hours. I hate to do this to you, but I really think we've got to get you over to Uncle Harold. I've brought you some coffee.'

She sat up properly, and took the cup from him. He perched on the end of the bed and watched her while she drank. She still looked extremely tired and somehow crumpled, but the main thing was, she was there. 'It couldn't wait, could it?' she asked. 'I feel like shit.'

'Darling, I daren't. He's got nuttier and nuttier ever since all this blew up. If he hasn't got his paroxysms over with, I'm afraid he'll make a scene at the funeral, and it would cause so much trouble. It wouldn't be funny if it all went pear-shaped, because May would be devastated. She adored Neville. It's her I'm worried about really, not upsetting the Rotary Club.'

'Well, I suppose we'd better,' said Melita resignedly.

'Why not have a nice hot bath? I've had the water on for the last hour, and I bought some aromatherapy bath-oil for you. It's supposed to energise and invigorate.'

'Michael, the way I'm feeling, getting me energised would take more like what Our Lord did for Lazarus.' She got wearily to her feet, and wrapped herself in Michael's dressing-gown. A moment later, he heard the water running.

He lay face-down on the bed, in the warm spot, breathing in the smell of her hair on the pillow. For two pins, he would have gone to sleep himself. The long drive down to London and back had been unbelievably tiring, especially on top of days of organisation. Even a simple ceremony at Dalston crematorium followed by a small reception at the Balmoral Hotel seemed to need an extraordinary amount of decision-making. Surely their managers must have some kind of Plan A, given that every funeral he had ever attended had involved 'Amazing Grace' and 'The Lord's my Shepherd' at the crem, and Dundee cake, ham, and egg-and-cress sandwiches at the hotel? So why did they want to check every last bloody thing? He had kept trying to tell them, all he wanted was for there to be what people expected, but they were relentless; every detail had to be approved.

Something poked him sharply in the ribs, and he realised he

had nodded off. Melita was standing there in a warm penumbra of rosemary-and-neroli essential oils, looking rather more like herself. 'Don't you go to sleep now,' she warned.

'Sorry, love.' He reached out a hand to her, and she hauled him to his feet, then heaved her suitcase onto the bed and opened it.

'I know this is hard on you, sweetheart,' she said, pulling out a dark-blue cotton jumper. 'Now I'm here, I'll try to be some help.'

She took off his robe, and began to dress. He looked at her smoothly twisting brown torso, adorned with a black lace bra, as she pulled the jumper over her head, and wished devoutly that they weren't going anywhere at all.

They walked down Criffel Street together. Melita's hand was tucked under his arm, and he was braced for curious glances, but nobody much was about. She was wearing a puffy dark-green coat which came down to her calves and reminded him of the lagging on a boiler. 'I hope to God you haven't had to buy warm clothes,' he said, suddenly focusing on the fact that it was an unlikely thing for her to own.

She smiled at him reassuringly. 'Remember I studied up in Canada? I kept some stuff in case I needed it again someday. Actually, I'm almost too warm. It's quite pleasant out.'

'It's not bad, is it? But it's very changeable at this time of year. We get a day or two of rain, or even hail, then a patch of sun. I'm just crossing my fingers this holds till tomorrow.'

They were at Great-Uncle Harold's gate. 'Here goes,' he said, as they walked up the path. 'I apologise in advance. Try not to get too cross with the poor old coot, even if he's outrageous. Remember he's just turned eighty-eight.'

He rang the bell, and the housekeeper answered.

'Sorry to be calling so late, Mrs Whitrigg, but he knows we're coming. This is my friend Melita Palaeologue.' He was watching her carefully; sensitive to any possible slighting of Melita, any look of distaste, but she seemed her cheerful self.

'I know, lad. He's been talking about it all day. Pleased to meet you, pet. Can I take your coat for you?'

'Thank you.' Melita shrugged out of her coat while Michael got rid of his. Mrs Whitrigg took both garments and turned away with a billowing armful of fabric.

'Just go on up,' she advised, walking down the hall to the coat-stand.

Michael went up the familiar stairs and opened the door, Melita following at his heels.

'Uncle?'

'Is that Michael?' Harold Boumphrey was sitting in his chair by the cheerfully blazing fire, in a pool of light from a standard lamp at his shoulder; the great room was otherwise in darkness. Unusually, there was no book to be seen anywhere in his vicinity.

'Yes. I've brought someone to see you.'

Harold struggled to his feet, peering into the gloom as they walked forward. Their feet made no noise on the thick carpet. He can't see her, Michael realised. Melita, in deference to his bereaved state, was dressed from head to foot in navy, and was all but invisible. He stepped to one side and put out a hand towards her. 'Melita, this is my great-uncle Harold Boumphrey. Harold, Dr Melita Palaeologue.'

Harold took a step or two forward. 'Shiloh,' he said hoarsely. 'The Child of the Promise. Verily I say unto you, this is the Day, and the Day-Star.' He fell clumsily to his knees.

'Oh, Christ,' said Michael, hoping that the old man hadn't done himself a mischief.

Harold did not move. He seemed to be praying; his hands were clasped, his glasses had fogged over, and tears were coursing down his cheeks.

'Hallo, Mr Boumphrey,' said Melita.

Harold fumbled his glasses off and mopped at them with a spotty silk handkerchief, his hands trembling, peering up at her with swimming eyes.

A small vertical crease appeared between her brows. 'Please get up', she said gently.

'Your Majesty,' he confessed, 'I am not at all sure that I can.'

'Come on, let me give you a hand.' Michael stepped forward and tried to heave the old man to his feet. It took both of them, one on either side, to get him up and back to his chair.

'Uncle, are you all right?' Michael asked, alarmed.

Harold ignored him, wallowing feebly in his chair, still leaking the easy tears of great old age. 'The time fore-ordained unto the peoples and kindreds of the earth is now come,' he pronounced, his voice louder and more vibrant than it had been in years. 'The promises of God have all been fulfilled. Out of Zion hath gone forth the Law of God, and Jerusalem, and the hills and land thereof, are filled with the glory of His Revelation! It behoves every man to gaze with an unbiased mind upon the sign of His Revelation, the proof of His Mission, and the token of His glory. O Lord, now lettest thou thy servant depart in peace, according to thy word. For mine eyes have seen my salvation.'

'I hope not, Mr Boumphrey,' said Melita, standing in front of the fire, 'one funeral in a week's enough for anyone to handle.'

He sat up straight, distressed. 'But I am forgetting myself, Your Majesty. May I have the honour of offering you a chair? I fear I cannot rise again.' He made a feeble attempt to do so, and she put out her hand to prevent him.

'Please, don't worry about it. Just relax.'

She was being very gentle with the old man, thought Michael, touched and relieved. General respect for age, probably.

'I apologise most humbly, Your Majesty, I had hoped to do you all the honour that lies in my power. And here I am, sitting while you stand!'

'That's OK,' she said, sitting down opposite him.

'I'll go and put the lights on,' said Michael. It's all very well for old men to dream dreams, but he was afraid that, sitting alone in the dark, his uncle had wandered off down strange, private pathways of obsession.

'The Rose of England,' said Harold, as Michael went round the room, click, click, click, turning on every light there was. No dark corners, no cobwebs, no strange lairs for forgotten dreams.

Melita laughed. Michael had forgotten how good her posture was; she was sitting forward in the saggy old armchair with her back as straight as a ruler. 'You don't get black roses, Mr Boumphrey.' He had found her face hard to read when he first knew her. Standing as he was, leaning against the mantel, watching the two profiles, he saw that inscrutability was a defence for her. She looked like a statue of Isis, still and self-contained, while Harold in his enthusiasm made him think of the Mad Hatter's grandpa.

'Oh, my dear young lady – forgive me – Your Majesty, how little any of that matters! You are the one for whom the nations have waited, do you not know your power?'

'Mr Boumphrey, all I know about is plants.'

'You will come to understand yourself,' said Harold with complete authority. 'Was not the Divine Wisdom born in the body of a prostitute?'

'It was?'

'The legend of Simon Magus,' put in Michael hastily. 'I'll fill in later.'

Harold ignored him. 'When did Sophia, the Shekinah of the Almighty, stir in the mind of that young woman? I think we may assume that she was not *consciously* the vehicle of the Lord in the time of her degradation. Your Majesty, I do not, of course, intend a direct parallel, it is perfectly obvious that you are a gentlewoman. But if I may, I would venture to remind Your Majesty that there may be depths in the mind we know nothing of, until the Lord chooses to reveal them.'

'That's so,' she conceded. 'You see it in the gospels, even.

Matthew twenty-six. The thing is, Mr Boumphrey, I'm telling you I don't know any of this in my heart. I'm just here to help Michael through with getting his Daddy decently buried.'

'Wait, my dear. Wait and trust. Your power *will* come upon you. The mighty wings of your own glory and majesty will overshadow you, and you will walk with angels at your right and your left hand.' Harold's face was incandescent with belief.

Melita stood up. 'Could be. But not just yet. I've got a job to do.' She got up, went over to Harold, and held out her hand. 'Goodbye, Mr Boumphrey. We need to go now. Thanks for everything. I hope I haven't made you sad.'

'Uncle Harold, I'd better take Melita home. She must be absolutely exhausted,' Michael chipped in hastily.

Harold did not reply directly, but he took Melita's proffered hand. He looked at it, lying small and dark in his soft old palm, and kissed it, in silence. Michael saw the teardrops that fell on it, and his heart contracted with love when she did not wipe them off.

'I'll see you tomorrow, Uncle,' he said.

Harold did not answer. He was lying back in his chair, eyes shut. Quietly, they walked away, and Michael closed the door softly behind them.

When they got to the bottom of the stairs, Michael went down to the kitchen, knocked, and put his head round the door. 'Mrs Whitrigg?'

'Yes, lad?'

As he had more or less expected, she was sitting very snug by the fire, with the telly on, and doing the puzzles in *Bella*. 'Just to tell you we're off now. Maybe you should look in on Uncle Harold? He's in quite a state.'

'I'll do that, pet. I know he's been working himself up. I'll take him a cup of tea in a bit. I didn't think to say, but I'm sorry about your dad. He was always very well-spoken, he'll be missed.'

'Thanks, Mrs Whitrigg. Don't bother to get up, I know where the coats are.'

He put Melita into her green lagging, and shrugged on his own charcoal overcoat. She said nothing, and he was desperate to get her out of the house.

The visit had taken the last of the day. They walked up to Neville's house in the orange glare of the street-lights. He had no idea what she was thinking.

He let them both into the house, and shut the door behind them. 'Melita, you've been absolutely wonderful,' he said. 'I couldn't be more grateful. Are you ravenous? Do you want a drink? What can I get you?'

'How about we go upstairs?' she said.

'Darling, I've been awake nearly as long as you have,' he said, 'don't expect miracles.'

She put her arms around him, and he hugged her back. It was like cuddling a duvet. 'Sweetheart. I just need a bit of human kindness.'

'Oh, God. Yes, I see it could all take you like that. Come on then. I was hatching schemes earlier, when you were putting your clothes on. I just hope it isn't too late.'

They went up to the spare room, which still smelt faintly of rosemary and orange, Michael removed her puffy coat, and tossed it out on the landing out of the way, then gratified his own impulse of earlier in the evening by taking her sweater off, followed by her bra. After a while, she fended him off so that she could deal with the rest of her clothes while he got his own kit off. She stepped naked out of a pool of dark-blue cloth and he stopped to stare, halfway through unbuckling his belt. Day-spring, he thought; dark and compact, she was to him the living image of human beauty, terrible as an army with banners, the bright shadow of incarnate love. Melita. The moment passed; she smiled, he scrambled out of his trousers, and they fell together onto the rumpled bed.

'That could've gone worse,' remarked Michael some time later. 'I'm quite surprised at myself. A tribute to your charms. Maybe old Harold's right, and you can work miracles after all.' They were sitting cross-legged, facing each other, with a miscellaneous feast on a tray between them which he had just brought up from the kitchen; cold meat, crackers, cheese, chocolate, anything portable he could find; in this limbo of non-time, neither of them wanted to get up and have a proper meal – dinner, lunch, possibly break-fast? Somewhere out there were the immediate horrors of the funeral, and the proximate horrors of Melita's return to Barbados, to say nothing of an ocean of unreason with Harold Boumphrey as its prophet, but in the rosemary-and-sex-scented fug of the spare room, they had achieved a temporary haven.

'He's kind,' she said, peeling a clementine. 'I wasn't expecting that – he's not at all like my grandpapa. I can't actually bring myself to encourage him, but if he can just go on believing that I might sort of manifest my destiny some time, he'll die hoping. I wouldn't take that away from a man, 'less I had to.'

'I think that's all he wants,' he said. 'Well, of course not. What he wants is for you to topple the governments of the world, and tons of fun stuff like that. But the thing is, if you don't actively discourage him, he'll be happy enough to go on waiting. And remember, he can't go on for ever.'

'I know he's wrong,' she said, 'but it looks as if he can work his dreams around me. That's good. I can live with it.'

'Talking of dreams,' he said, 'I need to tell you how things are going.'

'Sweetheart, I'm not going to be awake much longer.'

'Just quickly. I'm going to try your story on the *Observer*. One of the Sunday papers, which still takes long, serious pieces. Do you mind?'

'It's a bit late for me to mind. We agreed. I can't say I'm looking forward to it all, but at least it'll be going down over here, when

I'm safely back in Barbados. You haven't written it up yet, have you?'

'No. I've got my notes, of course, and I started putting it roughly into shape before all this stuff blew up with my father, but it's going to take a few days' work to get it right. I don't want to touch it while you're here, so I imagine I'll get it off in ten days to a fortnight, and I suppose they'll run it the following week. Once we've got through tomorrow, we can take a little break. I've done most of the mopping up now, so we can go anywhere you fancy. We don't even have to stay in this awful house if you don't want to.'

'I want to see what's important to you. Can we go to Cartmel?'

'God. I've never been back, you know. But it'd be different if you were with me, holding my hand and reminding me I wasn't stuck there any more. It'd be good for me, I might stop dreaming about the bloody place.'

'We've all got things we need to face up to,' she said, 'but it's easier with two.' She untucked her legs and picked up the tray. 'You're finished with this, sugar?'

'Yes. Let me take it downstairs, though. It's freezing down there.'

'Michael, I may be Bajan, but I'm not a blasted frangipani. Cold won't kill me.'

'I know. But I don't want anything horrible to happen to you ever.'

She laughed, and gave him the tray. 'Sweet. But Michael. Don't mama-hen me. I need my space.'

Half-way through October, Michael was sitting in his college room in Oxford entirely surrounded by newsprint. The phone was not ringing, for the sole reason that all his calls were being routed via the Porter's Lodge, greatly to the irritation of Mervyn the Head Porter, who was having to keep one more person on duty than usual just to cope with them. The college had been under siege for a week: all external gates and doors were locked, and everyone from the cleaning ladies to the Regius Professor of Divinity was being forced to come and go via the Porter's Lodge and to present identification to gain admittance, annoying everyone still more, while Michael himself was camping out in a college guest-room, effectively a prisoner.

It left him in a strange oasis of calm. He had had to ask the university computing services to suspend his email registration for the duration and to take out a private account with Yahoo, but the only people who knew this address were ones he had person-ally told. Without incoming email and phone calls, his days felt strangely old-fashioned and if it had not been for the daily sack of mail brought to him by one of the porters, rather pleasantly manageable. However, the other downside was that he was completely out of contact with Melita. She was not in her flat, and according to the UWI switchboard, she was on leave. He suspected that she was somewhere on the east coast, staying with relatives, unable to ring him, and like himself, without access to her email: he had sent her a message from his new Yahoo account and it had bounced back as 'user unknown'. He was left hoping that she would write, but so far she had not done so, or if she had, the letter had not got through yet.

He had sent an outline of his story to the *Observer* soon after returning to Oxford, and realised shortly after doing so that he had made an important mistake. He had naïvely imagined that the nature of news meant that papers reacted very quickly to incoming information, and he had intended that all the hoopla should be over before the undergraduates came back for the new term. But though the editor had taken his story with alacrity, he had wanted to do his own checking, and had also sent people over to Barbados to interview and photograph Melita. So in fact, the article had appeared only on the previous Sunday, after teaching had started, and since then, every journalist in England had tried to speak to him, or so it seemed, to the vast inconvenience of all his colleagues. Several had even found their way over to Middelburg, where the resulting clash of cultures had, he imagined, been instructive if not particularly pleasant.

Corinne, never one to miss an opportunity, had heeded the warning he sent her and hurried south in the hopes of taking the pressure off the archivist and steering the investigations in ways useful to herself. Being highly photogenic and in command of excellent, idiomatic English, she had done very well. To her credit, she had emphasised the co-operation and friendship which had caused one discovery to lead to another; if her reported remarks gave the impression that she had been looking for a lost heir all along, that was forgivable, and in any case, it was important to bear in mind that the journalists who reported her might have found the truth too complicated or insufficiently sexy.

Even *The Female Rosicrucian* had so far received only perfunctory attention, to his regret; he had begun to get fond of the play for its own sake, and he would have been pleased to see Aphra Behn's profile rising outside the academy. If Corinne had tried to explain to anyone that Pelagius's thesis was a great work of scholarship, something which he knew Theodoor felt strongly about, then her explanations had fallen on deaf ears. The only documents from the Dutch end which excited anyone were the three surviving love-letters from Elizabeth to Pelagius, which had the crucial advantage of being not very long and in comprehensible English; they had been quoted by a good few papers and published in full in that Friday's *TLS* with a commentary by Germaine Greer. The *TLS* does not generally deal in 'hold the front page' journalism, Michael reflected, as he put the cutting into a cardboard folder and labelled it. They had had his own essay on *The Female Rosicrucian* for three months, and still hadn't told him when they planned to print it. Germaine's piece was a testimony to her powers of persuasion, but he also wondered what poor sod had been told that his own essay must be held over for an indefinite length of time to make room for it.

The original Melpomene had been the Muse of Tragedy, but what her twenty-first-century avatar seemed to be presiding over was farce of the lowest description. The new millennium looked unlikely to be any shorter of appalling events than its predecessor, but as far as cultural responses were concerned, the temper of the times continued to be too postmodern to allow anything else. Reactions to Melita covered a fairly wide range, but the gamut ran from the trivialising to the deranged. The red-tops had all retold the story in shorter and simpler forms, with or without photographs of Corinne and/or Elizabeth of Bohemia, and as was inevitable, the weekend papers were producing a great deal of comment from professional opinion-holders of one kind or another. He was working through the papers collecting the stories, sub-divided into 'reportage' and 'comment', with comment further divided into 'pro' or 'con', depending on whether they were for or against Melita's claim to be the rightful heir; so far, the cons were coming out well ahead, though with some interesting individual takes.

He turned to Saturday's *Telegraph*, hoping that Germaine would have returned to the subject in her column, as indeed she had:

In this day and age, who cares any more who's Queen of England? When the monarch still had some vestige of legislative function, it might have mattered very much. And it would have mattered nearly thirty years ago, before the cracks had appeared in the House of Windsor and round about the time Enoch Powell was ranting on about 'rivers of blood', if anyone had known that one of the young black men who came to this country to do the jobs the Brits wouldn't do any more was the rightful King of England. If this debate had arisen in the early Seventies, when all kinds of imme-morial truths found themselves up for questioning, it might even have precipitated this over-sceptred isle into rethinking its grotesque devotion to the monarchy. Now that the royal family has degenerated into a freakshow run by the tabloids, Dr Palaeologue should thank her lucky stars she's got a real job. She is better employed as a professional botanist than wearing funny hats, opening factories, and raising dysfunctional kids.

It was hard to see if she was for or against, but on the whole, the thrust seemed to be against, if only on the grounds that she thought Melita would have a nicer time as she was.

He opened the *Guardian Magazine* next, handling it with the circumspection of a bomb disposal expert dealing with a suspicious parcel.

Suddenly we seem to be bursting at the seams with queens – though we're used to that here in Brighton. The prospect of having a young black woman instead of mumsy Liz is superficially appealing, if only for the look on Prince Philip's face when they explained it to him, but in the unlikely event of Queen Melita being crowned, wouldn't there be some corner of your mind that suspected that this was yet another of Tony Blair's cack-handed attempts to appeal to the kids? However, to work at all, it'd have to depend on the key question, can monarchs be fanciable? I'm firmly of the opinion that they come out of the box frumpy and grannyish, so Dr Palaeologue is out of the running straight off. The boyf. disagrees, citing Elizabeth I, but he loses because it's clear he's really thinking of Miranda Richardson in *Blackadder*. The little we can glean about the Barbadian botanist suggests that she's far too wise to claim the throne, regardless of constitutional niceties. But it's telling that none of the self-appointed constitutional experts wants to answer how Queen Melita would actually seize power with an army consisting of two university lecturers – hardly enough to storm Buckingham Palace, although at least they could share a taxi. The other traditional method of dealing with surplus queens, a bloke with a big axe, might be a bit rich even for our jaded tabloids. Much fairer, and let's face it, more attuned to our culture, would be to rig up Buck House with cameras, put the two royals in there for a month, and let us all vote. The BBC are still looking for a killer response to *Popstars*, and *Royal Big Brother* would fit the bill nicely. The winner gets the crown, the loser gets to be a presenter on Channel Five. Or would that be the other way round?

Ouch, he thought. Pro or con? It was hard to tell. He picked up Saturday's *Indie*, hoping for something a bit more rational, and found it was illustrating its independent-mindedness with a worrying call to arms:

The quiet world of scholarship has presented us with an opportunity for justice when we were least expecting it. The quietest of revolutionaries, a mild-mannered Oxford don and a Dutch academic, have forced us to ask, is it time for a change? Should we be looking forward to seeing Queen Melita on the stamps? According to MORI, the Queen herself is as popular as she has ever been – more than 80% of Britons feel loyal towards her – but at the same time, only a quarter think there will still be a monarchy in a hundred years' time. Those who are looking forward to seeing Charles step into her place are increasingly outnumbered by those who see the Windsors as the symbol of everything that's backward-looking about Britain today. All those who feel that the royal family is out of touch would find Melita a fitting figurehead for today's multi-cultural and multi-ethnic Britain.

Could be, he thought, but what do they want anyone to do? The crack about sharing a taxi was rankling a little. Are they expecting Charles to fall on his sword? he wondered. For immediate purposes, it counted as pro.

As he had expected, the *Mail* was taking a very different line.

Whatever the merits of Melita Palaeologue's claim, we must face facts. Monarchy in Britain today is a job, and a tough one. Again and again in recent history, we've seen that the people who have married into 'the Firm', as the Queen calls it, have found it hard going. Fairy-tale weddings have been followed by nightmare divorces. The lesson we've all learned is, you need to be born to it, not because there's such a thing as royal genes, but because the Windsors are trained to cope from childhood. What chance would a young academic from a sleepy little coral island have of coping with the pressure?

Well, Melita would probably agree with the general trend of this one, though she'd be spitting feathers at the implication that Barbados was some kind of primitive culture. Definitely con.

The Times surprised him:

One of the strangest features of this story is that Dr Melita Palaeologue seems to be far more like Her Majesty the Queen than the Queen's own children are. Compared to the antics of the younger Windsors, Melita's life-style makes her looks like the answer to a monarchist's prayer. She is publicity-shy, just like Her Majesty, but sources close to her assure us that she is also, like her, an Anglican and a regular churchgoer who does not smoke or take drugs, and rarely drinks. Her name has not been romantically linked with anyone's since her student days

– thank God for that, thought Michael fervently, if anyone realised that he and Melita were engaged, he'd have media people abseiling into the college from helicopters –

she spends most of her leisure time with her family, and she is hardworking, educated and conscientious. She is even a scientist, and despite the importance of science to our collective survival, there are precious few scientists among this country's opinion-formers. Compared with the scandal-rocked house of Windsor, she looks like a throwback to better days, and perhaps, like hope for the future.

I'll put that down as a 'pro', decided Michael. It was distinctly worrying. The Murdoch papers were showing definite anti-Windsor tendencies, and doubtless if Melita had been persuaded to get her kit off, the *Sun* and the *Star* would have been right behind her: was there any chance that some lunatic shift in public opinion would actually force her to come forward?

Private Eye was bracing:

The emergence of Melita Palaeologue as a claimant to the throne of England has sent shivers of delight through the country's prolier-than-thou liberals. But the news of the first serious royal pretender since Bonnie Prince Charlie has left Brenda remarkably unperturbed. Could it be that she's already calculated that nothing could firm up support for the old firm more than the prospect of their greatest asset being replaced by a black colonial academic? Charles, meanwhile, surely now realises that any lingering hopes he had nurtured of persuading Mummy to abdicate are dead in the water. Abdication would blow the issue of precedence wide open. It looks increasingly as if Brenda's booked herself the gig for life.

The *Guardian* was still more reassuring. Under the headline 'HOUSE OF WINDSOR, PLC', somebody sensible pointed out that

in today's world, monarchy is big business. The Hanoverian kings of the eighteenth century were more interested in ready cash than capital, so they sold off their assets, the Crown Lands, to Government in exchange for a salary, the so-called Civil List, a deal which, with hindsight, looks a bit like selling Manhattan for a handful of beads. The profits from the Crown Estate last year exceeded £147m, which went straight to the Chancellor, while the Civil List is currently running at £7.9m, on which the Queen and Prince Charles now voluntarily pay tax. If we relate the two sums to one another, as the Windors are understandably anxious that we should, this represents an overall return for Gordon Brown of approximately 2000% on annual expenditure. Moreover, we, as taxpayers, benefit to a surprising extent from the present setup. The profits from showing Buckingham Palace, Windsor and Holyrood (£4.2m last year) go to fund the Royal Collection, which receives no State funding, and is increasingly accessible to the public: the new Queen's Gallery will shortly be opening at Buckingham Palace. Thus, though a republican might argue that the Crown Lands, the Crown Jewels and the royal picture collection would be just as much national assets, if not more so, if the Windsors were invited to seek alternative employment, there can certainly be very little governmental appetite for change for its own sake, even in the interests of youth-appeal. Blair may be seeking to drive an ever harder bargain with 'the Firm', but pomp and pageantry, the royal mystique, bring in too much tourist revenue to be meddled with. Though the idea of a black queen sounds funky and superficially attractive, there is a great deal at stake, and with freebies like the Royal Yacht and the Royal Train now things of the past, the Windsors are looking like an increasingly good bargain.

'Con', oh excellent, thought Michael, thank God for the abstract approach, it was the first article he felt he had learned anything from. Furthermore, he was delighted to find that it illustrated New Labour's irritating tendency to claim the high moral ground while simultaneously benefiting to a surprising extent from corruption inherent in the status quo.

So much for the papers, but apart from the professional opinion-formers, there there were plenty of people out there who wanted to share their views, and there were hundreds of letters: if he had not temporarily closed his account, there would doubtless also have been hundreds of emails. The letters by themselves covered an inconceivably wide range of possible opinion: looking at them was like shaking a tree and watching the nuts fall out. He sorted them by category as he opened them: they made an interesting archive in themselves, and also he found that thinking of them as essentially documents rather than communications addressed to himself made the more painful ones easier to handle.

One of the larger files, as he had anticipated, contained letters, by no means all of them illiterate, originating from white suprema-cists of one kind or another; after wading through a few of these communications, if his eye lighted on the words 'coon', 'nigger', 'jig', or 'nig-nog' as he was opening a letter, he stuck it in a file unread in the interests of his own mental health. A smaller number were from black individuals or organisations, mostly taking the view that if Melita were not immediately crowned as Queen of England, black Britons should rise as one and storm the palace, though some took a theological line, and were apparently content that her kingdom need not be in this world. There were also letters from republicans and anarchists, execrating him for attempting to lend modern credibility to the concept of monarchy.

Considerably larger numbers told him he should be ashamed to be an Englishman, and it was people like him who were bringing the country to its knees. A few of these contained death threats, some of them horribly explicit, which he could only hope repres-ented nothing more serious than violent fantasy based on unsuit-able reading. He began to feel grateful that the Church of England had never evolved the concept of the *fatwa*. There were, he knew, further shedloads of correspondence of a similar nature going to the Master, urging that he should be sacked immediately, or, at the very least, insulated from contact with impressionable youth; some of them, he suspected, from Ellen Lorimer and her mates. A surprising number of correspondents started from the belief that the queen had personally ordered the assassination of Princess Diana and Dodi Al-Fayed, and assumed that he would be happy to involve himself in some action of retributive justice – these he put to one side, along with the death threats, wondering if he ought to send them on to the Special Branch.

Then there were the letters it was harder to define. All kinds and varieties of the bewildered, anguished, celebratory, anarchically gleeful or simply mad. Among the latter, his personal favourites were an informative and scholarly one, possibly on the level, which pointed out that even the present queen had black ancestors (via the wife of George III, descended from the African mistress of a Portuguese king), and three from people who believed some version of the theory that the House of Windsor, along with other notables including William F. Buckley Jr and President Bush, were members of a shape-shifting alien master-race from Sirius. Two of these took the view that Elizabeth of Bohemia had let the side down by marrying a human being, and Melita was therefore a mere nobody, while the third informed him that since Pelagius had self-evidently been an Egyptian Mason and priest-king, Melita was therefore one of the aliens, and probably the Dark Goddess Hecate, whose arrival on earth had been announced by the ritual sacrifice of Princess Diana. Its author, in a manner familiar to him from Harold's correspondents, did not ask him if he had any more information about Pelagius, but seemed, rather, determined to instruct him. He laid a small bet with himself that within six months, the man would have published a book called *The Pelagius Code*.

All in all, the letters suggested that there were worryingly large numbers of people out there whose mental competence was, to say the least, questionable. But even leaving the nutters aside, the correspondence was sobering. It was generally supposed in academic circles that the postmodern mentality was essentially sceptical, but the Melita furore was forcing him to revise his own views. Either Lyotard was wrong, or the majority of the population was not postmodern. Belief had become highly idiosyncratic, but there was as much of it about as ever. Furthermore, the correspondence suggested strongly that his initial assumption that the mass of the population had become indifferent to the monarchy had been a serious error. Even a thousand-odd letters was a small sample of the millions who lived in Britain, but all the same, they suggested that to many, the royal family was a cherished institution, while even those who believed Prince Charles to be the Antichrist, of whom there were one or two, at least still thought he mattered.

He had been right about one thing: it was no longer true that the monarchy united the British people, if it ever had done. But the challenge that Melita represented showed it to be, to a far greater extent than he had imagined, a fulcrum or a still centre around which hopes, fantasies and ideals of all kinds still swung. If it was a mythical construct, it was one which Britons seemed bizarrely reluctant to relinquish, and trying to demystify it was like trying to convince a bumblebee that it was too aerodynamically inefficient to fly. The best he could hope for was that one day inertia and indifference would triumph, and the nation would wake up wondering why it had ever been bothered.

Coda

It was December before Michael and Natty met again. Michael had had to go straight from mopping up his father's affairs into term, and similarly, Natty had gone straight from Glasgow to his semester at UEA; then during term itself, both had been too hard-pressed to consider an excursion. But they both very much wanted to see the Upton House *Visit of the Magi*, and there was a window of a few days after they had both finished teaching and before Natty flew home. Once politely but firmly reminded of the terms of their charter with respect to scholarly visits, the National Trust had yielded to the persuasiveness of letters on Oxford college paper, and agreed to open up for them, by appointment.

Since Upton House was slightly north-east of Banbury, which was only forty minutes up the motorway from Oxford, the obvious arrangement was for Natty to get himself across to Oxford, and meet Michael there mid-morning, which he duly did. It was a nasty day, and cold gusts of rain were rattling on the forecourt of Oxford Station as Natty's train drew in. Michael saw on Natty's face pleasure which mirrored his own as they met and shook hands.

'I thought we'd go on after Upton, and have lunch at the pub at Edge Hill, which is just a bit further up the same road,' said Michael, once they had negotiated North Oxford, and were fairly launched onto the M40. 'It's a Civil War site. The Edge is a great knife-edged escarpment, and from the top, you can see half Warwickshire like a patchwork quilt. The story goes that Rupert of the Rhine hurled himself down the Edge with three thousand cavalry, and smashed the parliament-men by sheer momentum.

They were at the bottom, you see, thinking they were safe because the ridge was so steep.'

'The story? Sounds from the way you put it there's another version,' Natty commented.

'Yes – one of the other commanders was in such pain from his gallstones he just charged down the slope hoping he'd kill himself. Horses are nervous beasts, so when he started crashing downhill, he startled them, and they just followed him pell-mell. But gall-stones and Merrie England don't go together, so the Rupert version's the one in the Tourist Board hand-outs. In the eighteenth century, an antiquarian called Sanderson Millar built a rather charming Gothick sham castle just at the most dramatic point, and it's now a pub full of civil war tat. It's a complete fake, but the view's wonderful, and the food's not bad.'

'But a bit theme-parky? I get the impression that this bit of England's living on its past,' said Natty.

'Fair comment. We can't afford not to. You were telling me in the summer that the Bajan economy depends on tourists, but you'd be surprised how true that is over here. We make billions off vis-itors, and every time there's a wobble it all starts falling to bits. We saw that in Cumbria, of course, last year. Without visitors, the place wasn't sustainable. Home's mostly eighteenth-century, because of the Lake Poets, but round here, we're supposed to be in Merrie England. The next junction of the motorway is "Historic Warwick", Middle Ages and knights in armour, and then you get "Shakespeare's Stratford", timber-framed buildings, ruffs and farthingales. Shakespeare did most of his work under James in actual fact, but we'd rather remember Elizabeth. Generally, the story we're trying to tell hereabouts is that nothing much happened since the first half of the seventeenth century.'

'Talking of marketing the past,' said Natty, 'how've you-all been coping? I kind of lost track after I came over to England, I was just too busy.'

'Oh, God. It was a circus. You have to remember that for most
of the late summer, the big stories in the English papers were
about murdered schoolgirls and a major cock-up with this year's
A Levels. It went on and on, and it was all incredibly depressing,
so when the Melita story broke, the hacks were so glad to have
something different the college was practically surrounded. I was
under siege for a fortnight, and we had to get the porters to check
everyone in and out. Of course, it was quite good publicity for us
– I mean, it was actually a story which related to someone doing
a bit of research, instead of a scandal about sex, drugs or admissions, which is what usually brings the journos round our way.
Even though it was a bloody nuisance, in the end the college was
really quite pleased with me.'

'I'm not surprised.'

'It was much worse for Melita – she was forced to take leave
of absence for almost two months after the story broke – UWI
just had to beg her to stay away. It's all died down now, of course.
When she wouldn't co-operate with the chat-show people and the
magazines, they had to drop it in the end. They were offering her
obscene sums of money, absolutely mad, but she just dug her toes
in. She was livid with me, of course, but she forgave me in the
end, and overall, our strategy seems to have worked. Someone
wants to do a documentary now, but so far, she's refused to talk
to them. The thing is, because she's stayed so aloof, we've been
able to ride over the interest in personalities, and raise the question of the issues. After a while, people started writing serious
think-pieces about the idea of the monarchy.'

'Which is what you wanted. There was that *Panorama* thing,
Paxo grilling Prince Charles on the future of the monarchy? I
caught that.'

'You wouldn't believe how hard they tried to get Melita to come
over and make it a two-hander,' said Michael. 'Paxman was so
surprised anyone would turn him down he was almost polite.'

'I'll bet. And your story drew a lot of attention in the black community. I did hear some stuff from my friends.'

'Oh, yes. You'd know more about that than I do, but I was certainly answering questions from black journalists. Anyway, apart from that side of it, I think we got somewhere politically. Melita's done her bit for justice by strengthening the PM's hand, though it's ironic to think that the Babbling Butler has probably helped the cause just about as much by being unprincipled and stupid. On the one hand, that fool Burrell's broadcast to the world that the palace is wall-to-wall with sleazebombs, fantasists and sexual weirdoes, which damages the argument that they've a right to rule because they're good at it, and on the other, just by existing, Melita's made it absolutely clear that the present regime is based on expediency, and the rest is mystique, which is to say, flim-flam. It's not that this is exactly news, the important thing is, for the first time, everyone who reads a paper at all's had their noses rubbed in it.'

'It strikes me that for a man who takes the high moral ground about spin, you're not too bad at it yourself,' said Natty drily.

'Spin is storytelling,' Michael retorted, 'and what academics in the humanities spend their whole time doing is looking at stories. If you wanted to be pompous, you could say that rhetoric's the great human art. What's so depressing about this government is they're so bloody bad at it that they're putting the whole notion into disrepute. They don't seem to realise that if a story's still revolving when it hits the news-desks, people start to worry.'

'It's no better anywhere else. Our politicians are snake-oil salesmen, psychos, or plain old-fashioned crooks. But what you're saying is, after all this, Melita's changed nothing? I'm a little sad about that.'

'What did you want?' Michael challenged. 'I went through a phase of thinking something ought to have happened, but after I'd waded through shedloads of anti-establishment paranoia, it dawned on me that it had never occurred to me for a second to wonder if either of us was in physical danger. And after all, generally speaking, you can't go upsetting a multimillion-pound family firm without starting to look three times before you cross the road. But I wasn't, and that's when I realised I hadn't ever seriously imagined that they'd think we were a threat. Were you wanting to see Melita beheaded on Tower Hill because it'd make a good ending for your novel? I've a vague idea treason still carries the death penalty.'

Natty looked as if he wanted to say something, but Michael wanted to finish his train of thought, and carried on. 'Only joking. I've had to think about what we've actually achieved, if anything, because of all the time I was banged up in college with nothing else to do. Yes, of course Melita's not Queen of England, and people said some incredibly stupid things about why she was or wasn't. But after living through the whole furore, I've ended up going back to where I started. It doesn't matter a damn who's Queen of England, and after everything we've heard about palace life in the last couple of months, I'm just glad it's not her. But remember, she's not the only thing that happened. All those documents turned up. The journalists ignored them, apart from the love-letters, but in the long term, I think they were absolutely wrong.'

'I think I'm with you,' said Natty. 'I enjoyed what I caught of the freakshow, but I was always more interested in Pelagius than in all this stuff about kings and queens. I thought it might matter that he'd had a son, but I've always been sure it mattered he existed, and he had an idea. That's why I wanted to write about him. So, if we go back to thinking about justice, you're saying it's not being a king which makes him important. It's writing a book about Africans and God. We've got to get it away from your guy in Holland.'

'We meaning black people?' Natty did not bother to acknowledge this with more than a flicker of the eye. 'Natty, I hope you realise we means you. If you're politically opposed to the idea of a white Dutchman as Pelagius's interpreter, you're going to have to do it yourself. OK, Theodoor's student and I will do the translation and the context. Let's face it, you're going to need all that. But we'll only reach a handful of people, almost none of them black, because our book's going to be scholarly and technical. So if you think it's really the ideas that are Pelagius's heritage, it's you that's going to have to take on his mantle, and be his heir. Not Melita. She can only write about plants, bless her.'

'Meaning?'

'Do what you were going to do anyway. Write your novel. Out of all of us, it's you who can tell people that in the early days of Atlantic slavery, there was a man who stood up and insisted he and his people were the children of God. In the seventeenth century, it took a king to have that much bottle, but everything's different now. Nobody cares about theologians, and nobody cares about academics either. Melita can do bugger-all about justice in the twenty-first century, but maybe you can.'

'Maybe.' The conversation was evidently making Natty uncomfortable. 'But what about you and Melita, anyway? Anything opening up on the job front?'

'I've done all the finding out I can, and there's a senior professor retiring at Kew. I can't even think about it in case it all goes wrong, but the way things are at the moment with academic funding, I think they'll be freezing the Chair, and looking to recruit at a junior level.'

'So there's some hope?'

'Yes. Melita doesn't really want to leave Barbados, but we love each other, and this is a much bigger system. We can only pray that it works, and that I can get a job in London. Rumour has it there might be something coming up at Birkbeck, which I think I'd find much more congenial than Oxford. And if Melita can't stand it here, we might be able to get across to the States. The ironic thing is, this discovery's given me a huge professional boost. I've now got a black studies/post-colonial presence, practically whether I like it or not. I think I might be able to get a job in America.'

As they came off the roundabout at Banbury, the weather seemed to be worsening: the wind was dropping, but the sky was filling up with slaty, heavy-looking clouds, and an occasional spatter of cold rain hit the windscreen. Natty turned his collar up, an automatic gesture, so Michael put on the heater.

'I think it might snow,' remarked Michael, 'it'll be the first snow this winter.'

'Don't say it,' moaned Natty.

They turned off the motorway and threaded through outer Banbury, pebble-dashed and nondescript, but once they were out of the town, the road began to climb the escarpment which fell away so abruptly at Edge Hill, running between gaunt hedgerows studded with bare trees, while winter rooks circled against the darkening sky. Upton must be somewhere on this great slope. A little further, and suddenly they came upon a small sign pointing left, and almost at once, tall wrought-iron gates. A long, dead-straight drive unrolled in front of them, stretching away between strips of shaved grass backed by yews and holly, with a big, lowish house just visible at half a mile's distance behind a high yew hedge, like an eighteenth-century painting. There was a forbidding sign saying 'House Not Open to the Public', but the gates were standing open; they were in good time for their appointment.

Michael turned down the drive. Just before he reached the front courtyard, a quadrangle of tall yew with a gap to allow cars to enter, he braked abruptly; an elderly black man who seemed to be wearing at least two coats tied round the middle with string was standing absolutely still in the shrubbery which half-concealed the entrance to the visitors' car-park.

'Sorry,' he said to Natty, who had had to put out a hand to keep his head from banging on the roof, 'I thought he might step out.'

'Who?'

'That tramp. He must have seen the gates were open. He'd better not get himself shut in.'

It was a strange, nondescript building, thought Michael as they entered the square of yew, the wheels of his car crunching on the gravel. Though the light ochre Hornton stone, set off with white-painted windows, had a superficially unifying effect, the façade was not harmonious, and the great broken pediment over the front entrance made it look like a giant clock. The snowy light did not suit it; that colour of stone would look at its best in spring, and might be fine in summer.

The National Trust representative opened the door and came out, having heard the car, and took them into the chilly, stone-flagged front hall. Once they had introduced themselves and shaken hands, they fell silent, looking around them. The atmosphere of an empty house filled with beautiful things folded about them softly like a Victorian cashmere shawl too good to wear. Natty's face showed nothing but casual interest, but Michael found himself reacting, against his will, to the idea of the deserted great house discovered under the fading light of a snowy day, something out of the world of de la Mare, or pre-war thrillers. Somewhere about, there ought to be an exquisitely boyish, frightened girl, or an obese, sinister alien.

'You might like to know there's a rather odd-looking man wandering about outside,' said Michael, after a while, since their host was beginning to seem anxious to move them on.

'An elderly black chap?' They nodded. 'That's only Old Riley,' said the Trust man casually. 'He just goes up and down the road, rain or shine. He scrounges bits of junk, but he's never broken in anywhere, and he's never done any harm anyone knows of. He lives in an ancient caravan behind a garage, down Ratley way. I think they let him stay there as a sort of nightwatchman.'

'How does anyone end up like that?' said Natty. 'I'd like to know more about him. Does anyone know where he's from?'

'He doesn't like to talk,' said the other man, 'not to anyone like me, anyway. He's afraid of the so-called caring services, I think. He's not got much, but he's got his pride, I suppose, and he's determined to hang onto it. Now, if you'd like to follow me . . . ?'

The representative, with impersonal politeness, took the trouble to walk them through part of the house, though he knew their concern was only with the one picture. So they dutifully admired the Long Gallery, sea-green and subaqueous with its blinds drawn against the light, which featured, Michael privately thought, some of the most optimistically attributed minor-league Dutch paintings ever seen outside an auction house. Michael was still preoccupied with Old Riley, which made it difficult to come up with the *mot juste* on demand, but since Natty was quite clearly thinking about something else, he felt he had at least to make a show of connoisseurship, to make a return for the Trust man's courtesy.

The three men trooped down a flight of oaken stairs to a landing completely lined with glass cabinets full of Sèvres porcelain, and turned left into a small green-damask-hung space which, as they entered it, revealed itself as a curious tunnel-like passage leading to the room simply called the Picture Gallery, which was on a lower level still. As they walked down the room, Michael could see the room beyond, and the triptych on the far wall.

They went down another short flight of stairs into the gallery, a beautiful space, also hung with green damask, which had started life as a squash court, and still featured a tiny viewing balcony in one corner and natural light delivered by glass skylights in the roof. It held a single row of smallish pictures, hung fairly low, and was furnished with a long Jacobean table, a console table, a Knole sofa, and some chairs disposed against the walls at intervals. Since the pictures were for the most part fifteenth-century, with the intense, transparent colours of that period, they glowed against the damask like cut gemstones, forming a frieze of angular, pale-skinned figures dressed in priceless silks and furs all around the room. Whether they were staring into space as 'Portrait of a young man' or elaborately spearing a dragon as 'St George', they all held the same contained, nonchalant energy.

'There's your Bosch,' said the National Trust man, unnecessarily. The picture came as a bit of a shock; after having seen Philip II's version of Bosch's *Epiphany* some years before in the Prado, Michael had unconsciously been looking for something about five feet tall, but this picture was barely half the size. They circled the banqueting-table, Michael and Natty going one way, and the Trust man the other, and all three came to rest in front of it.

'Pelagius,' said Natty, as if in greeting. He put up a hand as if he half-thought of touching the painting.

'It's not actually a copy,' said Michael, fascinated. 'The side-panels are completely different from the ones in the Prado. I think it's a studio version, perhaps for a side altar somewhere. Or maybe a domestic chapel.'

The National Trust man began saying sensible things about the cult of the Three Kings of Cologne in the early sixteenth century, but neither Michael nor Natty was really listening. The painting absorbed all their attention, the glassy city on the horizon, the hovel which barely sheltered the Holy Family, the crystal in the black king's hand.

'It feels real,' said Natty, staring at the picture as if he hoped it would talk back, 'not like a copy. Pelagius was looking at this, and what he saw was himself. It's a Nigerian face, all right. You get guys who look like that all up and down West Equatorial Africa, with that round face and those little ears. He was standing here, where I'm standing, looking at this picture. In Holland, I suppose, about 350 years ago.'

'This is a picture of a person,' said Michael. Stories, stories. He and Natty were standing there longing to be seduced by this picture, and it was seductive, no doubt about it; catching the Black King's troubled gaze, he could not but feel that they had some sort of rapport.

The room seemed obscurely to darken. He blinked, puzzled; it was as if some influence had come out of the picture. It was only when he looked up that he saw it really had got darker, the sky had turned black, and the skylights were starred with wet spatters of snow.

'Where did it come from?' he asked, mostly for the sake of something to say.

'We haven't the whole history. Elizabeth of Bohemia's Bosch was with her in Leicester House where she died, because it's in the inventory. Some of her bits and bobs were sent off to Heidelberg, because her son was nagging for them, and her friend Lord Craven got some portraits to remember her by, but Charles II will've got all the rest. He hadn't quite the eye for a picture his father had, and of course, his taste was very French. He kept some family pics, but I doubt if he'd've wanted anything Flemish earlier than Rubens, so he probably sold it, swopped it or gave it away. Bernard Berenson found it at Casteel Walenburgh, where he got quite a few nice things – the owner was a Dutch collector with a habit of selling things on whenever he wanted some cash for something new. This chap said he'd bought the triptych in England some time in the 1890s, which is why we've tended to think it must be Elizabeth's copy, but he never said exactly where. Berenson couldn't persuade Mrs Jack to fancy it, though, so he flogged it to Lord Bearstead, and it ended up here. Just as well, or you'd have had to go to Boston.'

Natty, looking rather irritated by this learned chatter, said, 'Let me get this straight. Elizabeth's Bosch disappears when she dies, which is in the 1660s, right? Then a Dutchman buys a Bosch in England in the 1890s, and the rest is guesswork.'

'That's about the size of it,' said the Trust man rather stiffly. 'One version vanishes, another bobs up, so the principle of Occam's razor says they're the same. Of course, there could have been two. There could have been a dozen, if you like.'

'No, it's the one,' said Natty, with certainty. 'Hey, Pelagius. What a lot you started.'

'We'll be able to get a good photograph of the central panel, will we?' asked Michael. 'Have you got one?'

'Yes, of course. I'd rather do all the paperwork by letter, if you wouldn't mind dropping me a line. We've got a postcard of it, actually, so you can take a couple of those to be going on with.'

Michael looked at his watch. 'Thanks very much. We mustn't keep you, we've taken quite enough of your time. Mr Polgreen's got to get back to Barbados, you see, so this was his only chance.'

Reluctantly, Natty picked up the hint and the three men turned away from the picture and began trailing back through the house.

'It's turned out to be rather a dreadful day,' observed the Trust man, unlocking the front door to let them out. Snow was falling quite thickly now, in ungraceful wet clots, some of it beginning to lie on the gravel and the dark thatch of the yew hedge. 'You'll be looking forward to getting back to Barbados.'

'Yes, but I wouldn't have missed this for anything,' said Natty, shaking hands.

They turned up their coat-collars, and as the door shut behind them, hurried down the slippery stone steps towards the car.

'Christ, it's Pelagius,' said Natty. The old man was standing just outside the enclosure of yew, staring at them with something of the hurt, lost expression of the Black King. Flakes of snow gleamed in his grizzled hair, and he held something in his hand; the light caught on it as he moved, and Michael realised it was an old wing-mirror. Impulsively, Natty started towards him. 'Hey, man. Can we carry you somewhere? It's a bitch of a day to be walking.'

Michael found himself waiting, one hand on the door of the car, with snow going down the back of his neck, straining with anxiety to hear the old man's voice.

Old Riley shook his head and retreated. A few steps, and his tall, dark figure was swallowed up in the shrubbery. Another man dispossessed by the accidents of personal history, like Pelagius, another untold story, or another man insisting on his right not to be scrutable by those who trade in stories. More simply, he was perhaps, like Neville, insisting on his right to be his own man. Michael looked into the darkness between two trees into which Old Riley had vanished. A gust of snow swirled between them. 'Then to the elements at last be free,' he said under his breath.

'You know the way runaway slaves went to live in the mountains?' said Natty, who had not heard him. 'The maroons. It's like he's doing that in England.'

'Natty, he doesn't want to talk to us. You're the enemy too,' said Michael. 'Come on, get in. He's gone, and we're getting wet.'

Natty did not reply, but he got into the car and they sat together for a moment looking out at the snow. It fell softly on the deserted house, on the empty park, on darkening Oxfordshire. Now flakes were beginning to settle on the windscreen, like the frangipani petals which starred the emperor's tomb, ten thousand leagues and half a world away.

Acknowledgements

The dedication of this book reflects how much it owes to a series of conversations which have been going on for more than twenty-five years and are part of the texture of my life. For all that time, Nick Graham has made me think about Cumbria, while John Gilmore and, more recently, Marita Browne-Gilmore, have done the same for Barbados. Without those three people, this book could hardly have happened.

In addition, I am grateful to a number of Cumbrians, notably Di and Brian Dawes (and to the works of Alfred Lauck Parsons, the late Messiah of Allonby, by Maryport, to which Nick introduced me), and to all those who have shared with me their knowledge of Barbados, its history, and its people; especially George Lamming, Evelyn O'Callaghan, and Theo and Margaret Williams.

Among the academic sources for this book, I should particularly like to acknowledge debts to Peter Linebaugh and Marcus Rediker, *The Many-Headed Hydra: Soldiers, Slaves, Commoners, and the Hidden History of the Revolutionary Atlantic*, Penelope Honeychurch, *Caribbean Wild Plants and their Uses*, Jacobus Capitein, *Political-theological dissertation examining the question: is slavery compatible with Christian freedom, or not?*, John Gilmore *et al.*, *A–Z of Barbadian Heritage*, Jill Sheppard, *The Redlegs of Barbados*, Jerome Handler, *The Unappropriated People*, Stephen Jay Gould, *The Mismeasure of Man*, Luigi Luca Cavalli-Sforza, *Genes, Peoples and Languages*, and Richard Lewontin, *Human Diversity*.

On other matters, James Kelly, Defoe specialist, was generous with information about Defoe and Holland, including the tale of the civet-cats; and Adriaan van der Weel was endlessly helpful in extending my knowledge of Dutch culture, Dutch universities and hypertext. Matthew Cobb straightened me out on genetics. I have also received help from the personnel of the Barbados Museum and Historical Society, the Barbados National Archives, the Cumbria County Record Office, and the Zeeuws Archief in Middelburg. Thanks are also due for a variety of reasons to Sarah Ballard, Andrew Biswell, Prezident Brown, Patricia Brückmann, Elizabeth Clarke, Peter Davidson, Dan Franklin, Betty Hagglund, Arnold Hunt, Pat Kavanagh, Jonathan Key, Sheilah and Irvin Klegerman, Carol Morley, David Norbrook, Jamie Reid Baxter, Alison Shell, Nigel Smith and Tine Wanning. And in particular, to Peter Davidson, who wrote me the lyric in Chapter VI with truly early modern generosity, and Jonathan Key, who contributed two elegant parodies to the collection in Chapter XII. I am also grateful to a certain very gracious lady whose name I have taken in vain more than once (no, not that one; another).

However, I should like to stress that I have no personal acquaintance in the University of Utrecht, and that my invented 'Book History project' bears, as far as I know, no resemblance to any studies at that university. Nothing said in this book about the University of Utrecht, Balliol College and the University of Oxford more generally, or the Cave Hill campus of the University of the West Indies, is intended as a portrait of the actual inner life of these institutions, or of any specific individuals attached to any of them.

Much of the preliminary thinking for this book was indebted to the late Stephen Jay Gould, a doughty supporter of the principle that humankind was created equal, and a champion of the distinction between myths and facts who never denied the importance of stories in human affairs.